GULF COAST CITY

BY DAVID LLOYD

www.DavidLloydNovels.com

Published by Premier Press Publishing and Palmetto Publishing Group through Amazon

Edited by Better Beta Reads - Deb Rhodes
Beta Readers - Better Beta Reads and Quiethouse Editing

Cover Design by Kimberly Lee Common and Mitransh Singh Parihar

ISBN-13: 978-0-9978069-1-5
ISBN-10: 0-9978069-1-5

Table of Contents

CHAPTER 1
TINSLEY, SOUTH CAROLINA

"You've got ten minutes. Tamar will be fine…"
—Jennifer

Jacob Carmichael was surprised to see his hands shaking as he looked for his sister's number on the speed dial. He fumbled around with his cell phone until he found what he needed.

It was December, 1994 in the small southern town of Tinsley, South Carolina. Christmas was always a festive time and young Jacob was doing an internship at his church. He was delighted to be serving the Lord in his hometown, but a little anxious too.

He phoned his sister, Tamar, because he thought she'd be willing to help. Ever since they were children,.Jacob knew he could count on his older sister. His parents died in a car accident when he was a teenager, so Tamar had to assist with everything from cooking to schoolwork. Today was no exception and she picked up on the first ring.

"Hey, Jacob," she answered in her pleasant voice.

"Hey Tamar, I need your help."

"I figured you'd be calling me at some point today." Fifteen years older than Jacob, she often found herself playing more of a motherly role. "What do you need?"

"Can you meet me at the church at six? I have to pick up the money, then go buy all the Christmas presents for the kids."

Every year the congregation of Tinsley Baptist Church generously donated, so the impoverished children of Tinsley could receive presents on Christmas day. Jacob was in charge of coordinating the event this year.

"I thought Miss Jennifer was gonna help you." Tamar sounded surprised.

"Well can you believe it? She's sick."

"Really? Well can't you ask Pastor Mike?"

"He had to go to Greenville."

"Oh my, Jacob. You know, sometimes you have the worst luck."

"I know, don't remind me." Jacob stroked his smooth face to see if he needed to shave. He could probably go one more day. "But will ya help me?"

"Of course I'll help you, little brother. Don't I always?"

"Yes, you do." Jacob's face brightened. "And thanks, I owe ya."

"Yes, you do." Tamar smiled.

"Okay great. Well, I gotta get over to Jennifer's first because she begged me to come by and check on her."

"You be careful with her, Jacob. I know you think she's a sweet innocent Christian girl but she's had her eye on you for a while now."

"Yeah yeah, I hear ya."

"And don't you be late getting to the church this evening either."

* * *

Tinsley was a typical small Southern town where everybody knew each other. At twenty-one, Jacob already had a great reputation in the town of always being obliging. He was studying Christian Ministries at Bob Jones University in Greenville and was about to graduate and hopefully become a pastor himself. Pastor Mike knew Jacob was a kindhearted person, so when he saw his application to intern at the church he didn't have to think twice about giving him the position.

After Jacob hung up with Tamar, he jumped in his old rusty pick-up and headed to Jennifer's house. He sped through the center of town past the statue of General George Tinsley, a famous general from the Civil War and native South Carolinian. He felt an obligation to go over to Jennifer's to see how she was feeling. They had known each other all their lives but became close in college and had been working together now for three months. For Jacob, their relationship was strictly a friendship, but he had a feeling she wanted more.

When he arrived at Jennifer's small brick ranch style house it was 5:20 pm. He couldn't be late for his appointment with Tamar, so he quickly strode through the grass that the winter had browned up to her front porch, shivering.

He knocked on Jennifer's door and tried to relax as he breathed in the fresh smell of pine needles. When she opened, Jacob's eyes widened with surprise. Jennifer, who was supposed to have the flu, wore the smallest T-shirt she probably owned, and almost nothing else. Jacob's eyes trailed up her toned legs and stopped right below the forbidden place that any man, let alone an aspiring pastor, should see. He didn't have to use his imagination to guess what color her panties were. He saw that they were clearly black satin and didn't leave much to the imagination.

"I – I..." He stuttered.

"Why don't you come on in Jacob," Jennifer said with her sweet South Carolina accent, and devious smile. "You're gonna catch a chill out there."

"Okay, sure." Jacob replied, forgetting about the cold winter air. "I only have time to check to see if ya need anything. You know, since you're not feeling good."

Jennifer welcomed him into her house, decorated with her framed cross stitch pictures hanging on every wall. Her favorite subject was churches of the South. In the corner of the room was a wooden rocking chair that used to be her grandmother's, and in front of the couch a coffee table was decorated with homemade candles.

When she gently placed her hand on his shoulder, Jacob jumped. Noticing his discomfiture, she laughed and said, "I'm just trying to take your coat for you, honey."

"Oh sorry," Jacob said and chewed his bottom lip until it turned white.

He found Jennifer very attractive with her curly blonde hair, sensuous red lips, and enormous breasts. But for him, she was just too voluptuous for a future pastor to be seen with. He was looking for a more conservative lady to make his wife. But he was still human and still had the same lustful thoughts of 21-year-old men who weren't of the cloth.

"Do you mind if I use your bathroom?" Jacob asked, averting his gaze from her tempting body while he contemplated his escape.

"Sure, silly," Jennifer answered with a giggle. She pushed several long curly strands of hair away from her pretty round face to reveal her bright blue eyes. "You don't have to be all formal."

He quickly disappeared into Jennifer's bathroom and began to gather his thoughts. He glanced around at the girly pink bathroom, feeling jittery, then studied himself in the mirror. He wondered what it was Jennifer found attractive in him because he didn't see anything to be enamored with. He was only just out of the acne stage, so at least he no longer had to worry about that. But he still didn't have the confidence of being a grown man. Jacob parted his hair on the side and combed it over. He was trying to look more mature, even though he looked a little silly.

Jennifer was on the other side of the door fantasizing over his broad shoulders, dreamy blue eyes, and wavy blonde hair. To her, he was the perfect Southern gentleman. And even though he could be a bit of a klutz, because he always tried so hard to be helpful, she found this endearing.

Jacob sensed she was pacing the floor outside the door licking her lips at the chance to pounce. He couldn't hide in there all evening so he gave the toilet a useless flush, took a deep breath, then crept out the door.

Jennifer was right back in his face to greet him. "Jacob, don't you think this is the coldest winter we've ever had in South Carolina?"

"Uh, I don't know," he replied. "I remember the winter of '78 when we had all that snow on the ground."

"Yeah, but we were only little kids then. I'm talking about the coldest winter we've had recently."

"Ah well, this is the coldest one then, I guess." Jacob was stumbling over his words because he was still suspicious of the vibes he was picking up. He hoped that as a devout Baptist, she would save herself for marriage, though considering the sultry looks she was sending him, he was beginning to doubt she had any such intentions.

Jennifer sat down on her cozy leather couch and wrapped a knitted blanket around her shoulders and breasts. Jacob breathed out a sigh of relief. He was glad to see at least she was trying to cover up. Then she said in a seductive voice, "I'm so cold. Will you come over here and warm me up?"

He stood up straight and nervous, still only a couple of feet from her bathroom door. He didn't want to go over there because he was sure Jennifer wanted more than just his body heat. He ignored the spike that was forming in his pants and replied, "Why don't I turn up your heater for you?"

"I tried that, but it doesn't wanna get any hotter in here."

Needing more heat was not Jacob's problem, and a bead of sweat rolled down his cheek. He was looking at her front door, still planning his escape, when she said, "Oh come over here silly, I'm not gonna bite you. How long have we known each other now?"

"I don't know. Forever, I guess, but you wouldn't talk to me before my freshman year at Bob Jones."

"So we've been friends for like four years?"

"Yeah something like that."

"Well, then you used to keep me warm at our strict Christian college where boys and girls weren't allowed to be anywhere near each other. Why can't you come keep me warm now? I used to call you my snuggle bunny. Don't you remember that?" Jennifer giggled, and his face flushed as he recalled her embarrassing him in front of his friends.

She was not going to take no for an answer, and Jacob was reluctantly aroused too. He found himself being pulled closer where he sat down next to her on the couch.

***

Tamar arrived at the church to meet Jacob. A petite brunette, she was a modest lady who always kept a neat appearance. A devout Christian, just like Jacob, she didn't believe in flaunting her body to get what she wanted. Tamar got out of her car and zipped her coat up tightly as she walked towards the large brick church. Though nearly completely dark outside, Tamar was not the least bit scared. Tinsley was just not that type of place. She was about to open the church door when someone startled her.

"Ma'am, you wouldn't have anything for me to eat would ya?" A tall malnourished looking man with salt and pepper hair appeared out of the shadows. Tamar immediately noticed he wasn't wearing a coat. "Sorry ma'am, but I ain't eaten in three days." Even though the man was skinny he still had well-toned muscles as if he'd been doing manual labor all his life. Besides the fact that Tamar knew everyone in Tinsley, she could tell this man wasn't from here because he'd obviously just recently been in the sun.

This made Tamar very uneasy, but she had to be a good Christian and help. "Why sure, sir," she replied and took a step back. "Let me see if there's anything in our kitchen for you." Tamar wanted the strange man to wait outside, but he followed her through the steel church door. She felt rude making him freeze out in the night air, so she didn't try to stop him.

As she walked on the tile floors down the dark hallway, the stranger followed behind. She was getting more uneasy so she said, "I'm Tamar, what's your name?"

"Carl," the man replied in a deep voice. He wasn't being unfriendly, but his lack of emotion livened up Tamar's pulse as she clutched her purse.

"And where are you from, Carl?"

"Kentucky," Carl answered. Now, this really frightened Tamar because no one from Kentucky would have such a dark suntan in December. She tried to stay calm, convincing herself that maybe he just got back from Florida.

* * *

Hoping Jacob would get here soon, Tamar looked at her watch which said

5:50. At the same time, still fidgeting on Jennifer's couch, Jacob looked at a clock on the wall that also said 5:50. Jennifer had been continuously giving him *take me to bed* looks so he said, "Wow it's ten till six already. I better get going or Tamar will be worrying about me."

Jennifer pulled him closer and whispered, "You've got ten minutes. Tamar will be fine."

The shots were being called from below the belt now, and concern for his sister was his last priority. He wasn't going to fight his desires any longer, and Jennifer knew it. She put her arms around him and started kissing his face. Jacob was lost in the moment, no one else mattered except Jennifer. Now that she knew he was all hers, she pulled him even closer and rammed her tongue down his throat. Jacob was out of control. Nothing was going to pull him away. Not an earthquake, not a snow storm and not his strong Christian beliefs. Their hands were all over each other now, and they were about to take it to the next level.

Jennifer looked up at Jacob and said, "I've wanted to be with you for years. You are so cute and so sexy." She grabbed his hands and put them on her breasts.

No girl had ever spoken to him like this before, and he loved it. Even though he was a virgin, instinct took over and he could not stop this runaway train. Jacob was just about to unzip his pants when he heard a loud bang outside. It was enough to jolt him back to reality.

He jumped up and wiped the lipstick from his mouth. "I gotta go Jennifer, sorry."

"Aw Jacob, you just got here. Can't you call Tamar's cell and tell her I'm really sick?"

"No, I really gotta go." Jacob walked swiftly out of Jennifer's house, into the dark, and jumped in his truck. *What a close call that was,* he thought. *I made a vow to God not to be sexually immoral. I know I can wait until I'm married.* He stepped on the gas and headed down the dark windy road towards his church.

* * *

Tamar was now inside the large church kitchen with the strange visitor with the dark suntan. He was pacing around anxiously. She looked up at him nervously and said, "We have a lot of food in the fridge over here, Carl. You can make yourself a sandwich if you'd like." Her voice was shaking although she was projecting calmness. "My brother will be here any second so he can take you somewhere if you need that." Tamar was hoping, if Carl had any wicked intentions, he'd put them aside after hearing Jacob was on his way to the church.

Her comments had no effect on Carl. He moved in closer then looked at her with his evil eyes and said, "I've been prowling around like a roaring lion, seeking someone to devour."

Before Tamar could make sense of what Carl had just said, he violently punched her face. She hunched over in excruciating pain, blood dripping from her nose. Tears and sweat stung her eyes as ice-cold terror entered her veins. "No Carl, please!" she screamed.

Carl showed no emotion. He pushed Tamar down onto the cold tile floor then got on top of her. She tried to fight him off as more tears poured out of her eyes. He was way too strong. He pulled some rope out of his coat and wrapped it tightly around Tamar's wrists. Then he yanked her up so she was standing upright shaking. "I know the church has money. Where is it?"

Tamar gasped for air as she tried to speak. "Wait, wait," she pleaded. The emotionless Carl paused, curious to hear what she had to say. "Wait, Carl." Tamar could still barely speak, her wrists throbbing and hands numb. "Carl, why are you doing this?" This was all Tamar wanted to know. Why was this strange man acting so cruel?

Carl looked at the crucifix hanging around Tamar's neck and said, "Be sober-minded; be watchful. Your adversary the devil prowls around like a roaring lion, seeking someone to devour."

Carl seemed to have no intention of stopping his evil behavior and appeared to be enjoying it. He grabbed the rope and yanked Tamar closer to him. "I said, where's the money?"

Tamar's bottom lip trembled with fear. She couldn't muster up the words so she pointed with her eyes down the hall to the left. Carl tightened the rope and dragged her behind him as they left the kitchen and headed towards the church business office.

A few terrifying steps down the hall and they were inside the office. There was no need for Carl to ask for the combination or key to the safe. There wasn't one. There was no need to ask where the money was hidden because it was right there on the wooden desk in a large bank envelope. Five thousand dollars cash. Carl smiled, obviously thinking this is way too easy. Tamar was shaking profusely, and Carl was enjoying the moment until he heard someone walking down the hallway. It was Tamar's brother, Jacob.

Carl grabbed the bank envelope and escaped down the hall and out the steel door. Jacob heard the slam as Carl disappeared into the darkness, so he called out, "Tamar, is that you? Hey I know I'm late and I know you're gonna be mad, but Jennifer was really sick." He quickly imagined Jennifer waiting for him in her tiny T-shirt, curled up on her couch. He smiled, then thought, *You are such a stud.*

When Jacob got to the business office he opened the door and saw his sister crying and struggling to get out of the ropes. A sharp pain knifed his heart as he froze. A drop of blood fell from Tamar's nose and stained the freshly cleaned white tile floor. He looked at Tamar and yelled out. "Oh my God, what happened?"

"I just wanted to help him. He said he was hungry." Tears were gushing out while Tamar's entire body shook, an image Jacob would never forget.

"Who, what? Who was hungry?"

"He said his name was Carl and he hadn't eaten in days." Tamar checked her nose with her fingers to see if the blood had stopped. She seemed satisfied that it had.

Jacob was about to give her a protective brother lecture about opening up to strangers then it occurred to him that he was half an hour late. His face blushed as he remembered why. "I should call the sheriff." He sat down as his knees suddenly weakened. He struggled to grab his cell phone out of his jeans pocket. Tears blurred his sight as he fumbled to dial 911.

***

Twenty minutes later the entire police force of Tinsley, South Carolina descended onto Tinsley Baptist Church. This consisted of one sheriff patrol car driven by the sheriff of Tinsley, Mr. Ryan Crepps. He was a bony middle-aged man with dark hair and dark eyes. Without an ounce of fat on his body he still moved like a turtle.

He stood up from his patrol car as Jacob ran towards him. "Did you call 911, Jacob?" Sheriff Crepps asked calmly.

"Yes, I did! Tamar has been attacked by a crazy man!" Jacob felt hysterical.

Sheriff Crepps was scratching his chin trying to make sense of what he'd just heard. "Do what?" he asked.

"I said Tamar was attacked by some lunatic. He broke into the church and punched her, then took the church offering!"

"You don't say?" The full force of what had just happened still had not hit Sheriff Crepps.

"Sheriff, you gotta get this guy! He's dangerous and he's gonna attack someone else!"

Tamar stumbled out of the church, with her hand over her swollen eye. Her lower lip was quivering and dried tears covered her face. When she got closer, Sheriff Crepps shined his flashlight on her then stepped back when he saw the damage that Carl had done.

"What the..." It finally hit the sheriff. "What the hell happened, Tamar?"

"I've been trying to tell you, Sheriff!" Jacob barked.

Sheriff Crepps picked up his radio and called out to Mary Lois, the administrative assistant and the other half of the Tinsley Sheriff Department. "Mary Lois, can you get on to South Carolina Highway Patrol and let 'em know to look out for a dangerous suspect… hold on a sec." Sheriff Crepps looked at Tamar and asked. "How'd this guy look? Was he white, black, old, young?"

Tamar was shaking from the cold and the traumatic event she'd just experienced, so Jacob jumped in. "He was white and skinny, right Tamar?"

Tamar nodded, then Jacob asked. "Was he old or young?"

"Maybe in his forties," Tamar whimpered.

"Okay great," Sheriff Crepps replied, then got back onto his radio. "Mary Lois, tell South Carolina HP to be on the lookout for a middle-aged white male who's… hold on again, Mary Lois." Sheriff Crepps looked at Tamar and asked, "You said he was skinny, right?"

"Yes." Tamar replied. "He was skinny but had well-toned muscles."

"Okay thank ya." Sheriff Crepps got back onto the radio. "Mary Lois, the guy was skinny but had muscles too."

Mary Lois came back on the radio. "What happened Ryan?"

"Tamar Carmichael was attacked but I can't get into all that now." Sheriff Crepps put down his radio then scratched his head while he planned his next move. Mary Lois could be heard in the background saying, "Oh my Lord. Is she okay Ryan?"

"Don't you think we should go look for him?" Jacob interrupted.

Sheriff Crepps looked at him as he pondered what he had just heard. "I tell ya what, why don't you and Tamar hop in the patrol car with me. Tamar, do you need medical assistance? You don't look so good."

"No, I'm fine Sheriff," Tamar replied as she looked down at the ground and wiped away a stray tear.

"Then why don't y'all hop on in and we'll go look for this fella."

Jacob sat in the front seat and Tamar sat in the back as they headed into town. Sheriff Crepps reached into the glove compartment and pulled out an ice pack. Then he snapped it to make it cold before giving it to Tamar. She held it on her face while he asked her to expound on what had happened. Tamar explained how she had agreed to meet Jacob at 6 pm so they could pick up the money to shop for the kids. Jacob hung his head in shame as they drove past the statue of General George Tinsley.

Sheriff Crepps looked in the mirror at Tamar and said, "Honey, I'm gonna leave you with Mary Lois at the police station. You don't look too good to me."

Tamar nodded her head in approval but Jacob was still squirming in his seat. He cried out, "But if we leave Tamar at the station, who is gonna identify the guy?"

Sheriff Crepps was still moving at a snail's pace. He said, "Don't worry Jacob. I have enough of a description to go on. Besides, I know how everyone looks here in town, so this guy won't be hard to spot."

As Sheriff Crepps pulled into the police station, Jacob didn't see any point in arguing. Mary Lois was waiting outside with her hand over her mouth. "Oh, my darlin' Tamar!" she cried. "What on earth happened to you, baby?" Hearing this made Tamar begin crying again. She ran to Mary Lois's chubby arms and let her console her.

Sheriff Crepps put his hand on Jacob's shoulder and said, "I'll be right back, buddy. Stay here."

As Sheriff Crepps walked off, Mary Lois, who was Sheriff Crepp's aunt, started asking all kinds of questions. Jacob, still stricken with guilt, had to explain everything to Mary Lois while Tamar sunk her head into her bosom. He was relieved when Sheriff Crepps returned. Now he appeared ready for action with a holster around his waist with his pistol attached.

He put his hand on Jacob's shoulder and said, "Why don't you stay here and help Mary Lois take care of Tamar."

"Oh no!" Jacob argued. "I'm going with you Sheriff."

The Sheriff knew Jacob wasn't going to budge so he gave him a stern look and said, "Okay, let's go get him then." The two men jumped into the patrol car and headed out on their search. The police radio inside the patrol car was blowing up with conversations from the South Carolina Highway Patrol. They were looking for any drifter in the area that fit Carl's description and couldn't wait to pounce. During Sheriff Crepp's thirty years with the Tinsley Sheriff Department, the most serious crimes he'd dealt with were mostly drunken fights at *The General* bar. One would never know from looking at him, but he was excited to finally be doing some real police work.

"Ryan?" Mary Lois called on the radio. "Ryan?"

Sheriff Crepps picked up the mic. "Don't you think you should call me Sheriff, Mary Lois. SCHP is all over the radio tonight."

"Yes, Sheriff."

"What do you want, Mary Lois?" Sheriff Crepps asked.

"Miss Annie just phoned over here and said someone matching the suspect's description just walked into her diner."

Sheriff Crepps said, "How does Miss Annie know the suspect's description?"

"I called Miss Annie a while back to see if she'd seen anyone suspicious around town, then she called me here, just a few minutes ago, and said that she had."

Sheriff Crepps rolled his eyes then put down the radio microphone and dropped the gas pedal to the floor. He looked over at Jacob and said, "Hold on tight, this might be our man."

Jacob's heart started to thump. "I sure hope so."

"Now when we get there, you just stay in the car, Jacob. You're too young and too emotionally connected to get involved in this. Ya understand?"

"Yes sir," Jacob responded as he gripped onto his seat while the patrol car weaved around a pickup truck puttering down the road.

When they arrived at Miss Annie's Diner, Sheriff Crepps turned off his headlights. He pulled up to the window of the small restaurant and they looked inside. Sitting alone at one of the tables was a skinny man with well-toned muscles and a dark suntan. He had salt and pepper hair, just as Tamar had described. On the table, next to his supper, appeared to be the bag that contained the church offering for the impoverished children of Tinsley.

Raw anger came over Jacob and he couldn't control his actions. Ignoring Sheriff Crepp's orders, he jumped out of the patrol car and rushed into Miss Annie's Diner. The lights were bright inside, and only a handful of customers were eating at the restaurant that boasted having the best barbecue in upstate South Carolina.

Jacob was full of rage and wanted revenge for his sister. And he wanted to make amends for arriving late to the church. He locked eyes with Carl and charged at him. Carl was chewing on a chicken bone just as calm as he could be.

When Jacob got to his table, he took a full swing and connected with Carl's jaw. He fell out of his chair and hit the floor. Then he stood back up and dusted himself off, unfazed. He brushed over his jaw with his hand then said, "I knew you'd come lookin' for me, church boy. But you're too late I done got rid of all your money."

Jacob tried to take another swing, but this time Carl caught his fist and didn't let go. He twisted his arm behind his back, then pulled out a large hunting knife and put it up to his throat.

Sheriff Crepps was inside the restaurant now with his pistol drawn. He pointed it at Carl and started slowly walking towards him.

"I'll kill the church boy. Don't come near me cop."

"Take it easy." Sheriff Crepps, continued to creep towards Carl, his pistol was still pointing at his face.

Carl yanked Jacob's arm up behind his back and he yelped in pain. Then he put his knife closer to Jacob's neck and pushed the blade against his throat. Small droplets of blood started to trickle out of Jacob's neck onto the collar of his shirt.

"Take it easy," Sheriff Crepps whispered with his pistol still pointing at Carl.

Carl started making his way toward the door of the diner as the handful of customers, wait staff, cooks and Miss Annie stood wide-eyed and frozen. Sheriff Crepps was the only one still doing his job, and he continued to slowly pursue the suspect and his hostage.

Carl got to the door and put one hand on the door handle and the other stayed on the knife that was digging into Jacob's throat. His eyes roamed around the restaurant then he spoke. "I bet you're all wondering why I came to your church and stole all your money. Well I'm gonna tell you all right now and you can tell your family and your friends to be sober minded and be watchful because the devil prowls around like a roaring li--"

BANG!! Sheriff Crepp's pistol went off and the bullet sank into Carl's skull. He fell back onto the floor, and Jacob ran to safety.

CHAPTER 2
BOB JONES UNIVERSITY, GREENVILLE, SOUTH CAROLINA

"... why does there have to be so much evil in the world?"
—Jacob Carmichael

Four Months after the assault and robbery of Tamar Carmichael at Tinsley Baptist Church, the town of Tinsley, South Carolina was still in shock. Her brother Jacob was back at Bob Jones University, guilt-ridden and failing every class. Tamar had survived a terrifying and unexpected attack and had come out stronger.

Sheriff Crepps was now a hero for catching up to Carl so quickly. With no choice but to protect Jacob and the occupants of Miss Annie's Diner, he had to pull out his firearm to stop Carl's advance. The town was happy that one less lunatic was in the world, but Jacob and Tamar were left without answers. *Why was he in Tinsley and why had he come into their church?*

In addition to working as an administrative assistant at Tinsley Baptist church, Tamar was also a part time professor of theology at Bob Jones University in Greenville. She was in her mid-thirties, single, but not by choice. She just hadn't found the right man yet. She knew a lot of single men but always ended up playing a motherly role in their lives, helping them with their problems, instead of becoming a lover.

Jacob was sitting in the dark on his unmade bed, alone in his messy dorm room. Its appearance matched the sadness that was living in his heart, every day since the incident at the church.

He heard a knock at his door and was intending on ignoring it when Tamar called out, "I know you're in there Jacob. Pastor Mike and I drove an hour from Tinsley just to see you."

Jacob couldn't help but smile as a warm feeling came over him. He felt indebted to Pastor Mike because he was the one who'd arranged for his internship at their church. Even though Pastor Mike put an abrupt end to Jacob's position the day after Carl stole $5000, he never scolded him for it.

He opened his door and Tamar and Pastor Mike walked in.

"Hey, Tamar," Jacob said softly. "Hey, Pastor Mike." He sounded like he hadn't spoken in months.

Tamar and Pastor Mike noticed his appearance had deteriorated immensely since they'd last seen him. His face was gaunt. His hair was messy, and he had dark circles under his eyes.

"Hi Jacob, it's good to see you." Tamar gave Jacob a hug and discreetly pinched her nose as she got a whiff of his body odor. She was sure he hadn't properly bathed since she'd last seen him. Pastor Mike shook Jacob's hand with a confident grip and pleasant smile.

"It's good to see y'all too," Jacob said as he moved some dirty clothes out of the way and quickly hid an empty whiskey bottle. He blushed a little, hoping his guests hadn't seen it. He pulled up a milk crate for Tamar to sit on and gave Pastor Mike his only chair.

"Jacob, I'm not gonna beat around the bush because frankly, I don't have time." Tamar motioned for him to sit on his unmade bed. "There's a lot of people out there who love you and are very worried about you. And I'm one of them."

"I know but--"

Tamar put her hand up. "Look, doing what you're doing is not gonna help you move on with your life."

"I just don't see the point anymore," Jacob replied.

"Well, Jacob, flunking out of college is not the answer. This is your last semester, right? After you graduate you can begin your life and start being a productive member of society. Isn't this what you want?" Since their mother and father had died in Amsterdam, Tamar often sounded more like his mom than his older sister.

Jacob had always wanted to become a pastor, but now he was ridden with guilt. If he'd been at the church when he said he would, his sister would not have been attacked and he wouldn't have ruined Christmas for so many poor children and their parents. Instead, he'd surrendered to lust. Jacob paused for a second to put his fingers on his eyelids, hoping the tears wouldn't spill out. Then he asked, "Pastor Mike, why does there have to be so much evil in the world?"

Forty-year-old Pastor Mike, a former college football lineman, had a chiseled face, was bald by choice and stocky. He liked to spend time in the gym working his muscles. Jacob used to join him occasionally, but always wondered how he had time to work out. Every time Pastor Mike was in the gym he always ran into someone he knew and had to spend all his time talking about the next church social, baptism or wedding.

"That isn't an easy question to answer, my friend." Pastor Mike scratched his scalp as he thought about how he was going to present his explanation. "You know, I've been asked this question a lot over the years, and I still don't know the answer for sure. But I do know this; God is real but so is Satan, and the evil we see all around us comes from him, not from God. The Bible says, *God cannot be tempted by evil, nor does he tempt anyone; but each one is tempted when, by his own evil desire, he is dragged away and enticed.* Someday the warfare between good and evil, between God and Satan, will be over, and Christ will emerge victorious. In the meantime, God calls us to be faithful to Him, and never give in to evil or sin."

Jacob took a deep breath and looked at the tile floor as he thought about what Pastor Mike had just said. He continued looking down at the floor, that desperately needed mopping, then said. "I know what you're saying Pastor, but I just can't come to grips with what happened. I have a hard time concentrating in my classes, especially after what I did to my sister."

"Jacob, you did not do anything to me." Tamar lifted her hands in the air as if she was at the end of her rope trying to convince Jacob. "It was Satan who did this, not you."

"Well I sure as heck was responsible for our parents' death. I was out drinking in Amsterdam and forgot how to get back to their hotel. I called them around midnight--"

"Jacob, we know the story but this was five years ago," Tamar interrupted.

"If they didn't have to come pick me up they wouldn't have gotten into the accident. You know Dad could never see at night."

Tamar eyes filled with tears, so Pastor Mike jumped in, "Jacob no one is to blame for this, it just happened. It was terrible, I know, but remember God's love is Divine. He didn't punish you for going out and doing what almost all teenagers do."

Jacob looked down, took a deep breath, then exhaled. "Look, guys, I have to tell you something." He looked up at Tamar and Pastor Mike whose eyes were glued to him. "I never told y'all the reason I was late to the church because I was ashamed. But I feel like I should tell y'all now." He took another breath then looked at Tamar. "I was fooling around with Jennifer instead of meeting you at six like I'd promised. I could'a prevented the whole thing."

Tamar's face tightened as she started tensing her fists, still locking eyes with Jacob. This newsflash hurt, and her immediate thought was to give her brother a thump. Luckily, Pastor Mike was sitting in the middle of them as the referee. He said, "Jacob, we are all human and God knows this. We all sin and every one of Jesus's disciples sinned as well."

"Yes, I know, but I feel so guilty I can't bear to think about it." Jacob brushed a tear away from his cheek. "I don't think I can be a pastor anymore. Every time I go inside our church all I can think about is that monster who tied up my sister. How could God let him into the church and why didn't He protect her?"

Pastor Mike's face was an open book. He truly cared about Jacob and wanted him to get back on the right track. "I can't answer those questions, you know that. In fact, no one can. The only way you'll be able to find answers is through prayer."

Jacob was still fixating on the floor. The tears had stopped but his eyes were still misty. "I haven't prayed since that night and I don't think I will pray again."

Tamar rubbed the back of her neck as she thought for a moment. She'd had time to absorb the new information Jacob had just presented and had come to terms with it. "Look, Jacob, I have a suggestion. I think you should leave South Carolina for a while and go in search of the answers to your questions. Pastor Mike could quote you scripture after scripture that talks about the issues you're dealing with, but I don't think this is what you want."

Jacob would not have listened to anyone else except his sister and Pastor Mike. He asked, "So if I leave, where should I go?"

Tamar leaned over, gently squeezing Jacob's shoulder, and said, "I know it'll be tough for you but I think you should go visit with my attacker's wife."

"What!" he jumped up from his bed and accidentally kicked over another empty whiskey bottle he'd forgotten to hide. Now he was confused. He clenched his fists as he replayed the events of his sister's attack. "His wife?" Jacob had no idea why Tamar would want him to do this. "Tamar, how could you be so disrespectful to me?"

"Look, I mean no disrespect. I only want what's best for you and I wouldn't insist you do this unless I thought it would be to your benefit."

"How the heck will this help me forget about what happened?" The tone in his voice had now turned to anger.

"Now Jacob, please don't take this the wrong way when I tell you, but Pastor Mike and I have met with Carl's wife--"

"What?" Jacob interrupted, and jumped back up from his bed just a split second after he'd sat back down. "Y'all met with that animal's wife?"

"Yes, we did. Carl's wife came to Tinsley after Sheriff Crepps shot him. You were already back at Bob Jones so I didn't feel the need to tell you. She had to claim his body. Now I know this doesn't excuse what he did, but they said he suffered from schizophrenia and other types of mental illnesses, such as depression and severe anxiety."

"I don't believe this. Are we supposed to feel sorry for this guy?"

"No, we're not, Jacob. And no one expects us to. But I think you should go down to Gulf Coast City, Florida, and when you're ready you should meet his wife, just like we did."

"But--" he felt the bile rise in his throat, and if it had been anyone but Tamar he would have told her to get out. He gritted his teeth and stared at the wall as if the wall was the one he was angry with.

"Let me finish Jacob, please. I think you should do this because I think it will help you like it helped me. You will see that the guy was not a monster, but a very mentally ill individual who was easily guided by Satan."

"I cannot believe what you're telling me. But I don't feel like you're giving me a choice." Jacob looked at Tamar for confirmation and she nodded. "I feel like you and Pastor Mike came here to gang up on me."

"Look, Jacob, we both know how hard this has been on you and we've both prayed on this. We feel the only way you can get past this is to face your demons and meet Carl's wife." Tamar put her hand on Jacob's shoulder and looked at him. "Will you do this for me?"

Jacob put his hand on top of Tamar's for just a second then lifted it to comb his hair with his fingers. "Where was it again?"

"Gulf Coast City. It's a small tourist town in the Florida panhandle."

"I don't know; I'll have to think about it. If I do go, and I'm not saying I will, don't expect me to go knock on his wife's door the first day I'm there, because I'm not ready for that." Jacob figured he'd more than likely have to give into Tamar's demands because he desperately wanted to earn her forgiveness. Even though she'd told him a hundred times she didn't blame him, it still ate at him every day.

Pastor Mike chimed in. "Tamar wouldn't ask you to do this Jacob if she didn't think it was good for you. You should head down there and when you're ready, go see Sue Ellen Dooley. Then try to forgive Carl, if you feel it in your heart, and try to make your peace. I only say this because forgiveness helps the forgiver more than the forgiven. I hope that makes sense."

Tamar and Pastor Mike left Jacob alone in his dorm room with a big decision to make. Jacob looked at the empty whiskey bottles that he'd hidden from his unexpected guests. He had a choice to make: continue sitting in his room drinking and feeling sorry for himself, or get out in the world and figure out how to move forward. Within a week, Jacob withdrew from his classes, packed his bags, and headed out on a Greyhound bus to Gulf Coast City.

CHAPTER 3
GULF COAST CITY, FLORIDA

"If the tourists knew what really happens in Gulf Coast City, they'd never come back."
—X-Man

Palm trees were everywhere and the damp air was still scorching hot at 9 pm. The Greyhound bus carrying Jacob Carmichael arrived in Gulf Coast City, Florida, five hundred miles from the foothills of South Carolina. Jacob looked out the window and saw a fountain clogged with beer cans and statues of dolphins on display. The water splashed on their backs as they jumped up in the air with smiles on their faces. He combed his wavy blonde hair nervously with his fingers as he stood up from the worn bus seat, anxious to make his exit. As he waited patiently for the other passengers to leave, Jacob thought about the statue of General George Tinsley back in his hometown. He thought, *We worship Civil War generals and they worship dolphins.*

"Man, I ain't gotta do shit!" A dirty homeless looking guy, in street rags was yelling at the bus driver. Jacob was trying to get off the bus while the filthy guy was trying to sneak his way on.

The grey-haired bus driver said, "You can't come on this bus without a ticket. Now get out of the way so the passengers can get off."

Jacob jumped off the bus and got away from there as fast as he could so the man, reeking of dried sweat and cheap wine, wouldn't follow him. He wondered if he'd made a mistake coming here.

He was outside for only a couple of minutes before the Florida heat and humidity caused him to perspire. He was in a whole new world now. Up in South Carolina they were still wearing long pants and enjoying spring, but here summer had already hit. *Maybe it never left.* Tourists and locals were gallivanting around in their tank tops and flip flops. He ran out of the bus station carrying one large suitcase and flagged down a taxi to get him the heck out of there.

When the yellow cab pulled over, Jacob was shocked to see such an old beat-up looking piece-of-junk. He hopped inside, wiped his sweat-soaked forehead and looked around. The taxi driver's ID card had the driver's name listed as Xavier, but when the dispatcher radioed in, she called him X-man.

"What happened? You just rob a bank or what?" X-man looked Jacob up and down in the rearview mirror, noticing he was out of breath.

"No," Jacob replied, as a single bead of perspiration trickled down his face, "I've been on that bus twenty hours straight and some nasty guy was trying to get on while we were trying to get off."

"No shit?" X-man sat behind the wheel with his wrinkled yellowed white T-shirt and started laughing. "Sounds like a typical Gulf Coast City local you're talkin about." X-man took off his ball cap to reveal a terribly receding hairline. So, to make up for this, it seemed like he kept his artificially-colored black hair extra-long in the back.

Jacob tried to get comfortable in the back seat without getting his button-down shirt dirty. X-man's taxi had a combined smell of tobacco and dirty laundry, with a hint of left out food. "Well, I was expecting things to be a lot livelier than back home, but not before I even got off the bus."

"So what you're sayin' is you thought this small town was all glitz and glamor just like they advertise to the tourists." X-man said laughingly with a silly expression on his face.

"Well no," Jacob answered calmly, not sure he wanted to be questioned by the forward taxi driver. "Actually, I meant more exciting but in a different type of way."

"Well anyway," the taxi driver announced loudly and proudly, "my name is X-man and let me be the first to welcome you to Gulf Coast City, the biggest small party town in North Florida."

"Why thank you, X-man," Jacob said, trying not to get too personal with his new acquaintance. "Do know where Oak Street is?"

"Sure, Oak Street is right up the road."

"Okay great," he said as he looked at the piece of paper that had Sue Ellen Dooley's address, and thought about how proud X-man was of his town. "Can you take me to a cheap motel that's close to Oak Street?"

"Naw man, you don't wanna do that." X-man shook his head as he looked back at him in the mirror. "The area around Oak Street ain't good. There's so many better places to stay than around there. Why don't you let me take you to Gulf of Mexico Boulevard? There's hot babes, plenty of cool bars, and it's right on the Gulf. All the tourists love it there."

"No, this is where I wanna go X-man." Jacob wasn't here on vacation and wasn't interested in partying on the beach.

"Okay man, you're the captain," X-man said with obvious disappointment.

As X-man continued driving down the road, Jacob looked around his taxi and was convinced that he more than likely lived inside his car. The dashboard was littered with McDonald's hamburger wrappers, and on the front passenger seat, a small laundry basket held wrinkled clothes.

X-man caught him looking around and asked, "Is this your first time in Gulf Coast City?"

Jacob was already nervously thinking, *I wonder if X-man can sense what I've been through the past four months*? He answered, "Yes, this is my first time."

"So where're you from?"

"Tinsley, South Carolina." He answered reluctantly, still not wanting to give out too much information but not wanting to be impolite either.

"Tinsley, South Carolina?" X-man asked as if no one from such a quiet town would ever want to visit this place. "Gulf Coast City is a lot different than Tinsley, I can tell you that."

"I'm surprised you've even heard of Tinsley," Jacob answered, and almost gave a hint of a grin. He didn't want to give away the reason he was here and was hoping X-man didn't only know about Tinsley from the news of his sister's attack. He convinced himself they'd never know about this way down to Florida. But just in case, he quickly changed the subject. "Gulf Coast City seems like a crazy place."

"So have ya moved here or are ya just on vacation?"

Jacob was not sure what to answer so he said, "I… I'm on an extended vacation."

"Well then let me tell ya something they probably didn't tell ya up there in ole Tinsley. If the tourists, who come here every year in the thousands, knew what really happens in Gulf Coast City, they'd get as far away from here as they could and would never come back."

Jacob wasn't really sure what X-man meant by all this, so he just replied, "Well that sounds really interesting."

When they both realized how silly he sounded, they burst out laughing. As Jacob started to relax, he noticed X-man was missing both his two front teeth. *What a crazy looking guy*, he thought. *Even his eyes look like he's whacked out of his mind.* He just hoped X-man could get him to a motel without driving off the road. He was curious about his new surroundings so he decided to ask. "But what do you mean by if the tourists really knew what this place was like they'd never come back? I don't get it."

"What I mean is this… all the local people here, who live downtown, are crazy. You see that house right there?" X-man slowed down as if he was the Gulf Coast City tour guide. Jacob looked out the window and X-man continued. "This sweet ole lady used to live there. She was like 80 years old. And these two dudes saw her one day sittin on the porch, mindin her own business, so they decided to go up there and rob her. They grabbed her and yanked her back inside her house, then dragged that poor sweet lady all around, makin her get jewelry and stuff for them."

"Did they get the guys? Was the lady okay?" Jacob's heart was racing.

"Naw man, they killed the lady. Don't ask me why because they didn't have to." X-man seemed upset.

"That's terrible," Jacob responded, "but did they get the guys?"

"Yeah, they got em. All the cops had to do was look around under the pier and there they were smokin crack. Yeah, I tell ya, most of the people here are either on the scam or too drunk or too high to know they're being scammed. The folks that get in my cab... I'm talking about the locals now. You follow? They're either a pimp, a hooker, a stripper, a drug dealer, a user or I don't know what."

X-man was laughing again now and Jacob was beginning to think he'd already been hitting the booze tonight. He hoped the motel wasn't too far away. X-man rolled down his window at the stop sign to spit out a glob of chewing tobacco, then he asked, "So I guess you're gonna be looking for some work down here, huh?"

Jacob thought about how the small amount of savings he had in his bank account was not going to last forever. His deceased parents had left him a small amount of savings to fall back on but he'd spent most of it on his college tuition.

He answered, "Yes, I guess I am." He wasn't really sure how to go about getting a job since all he really knew was working for the church. He asked the way he thought was customary. "Do you know anyone who's hiring?"

"Well, I don't know man, ya know. It's 1995 and folks 'round here are havin' a hard time findin' work with ole slick Willy in the White House. Ya know, on account of him lettin' in all the Mexicans." X-man looked at Jacob in the mirror to see if he was going to react, but he didn't because the Bible said to *Love one another: just as I have loved you.* X-man looked at Jacob's blank face and continued. "I ain't really got nothin' against 'em. In fact, I've even dated some beautiful senoritas myself. But some folks say they're stealin' our jobs."

"Well don't worry, I haven't decided if I'm gonna be here long enough to get a job anyway."

"Oh, okay. Hey, what about a car? Are you gonna rent one down here?"

"No, I don't have that kinda money."

"How you gonna get around?

Jacob didn't want to give out too many details, so he just said, "You know, I never thought about that." He was not intending to stay in Gulf Coast City very long and hadn't wanted to drive his old clunker all the way down to Florida, fearing it might not make it.

X-man looked at him like he was from a different planet. He paused for a second, pushed his chewing tobacco further back into his mouth and said, "Well you can always call me, ya know. But of course, that gets kinda expensive every time you wanna go out. I tell ya what, I have a bicycle I can sell ya if ya want."

"You know that might be a good idea." Jacob was realizing that he really hadn't planned too far ahead. He wasn't intending to do too much traveling around in Gulf Coast City. He mainly just wanted to follow his sister's wishes and meet with Carl Dooley's wife, Sue Ellen.

"Okay cool, I tell you what. Give me an extra $20 bucks when I drop you off tonight and I'll bring you a bicycle by early tomorrow mornin'. You'll probably still be asleep so I'll leave it outside your door so I don't have to wake ya up."

Jacob thought, *I've only been in Gulf Coast City less than an hour and I'm already experiencing my first scam.* But instead of saying no, he said, "Okay sure, that'll be great." He thought, *This will prove to Tamar, Pastor Mike, and the rest of the world that all people are basically evil if given the chance. And everyone is always just looking out for themselves.*

"Okay great. I'll bring it by tomorrow morning." X-man spit his tobacco into a McDonald's cup. Then he asked, "You see that sign right there?" He pointed out the window as he took his foot off the gas.

"That one?" Jacob asked.

"Yeah, can you read what it says?"

"Gulf Coast Jobs?" He could barely make out the writing on such a small sign. They were now in the older and poorer part of Gulf Coast City. The streets were mostly lined with small two-story apartments and everyone who lived in this area seemed to be on top of each other. The few houses around were small and neglected. The grass needed to be cut and the dwellings needed paint. Even the street lights looked as if they weren't pumping out as much light as downtown near the bus station.

X-man smiled as if Jacob had just answered a difficult question. "That's right. Gulf Coast Jobs is an employment agency."

Jacob looked out the window but didn't show much interest because the small row of old worn-down office buildings didn't look all that appealing.

X-man now had a proud look on his face. "I used to pick girls up from Gulf Coast Jobs from time to time and they were always young and sexy. I mean smokin-hot sexy." Jacob started to feel uncomfortable. "The owner there is this really shady Arab guy from Syria or Algeria or somewhere. Anyway, he runs these girls to the strip clubs, sets them up as escorts and Lord knows what else. And you know what else?" X-man looked around his cab as if he was checking to see if anyone else was listening. "They're all from Russia."

"Really?" Jacob was starting to liven up. He might have been exhausted from his long bus trip. He was definitely not here to chase girls, but he was still human and still an easily excitable young man.

"Yeah, man." X-man could tell he wanted to hear more. "Every year around this time Gulf Coast City gets flooded with hundreds of chicks from Russia, Belarus, Estonia, Ukraine. You know, hot chicks from all over the place."

"Wow, I like the sound of this," Jacob said, sitting straight up with a grin on his face. X-man was painting such an intriguing picture that he'd temporarily forgotten why he was here.

"Oh yeah, they come here for the tourists season and work in the hotels and the restaurants. It's really great, I tell ya, seein' all these hot chicks all over the place. They prance all around town in their tight little miniskirts and short-shorts. Man, do they have really amazin' legs. I guess they do a lot of walkin' in Russia that helps 'em stay all toned-up. Of course, the Russian dudes gotta come too. I think they're all college kids from over there and that shady Arab guy finds jobs for them."

"I'm definitely gonna have to check out Gulf Chicks Jobs," Jacob said as he started smiling.

"Not Gulf Chicks Jobs, man." X-man laughed. "Gulf Coast Jobs. I know where your mind is."

Jacob blushed. "Wow, I can't believe I said that."

X-man continued to drive deeper into the poor part of town. Jacob looked out the window as more and more dilapidated homes lined the road, all in various states of disrepair. Instead of boasting colorful flowers, the residents must have sat back and let the kudzu and weeds take over. Neighborhood street dogs roamed free along the broken sidewalks. Occasionally a dark figure would jump into the shadows when they saw X-man's taxi passing by. The surroundings continued to decline until X-man finally arrived at the motel he'd picked. When Jacob stepped out of the taxi to pay, he put his feet on some broken glass.

"Watch out now!" X-man cried out. "A lot of people like to party around here at night. If I was you, I'd head straight indoors."

Jacob tried to look around but everywhere was dark and the streetlights were dull. His new surroundings were quiet and creepy. "Thanks, and thanks for the ride X-man. Here's the extra $20 for that bicycle. By-the-way, my name's Jacob Carmichael."

X-man handed over his business card and said, "Nice to meet ya, Jacob. Here's my card. If ya ever need a ride around town or just wanna get crazy sometime, give me a holla." Jacob looked at the card, while X-man was peeling out of the parking lot, and chuckled when he saw what was on it. *Gulf Coast City Taxis - X-man - Licensed Driver*

He quickly checked into the seedy motel and paid the old man behind the bulletproof glass for a week's accommodation. The inside of his motel room was not much to look at with dirty carpet, peeling wallpaper and one bed underneath an old faded blanket. The place was only large enough to squeeze in one person and a few belongings, and he already didn't feel safe. The old windows could easily be opened by anyone who wanted to come inside to rob or attack him, and he had no idea who was lurking around outside. But it was cheap and close to the city center where he could easily jump on a bus to get the hell out of here. So he tried to convince himself that he was going to be safe as he tossed and turned in his bed. Tomorrow was going to be a very apprehensive day.

CHAPTER 4
SUE ELLEN DOOLEY'S HOUSE

"There's no way I'm going in there!"
—Jacob Carmichael

Ordinarily, Jacob would have slept in late and enjoyed the morning, like any other unemployed 21-year-old who'd just arrived in Florida, but he wanted to see if X-man had delivered on his promise. He crawled out of the motel bed and walked two feet to the window. He looked outside into the bright sun and to his surprise, there was a bicycle resting up against the wall. He was excited to see that X-man was a decent person after all. He rushed out into the sticky heat, wondering how the bicycle managed to stay out there without being stolen. *Maybe Someone was watching over him after all.*

He decided he was going to spend the day exploring his new surroundings. He thought about trying to find Sue Ellen Dooley's house, so he went back inside the motel room and picked up the piece of paper that had her address. He got on his bicycle and combed his wavy blonde hair to the side with his fingers. This would be enough grooming to keep him presentable for the entire day. He wiped an endless supply of sweat from his forehead and headed out on his wobbly old bicycle towards Oak Street.

Jacob remembered the path X-man had taken last night, so he retraced his steps until he was about a block away. When he reached the sign that said Oak Street, his stomach heaved and he said to himself, *No it's too early*. So he took a detour and headed towards the beach instead.

Last night he'd read a tourist pamphlet he'd found on the bus. Gulf Coast City is right on the beautiful Gulf of Mexico. The population of permanent residents is not much larger than Tinsley but when the tourists arrive in the Spring and Summer the size quadruples. They come from all over the world to see the clear turquoise water and soak up the sun, so Jacob decided he might as well check it out too.

When he reached the beach, he forgot to look for the white sand and clear water because bikini girls were all over the place. It was still cool up in South Carolina, but here everyone was walking around with bronze skin and perfect bodies. Jacob's mood perked up fast.

He spent the entire day sitting on the beach, sipping a few beers, eating half a hot dog from a sidewalk vendor and thinking about his problems. *What was he going to do with the rest of his life? He had made a vow to God that he was going to help people. He cared deeply about the human race but since his sister's attack, he had really gotten off track. Why was the madman in his hometown?* He hoped meeting Sue Ellen Dooley would give him the answers.

When evening rolled around, he got back on his bicycle and headed back towards his motel. He didn't feel safe being out after dark. The inhabitants of the neighborhood around his motel were not as happy-go-lucky as the tourists, who pranced carelessly around the beach. These people were either manual laborers, or unemployed doing Lord knows what, Jacob thought. They certainly didn't look like they wanted to make friends with the new kid in town, who was staying at the Shady Tree motel.

He decided he'd ride back along Oak Street and look for Sue Ellen and Carl's house. The scenic part of Gulf Coast City soon turned dismal as Jacob peddled away from the beach and back into the scary part of town.

When he arrived at Oak Street he started looking for house numbers to see how far away he was from 127. The first house he saw was 101, so he knew he was close. The houses were small and none of the occupants seemed to care about how they lived. *If they did*, he thought, *they'd do a better job of cutting their grass and painting their houses.* But no one seemed to have any desire to keep their home looking nice. Jacob peddled past 113, so he knew he was getting closer. He smelled what he thought was marijuana smoke coming from one of the houses and peddled a little faster.

Finally, he arrived at 127 Oak Street and he was sure that this was Sue Ellen Dooley's residence. His heart began to pound in his chest, and he tried to swallow but couldn't. He looked at the house for clues that would tell him more about the man who attacked his sister. But the house didn't give him anything. It was just a set of bricks in a poor neighborhood that nobody cared about. The weeds had taken over the front yard and were making their way onto the brick front porch. It appeared that whoever lived in there had to go through the carport to get inside. On the cracked driveway, someone had spray painted some words. Jacob peddled up the driveway to read what was written. *"LEAVE TOWN BITCH"* This made him nervous. But he had come over five hundred miles; even though someone obviously disliked Sue Ellen Dooley, this was not going to stop his search. With knees shaking and palms sweating, he got off his bicycle and wheeled it along Sue Ellen Dooley's driveway until he got to the brick steps of her front porch. He pushed down the kickstand with his foot, took a deep breath, then prepared himself to walk up towards the door.

He was about to take his first step onto the porch when a police car pulled into the driveway. Jacob froze. The engine stopped and a short stocky policeman got out of his patrol car. He was confident and arrogant; Jacob could already tell. He swaggered over to where Jacob was still frozen. His short sleeve shirt was rolled up to show his biceps and his hand rested on his gun, just in case.

"You wanna tell me what's going on here?" the police officer demanded with his strong Southern accent.

"I-- I," Jacob stuttered. He didn't know why but he already felt guilty. This policeman just seemed to bring it out of him.

"Is this your property, boy?"

"No sir," he said.

"Then you wanna tell me why you're lurking 'round here?" The bald policeman was oozing with condescension as he stared at him through his mirrored glasses.

"I'm not lurking around here." Jacob's face showed that he was a little insulted.

"Well, I saw you snooping 'round here earlier today and now you're back again. Seems to me like you're up to something."

"Look, officer." He paused to look at the policeman's badge. "Look officer Hunter--"

"That's Corporal Hunter boy!" The policeman was offended, and Jacob was surprised at how easily it had happened.

"Look, Corporal Hunter, I'm not snooping and I'm not lurking, I--" Jacob was just about to explain everything when Corporal Hunter's radio blasted and he put his hand in his face for him to be quiet.

"Corporal Hunter, please respond to a 10-17 at the Food Chief," Dispatch announced.

"Copy that. I'm en route." Corporal Hunter put down his radio and said to Jacob, "Don't let me catch you 'round here again or I'll lock you up." He jumped into his patrol car and took off down the street.

* * *

The next day Jacob wanted to do more exploring. He thought about riding past Sue Ellen's house again but couldn't get the courage to risk seeing Corporal Hunter. He really wanted to get out of the depressing motel, so he decided he'd ride around and maybe check out Gulf Coast Jobs. The words of X-man, the taxi driver, were still ringing in his head. *"These girls are smoking-hot sexy and they're all from Russia!"* He tried to force temptation away but he couldn't.

With visions of Russian strippers in his head, he got on his bicycle and headed towards the street where X-man had shown him the sign for Gulf Coast Jobs. His motel was not far away, and very soon Jacob was riding past this intriguing employment agency and seeing it for the first time in the daylight. It didn't seem as exciting as when X-man had presented it a couple of nights ago. It was definitely not a place where seasoned white collar professionals would go looking for work. *Only desperate manual laborers probably went here*, he thought.

He needed to keep his mind occupied and off of his sister's attacker, who'd lived only a few blocks away, so he rode down to the beach again to check out the cute girls and escape his life. He ended up doing the same routine every day for two weeks. He got up, rode past Gulf Coast Jobs, then went to the beach to drink beer and girl watch, then rode back to the motel by way of Sue Ellen Dooley's house. Hoping he wouldn't run into Corporal Hunter, he always did the same routine and never once deviated.

Today was going to be different; however, Jacob didn't know it yet. He got out of bed in the morning and got on his bike, which he was squeezing inside his motel room. Without showering, shaving or even washing his face, he combed his hair with his fingers and headed towards Gulf Coast Jobs.

When Jacob arrived at the employment agency, he saw a woman walking out the office door. He slammed on his bicycle's brakes so he could watch her. The woman was small and prematurely grey, so he immediately knew she wasn't one of the strippers that X-man had talked about.

He got closer so he could learn more about this mysterious person. And as he did, he realized he knew who she was. He recognized her from the newspaper photograph back in Tinsley. Walking right past him was Sue Ellen Dooley. *She must work at Gulf Coast Jobs*, he thought. He could feel his heart racing so he got back on his bicycle and pedaled back to the motel to get away.

CHAPTER 5
THE JOB INTERVIEW

"Necesitamos un Trabajo."
—Anonymous

When Jacob got back to his motel, he'd calmed himself down and curiosity was eating away at him. He had to find out more about Sue Ellen Dooley. He showered and shaved for the first time in weeks - psyched himself up, got properly dressed and ran out the door. He wore a white shirt, black tie and a pair of black slacks. He was proud that he was able to steam out the wrinkles in his shirt from the hot shower, and thought he looked professional. Everyone who saw him most likely thought he was a Jehovah's Witness. He didn't have a car so he couldn't exactly arrive in style, and of course riding on his bicycle made him look even more like a Jehovah's Witness. All he needed was a Bible in his hand and people would be getting nervous that he was going to knock on their door.

He was determined to find out more about Sue Ellen Dooley. Since he didn't want to go to her house for fear of seeing the intimidating Corporal Hunter, he summoned up the courage to peddle towards Gulf Coast Jobs. His biggest concern was not to get too sweaty on the ride over. Half of Jacob was racing to get to Gulf Coast Jobs to find out what his sister's attacker's wife was doing and the other half kept saying, *Slow down, you don't want to arrive drenched in sweat.*

Fortunately, Gulf Coast Jobs was only four or five blocks away from his motel, so it was actually pretty close if he cut through some side roads. When he arrived, Jacob combed his hair to the side and decided the only way he could get inside was to apply for a job.

He walked up to the entrance of Gulf Coast Jobs and caught his reflection in the glass door. He quickly patted down the hairs that were still standing up from the bicycle ride, then checked to see if his part was on the side. Satisfied and with pride in his step, he entered the office.

When he got inside, he was very surprised. This place was not at all like X-man had described. No beautiful Russian girls sitting around waiting to go strip or escort, nothing exotic like he'd imagined, just a dusty waiting area and a woman sitting behind a desk. The small room was quiet and falling apart. His first impression was the same as the rest of the neighborhood. *No one here cares about the appearance of this place because if they did they'd at least keep it clean.* He knew they couldn't do much about the building being old, but someone could at least mop the tile floor and dust the wooden desk where the receptionist sat.

"May I help you?" the woman asked in what sounded like a Middle Eastern accent. When Jacob realized she'd been watching him fix his hair, he blushed.

She was probably in her early thirties, attractive, he thought, and later that day found out her name was Ada. She was Turkish, and co-owner of Gulf Coast Jobs. But when Jacob first walked in, all he thought was, she is just the receptionist. Still, he reluctantly found himself attracted to her shiny jet black hair, almost black eyes and shapely large breasts. He kept trying not to stare at her chest because he knew this would get him in trouble. Jacob's mind instantly went back to the last time he lost control around a voluptuous woman and he wasn't there to protect his sister.

Slightly annoyed, the receptionist asked again, "May I help you?"

"Yes," he said timidly. "I'm looking for a job or some work... anything you might have."

"What kind of work are you good at?" Ada asked in an impervious tone as she looked down at some papers on her desk.

"Well, I'm a semester away from graduating from Bob Jones University. My major is Theology and I intend to be a pastor after I graduate." Then Jacob thought, *I'm not even sure if I still believe in God, so why did I just tell her I want to be a pastor?* He quickly changed the subject. "I also visited Europe where I traveled around for about six weeks."

"Sounds interesting," Ada said, not really sounding impressed. "I'm from Holland. Well, originally I'm from Turkey, but I moved to Holland when I was fourteen."

"I visited Holland when I was in Europe," Jacob said hoping to establish some kind of connection with Ada.

"Where did you go, Amsterdam?"

"Yes," he said, realizing that now she probably thought he just wanted to party.

"Yeah, all the Americans go to Amsterdam."

Jacob got the feeling this woman was totally unimpressed with him. He wanted to tell Ada his parents used to go to Amsterdam to serve as missionaries, but he didn't want to answer the follow-up questions he knew she'd be asking. He'd have to tell her how they died suddenly in a car accident while he was over there visiting. He'd have to explain that they were on their way to pick him up from the bar when he was 16. He'd had too much to drink out in the red-light district, so he'd called and asked them to pick him up.

Ada gathered some papers and handed them over. "My husband traveled around Europe as well. He said it was fun." She gave Jacob a little hint of a smile.

"Maybe he and I can swap stories one day."

"Fill out these application forms and give them back to me when you're finished," Ada said with the enthusiasm of a cold fish.

So Jacob did what he was told and where the application asked, *"What type of job are you interested in"*, he wrote *"Anything."* He thought, *I might as well follow this all the way through, and even if they have me digging a ditch I won't care because I can find out more about Sue Ellen Dooley.* When he finished, he handed the employment application back to Ada, who began looking it over immediately.

While Ada appeared to be deciding whether to give Jacob a job, he sat on a creaky chair trying not to fidget. As he looked at the peeling wall paper while combing his hair to the side with his fingers, he thought, *if they're trying to make a good first impression, they're failing miserably.* He observed some of the signs posted on the walls that were mostly in Spanish. They all seemed to be explaining some sort of Florida state employment law.

The door swung open and four small Hispanic men walked inside. "Necesitamos un trabajo," one of the men said. Jacob didn't have a clue what he was saying.

Ada replied back at a louder volume, thinking, it seemed, that this would make it easier for the men to understand. "Gabriela will be here mañana." Jacob still had no idea what was going on, he began wondering if maybe this was not the place for him. He didn't speak Spanish and maybe these were the only type of employees they hired here.

He was sitting nervously on his hands, trying to stop fidgeting, and debating whether he should get up and leave, when he heard, "My name is Ada and my husband and I own Gulf Coast Jobs." She pointed at a dirty plastic chair in front of her desk and said, "Why don't you come back up here and have a seat. I'd like to hear more about your college and what kind of work experience you have."

He walked up to the dusty chair and sat down. "I did some missionary work with my parents, when I was in Europe, and I did an internship at Tinsley Baptist church in South Carolina."

"You say you interned at a church?" Ada asked suspiciously.

"Yes," he replied trying not to think about his past.

"And you only had one semester to go at your college and you dropped out?"

The hair on the back of Jacob's neck stood up as he could feel the bad memories coming back. "I-- I just needed a break so I decided to come to Florida for a while."

"Okay," Ada said. She realized she'd hit a nerve. And even though this was a job interview, she didn't seem to feel the need to pry too deep.

Ada continued to ask him basic interview questions. She wasn't listening to exactly what he was saying but more how he said it. She just wanted to see how well he paid attention to her questions, and how well he articulated his answers.

He must have done pretty well and Ada must have realized he was intelligent because she offered him a job right there on the spot. She announced, "We have an opening for an operations manager here at Gulf Coast Jobs. Would you be interested in this?"

Jacob couldn't believe how fast this was all happening. He had to make a split-second decision. He stalled for a second then said, "Yes, I'd be interested." He was thinking, *Wow she didn't even check my references.*

Ada explained, "This is a full-time position that pays minimum wage, plus commission."

"Sounds great, I'll take it."

"I haven't finished explaining yet." Ada was a little annoyed, and from what Jacob had seen so far, she *always* seemed a little annoyed. "You'll be in charge of all the temporary employees as well as help my husband and me build the business. This means that in addition to helping with staff recruitment, you'll also be calling on hotels and other businesses to explain how we can send them seasonal workers."

The more Jacob thought about this in the short time he'd been here, the more he realized this was the perfect job. If he was managing the operations, he could keep tabs on Sue Ellen Dooley. He'd be able to find out all about her and could see what type of a woman married a monster like Carl. When he was ready, he'd tell her who he was. Maybe this would somehow relieve the huge weight he'd been carrying on his chest.

He was just another anonymous person in Gulf Coast City, which he liked, and now he had a job. He could stay here as long as he wanted. He was a little suspicious of why Ada had offered him the job so quickly. Obviously, he wasn't going to inquire because she might change her mind. After seeing the four Hispanic men enter earlier, and remembering X-man's comments about the Russians, he assumed that maybe they didn't get a lot of Americans applying for work. Maybe Ada and her husband just offered the job to the first English speaking college kid who entered their office, he didn't know. At this point, he didn't care because he was perking up at the thought of once again doing something meaningful with his life.

Ada asked, "Can you be here first thing tomorrow to begin training?"

"I sure can," Jacob answered immediately. "Thank you."

They both said goodbye and Jacob walked out the door grinning from ear to ear. He got on his bicycle as the midday's steamy heat bore down on him, and pedaled back to his motel. He was looking forward to returning tomorrow.

CHAPTER 6
GULF COAST JOBS

"Don't the police do anything about this?"
—Jacob Carmichael

The next day Jacob peddled into Gulf Coast Jobs early, and even though the surrounding area was as beautiful as the city dump, he was excited to be starting his first day at work. Ada introduced him to Gabriela and said he'd be shadowing her most of the day. Gabriela was the secretary and receptionist for Gulf Coast Jobs. She was a 30-year-old Puerto Rican lady with curly black hair. She was a little plump with a friendly smile, kind face, and bubbly personality. She was the type of person that was easy to make laugh, and because of this, was always laughing. Gabriela spoke Spanish and English, which was a big plus in this business because most of the manual laborers were Hispanic.

The first thing Gabriela told Jacob was none of the Hispanic workers were legal, meaning of the twenty Mexican, Guatemalan, and Honduran workers employed by Gulf Coast Jobs, not one was legally eligible to be employed in the United States.

"How could that be?" Jacob asked Gabriela. "They all have green cards. I've seen them."

Gabriela was enjoying feeling important. "All the Latin people go to the same guy here in Gulf Coast City and pay him $100 for a fake green card and social security number. It takes him about thirty minutes to give them what they want and he has customers lined up around the block."

"Don't the police do anything about this?" He asked, remembering he was no longer in Tinsley, South Carolina and realizing he must sound naive.

"They do, but less than a week after they haul their butt to jail, someone always steps in to take their place." Gabriela smiled as she explained. "Besides, do you really think the United States would hand out green cards to Hispanics who don't speak English?"

Gabriela's comments made a lot of sense and none of the Hispanic employees at Gulf Coast Jobs spoke any more than very basic English. Jacob had already noticed that almost everyone who came in this place was not American. They were immigrants, mostly from Latin countries and occasionally Russia or Eastern Europe.

He continued conversing with Gabriela, and while he did, he noticed she had a small TV that appeared to be hidden in her desk drawer. When he asked her about it she started laughing and said, "You know Jacob, for when it gets slow and boring in here I can watch my soap operas." They both laughed and he thought Gabriela was a really nice person. It seemed like the two of them were going to get along really well.

Later in the day, Jacob met Ada's husband and co-owner of Gulf Coast Jobs. His name was Mustapha, and just as X-man had described, he was an obese, dark-skinned Middle Easterner with a bald head and dark eyes. X-man claimed Mustapha was from Syria or Algeria, but he was actually from Libya. Mustapha was in his thirties but looked a lot older due to his excessive smoking and extra weight. Even though he had a slight accent, his English was perfect. Jacob liked the guy but still felt intimidated around him.

Mustapha asked Jacob to come with him so they could have a chat. They walked back to his office which was right behind the small waiting room, and just like everywhere else in this employment agency, it had peeling green wall-paper and dusty old furniture. They both sat down and while Jacob was trying to get comfortable, Mustapha asked. "Do you mind if I smoke?"

Of course, Jacob minded. He didn't want to breathe in Mustapha's nasty cigarette smoke while he sat in his tiny office. But this was his first day at work, and he was meeting with his new boss for the first time, so he politely replied, "No, I don't mind. Go right ahead."

Mustapha was the only guy Jacob knew who produced an all-out attack on three of the five senses. He attacked the sense of smell because he was a heavy smoker and the stench stayed on him. His deodorant habits, or lack of, weren't covering his musky odor; to mask the cigarette smell he blasted his body with cheap cologne. He attacked the sense of sight with the outrageous outfits he wore. He was almost 6 feet and 275 pounds, but instead of wearing some manly looking clothes, he wore brightly colored silk shirts and silk pants. Today he wore a bright yellow silk shirt with matching silk pants. Mustapha also attacked the sense of hearing because when he spoke it was always at full volume. He had a commanding deep voice, and he spoke as if he was in charge of something big.

Mustapha leaned back in his creaky wooden chair like he was the admiral of a large ship, and said, "Jacob, I'd like to take some time to sit with you so I can explain the philosophy behind my employment agency, and let you know how Ada and I think you will fit into all this."

Mustapha exhaled his smoke just as Jacob swatted away a fly. Realizing Mustapha probably thought he was disgusted by his nasty habit, he quickly replied, "Sounds good," and tried to look relaxed.

Mustapha continued, unfazed. "You see, Jacob, Ada and I started this employment agency because we are both Christians. We want to help other less fortunate people find jobs which will help them bring happiness and dignity to their lives. The reason we came to the United States was because we were granted refugee visas which allow us to take up residence in this country, as well as legally gain employment or start a business. In Libya, we were persecuted for our Christian beliefs, so we applied for visas to USA."

Mustapha also told him his family was very poor back in Libya and he and Ada had to do terrible things to other humans just to survive. "That's awful that this happened to you and poor Ada back in Libya," Jacob said, hoping he'd give him the details, but Mustapha started talking about his life in America instead.

"It hasn't always been easy for me here in USA either," Mustapha said, as he took another big drag on his cigarette, then exhaled the smoke so he could add to the already polluted small office.

"When I first moved to USA with my wife and four children, we lived in Miami and I had to work in a hot kitchen washing dishes after walking an hour to work. Ada, of course, had to stay home and look after the kids so she couldn't contribute."

Jacob figured now was a good time to try to establish some common ground with his new boss, so he told Mustapha, "I too was brought up by strong Christian parents and my faith is very important to me." He was struggling with his faith, but he didn't want to tell Mustapha this. He was tired of feeling guilty every time he lusted after a beautiful girl because he remembered how this had opened the door to the violent attack on Tamar. He was tired of feeling guilty the day after he drank alcohol because he remembered how his parents would still be alive if they hadn't come to pick him up when he was drunk.

Mustapha seemed happy to hear that they shared the same Christian beliefs. He smiled and said, "Jacob, I can already tell you have a real talent for this type business. I can see you being very successful working for Gulf Coast Jobs."

Mustapha had one employment agency in Gulf Coast City and had just recently opened another office in Columbus, Ohio. Mustapha and Jacob talked about opening many offices across the country. He told Jacob he was getting in on the ground floor, and as the business grew he would someday be helping him run multiple offices throughout the country. Jacob, of course, wasn't sure if he'd work here a day, a week or forever, but he was happy that his new boss was taking an interest in him.

For the most part, he felt good about being here. He smiled as Mustapha explained in detail exactly how he was supposed to help recruit temporary staff, as well as assist with growing the business. This meant lots of sales calls to hotels looking for housekeepers and laundry attendants, and golf courses looking for maintenance staff. Landscaping companies were in need of temporary workers too, especially during the summer season. Restaurants were another source of business for Gulf Coast Jobs because they were always looking for extra employees for anything from dishwashing to wait staff. Gulf Coast Jobs was doing quite a bit of business already, but Mustapha wanted Jacob to get him more.

Just as Jacob thought the office couldn't get any smokier unless the place was on fire, Mustapha decided to light another cigarette. Then he asked, "Where are you living now?"

Feeling a little embarrassed, he answered, "I'm in the Shady Tree Motel."

Mustapha looked down his nose and asked, "Do you mean that trashy motel a few blocks from here?"

"That's right, but I'm looking to get out of there as soon as I can," Jacob said, hoping to save himself some dignity.

"We gotta get you outta there, Jacob. You're gonna get mugged before I can even get you ready for work." Before he could reply, Mustapha got up and said, "I have a meeting I have to go to with the landlord of this office. We'll continue this conversation later, okay? You know what? While I'm there, I'll ask the landlord if he has a better place he can rent you. You'll like this guy. We all call him Hamid the Mustache."

Before Jacob could ask why they called the landlord this, Mustapha hurried out of his smoky office and he watched his fat jiggling as he waddled out to his SUV.

* * *

Jacob spent the first week at Gulf Coast Jobs getting to know the business, the customers and how he fit into all this. It was mostly routine stuff, like helping job seekers fill out application forms and meeting some of their customers from the hotels, restaurants and golf courses.

But there was a little excitement, even the first week. It wasn't long before he got a hint of what his new life in Gulf Coast City was going to be like. The Russian stripper girls, that X-man had talked about, didn't show up, but the next best thing did.

Karina, Olga, and Lilianna were from Belarus. They had arrived in Gulf Coast City three weeks ago, and were desperately seeking employment. They were attending college at the University of Minsk and were able to come to the United States on what's called a J-1 Visa. This visa is called the *"Work and Travel"* visa and is granted to foreign college students so they can come over to the USA to work for a while, then travel around before they go back to their countries. Usually, students on the J-1 Visa already have a job lined up before they arrive in the United States. The Belarus girls thought they had a job waiting for them, but when they got to Gulf Coast City, surprisingly, they found out they did not.

Mustapha introduced Jacob to the Belarus girls in the front lobby of Gulf Coast Jobs, and suggested he take all three of them back to his office for an interview. Jacob obviously was happy to do this, and was beginning to really enjoy his new job. Jennifer was the last gorgeous girl who'd spoken with him, and now there were three sitting in his small office looking right at him.

Lilianna was the stereotypical confident Russian blonde with green cat-like eyes, although Jacob had to keep reminding himself she was from Belarus. She was the spokeswoman for the girls because of her confidence in herself, as well as the fact she had the best grasp of the English language.

Olga was also quite stunning with crystal blue eyes and long luxurious lashes. She had long blonde hair, just like Lilianna, except hers was in a ponytail. She seemed a little colder towards him than the other two, so he didn't fancy spending much time conversing with her.

Out of the three girls, he instantly took a personal interest in Karina. She came off as shy and quiet, but he found that enticing. To Jacob, she had the whole package, with her long dark-chocolate, wavy hair and athletic but very amazing legs. He imagined her playing tennis all day, so this was probably why she looked so breathtaking. She was wearing a fetching but professional business skirt, but since her legs were so long, when she sat down it appeared as if she was wearing a seductive miniskirt. From the very beginning, he couldn't take his eyes off of her.

Jacob asked Lilianna, "Why did you girls come to Gulf Coast Jobs?"

Lilianna had a friendly personality and was pleased to answer all Jacob's questions. She said in a harsh Belarus accent that sounded, to Jacob, the same as a Russian accent, "A crooked Russian company charged each of us $2000 for J-1 Visa, plane ticket to USA, and guarantee of job in Gulf Coast City."

"Wow," he said, legitimately surprised. "That's a lot of money just to come over here."

Lilianna explained, "We were so excited to come here for first time. The Russian company promised us they'd have job waiting at Gulf Coast City Sea Aquarium. So as soon as we arrive we go to Aquarium but no one there was expecting for us. Then we found out about Gulf Coast Jobs so we come to here."

"How could the Sea Aquarium not know you were coming?" he asked Lilianna, as he brushed under his chin with his fingers, realizing that most of his questions this week seemed like he knew almost nothing about how the real world worked.

Lilianna was proud to answer his question, mostly he suspected because she enjoyed showing him that she knew English better than Karina and Olga. "This happens all the time, Jacob. Work and Travel companies, mostly from Russia, come to universities and promise students huge opportunities in USA. Even though we students know this is probably not always true opportunity, we must take chance because this is only way we can get visa to come to USA."

"Well, you ladies won't find any dishonesty here," Jacob said, secretly hoping this would score him points with Karina as well as put his job applicants at ease.

He focused his attention back on the long explanation that Lilianna was giving. "When we come to USA most students start out in minus, you know, below zero dollars. You understand?"

"Of course," he answered with a reassuring smile.

"And for us girls, we now stay in motel room that has very expensive cost for students on low budget," Lilianna continued to explain as she locked her cat-eyes on Jacob.

Jacob listened and nodded, hoping he was not giving any indication that his 21-year-old brain was picturing what it would be like to knock on their motel door and get invited in by three beautiful Belarus ladies wearing only their skimpy pajamas. He quickly came back to earth as he realized a small piece of drool was about to fall from the corner of his mouth. He sucked in quickly and was able to get it back in his mouth to avoid a potentially embarrassing moment. He nodded in agreement, as he blushed, to whatever Lilianna was still talking about, then looked over at Olga. She seemed very distant and disinterested in their conversation. Occasionally, she'd look at her watch as if she had some important date to keep and wanted to make sure he didn't spoil it for her.

Karina seemed engaged and interested in everything Lilianna was saying. Every time Jacob tried to make humorous comments it appeared that Karina would laugh whether she thought they were funny or not. He felt like this was a good sign that she might be interested in him. He knew he was getting way too far ahead of himself, so he focused his attention back on Lilianna.

Lilianna asked, "Would it be possible to find us two or even three works... I mean jobs? Also, does Gulf Coast Jobs provided affordable housing for foreign students?"

"When will y'all sleep?" Jacob asked.

All three girls answered with a giggle, "We will sleep when we get back to Belarus."

He realized then that these young ladies were in desperate need of his help, so he tried to put the fantasies about the girls aside long enough to make an effort to help them.

"Give me a second ladies," he said in an earnest tone, then walked out of his office to search for Mustapha.

He found him in his office with his wife Ada and asked if he could think of anything they could do to help these girls.

"Yes Jacob, I can probably help them," Mustapha replied with his deep confident voice. "I have a friend whose name is Suma. He's from Turkey and the owner of Happy Suma's. It's right in the center of Gulf Coast City close to the beach. Happy Suma's is basically a convenience store and small restaurant, so he's always looking for attractive girls to work for him." He paused for a moment while a glob of ash dropped off the cigarette dangling from his puffy lips.

"Wow," Jacob said, happy he could go back to the girls to deliver the good news. "Let me go back to my office and run this past them."

Mustapha put up his hand to stop Jacob. "I know what I'm doing here. He also owns a small motel that he rents out to foreign students every year. Why don't you tell them about Happy Suma's then take them back to their motel. Let them shower up and put on evening clothes. Then you and I will go back over there so we can take them to meet my friend Suma tonight. We'll see if he has jobs and a place for them."

Jacob didn't know who Suma was but anything that involved going back to the motel of the Belarus girls, and helping them out, sounded great to him.

"Sounds good," he said. He went back to present this amazing idea to the girls. Needless to say, they were very excited. Mustapha lent Jacob his SUV, so he drove the girls back to their motel. For a second, he secretly and unrealistically hoped they'd invite him inside, but he cleared his mind of impure thoughts and kept it professional. The girls jumped out of the SUV and ran into their motel but not before they said thank you many times. Jacob could tell they were happy, grateful and looking forward to their trip to Happy Suma's.

* * *

He went back to work counting the minutes until it was time to collect the girls again. When the time finally came, Mustapha said, "Hold on Jacob. I'm coming with you." His wife Ada had already left to take care of their four children and she would meet them later at Happy Suma's.

On the way over to the girls' motel with Mustapha, Jacob decided to ask about Sue Ellen Dooley. He assumed he had to be careful with his words so he started out vague. "Mustapha the first day I was at Gulf Coast Jobs, I met this lady who was very nice to me. I think her name was Sue Ellen. You wouldn't happen to know her, would you?"

"Sue Ellen Dooley?" Mustapha shot up in his seat.

"Yes, I think so," Jacob said calmly, as a dagger hit him in the heart.

"Of course I know her. I know all my employees. What's this all about, Jacob?"

He started to fidget. "Oh, nothing. Like I said, she was very nice and you know, I'm new in town and don't really have a lot of friends."

"Well, I tell you what Jacob, she is one friend you do not want to have, I can tell you that!" He gripped the steering wheel tight as he gritted his teeth and reached for his pack of cigarettes.

From Mustapha's reaction, Jacob was sure he knew her husband, so he quickly tried to change the subject. "I was just curious about her that's all, but it's no big deal."

Mustapha must have realized he'd been a little hard on Jacob so he unclenched his fist from the steering wheel and lightened up his tone. "Look, I don't know how much you know about Sue Ellen Dooley but she has a really bad reputation in this town."

"Oh, I didn't know," Jacob said.

"That's right, and even though this town seems big with all the tourists here, most of the locals all know each other. And no one, I mean no one in this town will give her a job because her husband was an evil man."

"Okay," Jacob said calmly, while his heart was about to beat out of his chest.

"But I found a way to make her situation work to my advantage. This is what being a great business man…" *like me*, Jacob was sure Mustapha wanted to say… "is all about."

"I see," he responded.

"You see, Sue Ellen used to work as an accountant but she was fired around Christmas because of something her husband did. After that the whole town shunned her, and she couldn't get a job anywhere." He put a cigarette in his mouth and torched it with his fancy lighter. He didn't bother asking if Jacob minded. "But I was the one who saw this as an opportunity. Now she works for me cutting grass and I pay her under the table," Mustapha boasted. "You want to know how much I pay her?"

"How much?"

"Three bucks an hour," he announced proudly. "What do you think about that?"

Jacob thought Mustapha was cruel. "Isn't that below minimum wage, and illegal?"

Mustapha almost started choking on his cigarette. "Well let's get over to see the girls and focus on your job, okay?" He sounded angry and was pulling rank on Jacob now.

When they arrived at the motel, Mustapha jumped out of his SUV and walked into the motel room like he owned the place. Maybe he knocked first but to Jacob it didn't seem like it. The girls were all dolled up and ready to go. Jacob had said put on some evening clothes which appeared to translate into Russian as put on skimpier, more revealing clothes than you wore during the day. He was not complaining as he breathed in three different types of perfume while everyone piled into Mustapha's SUV. As they headed towards Happy Suma's with Mustapha at the wheel, Jacob decided he liked the vanilla smelling perfume the best and hoped Karina was the one wearing it. Karina must have sensed Jacob gazing at her, and gave him a bashful smile.

CHAPTER 7
HAPPY SUMA'S

"To my Gulf Coast City homeboy..."
—Snoop Dogg

Happy Suma's was located one block inland from Gulf of Mexico Blvd, right on the busy Gulf Coast City strip. Half the building was a restaurant that serves hamburgers, pizza and beer and the other half was a convenience store.

Mustapha's SUV pulled into the parking lot of Happy Suma's and Suma, the proud Turkish owner and his wife, Azra, could be seen through the large windows. When Suma recognized Mustapha, he jumped up and hustled over to the door to greet everyone. Suma was a heavyset guy, when he heartily shook Jacob's hand, it hurt from his tight grip. Jacob noticed Suma was missing part of his thumb, and two of his fingers, which was surprising considering how tight his grip was. He had wiry white hair, dark leathery skin and his left eye was lazy so Jacob never knew exactly where he should look. Jacob guessed Suma was probably in his mid-50s.

Ada was already talking with Suma's petite Turkish wife, Azra, while her four young kids were running around the small restaurant annoying the customers. Suma told everyone to come over to the large table already set up for a feast. Mustapha and Suma both gave each other a pat on the back and it appeared they were good friends. Mustapha greeted Suma in Arabic before explaining in English that the Belarus girls were looking for jobs and a cheap place to stay, and asked if he could help.

Suma replied as he wiggled the hand that was missing fingers, "Well, it just so happens I have a room available at my motel and I need one waitress. But she has to speak perfect or almost perfect English. So which one of you ladies speaks the best English?"

Karina was generous and pointed at self-assured Lilianna, while Olga asked, "Can you repeat question and speak slowly?"

Suma roared with laughter, which seemed typical of his demeanor, and offered Lilianna a chance to try out for the waitress position by serving everyone tonight. Lilianna's face brightened as she gladly accepted. Suma's wife, Azra, got up from the table and took Lilianna back to the kitchen for some training. As Lilianna walked off with a big grin on her face, the other girls sat down at the table with sunken faces. Suma turned his attention to Jacob and asked, "So what brings you to Gulf Coast City?"

"I was bored living in the small town where I'm from in South Carolina." Jacob looked at Suma's right eye, hoping it was the one he was supposed to focus on. "I decided to move here because it seems like an exciting vacation destination." There was no way he was going to tell Suma the real reason in front of everyone.

Suma continued his friendly grin and seemed satisfied with his answer so he asked, "How do you like working at Gulf Coast Jobs?"

"I think it's great," Jacob said with a smile. He wasn't lying, and even though his boss was sitting right next to him, he still didn't feel like he was overacting his enthusiasm. "I'm meeting a lot of interesting people and feel like I can help a lot of them."

Suma let out a roaring laugh, as if to say, *That's funny and I know you had to say that because Mustapha is sitting close to you.* He motioned for everyone to stand up and said, "Let me give you guys a tour of my restaurant. Lilianna is probably busy with Azra so Jacob, Karina and what's your name again?"

"Olga," she replied quietly.

"Olga!" Suma yelled out with an amused smile. "Why is everyone from Russia called Olga?"

"She's from Belarus," Ada chimed in with her quiet voice, sounding slightly annoyed. Jacob decided she seemed quiet because Mustapha and Suma were so loud.

"Oh, Belarus. So sorry Olga. Anyway, Jacob from South Carolina and Karina and Olga, from Belarus, come follow me. My place is nothing fancy, but I give you a tour of Happy Suma's anyway."

He showed everyone the kitchen as they walked past a small unisex restroom which had only one toilet. There was a sign on the door saying, *'Restrooms are for Customers Only'*.

Then Suma brought everyone back into the dining room, which had about ten tables, and showed them some pictures he had hanging on the wall. The pictures were large framed photographs taken inside Happy Suma's. Jacob noticed that every picture had the same person in it. It was the famous rapper, Snoop Dogg. One, in particular, had the rapper with his arm around Suma as if they were best buddies.

"You're friends with Snoop Dogg?" Jacob asked.

Suma replied back with a proud grin. "Snoop Dogg was performing at the Electric Dolphin and he stopped by Happy Suma's because he knows a great hang out when he sees one."

"Wow, that's pretty cool," Jacob said as Karina and Olga moved in closer.

"We made good money that night, remember Azra?"

Azra was too busy talking to Lilianna to answer, and Jacob sensed that she'd heard all this before. He had the feeling this was going to be a long story so he took the opportunity to get closer to Karina. She was playing with her long dark hair and sneaking glimpses of him when she thought he wasn't looking.

Suma continued, "There must have been five hundred kids all hanging around that club to get a glimpse of Snoop Dogg. So Snoop Dogg snuck away with his posse." He was trying to be cool now. "And they all showed up over here."

Jacob asked with a sly smile, "Those big bongs you have for sale over there in your convenience store wouldn't be the reason Snoop Dogg came to see you, would it?"

Another thing each picture had in common besides Snoop Dogg, was they were all holding on to the same water bongs that Suma had for sale in his attached convenience store.

"That's right Jacob," Suma announced as if he had won a contest. "Snoop Dogg bought water bongs from me and he also ate famous Happy Suma's pizza. I get these bongs cheap from my supplier at Gulf Coast City Imports."

Jacob looked a little closer at the photograph and saw that Snoop Dogg had signed it, "To my Gulf Coast City home boy, Suma."

Suma's story could have gone on indefinitely. As the smell of delicious olive-oil-enriched chicken kabab got stronger, Jacob's stomach started to rumble. Then a small-framed dark haired Middle Easterner, in his mid-30s, entered the restaurant. He clicked his key fob to set the alarm, and also to make a noise that would draw everyone's attention to his brand-new BMW outside. Jacob could immediately tell he was going all out trying to impress everyone in sight, as he was too well-dressed to be on the strip of this beach town.

"Hamid the Mustache!" Suma yelled across the restaurant. "How are you, my Libyan friend? We were just talking about you."

While Hamid arrogantly looked around to see who was watching him, Jacob could definitely see why Suma and Mustapha called him the Mustache. He had a large dark black mustache that seemed to cover his entire mouth.

Suma put his arm around Hamid and walked him over. He said, "This is Jacob, who just started working with Mustapha. And these two lovely ladies are Karina and Olga from Russia. I mean Belarus." Suma corrected himself after the girls jokingly gave him an irritated look.

Hamid shook Jacob's hand first with a firm grasp. Then he shook Karina and Olga's hands. The way Hamid the Mustache looked at Karina and Olga convinced Jacob that this guy was a wolf on the prowl.

"Nice to meet you, Jacob, and ladies," Hamid said in a harsh but high pitched Libyan accent.

Suma took center stage again. "Hamid has an import business and he is the one that can get me these water bongs at such a great price. You tell them, Hamid."

Hamid responded with his barely understandable voice. "Yes, I own Gulf Coast City Imports and we import from China and sell all over Florida. I have the big warehouse on Third Avenue South. Maybe you saw it already, I don't know. Anyway, how long have you girls been here, huh?" It was obvious Hamid had decided to hit on the girls, there really wasn't anything Jacob could do about it.

"We arrive to here only few of weeks ago," Karina answered with a disinterested air, which gave Jacob a big sense of relief. She sounded about as enthusiastic as Olga had back in his office earlier today. Then Karina looked over at Jacob hoping he'd come to the rescue.

Just in time, Lilianna showed up with a sizzling plate of Turkish food, and Karina was able to make her escape. Suma was doing most of the talking now until Mustapha chimed in, with the help of Ada, and started telling everyone about Ada's sister. She lived in Turkey and desperately wanted to come to the United States. They showed everyone pictures, and Jacob saw that she was about his age and quite stunning. As soon as Mustapha saw Jacob's eyes appear to brighten he asked, "Would you like to marry her?"

His jaw dropped. "I'm sorry, what?"

"If you marry my sister she will pay you," said Ada, as both Mustapha and she leaned in uncomfortably closer.

Then Mustapha took over. "It will be a business arrangement, but she will also be your wife. She will cook and clean and help you with the rent. When she gets a job, she'll share the money she earns with you."

Ada added, "Maybe you two will fall in love like Azra's sister Nilgün and her American husband."

Feeling like he was being given the high-pressure sales pitch, he asked, "Does her American husband have a business relationship with Nilgün?"

"They did," answered Mustapha, "but now they are in love."

Jacob combed his hair to the side with his fingers, suspicious of the whole idea. He started to get the feeling that Mustapha, Ada, Suma and Azra had already discussed trying to get him to marry Ada's sister prior to his arrival at Happy Suma's. This may have been the entire reason he was invited over for supper.

He didn't know what to make of all this so he looked more closely at Yousra's photo. He noticed her curly black hair and sweet face. In the picture, she had her hands on her curvy hips and he imagined her parading around Happy Suma's commanding attention from all the male customers. He couldn't help but start daydreaming about what it would be like to have her show up on his doorstep saying, *"Hello I'm your fiancée! I'm ready to get married to you so I can get my green card."* Jacob was miles away, he realized he had a silly gaze on his face and he blushed when he realized everyone at the table had stopped talking.

A young African American man and his white girlfriend had just walked into Happy Suma's and were walking towards them. The girl was definitely still in her teens and had a great sun-tan, despite being a red-head. She was wearing low-cut Brazilian style jeans and a half shirt that showed off her stomach. The black guy looked like he was in his 30s with braided hair. His Sean John jeans were way too big for him and seemed to be hanging down around his knees. From the smug look on his face, Jacob could tell that this guy obviously thought he was something special. The girl was hanging all over him as if she was in heat. The guy had his arm around her, and she was playing with his gold necklace and rubbing his chest.

When the couple reached the table, the young man made eye contact with Suma. "Yo Suma, you think my girl here can use y'all's bathroom even though the sign say it fo customers only?"

"Go ahead Winston," Suma said lightheartedly.

Winston and his girlfriend walked off towards the small restroom, and everyone continued eating. Lilianna came out again and seemed as if she was getting the hang of her new waitressing job. She asked, "Does everyone want ice in your iced tea?"

Suma yelled out, "Lilianna, the reason they call it iced tea is because it's tea with ice in it!" At first Lilianna was upset because she thought Suma was mad. Then he smiled and she realized he was only joking.

Hamid the Mustache took this as an opportunity to make a move on Lilianna. He took a $100 bill out of his wallet and put it on the table, then watched Lilianna blush as she picked it up. This was the first time Jacob saw anyone tip the waitress *before* the meal was over, and it was also the largest tip he'd ever seen. Hamid continued to direct his attention towards Lilianna as he said, "In addition to owning a business that supplies clothes, souvenirs and of course water bongs to the beachwear stores, I also have connections with a modeling agency in Miami."

"Really?" Lilianna's cat-eyes lit up.

"That's right," Hamid bragged, with a conceited look on his face. "If you want, I can make a phone call to my associates in Miami and they'll put you on a plane and get you set up in a condo in Miami Beach. You'll have to share with the other models of course, but I'm sure you'll love it."

Jacob was convinced Hamid the Mustache was exaggerating, but he was doing such a great job of describing this agency that Lilianna was really buying into it. Jacob looked over at Karina and Olga, they seemed to be totally intrigued as well. He was wishing Hamid would just leave because he was spoiling his chances of getting into a conversation with Karina.

"Winston!" Suma yelled. "What is he doing? Didn't he say his girlfriend needed the restroom? Where is he? Wait a minute!" Suma got up from the table and walked to the back of the restaurant towards the restroom. Then everyone heard, "Winston you and your girlfriend need to get out of there right now!"

When Winston and his girlfriend came out of the restroom, they were frantically pulling up their clothes, so Suma laid into them both. "What the heck do you guys think you're doing in there?"

"Yo, sorry Suma," Winston whispered and seemed proud that he'd been caught.

Suma was trying to act mad, but everyone could tell he was having a hard time, and couldn't help smiling.

Winston and his girlfriend made a quick exit and Suma asked Lilianna to bring out the dessert. It was now pretty late so after the huge meal everyone said their goodbyes and left Suma from Happy Suma's for the night. Mustapha told Jacob to take the girls home and drive his SUV to work tomorrow. When Mustapha said he'd ride home with Ada and the kids, he definitely didn't get an argument from his new operations manager.

Jacob and the three Belarus girls piled into Mustapha's black Ford Exhibition and he drove them back to their motel. The girls were buzzing about their night out and Lilianna was talking about her new job.

Karina was sitting up front with Jacob, just like he'd hoped. She thanked him for finding them a better motel at Happy Suma's then asked in her soft voice, "Jacob can you help Olga and me find good job, just like you did for Lilianna?"

Jacob reassuringly said, "I will definitely try my best," hoping like hell Mustapha would come up with something so he could help them.

As he drove through the bright lights of town to the girls' motel, he kept catching Karina looking at him and playing with her hair. He felt like this was a really good sign. He decided to ask, "So why did you decide to come to the USA?"

Karina swallowed a huge lump then answered, "My mom is very sick back in Minsk and I need to get money for her operation."

"Oh no, what's wrong with your mom?"

Karina's English was good, and definitely better than Olga's, but not totally fluent. When she tried to give the details, she couldn't find the correct words. He quickly changed the subject when he saw her eyes starting to mist.

They arrived at the motel and he felt his heart begin to race. When the girls climbed out of Mustapha's SUV, he got out with them. Now he was almost trembling. He was hoping Karina's smiles were not just her way of being polite. If he misread any of her signals he could be in for a major embarrassment in the next few seconds.

He continued the small talk with Karina, as they walked closer to the motel room. Then Lilianna and Olga stepped inside which he felt for sure was off limits.

Just as Karina was about to step through the door, Jacob gently grabbed her arm and said, "Can I have a quick word with you in private?"

Though she seemed startled by the request, she smiled at him. Jacob paused for what seemed like forever trying to figure out his next move. Lilianna caught onto what he was trying to accomplish, and closed the motel door to give them some privacy. She gave him one last smile as the door shut as if to say, *Good luck with Karina.*

Anxiously, Jacob began to make his play. He felt the past try to push its way into his thoughts and dominate his feelings. He thought about Jennifer sitting seductively on her couch, recalling how fast that situation got out of hand. He fought hard with his conscience and was determined not to let it win. He didn't have anywhere to go tonight. Tomorrow was Saturday and he had the day off. There was nothing wrong with getting closer to a respectable young lady.

He turned to face Karina then looked into her curious eyes and said, "Um… I just wanted to say I know we didn't get to spend much time with each other tonight, but I still enjoyed it." Karina brushed her hair away from her face and started to get giggly. He leaned in closer and breathed in her vanilla perfume. He kept getting closer to Karina's face and kept watching to see if she was going to reject him. But she never did. In fact, the closer he got the more her face lit up. He directed his lips towards her cheek but Karina turned at the last second. Their lips both met perfectly. He ran his fingers through her hair and savored the moment.

It was as if they were both destined for this kiss as far back as when Jacob was packing his bags in Tinsley, South Carolina, and Karina was packing her bags in Minsk, Belarus. After their kiss, Karina looked up at him beaming. He knew then that Karina must have wanted to get closer just as much as he did. They embraced in silence for a little while longer while Jacob stroked her hair and breathed in her perfume.

Soon afterward, Jacob felt like the mission had been accomplished for the night, so he decided to make a move back to Mustapha's SUV. He hadn't connected with a woman since his night with Jennifer, while his sister was being tied-up and dragged around the church. Now he couldn't stop the memories from flooding back into his mind. He definitely didn't want to ruin what he'd just started by sticking around, so he thanked Karina for a great night and she did the same. He told her he was looking forward to seeing her tomorrow and wished her a good night. Then he walked off quickly and jumped into Mustapha's SUV. He could feel a panic attack trying to break through as he thought about his sister. He sped off towards his motel to ease his anxiety with a large gulp of Jack Daniels.

CHAPTER 8

GULF COAST JOBS

"The prostitute and the prostitute-user disgust God by their degrading and destructive activities."
—*Jacob Carmichael*

At 6:30 am Saturday morning, the motel alarm clock went off and shot Jacob up in his bed. When he realized where he was, he felt a headache throbbing through his forehead. He looked at the empty Jack Daniels bottle on the floor and didn't have to wonder why he was fumbling for the aspirin like he used to do back at Bob Jones University. He rubbed the back of his head and started looking for a clean button down shirt, then realized he had the day off. He laid back down on his uncomfortable bed and thought about Karina and their first kiss.

He couldn't stay in bed because he was too excited. He jumped up and hopped in the shower. When he was finished, he looked for the cleanest pair of shorts and polo shirt he had, put them on then headed out the door with his bicycle. The sun was just coming up as he peddled to Karina's motel.

He felt foolish. *What if she's still in bed?* It was still very early and the aspirin hadn't had the chance to numb his headache yet. He decided he'd at least ride by her motel and see if there were any signs of her being awake.

When he arrived, the motel was quiet. No cars were driving by and none of the other motel guests were out and about. Jacob stood balancing his bicycle between his legs and gazed with longing at Karina's motel room door. He was about to leave and come back later when her door opened. It was Karina, dressed in a red skirt and black T-shirt with a picture of a lion on it. She had a paper bag with her and seemed to be in a hurry. Jacob considered getting out of there to hide but he was busted. Karina saw him and froze. He didn't have a choice so he peddled over to her.

"What are you doing so early?" Karina asked.

"I get up early every morning to ride my bike to get some exercise," he lied.

"Do you always ride past this motel?"

"Not always, you know. I like to take different routes."

"Okay." Karina smiled. She was quiet and shy and Jacob liked this.

"Where're you going?" he asked.

"I'm going to feed ytok."

"You're gonna feed what?"

"Ytok." Karina laughed.

"U-took?" Jacob asked.

"Yes, ytok."

"What's a u-took?"

"You'll have to follow me to find out."

So Jacob followed Karina and found out that ytok was Russian for ducks. Karina liked to get up early and feed the ducks near her motel, every morning when it was quiet and the tourists hadn't scared them away. Jacob and Karina spent the rest of the morning feeding the ducks, and the rest of the weekend together. Except at night, of course, when they both gave the other a goodnight kiss and went back to their own motels. It was a delightful weekend and Jacob never wanted it to end, but Monday morning eventually rolled around. They said their goodbyes Sunday night with Karina promising she'd come by and visit with Jacob at Gulf Coast Jobs.

* * *

Jacob got to work early and hangover free, anxiously waiting for Karina to walk through the door. He wasn't in the mood to do any work or see anybody except of course the sweet young lady from Belarus. He spent most of the morning helping new job applicants fill out employment applications and answering their questions.

Most of the applicants were either Hispanics, Eastern European or Russian students. Gabriela helped most of the Hispanics, and Jacob helped the students. Gabriela was busy talking to a Costa Rican lady, who evidently was a hotel housekeeper that Gulf Coast Jobs employed. The lady's name was Lydia, and she was having an intense conversation in Spanish with Gabriela, which Jacob didn't understand. He assumed Gabriela had it under control, so he decided to focus on the foreign students. The girls were much more attractive than Lydia and they spoke English. Jacob met several more young college girls from Poland, Ukraine and Russia. They were very enjoyable to speak with, and were all hoping to get seasonal work. But as intriguing as most of them were, he kept it professional. He already had his heart set on Karina.

In addition to the young ladies that were applying for work, there were also the foreign college guys. Obviously, they were less entertaining for Jacob. There was Sergei, an enormous Estonian bulging with muscles, who had his heart set on becoming a houseman in a top-notch hotel. Someone must have told him this was the best paying job in Gulf Coast City. "I will not accept anything lower," Sergei demanded. Hiding his vexation, Jacob made sure Sergei put this on his application and told him he'd get in touch if anyone called.

Jacob held out for Karina as long as he could before going to lunch, but she didn't show. He rode his bicycle back to his motel and grabbed the sandwich he'd forgotten to bring with him in the morning, then quickly rode back to Gulf Coast Jobs. When he got back, he went straight to his office and made a few phone calls to hotels trying to drum up some business for Gulf Coast Jobs to send housekeepers.

Mustapha and Ada had been out of the office all day. Gabriela covered up front while Jacob hid in his back office. At one point during the day,

Gabriela was laughing so loud that Jacob got up from his desk to see what was going on. As he got closer to her desk he heard a bunch of women yelling at each other in Spanish. Then he realized the noise was coming from a television. Gabriela had been watching her Spanish soap opera on her secret portable TV most of the day and was laughing her head off.

Jacob asked Gabriela, "What the heck are you watching?"

She replied, "Prisonera," as she was still laughing.

"What?"

"Prisionera."

"Prisionera?"

"Si, I mean yes."

"What the heck is Prisionera?"

"It's a Spanish speaking soap opera. You wouldn't like it."

"What's it about?"

"This girl called Guadalupe Santos is only a teenager but she has to go to prison for thirty years. When she's in the prison she gives birth to a baby girl but the guards take her away and give her to Guadalupe's sister--"

"You're right, I probably wouldn't like it," Jacob interrupted. He went back to hide in his office; later feeling a little guilty for cutting Gabriela off like that.

Around 4:30 there was a phone call from Gabriela. "Jacob, you have some visitors. They say they're looking for work and you told them to come see you."

"Send them back," he said, trying to act professional and not wanting Gabriela to think he was mixing business with pleasure. Gabriela, of course, was laughing when she delivered the message. But since Gabriela was always laughing, he didn't know if it was because she knew Karina and he had something going on, or because Gabriela always acted like this. He combed his wavy blonde hair with his fingers, then quickly looked in the mirror as he prepared for Karina. Gabriela said visitors, so Jacob assumed Karina had brought Olga. Now there was a knock on his office door.

"Come in," Jacob commanded, trying to sound important.

"What up cuz?" Winston said as he strutted into Jacob's office with the same teenager he'd been caught with, in Suma's restroom, Friday night.

"Winston?" Jacob moaned with disappointment.

"Yo, playa, don't sound so happy to see me."

"Sorry Winston, I thought you were someone else."

"Hey, I told your secretary up there, I was lookin fo a job, 'cause I knew this way I'd be able to holla at ya."

"About what?" Jacob sat up in his chair.

"Ok Mr. Jacob, hear me out on dis now. I have a bidness proposition for you and Suma says you'd be interested in dis."

"Aren't you going to introduce me to your lady friend?" Jacob asked.

"I'm gettin to all that now Jacob..."

"Oh okay."

"Anyways, I sort of have dis bidness, you know what I'm sayin' with my girl here. Well she and a couple of other honeys we kinda have dis bidness--"

Jacob interrupted Winston and asked, "What kinda business?" He was definitely interested in hearing more about what the petite but curvy redhead did with Winston.

"Ok, here it is. I sort of run this escort agency and I need to get a bidness license but the folks at the bidness office fo Gulf Coast City, they know me, you know what I'm sayin'?"

When Winston said escort agency, Jacob couldn't help but get a little excited to see what this was all about. This was all new to him. Of course, he knew he had to keep it professional so he sat calmly behind his desk and continued listening.

"Like I'm sayin', I run this escort agency and I send some honeys out to the hotels, you know. It's all legal and the police, they don't bother me as long as I have a bidness license."

Jacob had never heard anyone talk about things like this and was really excited to hear more. He knew he couldn't let Winston know this, so he said, "Then why don't you get a business license?"

Winston's girlfriend gave him an inviting look and Winston continued. "Well the bidness office, fo Gulf Coast City, they won't give me no bidness license 'cause I got dis criminal record, you know what I'm sayin'?"

"I see, but what do you want me to do about that?" Jacob wanted to help but was not about to cross the line.

"Well, if you was to get me the license then me and you could be bidness partners."

Jacob blushed; he felt sure Winston was talking about more than just escorts. He had to put his foot down because his Christian beliefs, that he'd been resisting lately, suddenly arose. "Winston, I gotta tell ya, prostitution is a vile business. And the Bible says, *The prostitute and the prostitute-user disgust God by their degrading and destructive activities.*"

"Ah man, but how am I gonna pay my bills? Is God gonna send me a check?"

Jacob shook his head while the redhead girl smiled and looked at him as if he was from another planet. Then he said, "The Bible also says, *The man who uses a prostitute is unfaithful to God's standards and therefore to God himself.*"

Winston motioned for his girlfriend to leave with him. He knew it was pointless trying to change Jacob's mind. "Okay cuz, I'll holla at ya later."

Jacob stood up and said, "Look Winston, I know I sometimes come on too strong. It's my upbringing. I'm not really so straight. You understand?"

"Sure man. I heard you was real religious but I didn't believe it. We gotta go but I'll still holla at ya." Winston and the redhead quickly walked out the door leaving Jacob alone, trying to figure out what had just happened.

CHAPTER 9
X-MAN'S TAXI

"... You could say I'm more of a lover than a fighter."
—Jacob Carmichael

The rest of the day was uneventful and ended without the emergence of Karina. Disappointed, Jacob walked outside and locked up the office. All he could see was overgrown weeds and palm trees as he bicycled home that evening. The palm trees were the only picturesque inhabitants of this area. Between the job applicants, hotel managers, and crazy sinful Winston, he was absolutely worn out.

* * *

Jacob came running through the front door of Gulf Coast Jobs the next morning. It was raining outside and he was soaked. Mustapha called him into his office before he could figure out a way to get dry. "You remember Hamid who everyone calls Hamid the Mustache? Remember you met him at Happy Suma's?"

"Sure," he said as he imagined Hamid flirting with the girls and trying to get Karina to model for him.

"If you remember, I told you Hamid owns the building that we're in." Before Jacob could answer Mustapha said, "He also has a nice little townhouse near the beach that he'd like to show you. He thinks you might enjoy staying there."

Even though Hamid the Mustache was the last guy Jacob wanted to see again, he thought a cool townhouse was exactly what he needed. This would definitely help him with his social life, and since he had no immediate plans to return to his hometown of Tinsley, he couldn't stay in that motel forever. There was nothing for him now in Tinsley but bad memories. If he went back, everywhere he'd look and everyone he'd talk to would remind him of Carl Dooley attacking his sister, while he was giving into his lust.

Mustapha continued. "It's fully furnished so you could move there today if you want. You know, just like we talked about." Mustapha saw his eyes light up so he asked, "What do you think about that?"

"That sounds great!"

So Mustapha and Jacob jumped into his SUV and headed over to the Shady Tree Motel to get his suitcase, then rode over to the beach to see the townhouse. When Jacob saw the place, and Mustapha told him the low price Hamid the Mustache was willing to charge for rent, he couldn't refuse.

He immediately moved into the quaint townhouse decorated in a beach motif, only a block away from the Gulf of Mexico. The furniture was used but still in good enough shape to satisfy Jacob's needs. The neighborhood seemed quiet and safe. It looked like most of the other townhouses either housed retirees, or families renting a place for a week's vacation.

Next, they headed over to the Belarus girls' motel. Jacob wondered how Mustapha knew the girls were going to be there, but didn't fret on it too much because he was going to see Karina. With a smile on his face, he was really enjoying his job today.

When they got to the ramshackle motel, Mustapha jumped out and walked straight into the girls' room. Last time he did this, Jacob wasn't sure if he knocked first, but this time he was sure Mustapha definitely did not. Jacob followed behind and soon heard the beat of loud dance music playing and saw overstuffed Mustapha dancing with Olga with a silly smile on his face. *Boy, does this guy move quick*, he thought. *And what about the fact he's married with four kids?* At the time, he really didn't think too much about this because all he wanted to do was see Karina and continue what they'd started. He looked around the room for her but she wasn't there.

Olga whispered something in Mustapha's ear. He looked up and announced, "Olga says Karina and Lilianna aren't here. She says they're over at that big white house on Oak street. Do you know where that is?"

"It's that really old house, right? It's kinda all beat up and in desperate need of paint." Jacob had already seen the place. It was in the old part of town just a few blocks from where Sue Ellen Dooley lived. He'd passed it over a hundred times as he rode his bicycle past Sue Ellen's house.

"That's the one," said Mustapha. "It's also owned by Hamid the Mustache and Olga says a lot of Russian students--" Olga jabbed him in the side and Mustapha smiled. "I mean, Russian and Belarusian students live there." Mustapha was sweating and still dancing with Olga with his tongue hanging out. "Why don't you take my SUV and go down there and find Lilianna and Karina so you can take them over to Happy Suma's motel. I'll stay here so I can talk to Olga about a job I have for her."

Jacob suspected Mustapha was full of crap about a job for Olga and was pretty sure the only job he had in mind was a blow job. But he was happy to go look for Karina, so he jumped into Mustapha's SUV and headed to Oak street.

He felt like a big shot pulling up to the house in Mustapha's big black Ford Exhibition. It wasn't brand new, maybe two or three years old, but it looked pretty cool. And for the Russian and Eastern European students this big American car must have looked super cool too. At least that's what he was hoping.

When he was outside the house, he tried to make as much noise as he could, hoping Karina would see him and be impressed. He remembered Hamid the Mustache had done the same thing with his BMW at Happy Suma's, and the girls all seemed to be interested in seeing whose car it was.

The plantation style house was massive but outdated and beyond neglected. With the peeling paint and sagging wrap-around porch, the house looked as if it belonged to a bygone era where no one had cared about it for a long time. When it was first built over 100 years ago, it was probably owned by one of the richest guys in Gulf Coast City. But now the place was in the forgotten part of town where none of its observers would be impressed.

He stepped up to the massive oak door and thought, *if Mustapha can walk right through without knocking so can I.* When he entered the house, he was immediately welcomed by over twenty tennis shoes as well as their sweaty odor. The place was quite spacious inside but filthy. With dirt, all over the wooden floor, he wondered why they even bothered taking off their shoes.

Jacob proceeded upstairs to follow some noise he'd heard. He knew there could very well be an army of foreign students up there after seeing the number of shoes inside the front door. Remembering what Lilianna had told him earlier, he was sure they'd packed the house with as many students, as possible, so they could pay minimal rent.

When Jacob got to the top of the creaky wooden stairs, he opened the door to one of the bedrooms. He did this without knocking, because this was his new cool thing, just like he'd seen Mustapha doing so many times. It was now around 10 am, but everyone was still lying around. There were five old mattresses spread out on the floor and each mattress had two horizontal students lazing on it. The mattresses didn't have any sheets, thus revealing the stains from previous occupants. He was up to fourteen people in his count of the room when he noticed two of the students appeared to be going at it under the blanket. He made eye contact with the pimple-faced guy who was laying on top of a girl and looked a little embarrassed.

Jacob's attention was suddenly drawn to the old tattered looking couches that were surrounding the beds. It was Karina. He should have been excited but instead he was devastated. Karina was not alone. She was sitting on one of the ripped couches snuggling up with Sergei the brawny Estonian. The guy who'd told him his biggest goal, for the summer, was to become a houseman in a hotel. He felt a sharp pain shoot through his heart.

He had to say something, so he asked softly, "Are you living here now?"

"Yes," Karina replied awkwardly. "We found good rent here so we move here." She tried to justify her decision.

"I guess you girls don't want to move into Suma's motel, huh?" he asked sheepishly.

Karina didn't even hear what he said because Sergei said something to her in Russian, no doubt about him, and she was trying not to laugh.

Without saying another word, Jacob got out of the house as fast as he could. He wanted to hit the nearest bar but it wasn't even 10:30 am yet. *How could Karina have done this to him?* He felt silly for feeling upset. The only thing he could do was go back to Gulf Coast Jobs and get back to work. What started out as a great day at his job, turned out to be the longest day since he'd been in Florida.

***

When the work day finally ended, Jacob jumped on his bicycle and rushed home so he could get ready to go out again. He had to hit the bar so he could forget about yet another dreadful ending to a love story that never even happened for him.

He picked up his cell phone and called the only guy he felt he could count on... X-man, the taxi driver. X-man picked up on the first ring, as if he'd been waiting for him to call, then said he'd be over in five minutes. This gave Jacob enough time to knock back a few shots of Jack Daniels before X-man showed up outside his townhouse. He didn't have to get out of his taxi to ring the doorbell because Jacob could already hear him blaring AC/DC's *"Back in Black."*

When he went outside X-man yelled out, "Hey, what's up buddy?" Jacob was sure all his new neighbors heard the commotion, but today he didn't care. He was ready to hit the bar and forget about Karina.

He replied back, slightly buzzed, and trying to be cool like X-man, "Yo, what's up?" Somehow he didn't feel like he sounded as hip as X-man, but X-man didn't seem like the type of guy to judge him.

"Hop on in man. Where're we going?"

He had just met Karina but he felt like she had just dropped a ton of bricks on him. Maybe this was just a silly excuse to justify getting drunk. He didn't know anymore. "I don't have a lot of money X-man, but I need to get hammered."

X-man thought for a minute then said, "I know just the place for you. Cheap pitchers of beer and $2.00 mixed drinks are at the Lazy Gator tonight. How's that sound?"

"That works for me."

X-man looked at him through the mirror of his beat-up taxi, while he stuffed his mouth with chewing tobacco. Then he finally asked what Jacob could tell was concerning him. "So I know this is probably a dumb-as-shit question, but why do you need to get drunk?"

"Why does anyone need to get drunk?"

"Well if they're alone, it's usually 'cause of a girl."

"You nailed it."

"That ain't good, Jacob. You just arrived here and you're already hung up on a girl?"

"That's right." He didn't feel embarrassed because as strange as it seemed, X-man appeared to be someone you could tell anything to and he wouldn't tease you for it.

"Yeah, I've had my share of heartbreak too, son. You'll get over it." X-man started deliberating to himself while he spit his tobacco into a cup. Then he looked back into the mirror and said, "If you don't mind me saying so Jacob, you seem a little different than other people I meet."

"Oh yeah, how do you mean?" he asked as he sat back and enjoyed the Jack Daniels coursing through his veins. The alcohol had already made it up to his head, numbing his brain.

"I don't know. You seem very sensitive for a big guy, and you seem like something deep is troubling you."

X-man was right, of course, and he knew it. He decided he'd have to put up an even bigger shell around himself so no one would ever discover what was bothering him. Since there was no way Jacob was going to explain his burden to X-man tonight, he responded by saying, "Well, you could say I'm more of a lover than a fighter."

They both laughed, and X-man dropped him in the Lazy Gator parking lot and sped off before Jacob could tell him about his new job.

CHAPTER 10

EXOTIC BEAUTIES

"Hi baby, you want a free VIP pass to Exotic Beauties?"
—Anonymous Exotic Dancer

When Jacob walked into the Lazy Gator, he noticed they had a long bar with all the big TVs that show whatever sport was hot at the time. It was mid-April of 1995 so the Atlanta Braves were on course to meet the Cleveland Indians in the World Series. The Braves were on tonight, and the bar was full of drunken dudes getting rowdy every time Greg Maddux pitched the ball. This was not Jacob's idea of a good time. He sat at the bar drinking and watching what seemed like everyone else having fun. Away from the baseball, couples were everywhere laughing, drinking and enjoying each other's company. His only companion was Jack and Coke and he was beginning to get more and more depressed. This was probably the second or third time he'd been inside a bar. He didn't have any friends in Gulf Coast City, and what he thought was going to turn into a summer romance, got shot down before it even got started.

Just as he was about to sink into deep intoxication, he saw four skinny scanty clad girls in short-shorts, out of the corner of his eye. They were not like the other girls at this bar. For starters, they were not dressed anywhere as conservatively as the other girls. Jacob could tell they were working tonight. At first, he thought they must be four local prostitutes, but realized they were from the self-proclaimed *"World's Largest Gentlemen's Club"* next door called Exotic Beauties.

After circling the crowded bar handing out postcards with a VIP pass to Exotic Beauties, a green-eyed leggy blonde came up to Jacob. "Hi baby, you wanna free VIP pass to Exotic Beauties?"

He sat up in his seat. "Where're you coming from?" he asked in as sober a voice as he could muster up.

"We're from Exotic Beauties. The owner of the club sent us out here to bring back some handsome men, since we're so slow tonight," the stripper replied, twirling her hair flirtatiously.

Jacob had a really good buzz so he was not going to quit staring at her. She gave him the impression that she was sad because business was slow tonight. She was trying to convince him that he needed to go over there and save the day by watching her perform and handing over all his cash. Even though he had never been to a gentlemen's club, he knew this was an act the skinny blonde with bright orange fingernails was performing. But after the day he'd just had, he felt like a strip club was exactly where he needed to go.

When the four short-short girls pranced out of the Lazy Gator, all the excitement seemed to walk out with them. Now it was back to reality, and couples having fun with no room for single losers like Jacob. He staggered out the door five minutes later and stumbled down the sidewalk through the steamy night heat and into the glass mirror doors of Exotic Beauties. After the dazzling bright lights from outside, Exotic Beauties was like a cave. Immediately inside and on the right, was what would be a coat check room up North. But here in Gulf Coast City, where you would rarely need to check your coat, this little room was used to take the entrance fee from their customers. He gripped tightly onto his VIP card feeling like he was pretty damn important.

"Can I help ya honey?" the puffy haired girl wearing white gloves and all white lingerie asked.

"Hi, I have a VIP pass," Jacob proudly replied.

"Well aren't you special darlin'."

"Why thank you." Jacob's face turned pink.

"There's no cover charge for you and I hope you have a great time." The girl smiled at Jacob as he walked away.

He beamed with importance as he made his way through another set of mirrored doors, at least until he saw about twenty more VIP cards scattered on the counter in front of him. But he didn't care because he was intoxicated and seconds away from entering the club which he knew would have sexy Gulf Coast City strippers dancing around and peeling off their clothes. For a 21-year-old, intoxicated virgin, this was going to be heaven. Jacob wondered if this was the place X-man, the taxi driver, referred to when he said he drove girls from Gulf Coast Jobs to the strip clubs. He hadn't seen that side of Gulf Coast Jobs yet and was wondering if it even existed.

After showing his ID to the bouncer, for what seemed like forever, Jacob was allowed to gain admittance. Everywhere was dark and the only lighting came from the strobe lights. The top 40 pop music of Tone Loc's *'Funky Cold Medina'* was blaring as he made a poor attempt to dance. And of course, the girls, as Jacob had expected, were slinking around in their revealing lingerie. They weren't drop dead gorgeous - some were a little over weight, others looked like they were at the end of their stripping careers but with the dim lighting and plenty of alcohol running through his veins they still looked quite inviting.

The more he looked around the more he realized the place was enormous. There were a few solitary drinkers at the bar watching the same baseball game as the Lazy Gator. But this was not the main attraction. Mirrors were on every wall. Beyond them were three walk-out stages with the iconic pole for the girls to swing around. The sign on the outside said *"World's Largest Gentlemen's Club"* and Jacob believed it. Two chubby blonde strippers were on stage dancing to the music. They started out in their black lingerie and strutted around entertaining a handful of men until they were down to only their G-strings. Stages two and three were empty and the place was kind of empty too. This club definitely needed more sensuous girls to liven up the place, which would consequently bring in more customers.

Jacob breathed in the lovely fragrance of ladies' perfume, and noticed that one stripper stood out from the rest. She was an incredibly exotic Latina, who was wearing a satin black teddy with shiny black panties underneath. She had lustrous dark eyes and silky black hair that went all the way down to her backside. She strolled around confidently swaying her hips up on stage, entertaining a few customers who had silly smiles on their faces. She glided around the stage then wrapped her hands around the dance pole. As she gripped the pole to do her twirl the small crowd of six men beamed, no doubt wishing they could be the one she was touching.

When her routine was finished, she stepped off the stage and caught him staring at her. Instead of ignoring him, she came closer and his pulse surged. When she was so close he could see the sparkling glitter makeup on her face, she spoke. "Hi, I'm Esmeralda."

Jacob breathed in Esmeralda's floral perfume and felt his entire body start to tingle. "What an alluring name you have, Esmeralda."

"Thank you." Esmeralda smiled as if she was a little embarrassed.

"Did you know that Esmeralda means emerald in Spanish?" He said, trying to impress this enchanting beauty.

"Yes, I know." Which sounded more like *Jes* I know. "I'm from Costa Rica so I speak es-Spanish."

"Oh I see," he said thinking, *I should go to Costa Rica if the girls are all as sexy as you.* He continued to try to impress Esmeralda. "Did you know that Victor Hugo used this name in his novel *'The Hunchback of Notre Dame'*?"

"No, I didn't know that," Esmeralda said, and Jacob felt like he had said something invigorating.

"Oh yes, Esmeralda is the Gypsy girl who Quasimodo is in love with."

Esmeralda looked down as if she was a little embarrassed and didn't know what to say.

"That's not your real name, is it?" Jacob asked as his face flushed.

"No, it's not." The stripper continued to look down at the carpeted floor, not wanting to hurt his feelings.

"Can I ask what your real name is?"

"Ana."

"Ana?"

"Jes."

"Why do strippers give out fake names?" he asked, even though he pretty much already knew the answer. This was his first time in a gentlemen's club and although he'd seen them in the movies and on TV, he was fidgety not knowing how he was supposed to act.

She smiled sympathetically at him and said, "The owner of this club makes us change our names because he es-says there's a lot of weirdos in here who will find out where we live and bother us."

"Then why did you tell me your real name so quickly? Maybe I'm a weirdo."

"I don't think you're a weirdo. Besides I know who you are."

"You do?" *How on earth does this smokin-hot super-sexy stripper know who I am?* he wondered.

"Jes, my sister works for you at your employment agency."

"She does?"

"My sister's one of the housekeepers that you send to the Sea Biscuit Inn."

"Really?" Jacob sat up straight with pride. "What's her name?"

"Lydia," she said as she moved closer to Jacob, waiting for him to pull out a chair for her to sit down.

Not picking up on the hint, he said, "Oh yeah, I know Lydia. She was in Gulf Coast Jobs the other day talking to Gabriela." He thought, *Lydia is nowhere near as beautiful as you.*

Ana took it upon herself to pull out a chair from under the table and sat down close to Jacob. One of her bare legs was now touching his trousers. "My sister es-says you're very nice."

Jacob's pulse rocketed, but he was able to play it cool. "Well, tell your sister I said thank you."

Ana presented a shy smile then looked down at their table, and she and Jacob didn't speak for a while. She was playing with the tablecloth and he was racking his brain trying to think of something to say so that his new companion would stay with him. The club was pumping out MC Hammer's '*Can't Touch This*', and was still not very crowded. Jacob wondered how the owner made any money. *That's it*, he thought, *I have something more I can talk to Ana about.* "What about your boss; what's he like?"

"His name is Brett and he's not as nice as you, but he talks a lot like you."

"Like me? What do you mean he talks like me?"

"He has the same accent as you."

"Oh. Is he a Southern boy?"

"Jes, I think so."

"So maybe he was raised in the South like me you mean?"

"Jes, I guess so."

Ana's smile showed her perfect white teeth, and every time she smiled she seemed incredibly sweet. There was only one other girl Jacob knew who had such a terrific smile, and that was Karina. But Karina wasn't here now and Ana was. And Karina had a boyfriend, and he was a little drunk, so he was all about Ana tonight.

"That's Brett over there," she whispered into Jacob's ear so she could overshadow the music. As she spoke, her warm breath was flowing into his entire body. Ana looked great and smelled delightful. He breathed in her floral aroma and really wanted to touch her. But although he'd never been inside a gentlemen's club, he certainly knew the rules. He and his friends had seen the movie '*Showgirls*' about a Las Vegas stripper several times. No matter what you DO NOT touch the girls. If you do touch the girls the big burly bouncer will throw you out of there so fast it will make your head spin.

There was more awkward silence and nothing to discuss with Ana, but luckily for Jacob, she stayed at their table and looked around like a lost puppy. Then a no-nonsense slightly older South American lady marched up to Jacob and Ana. She held out her hand, inviting a handshake from Jacob, and confidently said, "Hello sir, I'm Camille. My husband and I own Exotic Beauties." She was very stylish, wearing leather pants and a low-cut blouse that showed plenty of cleavage.

He looked over at Ana as she suddenly sat up straight. She seemed very nervous. Jacob responded calmly to Camille saying, "Hi, I'm Jacob Carmichael."

What struck him the most about Camille was she was classy and had beautiful black hair and piercing dark eyes, but he could tell she was caking on the makeup to fight the aging process. Of course, being around young strippers night after night certainly wouldn't make things any easier for her.

Camille asked, "So what do you do for a living, Mr. Carmichael?"

"Please call me Jacob."

"So what do you do for a living, Jacob?"

He answered proudly, "I'm the operations manager for Gulf Coast Jobs."

"Wow! That sounds impressive." Camille pulled out a chair and sat down.

"Thank you." Now he felt important and was glad to be impressing two exotic ladies.

Camille's eyes bore into Ana's and she said, "Esmeralda, why don't you go work the room." Ana shot up and was gone in a split second. Camille moved in closer to Jacob so she could ask him some questions. "So where do you get your employees from?"

He felt a sense of loss without Ana and had to readjust to his new host. "Um, we get them from all around the world."

"That's impressive. Do you have any employees from Colombia, South America?" Camille moved a little closer to Jacob.

"No, I don't think so. Is that where you're from?"

"Yes, it is." Camille moved even closer, and he started to get a little uncomfortable.

She noticed and said, "I'm having a hard time hearing you with the loud music."

This helped him relax so he continued, "Most of the people we hire are foreign college students that come here on the J-1 Visa from Russian, Poland, Ukraine, Belarus. You know, places like that."

"I came here on a J-1 Visa too. I think it was fifteen years ago. I immediately became an exotic dancer and I was going to go back to Colombia with a lot of money, but I met my husband Brett, and we got married."

"Wow that's a great story," Jacob said. He was trying to act impressed but he really wanted Camille to leave so Ana could come back.

"That's right, Brett came to see me almost every night when I was dancing. At first, I wasn't interested but he wore me down and I fell in love with him. Now we own the world's largest gentlemen's club."

"I guess Brett is a one in a million guy who got a stripper to fall in love with him."

Camille's face went grim. "Ahem, Jacob, inside Exotic Beauties we don't call them strippers. We call them dancers, or more specifically exotic dancers." Jacob was embarrassed but she didn't seem angry. "Let me go get my husband and introduce you to him."

Camille walked off and when she came back she had a short pudgy guy with her who had a beard that didn't suit him.

Jacob held out his hand. "Nice to meet you Brett. I've been enjoying speaking with your wife."

Camille interrupted, "This is not my husband. This is my husband's brother, Jamie."

Jamie stepped up and shook his hand. "How ya doin' dude?" Jamie was a small-town country boy who was way overdressed in his suit and tie.

"I'm doing good Jamie. Nice to meet you," Jacob replied. He really didn't want to be in this conversation and was searching around the club for Ana.

"Where you from dude?" Jamie asked.

"I grew up in Tinsley, South Carolina, but I live here now."

"That's cool. I'm from Dothan and my brother is too."

Jacob didn't care that Jamie was from Dothan but he felt he had to be polite, so he asked, "Where's Dothan? I've never heard of that."

"It's in Alabama. Ain't nothin' ever happens there. That's why me and Brett moved here."

Before he could reply he spotted an enormous guy, who must have been eighty pounds overweight, walking towards them. "Hey I'm Brett," the heavyset man said with his strong southern accent. "Camille tells me you work at Gulf Coast Jobs." Brett was so large that he almost made Mustapha and Suma look small. He had huge muscular legs that Jacob assumed he got from having to lug his massive belly around.

"That's right. I'm the operations manager."

"How's ole Mustapha doin these days?"

Jacob was surprised that Brett knew Mustapha. "Oh he's doing fine, you know."

"Why don't you let me give you a tour of our club."

He could tell Brett wasn't going to take no for an answer, and thought if Brett was going to give him the opportunity to see more half-naked girls, then why should he say no? He jumped up out of his seat and began following Brett around.

Brett pointed over to the far dance floor and said, "That's Runway number three. Right now, we are at Runway number one. We are the only gentlemen's club in the world that has three full dance runways."

Jacob could tell Brett was bragging, but he enjoyed being given a guided tour and was excited to see what was next. Ordinarily, he would be ashamed of where he was, but the alcohol and the fact he was hundreds of miles away from Tinsley gave him the feeling that he could explore and sin without being judged by the members of his church, Pastor Mike and his sister Tamar.

Brett called out, "Follow me, I'm gonna take you upstairs so I can show you the couch rooms and the hot tub rooms." Brett saw his eyes were taking everything in, so he didn't wait for him to answer.

As they both climbed the stairs, Jacob asked, "Why aren't more strippers working in here tonight? The place looks kinda empty, Brett."

Brett seemed to get a little annoyed, just as Camille had earlier, and interrupted Jacob. "Here at Exotic Beauties, we don't call them strippers." Brett paused for a minute to catch his breath from the stair climb. His face was ghostly white, a byproduct of working nights and sleeping days. The blood poured into his almost transparent face as he waited for his pulse to descend. Then he continued. "We call them dancers, or more precisely exotic dancers."

Jacob suddenly remembered Camille saying the same thing. Still feeling intoxicated, he felt like saying, *Excuse me for insulting your strippers, oh sorry, I mean exotic dancers.* Of course, he didn't respond, even though he was beginning to sense Brett's arrogance.

When they finally got to the top of the stairs, Brett's face was still flushed, looking like he had just climbed a mountain. He opened a door which led to a men's changing room, which then led to what he called the *'hot tub room'*. There was a dangerously underweight blonde girl standing behind a table with a small cash register on it. Jacob felt sorry for her because she didn't seem healthy. Brett said hello to the young lady then explained to him, "The dancers make a deal with the customers down on the main floor to go up to the *'hot tub room'*. If the customer is interested, he goes up the stairs with his dancer and she leads him to this cute young lady in the changing room who takes his money." The blonde girl forced a smile as married man Brett flirted a little. Then he continued, "Obviously, the customer can't jump into the hot tub with his clothes on and it's illegal for him to jump in naked, so the cashier sells him a pair of authentic Exotic Beauties swimming trunks." Brett was smirking at Jacob proudly. "Pretty good business, huh?"

"Sure is." Jacob had to admit he was impressed and a little envious of everything Brett had at this point. Between the alcohol in his system and all the affectionate girls he was seeing, he totally forgot about the tenth commandment, *"Thou shalt not covet."*

Brett continued bragging, "Of course, while they're in the hot tub the customer needs a drink, right?" Without waiting for him to answer, Brett pointed to the full bar that was behind the cashier.

Jacob didn't want Brett to notice he was envious as well as still a little drunk so he asked. "What does the girl do in the hot tub?"

"Whatever the two of them work out is between them. Camille and I stay out of this. Of course, we strongly advise the girls not to do anything illegal." Brett winked at him as if to say, *I can't be everywhere watching all the time.*

Brett led Jacob out of the hot tub room but not before they took a quick glimpse at a bikini-clad dancer and an older, slightly bald man sitting in the hot tub together drinking champagne. As they walked towards the couch rooms, Jacob couldn't help thinking, *I wonder what this stripper, I mean dancer, worked out with that dirty grandpa?*

Brett and Jacob were walking towards the couch rooms, which was the next stop on the tour, when Jacob felt a tap on his shoulder and turned around to see Winston.

"What up, playa?" Winston hollered.

Jacob was surprised. "What are you doing here?"

"I'm here for the bitches yo, you know what I'm sayin?"

He was uncomfortable hearing Winston talk like this, but he gave him the benefit of the doubt that he didn't mean anything unkind by it.

Brett told Jacob he had to get back to work and walked off without even acknowledging Winston. Unfazed, Winston motioned for Jacob to come downstairs with him towards the bar. When they arrived, Winston bought him another Jack and Coke then asked, "Yo, you wanna hit dis?" He held out a small piece of paper small enough to fit on the tip of his finger.

"What is it?" Jacob asked.

"It's acid, you know what I'm sayin?"

"Acid? LSD?"

"Yeah, baby!"

He had learned at Bob Jones University that LSD stood for lysergic acid diethylamide. The effects of LSD were always some kind of hallucination so with exotic dancers everywhere, why did he want this? He was enjoying looking at the girls and didn't need to hallucinate about them turning into little pink elephants. He was fine with drinking Jack Daniels and Coke and the feeling he was getting from this. The only hallucination he was hoping for right now was not to see Winston, Camille or Brett anymore.

"Now let me ask you this Winston, why the heck would I wanna take acid in a strip club?"

Winston snarled, "You better not let Miss Camille hear you call this place a strip club."

"Why not?" he asked. He'd already forgotten Camille and Brett's warnings that they didn't like to call the girls strippers.

"Well, Miss Camille and her husband Brett, they don't like to call these bitches strippers. They like to call them dancers or entertainers, you know what I'm sayin'?"

"No, not really." Jacob slurred his reply. He didn't want to give Winston the satisfaction of thinking he'd educated him on something.

"Well, they try to keep this place classy. And now Mustapha--"

Camille suddenly came back up to Jacob and asked, "Do you want a couch dance with Esmerelda?"

Without saying a word, Jacob leaped over to where Ana was standing. She took his hand and led him upstairs to the couch room where she could begin entertaining him in private.

He followed her to one of the back rooms where they were finally all alone. He sat down on the couch and she started wiggling her hips around him. Jacob started to quiver, then he remembered he left his Jack and Coke down at the bar near Winston. He needed more alcohol to calm his nerves, so he told her, "I'm very sorry, but I left my drink at the bar. Will you wait for me while I go and get it?"

"Of course," Ana said sweetly. She must have noticed Jacob was jumpy but she never laughed at him. Surely he wasn't the first customer of hers to get a little shaky when they knew her teddy was about to come off.

Jacob quickly walked back downstairs to the bar and found his liquid courage waiting right where he left it. Winston was leaning on the bar talking to Camille, and didn't seem interested in bothering him anymore.

When he got back to Ana, Blondie was playing the song *'Call me'*. Ana had her eyes closed and was really into the music.

"Call me (call me) on the line
Call me, call me any, anytime
Call me (call me) oh my love
When you're ready we can share the wine
Call me."

Ana still had on her black teddy and black panties, but Jacob knew soon she'd be peeling them off. She started dancing and stripping. First she was facing Jacob and showing off her gorgeous breasts. Then she turned around and stuck her heart-shaped tush in his face. She slowly started to pull down her panties to reveal her G-string then stopped and grabbed Jacob's crotch. It was only a split second but was enough to bring him to full attention. Jacob immediately chugged down the rest of his Jack Daniels and started to get really excited as he was sure that the show was just beginning. Ana had both arms in the air and was wiggling her hips and giving Jacob an *I-want-you-to-take-me-to-bed* look. She slowly crouched all the way down on the floor, still keeping the beat to the music. Now she was laying on her stomach and Jacob could see the tan lines of her beautiful bare bottom as she seductively looked back at him.

"So sexy," he kept saying over and over to himself. "So sexy, so sexy, so sexy..." He thought, *Ana has got to be the sexiest creature alive and for a few short minutes she's all mine.*

Then he started to feel dizzy and the room started to spin. He fell off the couch and everything blurred. He couldn't see anything for a few seconds but the strobe light flashing. When he was finally able to regain his focus, he looked up and Ana had turned into a fish! Jacob was no longer looking at beautiful Ana. He was looking at a five-foot-long fish with long black hair. And it was the ugliest fish he'd ever seen. It kept flipping and flopping on the floor and water kept splashing off its scaly body. And worst of all, Ana's sweet perfume was now replaced with the smell of an old dead fish.

Jacob freaked out and ran from the couch dance room and down the stairs. He was now in the center of the club, and for some reason decided to jump up onto Runway one. He nearly knocked over the girl putting on her act. Then right in front of everyone, he yelled, "A fish, Ana turned into a fish!"

Everyone started laughing hysterically. Then he looked down and all his clothes were gone... or so he thought.

The song that was playing now was *'Panama'* by Van Halen. Everyone remembers this song, but Jacob will always remember it a hundred times more than anyone who hasn't heard it under the influence of LSD. When *'Panama'* started to blare over the speakers, for some reason he thought he must be the next act on stage so he started dancing and imitating everything he'd seen the other strippers do. When Eddie Van Halen began his guitar solo, the hallucinations were attacking Jacob's brain in full force. He could actually see Eddie performing in the corner. Eddie was so into the solo that tears were running down his cheeks and his guitar had smoke pouring out of it. It seemed that his guitar was slowly starting to overheat from the intensity of the solo, and Jacob was loving it.

When he went up to the pole and started swinging around, Camille's brother-in-law, Jamie, came up on the stage. He pulled him off the pole and yelled out, "What in the hell are you doin, dude?"

At this point, Jacob was way too far gone to even try to speak. Jamie, Winston and Brett carried him out the door and put him in the back of Jamie's car. Winston jumped in and sat next to him and Jamie drove away. The car headed out of the parking lot and down the brightly lit street. Every time Jamie accelerated, Jacob's chest was thrown back into the seat and he thought they were going to take off into the air.

Jamie pulled into the Food Chief convenience store and Winston got out. Jacob felt like he was slowly coming down to earth, but was confused when it appeared that Winston was pulling the Food Chief cashier all around the store. He wasn't sure if the cashier was chasing Winston or if Winston was chasing the cashier. Or maybe he was just imagining the whole thing.

Then Jamie quickly pulled out of the brightly lit Food Chief parking lot and headed towards the beach where Jacob now lived.

When they got to his townhouse, Jamie had to practically carry him out of his car into his living room. Jamie examined Jacob's face. He was still on a different planet, although he was probably on one closer to earth than earlier tonight. Jamie smacked Jacob's cheek and said "Dude, don't go outside okay?"

Jacob looked back at Jamie and mumbled something incoherent.

Jamie shook him and said, "Look, dude, if you leave your townhouse tonight the little green men are gonna get you, ya hear?"

That was enough for Jacob to stay on his couch for the rest of the night until he finally passed out.

CHAPTER 11

THE FOOD CHIEF

"You gonna die tonight!"
—Winston Brown

The next morning, Jacob woke up on the floor of his townhouse with a pounding head. His brain felt as if it had been twisted and wrung out and hung up to dry. He struggled to get ready for work. Last night's events wreaked havoc on his mind and he desperately needed answers. He'd had a bad trip and wanted to know who'd drugged him and why. He strongly suspected Winston. Who else could it have been? He had left his drink next to him at the bar to follow Ana into the couch room. Winston would have had plenty of time to drop the LSD into his drink. He wanted to find Winston and confront him. He didn't know where to look but suspected someone at Exotic Beauties could help.

He rushed through the day doing his daily routine of sending the foreign students and Hispanic laborers to the Gulf Coast City hotels, golf courses, and landscaping jobs. The whole time he was counting the minutes until he could leave and get back to Exotic Beauties.

Finally, at 6 pm, when the work day was done, Jacob said goodbye to Gabriela and got on his bike to head home. He wanted to shower up then call X-man so he could taxi him to Exotic Beauties.

He'd gone about a block away from Gulf Coast Jobs when a police car flashed its lights behind him. Jacob assumed the cop wanted him to get out of the road, but she was actually looking for him.

The policewoman's name was Paula, he had met her earlier in the week when she had dropped in at Gulf Coast Jobs. She was a short-haired blonde, about 30ish, leaning on the overly muscular side. She'd told Jacob she was in charge of policing the businesses around this side of town. Paula mainly patrolled Gulf Coast City on her police bicycle. He had waved to her a couple of times and exchanged some words when he was also riding his bike. The other day she'd seen him driving Mustapha's SUV and complimented him on having a nice car. Jacob joked that the SUV was stolen, and she laughed. But she wasn't laughing today and neither was he.

"Hey Jacob," Paula called out from her police car. "Do you have time to come to the police station? I have something urgent I need to talk to you about."

Paula was asking, but he was pretty sure if he told her he was busy she'd insist he find the time. He started to wonder if she knew about the performance he'd pulled at Exotic Beauties last night. He began replaying the events in his mind, and vaguely remembered taking off all his clothes and doing a strip tease in front of everyone. *Surely she can't be here to arrest me for this.* An extra layer of sweat poured onto Jacob's forehead.

"Sure, I have time. What's going on?" He tried to sound casual.

"I'd really rather explain when we get to the station. Here, let me help you put your bike on my bike rack."

When he walked up to Paula's police car he hesitated because he couldn't tell if she wanted him to sit in the back or the front. Obviously, there was a big difference between sitting in the front seat or being a prisoner in the back. Paula noticed him standing there confused, and chuckled. "Come up front with me," she said and he blew out a sigh of relief.

When they got to the police station Jacob followed Paula inside where she led him into a meeting room that had about ten chairs around a table with a large TV mounted on the wall. Inside the room was another policeman, whom Jacob thought he recognized, and the chief of police himself. *Oh my gosh!* Jacob thought. *Why is the chief here?* He recognized the police chief as Joe White because he'd seen him on the news a couple of nights back. He was an older African American with white hair, square jaw and commanding face. Jacob couldn't recall what he was talking about on the news, but the chief gave the impression he was not playing around, and was ready to put all the bad guys in jail no matter what it took. Jacob just hoped that he was not going to be one of these bad guys.

Everyone sat down around the table and the chief of police began. "Jacob, I'm Chief of Gulf Coast City Police, Joe White," he said in a slow sing-song accent and deep voice. "I'd like to say thank ya for coming over here to speak with us."

As if I had a choice, Jacob thought.

"It's our understanding that you are in communication with a gentleman by the name of Winston Brown, is this correct?"

Jacob didn't know Winston's last name, but he was sure the chief was talking about the Winston he knew, who was always causing trouble. "Yes sir, I believe I know Winston."

Police Chief Joe White locked eyes with him so he could study every word and every movement. "Well now, Jacob, would you mind watching a video we have here from the Food Chief and let me know if you recognize anyone?"

He hoped he appeared calm on the outside, because inside he felt as if his head might explode. He scrambled to think what's significant about the Food Chief. Then he remembered this was where Jamie, from Exotic Beauties, had dropped Winston off last night. As he replayed the events of last night, he vaguely remembered Winston running around the Food Chief, but he had done nothing wrong. If Chief Joe White had a videotape of Exotic Beauties, now that would be a different story.

"Sure, I can do that," he said, pleasantly exhaling as he realized it wasn't him the police were after.

Police Chief Joe White asked Officer Paula to pop in the video tape while the other short stocky policeman glared at him. As the malicious-looking officer continued to bear down on his face, Jacob realized where he'd seen him before. This was the policeman who'd hounded him the first day he'd set foot on Sue Ellen Dooley's property.

As the tape began rolling, he noticed it was the security footage from inside the Food Chief. The video showed the clerk, who was a salt and pepper haired, white woman probably in her 40s. It also presented a quick view outside the door to the Food Chief. Jacob saw a car drive up and drop someone off. Then he realized the car was Jamie's Cadillac. And the guy getting out was definitely Winston. This was enough to jolt him up in his seat. Now he thought his heart was going to pound its way out of his chest, still not fully comprehending what was going on. He saw Winston walk inside the Food Chief and start peering around. He was jumpy and definitely under the influence. Jacob suspected he was on some kind of speed because his eyes were bouncing everywhere. First Winston looked at the cashier then he looked at the door, then he looked around the tiny convenience store. He did all this in about half a second, then he looked around again. It finally dawned on Jacob that Winston was going to rob this place.

Just as he realized what was going on, he saw Winston pull out a pistol and run up to the cashier and yell, "Give me all the motherfuckin money, bitch!"

"Oh Lord!" Jacob yelped. This was really happening. Winston put his pistol up against the cashier's head and grabbed the back of her shirt. Then he shoved her around the back of the store, occasionally throwing her into the wall if she didn't cooperate. Jacob wondered why he had to be overly rough with this poor woman. At first, the cashier didn't speak, but he could tell she was terrified and most probably in shock.

While the poor lady was gathering the money out of the cash register, Winston pushed the barrel of his pistol into her temple. He cocked back the hammer, then he yelled, "You gonna die tonight bitch, you gonna to die tonight!" Jacob could not believe it. Winston was no choir boy, but he had never appeared to be into committing such violence. Winston asked the cashier-- or rather demanded-- she unlock the safe. Jacob couldn't hear exactly what the petrified cashier was saying but it sounded like she was whispering, "I.. I can't do that."

Then Winston took his bullying to the next level. "You gonna to die tonight, bitch!" When Winston put his finger on the trigger of his pistol, Jacob thought, *oh my God, he is going to shoot this poor woman.* Winston stared at her with his evil eyes, then pushed her head down onto the counter with the barrel of his gun. The cashier laid her head on the counter, leaving her life in Winston's hands. "You gonna die tonight bitch!" Winston seemed to be enjoying the torment he was dishing out.

The cashier had tears in her eyes as she was begging for her life. "Please, I have children," she pleaded. But Winston didn't seem to care. He yanked her head up from the counter and pushed her into the cash register. "Please. You don't have to kill me," she cried out, as she handed him the dollar bills.

Winston grabbed the money from the woman's hands, and ran out the door. The cashier fell to the ground, and Police Chief Joe White got up and turned off the tape.

The chief gave Jacob a long stare, studying his reaction. He was frozen in his chair. He tried not to make too much eye contact with the chief, wondering why he was here. *Did the chief know he was in Jamie's car? Did he think he was in on this? Was he going to prison?* He sat frozen, waiting to learn his fate.

Then the chief spoke. "We know Winston came to see you this week at Gulf Coast Jobs, and we believe you can help us."

"Sure. Whatever y'all want." He exhaled. He was relieved the chief was not outright excusing him of being involved in the robbery but feared it was only a matter of time before he figured it out. He was terrified he might discover this was Jamie's car and then he'd somehow find out he was inside.

"What we need from you, Jacob, is to let us know when Winston comes back over to Gulf Coast Jobs. Now we know that Winston only got $89 out of the register, and he never got into the safe. So I'm sure he's burned through that already from his crack habit."

Crack, Jacob thought, *that's what made Winston act so crazy*. He had never seen anyone who had a crack habit before, except in the movies, of course. In the movie *Deep Cover,* with Laurence Fishburne, the crack addicts would have sold their own grandmother for a hit.

The chief gave Jacob a stern look and said, "If Winston comes to see you, maybe you can offer to get him some work."

"Can't you just go to his house and arrest him?" he asked, too terrified to get involved.

"We have already been to Winston's house but his wife says she hasn't seen him for a coupla weeks."

"Wife?" he echoed, "I didn't even know he was married."

"Oh yeah, Jacob. He has a young son and a baby girl too. Eighteen months old, I think."

"Wow, y'all really know a lot about Winston, don't you?" he said with surprise, not meaning to be disrespectful.

The malicious-looking stocky cop with the bald head snapped back, "This is our job! You think we're just playing a game here Jacob?" His perfectly pressed uniform boasted a shiny police badge and belt buckle, topped off with shoes polished to perfection.

The chief cut the overly ambitious policeman a glance that said *calm down.* Then he continued. "What I believe, Jacob, is you will see Winston before we do, and this is why we need your help."

Now Jacob's anxiety was back in high gear. Now that he knew the type of person Winston really was, what was to stop him from coming over to Gulf Coast Jobs with his gun? What if he started dragging him around his office like he did the poor cashier saying, *"You gonna die tonight!"*

Police Chief Joe White scratched the bottom of his chin then said, "What we need from you, Jacob, is to let us know when Winston is back at Gulf Coast Jobs so we can snatch him up. Now, this incident at the Food Chief is not Winston's first act of violence and it won't be his last. So what I need to know from you is, are you willing to do your part?"

"Of course," Jacob answered. What else could he say? Besides, now he really wanted Winston locked up too. Frightened Winston would come after him, he said, "Whatever y'all need, Chief." He looked at the mean cop who was still giving him the same malicious stare he'd been sending his way since he first entered the room. Paula seemed like the only sympathetic person in the meeting. She brushed a fallen blonde hair off of her uniform and nodded at Jacob to imply he'd done good.

The chief laid out his plan of attack. "Jacob, Corporal Hunter and Officer Paula are both gonna give you their business cards. When you make contact with Winston, I want you to call either Paula or Hunter, okay? If Hunter doesn't answer, I want you to call Paula and if Paula doesn't answer I want you to call Hunter. You understand? They patrol your area all the time and if one is working the night shift the other is usually working the day shift. When you make contact with them with information about Winston they will know what to do."

He nodded at Chief Joe White and once again said, "Okay Chief, I'll do whatever y'all want."

"Just go about your business normally, but keep an eye out for Winston."

Jacob asked, "What makes you so sure Winston will come my way again?"

"Don't worry about that. Pretty soon he'll run out of money and come waltzing into Gulf Coast Jobs looking for work. He's been getting day labor jobs there long before you came along and I don't think he's gonna stop anytime soon."

"Oh yeah? How do you know all that?" Jacob asked not meaning to be disrespectful, but knowing Corporal Hunter was going to come down on him for sure.

"We've had our eye on Winston for a long time, Jacob. We know what we're doing here. We just need a little cooperation from you to let us know his whereabouts." Police Chief Joe White put his hand on Jacob's shoulder and said, "You think you can do this for us?"

"Sure," he answered as if he had a choice.

The chief quickly wrapped things up and sent him on his way. Of course, he couldn't leave without Corporal Hunter and Officer Paula's cell phone numbers. And Corporal Hunter had to give him one last disgusted glance as he walked out of the police station. Jacob got on his bicycle and waved goodbye to Paula as he continued to head back to his townhouse.

CHAPTER 12

EXOTIC BEAUTIES

"You are a sick pig to do this to a woman."
—Camille Olson

When Jacob finally got back to his place, he showered then called X-man to come get him. X-man arrived at Jacob's townhouse in his usual rowdy fashion making sure he disturbed as many of the neighbors as he could. And even though Jacob already knew he was outside, X-man blew his horn three times to indicate he'd arrived.

As soon as Jacob walked out his door, X-man yelled out and gave him a toothless grin. "Hey, nice lookin' crib you got here man! So what's happenin'?"

"All kinds of stuff's happenin' X-man. All kinds of stuff."

"Well, don't just stand there Jacob, get in the damn taxi and fill me in!"

Jacob felt good to have someone to tell his problems to, even if he was a homeless looking taxi driver. "Not really sure where to start," he said.

"How 'bout since we last saw each other." X-man pulled out onto the street, one hand on the wheel and seat reclining as far back as it could without falling over.

"Well, a lot of stuff happened before we last saw each other. I just didn't have the chance to tell you last time." He sat up straight in the back seat.

"Well tell me now, son!" X-man was laughing and fidgeting around in the console trying to find his chewing tobacco.

"Okay, well you remember that employment agency you showed me on my first night here?"

"Gulf Coast Jobs?"

"Yep, that's the one and here's the thing. I work there now."

"No shit!" X-man laughed and looked like he was impressed.

"That's right. I'm the operations manager there," he bragged.

"No shit!"

"Yep, that's the good news but everything else is bad news."

"Bad news?" X-man eased up on the gas so he could focus on the problem. "What's going on?"

"You don't really want to hear my problems." Jacob was beginning to feel uneasy giving out personal details to a taxi driver.

"I know what you're thinking, Jacob. This guy just drives a taxi cab. What the hell does he know? But let me tell you somethin', I've been talkin' to people for a long time. They hop in my cab and we shoot the shit. Next thing you know they're at their destination and we've talked out their problems. It's great therapy, ya know. So don't just look at me as just a taxi driver, I'm your mobile psychologist." X-man loaded up the tobacco into his mouth and grinned.

They both laughed and Jacob loosened up enough to continue. "Well since you put it that way, I already met a girl and lost the girl in less than a week. And when you drove me to Exotic Beauties to drown my sorrows, things got even worse."

"Now, I dropped you off at the Lazy Gator. How'd you end up at Exotic Beauties?"

"Well these strippers came over to the Lazy Gator-- that part of the story doesn't really matter. Someone put LSD in my drink and really messed me up last night and I think it was this guy called Winston. Then today I got Police Chief Joe White, Officer Paula, and this cop called Corporal Hunter up my you-know-what, trying to make me help them put Winston in jail."

X-man's smile vanished as his face tensed. "Please tell me you ain't talkin' about Winston Brown."

Jacob remembered Police Chief Joe White referring to Winston as Winston Brown, so he said, "Yeah that's who I'm talking about."

"Jacob, Jacob, Jacob." X-man wasn't joking around anymore. "Jacob, this guy Winston is as bad as they come, buddy. You gotta get away from him. The guy runs around town pulling rip offs and all kinds of scams. I told you about guys like him the first night we met. And Winston, he's faster than Hershel so the police can't catch him."

"You lost me, X-man." He was worried but didn't want to show it. "You gotta me tell everything."

"Okay, Jacob I'm gonna tell you everythin I know about this guy and when I do, you gotta get the hell away from him, okay?"

"Okay."

X-man continued to drive down the road. He took a quick sip from his flask, no doubt some kind of liquor, so he could prepare to tell his story. Jacob had never seen anyone chew tobacco and drink at the same time, but he'd never seen anyone quite like X-man either. He tensed his face, stared at Jacob through the mirror and said, "Winston's daddy is Hershel Brown."

"Who's Hershel Brown?"

"You don't know who Hershel Brown is? Hershel Brown, man! He's the hot-shot running back who played for the University of Alabama."

"Okay, so what?"

"Winston's daddy was a great football player, man, and Winston was great too. He played at North Dothan High School and was the second leading rusher in Alabama."

"I thought you were gonna tell me bad things about this guy, X-man."

"I'm gettin' to that." X-man took another quick sip from his flask, swallowed, then spit his tobacco out the window. *Quite a talent*, Jacob thought. "Winston and Brett played football together at North Dothan High School."

"Brett?" Jacob's ears perked up.

"That's right, Jacob, Mr. Exotic Beauties himself was on the same football team, and Winston's best buddy. Now Winston helps Brett do all his dirty work."

Jacob wasn't sure what X-man meant but it certainly didn't sound good.

Another guy at their school was Corporal Hunter, although they didn't call him corporal obviously back then."

Jacob was impressed. "You know Corporal Hunter too?" *Who doesn't X-man know?*

X-man was back to laughing again. "That's right, Jacob. I know everybody! Your other new enemy Hunter, that mean sadistic son of bitch cop, was also on their football team and played halfback as well. Except Hunter was never as good as Winston and he's been jealous of him ever since."

"This explains why Corporal Hunter is so motivated to take Winston down," Jacob said. "But how did Winston go from being a great running back to where he is now?"

"Drugs my man, drugs."

He was surprised X-man knew all this. It seemed like X-man could have continued his storytelling all evening, but they'd arrived at the parking lot of Exotic Beauties. X-man brought his narrative to an end and Jacob thanked him for all the useful information he provided. X-man wished him good luck finding out who drugged him last night.

It was still early by gentlemen club standards, maybe 8:30 pm, when Jacob walked into Exotic Beauties. Three Mexican construction workers were at the bar watching a disinterested flabby bellied stripper dancing around the pole. The TVs on the wall were turned off and the top 40's music was at half volume.

Disregarding his Baptist beliefs as he often did lately, Jacob went up to the bar and ordered a Corona. As he waited for the bartender, he whispered to himself, *"The Bible says alcohol will bite like a servant and will make your mind utter perverse things."* Beefy Brett soon waddled up to Jacob and asked if he had a good time last night.

Jacob replied, "Yes, from what I remember," while fidgeting on his bar stool.

Showing no emotion, Brett said, "Follow me over here," then began leading Jacob upstairs to the couch room. At the top of the stairs, Brett did his usual stop to catch his breath and wipe his moist forehead. On the wall, there was a huge poster of Paula Abdul. He removed both thumbtacks at the bottom. Then he rolled up the poster half way so Jacob could see a small peep hole like most people have on their front door.

Brett's eyes bore into his as he said, "Camille and I saw everything last night."

"Oh yeah," Jacob said. He blushed.

"Damn right. Camille, Jamie and I watch all the time. You don't think we just let the girls in there unsupervised, do you?"

"I guess not," he said. He felt a lump in his throat and tried to swallow it down.

Camille appeared from down the hall, wearing a low-cut cleavage-highlighting blouse, and Brett waved her over. "Honey, why don't you see if Ana is back in the dressing room." Then Brett started studying Jacob's face.

Camille left and came back with Ana. She had on jeans and a t-shirt and Jacob was sure she was not here to strip for him. When she turned to look at Jacob he realized why. She had a huge black eye that covered the entire left side of her face.

"Oh my God!" Jacob cried out. "What happened?"

Ana's bottom lip was shaking and tears formed in her eyes then rolled down her cheek.

He was putting together another question for Ana when Brett yelled out, "You did this Jacob!"

"What?"

"Yes, you did this last night. What in the hell kinda guy are you anyway?"

"I, I..." Jacob didn't know what to say. He felt lightheaded.

Camille walked towards Jacob, ready to give him a slap, then yelled, "You are a sick pig to do this to a woman and you will pay for this, I can assure you!"

He could not believe what was happening. He swallowed the rock-sized lump in his throat. "If I did this, I didn't mean to. I was drugged--"

Camille glared at Jacob with her piercing dark eyes and said, "I don't want to hear your lousy excuses." Her fists were clenched, ready to pounce.

"Okay Camille, let's all calm down." Brett cut her off and Jacob hoped he was coming to his rescue. "Maybe we can work this out and the police don't have to get involved. Are you interested in hearing what I have to say?"

"Sure," Jacob said. What else was he going to say? He glanced at Ana and she looked like she was about to burst into tears. Then he turned to Camille and she looked like she wanted to kill him. Finally, Jacob glanced at Brett and he looked like he wanted to help.

Brett motioned for Ana to leave and said, "Okay, Ana would you mind leaving us now so we can talk to Jacob and try to straighten this out."

When Ana left, Brett began to lay out his plan. "Jacob, last night you were acting crazy, dude. What the hell were you on?" Before Jacob could spit out an answer Brett continued. "I don't care what you do when you're not in my club, but when you're here you must follow my rules."

"He must never hit a girl!" Camille yelled.

Brett put his hand on Camille's hand trying to calm her down. "Jacob look, ultimately I have to protect my girls. Now Camille wants to turn you into the police and Jamie wants to take you out back and stomp the shit outta you."

"What does Ana wanna do?" Jacob asked.

"Good question," Brett answered. "Ana is very upset because she feels like she had a connection with you and also you work where her sister works as a housekeeper, so she doesn't wanna jeopardize that. She does feel like you should be punished, I can tell you that. She wanted to phone the police last night but I asked her to wait until the morning to decide if that's what she really wants."

"What did she decide?" Jacob asked, fidgeting his hands.

"Well, she decided to give you a second chance." Jacob blew out a sigh of relief. "But although she is not interested in involving the cops at this time, she still thinks you should be punished."

"Okay." He was curious. "What does she have in mind?"

"Well, Jacob you may not know this, but Ana and her sister Lydia are in this country illegally. And even though she knows that you would be the one going to jail for attacking her, she is still a little worried about having her immigration status being reviewed."

"I understand." Jacob tried his best to show his true concern for Ana and Lydia. He realized that he hadn't taken into account anyone's feelings last night. He'd given into alcohol and lust and treated a lot of young ladies poorly. Shame swept through him.

Brett continued as if Jacob hadn't spoken. "So anyway, I've promoted Ana to floor manager here at Exotic Beauties, so she will be in charge of recruiting and managing the dancers. So now you will help her with recruiting. You will have a quota that you'll have to meet, and if you don't meet this quota, Ana may not be as understanding as you'd like."

"I don't understand."

"If you don't line up Ana's quota of girls she might decide to call the cops on you. Got it?"

"Yeah, I got it." This was definitely blackmail, but Brett worded it so perfectly that Jacob really didn't have a chance to say no. Camille and Brett knew that he had access to young Russian and Eastern European girls through Gulf Coast Jobs. He thought about what Brett had just told him, then it occurred to him that he wasn't the one in charge of Gulf Coast Jobs so he asked, "What about Mustapha, why don't you ask him?"

"I've worked with Mustapha in the past, but he really doesn't give me top priority. I might get a dancer here and a dancer there, but it's never enough. You, on the other hand, have a little more motivation to help out." What Brett meant was Mustapha didn't have the threat of going to jail hanging over his head so he wasn't going to work as hard as Jacob to recruit.

"Brett it's not as easy as you think. I can't just walk into Gulf Coast Jobs and tell Mustapha I'm gonna round up dancers. I work for him, remember? He doesn't work for me. If I--"

Brett interrupted. "I think you can find a way to convince Mustapha. Besides, he doesn't hang around Gulf Coast City all the time. He likes to get out of here and do his gambling."

"How do you know this?"

"Let's just say I know, 'cause I've worked a lot with Mustapha in the past. So you need to tell him that you're gonna start helping me. I'm sure he'll let you bring me a girl here and a girl there. And when he leaves town you ain't gonna have any more excuses not to bring me girls full time. You got it?"

"I thought I was doing this for Ana?" Jacob was suspicious.

"You know what I mean Jacob! I'm the one trying to help your ass here." Brett's face filled with blood. "Look, in the long run, this will work out for all of us. Instead of paying Mustapha for these girls, I will pay you directly. There's a lot of easy money to be made in this business and I'm happy to share it with you."

He still didn't feel like he could make himself do this. He appealed to Brett and Camille. "Look, guys, this was just a one-time thing for me. Last night when I came into Exotic Beauties was the first and last time I've ever been in a strip club. Besides, everything that goes on here is against my Christian beliefs. The Bible says that *Whoever looks on a woman to lust after her, has committed adultery in his heart.* I know I sound like a hypocrite, but I was a little drunk last night and I gave into temptation. I won't let it happen again so I really don't think I can help you even if I wanted to."

Brett was really angry now and his veins were popping out of his neck. "I don't give a flyin fuck what the Bible says! You're gonna bring me girls or your ass is going to jail. You got it? And one more thing. Don't even think about going back to Tinsley, South Carolina."

Jacob's eyes widened. *How does Brett know where I'm from?*

"That's right. You told Camille and Ana all about Tinsley last night so I decided to do some research on you. Your sister was attacked by Carl Dooley so this is probably why you came here, huh?"

Now Jacob was fighting back the tears but he was not going to give Brett or Camille the satisfaction. "So what are you trying to say here, Brett?"

"What I'm saying is if you decide to run back to South Carolina, I'll just tell the cops where they can find you."

Jacob didn't know what to say and he was trembling now. "Okay Brett, I'll try to do it."

"You better," Camille chipped in to show him she was just as serious as Brett.

Brett stood up and walked towards him with an angry look on his face. "Now get the fuck out of here." Jacob jumped up quickly and started to leave when Brett said, "I'll give you a week to work on this then I wanna see my first dancer."

CHAPTER 13

JACOBS'S TOWNHOUSE

"You think Brett be playin but he ain't."
—DeAndre Brown

Jacob went into work the next day. He was supposed to be focusing on some paperwork, but his mind was racing all over the place. He thought about the huge mess he was in now. He still hadn't contacted Sue Ellen Dooley to make his peace and now even if he wanted to go back to Tinsley he couldn't. Brett had made sure of this. He thought about trying to convince Mustapha to let him recruit dancers for Brett and Camille. He knew Mustapha had done this before for Exotic Beauties, but now he didn't. Jacob wondered why he quit. The reason was either he was not making enough money or Ada didn't like the idea of him being around all these young loose girls. His gut feeling was Ada probably didn't like all the floozies being around her husband. He decided he had to talk with Mustapha to determine if he'd give him permission to start recruiting again. Jacob asked Mustapha if they could have lunch together so they could talk and he agreed.

Mustapha and Jacob met at Happy Suma's later that day. Suma was there, but he was busy taking care of some business in the back of the restaurant so they didn't interact with him at all. Lilianna was their waitress, and of course, she was happy they were there, and expressed her gratitude for giving her such a great job.

"Hello Jacob and Mustapha," Lilianna greeted them with her Belarus accent. "What brings you two both to Happy Suma's?"

Mustapha acted cold. "We're here for a business meeting, Lilianna, and don't wish to be disturbed. Why don't you bring us both a cheeseburger and a Coke, and tell Suma I'll pay him later for this, okay?"

Jacob could tell Lilianna was a little upset with Mustapha as she walked back to the kitchen to place their order.

"Now, what is it you wanted to talk to me about?" Mustapha asked as he directed his attention back at Jacob.

Now was his chance to pitch the idea of once again recruiting foreign students to work at Exotic Beauties. He knew if he didn't convince Mustapha, Brett was more than likely going to come down on him hard. Jacob was not much of a salesman but he had to make a damn good presentation today.

"Mustapha, I've had a couple of meetings with Brett and Camille at Exotic Beauties and they are really interested in using our services to recruit J-1 Visa students to work at their club. They need a lot of girls and they're willing to pay us generously to recruit them. I know you've done business with them before and I thought--"

"No!" Mustapha barked. "No, I'm not interested in doing business with them anymore."

"But this is easy money and you did this before," he pleaded.

"I said no, Jacob. As I told you when we first met, I am a Christian. I was persecuted for my beliefs in Libya because my faith is very strong. Recruiting young girls to work at a gentlemen's club to take off their clothes and promote sex is sacrilegious and I will not play any part of this. I have already told Brett this, and he keeps throwing more and more money at me and I keep turning him down. Now he thinks he can get you to influence me because you are new and weak but I will not be torn from my beliefs no matter how much money Brett offers. My faith cannot be bought!"

Jacob was sure that Mustapha was only telling him this because he didn't have the courage to admit that Ada wouldn't allow him to help Brett anymore. He hadn't seen any Christian behavior at all from Mustapha except that he constantly told people this was what he was about. However, he felt that there was no way he was going to convince him to change his mind.

He wanted to tell Mustapha he didn't believe a single word he was saying, but he was too intimidated. He didn't even try to argue because Mustapha was so strong willed that he would never have changed his mind. He didn't know what he was going to do but he was sure Mustapha was not going to help him.

* * *

Every night for a week Jacob laid in his bed unable to sleep. He kept tossing and turning, trying to think of a way to either get Brett off his back or recruit J-1 Visa girls without Mustapha and Gulf Coast Jobs. He couldn't find an answer, and he was pretty sure Brett was not going to let him off the hook. About a week after his meeting with Brett, Camille and Ana, Jacob received a message to show him that Brett was not going to forget about him.

He had finally gone off to sleep in his small two-story townhouse when around 11:30 pm he woke up to a noise downstairs. It sounded like someone rummaging around. He began to panic although he wasn't sure if it might just be his neighbors, who liked to stay up all night. He laid still in his bed trying to listen to every sound. Then he heard footsteps coming up his stairs. The stairs were carpeted, so he could barely make out the patter of someone creeping up. He was still trying to decide if this was his imagination when he heard the door knob turn and his bedroom door open. It was pitch black and now he was totally frozen. He saw two dark figures slowly walking towards him and he suddenly realized this was really happening.

One of the intruders slithered up close and whispered, "Hey motherfucker, wake the fuck up." Jacob shot up in bed, his heart pounding so fast he thought it was going to burst out of his chest. When the intruder's evil brown eyes made contact with him, he couldn't speak. He couldn't move and he couldn't breathe. Both intruders had on ski masks so he couldn't determine their identity.

"Hey motherfucker, do you know why we is here?" The same intruder asked as he placed a knife up to his throat. The other intruder was hanging back observing like he was going to pounce any second. Jacob tried to speak but the lump in his throat was as big as a boulder.

"What's wrong motherfucker, you ain't got nothin' to say?" Both intruders started to laugh, but he was so scared he still couldn't breathe. His mind was racing and all kinds of thoughts kept rushing in and out of his head. *Do I run? Do I fight? Should I jump out of my bedroom window? Is there anything on my floor I can use as a weapon?*

"I asked you a motherfuckin' question, bitch. Do you know why we is here?"

The other intruder finally spoke. "He scared man." He was giggling and Jacob thought maybe he recognized his voice.

The first intruder looked at the second and whispered loudly, "Shut the fuck up man." Then he looked back at Jacob, pushing the knife into his neck, not yet breaking the skin and asked again, "Do you know why we is here?" He knew Jacob was too terrified to talk, so he continued. "You think Brett be playin' but he ain't. You better get him some bitches or he gonna show you what's what, motherfucker. He ain't playin'. Ya feel me?" Then the first intruder released the knife from Jacob's neck and pointed the tip towards his eyes. He moved the knife closer to his left eye. Jacob was completely frozen while he stared at the blade, only a millimeter from piercing his pupil. The intruder pulled the knife away a couple of inches then lunged the knife forward stopping just a millisecond before it stabbed his eye. He winced in agony until he realized the blade had not penetrated him. The intruder took the knife back again then lunged it forward and yelled, "I'll fuck you up, bitch!" Once again, the knife stopped just in time. "You better do as I say, motherfucker."

The other intruder moved in closer to him and whispered, "If you don't, you gonna die. You know what I'm sayin'?"

As soon as Jacob heard this he knew who this intruder was. The same chill ran down his spine as after he'd just seen the video of Winston holding up the Food Chief convenience store. The words *"You gonna die tonight"* had been haunting him ever since. He still didn't know who the other intruder was, but he was positive this guy was Winston. At first Jacob thought, *if I tell Winston "I know it's you", we can all have a good laugh about this and I can finally breathe.* Then he thought, *if I blow Winston's cover the other guy might push the knife into my eye for real.* He kept quiet and barely spit out the words, "Okay, I understand."

"You understand?" The first intruder asked again. "I think you're just fuckin with us. Yo stand up motherfucker." The first intruder and Winston didn't wait for Jacob to get up. Instead they grabbed both his arms and yanked him out of bed. He was only wearing his underpants. "Yo, nice tighty whities, bitch." The first intruder and Winston started to giggle and couldn't stop.

Winston and the other masked intruder turned around and exited Jacob's bedroom. He heard Winston saying, "Don't make us come back bitch," as they walked back down the stairs.

Jacob waited in his bed and strained his ears to hear them leave. Then he jumped up and turned on the lights. He wasn't sure if they were gone or not. He thought, *This is probably a stupid thing to do, but I should call the police.* He kept thinking, *The police will find out I beat Ana when they catch Winston and the other intruder*, but he dialed 911 anyway.

"911 what's your emergency?"

"Two guys just broke into my townhouse! Send the cops here now!" Jacob's body continued to shake.

"Okay sir, are you inside your place now?"

"Yes, I am. Please send someone quick! I don't know if they're still here!"

"A police unit has already been dispatched, sir. Do you know if the intruders have any weapons on them?"

"One has a knife."

The dispatcher should have said police units have been dispatched not unit because Jacob counted at least five Gulf Coast City police cars outside his townhouse within five minutes.

The first cop to get to his door was the overly ambitious, skinhead, who appeared to be on steroids. This of course was Corporal Hunter.

"What's going on?" He asked.

Right behind him was Officer Paula. "Are you okay Jacob?" He was glad to see Paula because he felt like she cared about people and she cared about him.

Before he could answer, two more male cops showed up, so Corporal Hunter felt like he had to act all macho. "Are you blind Paula? He looks okay to me." Jacob thought Corporal Hunter was really nasty and didn't have to act so hostile.

He sat down and looked up at Paula. "Physically I'm okay." He was still shaking and didn't want anyone to see him like this.

Paula looked at him with kind eyes. "Take it easy Jacob. I can tell you're upset."

Jacob was trying not to get too emotional as Paula and the rest of the Gulf Coast City police responders concentrated on him. Paula shined her flashlight on his face to see if he had been assaulted then said, "Take your time and tell us what's going on."

With his voice quivering, Jacob explained what happened. "I was lying in my bed when two guys broke in and came up the stairs and I'm pretty sure one of them was Winston. They pulled a knife on me and scared the shit out of me, Paula."

Corporal Hunter interrupted. "What do ya think they wanted? Did they rob you? Did they assault you?"

Jacob knew he couldn't tell the police the reason Winston and the other guy were there because then he'd incriminate himself, so he just replied, "No, I don't know what they wanted."

Corporal Hunter was starting to get suspicious as Paula continued to inspect Jacob to see if he was okay. He continued, "Why do you think one of the perpetrators was Winston?"

"Because he said *'You gonna die'* just like he did in the Food Chief robbery video."

He could tell he'd convinced Paula. "Are you sure that's what he said?'

"Yes, I'm sure."

Officer Paula put the radio up to her mouth to have dispatch notify the entire Gulf Coast City police force to be on the lookout for Winston Brown.

Corporal Hunter asked, "What did the other perpetrator look like?"

"I couldn't see his face because they both had on ski masks and it was dark. But I'd say he was probably a black guy because I sort of saw his hands."

The police stuck around for a little while longer but eventually said they had to leave. Paula told Jacob she would continue to drive by his townhouse all night, and to call 911 if Winston came back.

Now every police officer in Gulf Coast City was on the lookout for Winston and another black male. Officer Paula and Corporal Hunter were in their patrol cars hunting tirelessly for their suspects. Corporal Hunter searched all the hotspots where the local druggies hung out on this side of town. He figured if Winston had just broken into Jacob's townhouse, then he must be all pumped up on adrenaline. He'd be running around looking for something to calm himself down. There's no way Winston could hold onto a bag of pot for consumption after the townhouse break-in. For a drug addict like Winston, a bag of marijuana would be consumed within minutes after its purchase. This meant he would be hitting the street hard, trying to score. With a guy like Winston you really didn't have to be a super detective to find him, even though, for some reason, no one had been able to. You just had to think like him, so this is what Corporal Hunter did.

He drove his car up and down the areas he'd busted guys for drug activity before. He looked along Oak Street then turned onto Third Avenue South. As Corporal Hunter pulled his patrol car into the parking lot behind Gulf Coast Jobs he spotted three dark figures crouching down trying to hide. He would have just driven past without stopping, but he saw the flame from an apparent joint lighting up as one of the figures took a toke. He drove his car close to the three individuals, who were trying to remain inconspicuous as they enjoyed their weed. When Corporal Hunter turned on the patrol car spotlight, all three men shot up and began running. Corporal Hunter jumped out of his car and began pursuit on foot.

As he was running he got on his radio to call in more help. "All units in the area of Third Ave South near Gulf Coast Jobs please respond. Officer in pursuit of three black males."

Officer Paula responded, "I'm about two blocks from your location now."

Corporal Hunter was in an all-out sprint now as the three suspects were running through people's backyards and jumping over fences. When they split off into different directions, he continued his foot pursuit of the suspect he was sure was Winston. Anyone who saw Winston running tonight would never have doubted he was the son of the Alabama running back, Herschel Brown. Winston could really sprint fast, and amazingly with all the drugs he had in his system, didn't seem as though he was going to tire anytime soon. Corporal Hunter was not going to give up the chase because his ego was much stronger than Winston's legs. Winston was headed towards the Gulf of Mexico and the center of town. He seemed to think he could disappear into the crowd of all-night tourists on Gulf of Mexico Boulevard, or maybe he was so stoned out of his mind that his only plan was not to get caught.

Officer Paula pulled around the corner in her patrol car and ran right into DeAndre, Winston's cousin and partner-in-crime. He was not going to stop either, so Paula got out of her car and ran after him with the same intensity Corporal Hunter was applying to the Winston chase. DeAndre had a big frame and was not really built as well for running as Winston, but he was still way faster than Paula. She could work out in the park almost every afternoon with her girlfriend but she still would not be anywhere near as fast as DeAndre. He simply kept running until he was completely out of her sight and disappeared into the night. Paula had not identified DeAndre. All she could put in her report was she had pursued a large black male and lost him in the chase.

Officer Paula put her hands on her knees and bent down to catch her breath. She knew Corporal Hunter and the other male policemen were not going to go easy on her for this. If they captured Winston, they would use this against her anytime she tried to argue that a woman can be just as good of a police officer as a man. As she radioed in the result of her pursuit, she secretly hoped Winston would outrun Corporal Hunter as well. "Officer Paula, request pick up from Tenth Avenue South. Suspect lost in foot pursuit." She'd run for seven blocks but hadn't been able to make an arrest. Now she was so exhausted that she had to wait for another patrol car to come pick her up. She was sure that whoever would be coming to get her was going to rub this in her face.

Corporal Hunter, on the other hand, was still in a foot pursuit with Winston and gaining ground. Two other officers had joined the chase and Winston was finally starting to tire. He was headed north on the busiest part of Gulf of Mexico Boulevard in the direction of Happy Suma's. Tourists were oblivious to everything around them except the bright lights and loud music on the strip, so they just casually watched as three white policemen chased after a black man. Some of the tourists even cheered as Winston ran past. One particular tourist yelled out, "You better pick it up, homeboy. The fuzz is right on your tail!"

Winston crossed Gulf of Mexico Boulevard at the traffic lights and headed towards the water. The lights on the strip were so bright that it almost appeared to be daylight. The beach was much different. It was pitch black and quiet. Only a handful of couples were walking on the sand, looking at the moon as it glistened on the Gulf water. When Winston got to the beach he was impossible to see. He had dressed in all black so he wouldn't be spotted during the home invasion of Jacob's townhouse. Corporal Hunter and the other cops chased Winston to the beach, but by the time they got there he'd already disappeared. Corporal Hunter radioed in the results of his foot pursuit and the patrol car carrying Officer Paula came for him and the other two policemen.

When Officer Paula got out of the patrol car, Corporal Hunter looked as if he was disgusted to see her, so she said, "Looks like you guys had as much success as I did."

This made Corporal Hunter's blood boil because he was not about to be humiliated by a woman. "I'd say we were way more successful than you, Paula, because we identified our suspect. You have no idea who outran you, do you?" He looked at the other two policemen and they both chuckled.

CHAPTER 14
GULF COAST JOBS

"I'm heading up north for a while..."
—Mustapha

Jacob arrived at Gulf Coast Jobs at 9:30 am. He was supposed to clock-in at 8. He hurried through the door, bracing himself for his boss to chew him out. Mustapha was already there with a determined look on his face. He called Jacob into his office. "I'm heading up north for a while with Ada and the kids, and I need you to be in charge of things here while I'm gone."

This was music to Jacob's ears. He was so relieved that Mustapha and Ada would be out of the way. Now he could totally focus on recruiting foreign girls for Brett and keep his butt out of jail.

Mustapha took a deep drag from his cigarette then polluted his office as he leaned back in his chair. "Olga will be coming with us to take care of the kids while Ada and I conduct some business at our employment agency in Columbus."

From the very beginning, Jacob suspected there was something more than an employer/employee relationship going on between Mustapha and Olga, the Belarus student. But he didn't know for sure. When he told Jacob he was going on a business trip, Jacob kind of figured Mustapha would be seeking more pleasure than business.

Mustapha continued, "I need to get up to Columbus to check on the other employment agency I'm trying to get started up there. I will fill you in on this more when I get back, because I want you to be my operations manager up there as well."

"Okay. Sounds good," Jacob replied. He acted excited but wasn't really that enthusiastic. He suspected Mustapha was just trying to keep him interested in the business so he'd continue to work hard for him. But other than that, Mustapha didn't care about him at all.

"One more thing Jacob, on the way to Columbus we're all going to stop in Atlantic City to have a little fun."

Jacob thought this didn't make sense. If you looked at this geographically, Atlantic City, New Jersey is not on the way to Columbus, Ohio from Gulf Coast City, Florida. Jacob knew Mustapha was from Libya, but he figured even he knew this. He really didn't care and was just relieved that Mustapha was leaving.

"Okay, well y'all have fun," he said, trying to rush things along.

"You wanna know another reason why we're all going to Atlantic City?"

Not really. "Sure, why?"

"Ada is pregnant and she loves going up there to gamble," Mustapha said with a proud smile.

"Congratulations, Mustapha." Jacob forced a smile. "That's great news."

"Anyway, we gotta get going. I'll bring us back some cigars from New Jersey. I know a great place there that sells real Cubans and we'll celebrate properly."

"Sounds great," Jacob said with as much enthusiasm as he could muster up.

"Oh yeah, I almost forgot," Mustapha said as he motioned for Jacob to follow him outside into the bright sun. "Here's the keys to my minivan. It holds up to eight passengers, so if you need to transport people to work, I want you to use this."

"Oh okay," Jacob said. "I'll definitely be needing this, I'm sure."

Mustapha got in his SUV. Ada and the kids and of course Olga, the nanny, were already buckled up waiting. Jacob and Gabriela waved goodbye to the black SUV as it began the trip out of Gulf Coast City.

With Mustapha and Ada out of sight, Jacob immediately got to work on keeping Brett happy. He headed to the best place he could think of to start recruiting. Happy Suma's was at the center of Gulf Coast City and everyone passed through there at some point. Also, Suma seemed like a good egg that Jacob could trust, and was beginning to consider his friend. He'd stopped by Suma's quite a lot lately, during his lunch breaks, and Suma always made time to chat with him. His new Turkish friend was always happy to listen and made suggestions to his younger companion on how to succeed at his new job.

When he arrived at Happy Suma's, Suma was standing in the doorway with a huge grin on his face.

"Mr. Jacob from Gulf Coast Jobs, how are you doing my friend?" The happy stout Turk yelled out. He hadn't shaved for a day or two and was way underdressed for a restaurant owner. But they were at the beach, so he was able to get away with it. Suma asked, "What brings you to my humble little business?"

"I was hoping I could talk to you, Suma."

"Of course, my friend. Where's Mustapha today? He's not with you?"

"He's driving up to Atlantic City. I thought you would've known this," Jacob said with a surprised look on his face. They both sat down in one of the restaurant booths. Jacob gave a quick look in the reflection of the window to make sure his button-down shirt didn't have the same wrinkled look as Suma.

"Why do you think I would know this, Jacob?" Suma caught him comparing their outfits but wasn't offended.

"Well, I thought you and Mustapha were best friends."

"Why, because we both speak the same language, you assume we are best friends?"

Suma had a point. Just because he had heard Mustapha and Suma speaking Arabic didn't mean they were friends. he thought, *I'm not friends with everyone I speak English with so why would I assume it's the same for Suma?*

"I guess I just assumed it," he said.

Suma explained how he really felt about Mustapha and Jacob was happy to hear it. "Look Jacob, Mustapha comes into Happy Suma's from time to time and always has the same agenda. He knows I will treat him like a king so he uses this to try to impress whomever he's with. He does it with people he wants to do business with. He does it with girls and he does it with you. As for me, I'm just giving my customer what he wants. Besides, my father made me learn Arabic when I was a kid, and if I don't continue to speak it, I'll forget. I'm sure you understand."

"Sure I--"

"Mustapha is a real bullshit man if you wanna know what I really think about him." Suma didn't give Jacob a chance to finish. "He tries to con and swindle just about everyone he comes in contact with. You be careful with him, Jacob. He may act like he's your friend and he wants to set you up with Ada's sister, but don't you think he's just doing this out of the kindness of his heart because he's not. There's definitely something in it for him, believe me."

Suma rambled on but Jacob was glad to listen. He was convinced he could confide in him about his problems. He felt like if Suma thought he could help him he would.

Suma said, "You are not at all like Mustapha, Jacob. I know we don't know each other extremely well but I feel like we are becoming friends and I feel like I can trust you."

Jacob told Suma that he felt the same and they began a long conversation about Jacob's recent events. He told Suma about Winston holding up the Food Chief and how the police knew all about it. Then he told him about how he was pretty sure Winston and another guy broke into his townhouse last night.

"Why don't the police arrest him immediately and throw away the key?" Suma screamed, within earshot of his customers. But Suma didn't care. That day he was devoted to listening and helping Jacob. "The guy is scum, I tell you Jacob. What kind of a man brings his prostitute girlfriend to a public restroom for a blow job? He has a wife and children waiting for him at home. This is what's wrong with this country. They are way too liberal in the government and I blame President Clinton. In Turkey, the police would have beaten him before he even made it to the jail!"

Then Suma raised his right hand up in the air. Jacob saw his hand and remembered how shocked he was to discover, on the first night he met him, that he was missing part of his thumb and two of his fingers. "Do you see that I'm missing part of my thumb and parts of my fingers?"

Jacob nodded his head and softly said, "Yes," because he was a little embarrassed.

"Do you know why they are no longer connected to my hand?" Before he could answer, Suma looked him in the eyes and sternly said, "Because the police caught me stealing when I was a teenager back in Turkey. They knew I wouldn't get into a lot of trouble because I was so young, so they took me down a back alley in a bad part of town and four of them held me down while the fifth one cut off my thumb and fingers with his knife. It was so painful Jacob, and I will never forget it, but this one event changed my life forever. If the police had taken me straight to the jail, I would be out and back on the streets in no time and I'd go back to stealing with my silly friends. When my father found out what the police had done he told me that I deserved this because I'd brought shame to our family by stealing. The next month or so, after my father made some kind of a deal with someone in the United States Air Force, I was on a military airplane to USA."

"Really?" Jacob asked.

"Yes Jacob, really. My father used to be a janitor at the American Air Force base in Ankara. He'd worked there for over 30 years when the police caught me stealing. He'd made a lot of friends with some very powerful American Air Force generals. When he explained to them that the only way he could save his son from drugs and crime was to get me out of the country, they agreed to smuggle me out on one of those large military transport planes. They flew me all the way from Ankara to MacDill Air Force base in Tampa and I've been in Florida ever since."

Jacob knew it was going to be a long lunch because Suma was going to voice his strong opinions and tell him stories about everything he had to say. But he was overjoyed to finally have someone, besides X-man, who would listen to his problems. Besides, this was one incredible true story and he wasn't interested in going back to Gulf Coast Jobs anyway. He told Suma how someone had dropped LSD in his drink which caused him to beat on poor defenseless Ana. And he told Suma he suspected it was Winston.

Suma asked how Ana was doing so Jacob told him she had a black eye and was crying a lot.

"Is she going to press charges?" Suma asked.

"I don't think she will as long as I cooperate with her, Camille, and Brett."

"Cooperate, what does that mean?" Suma asked, with a scrunched forehead and confused face.

Jacob explained that Brett gave him a choice to either go to jail or recruit strippers for Exotic Beauties.

"How does this help Ana?" Suma was still confused.

"Brett said he promoted Ana to floor manager and now she will supervise the strippers and help recruit new ones."

"Something sounds fishy about this, Jacob. Ana gets beat up by you, but you don't remember anything. The next day Ana has a black eye and a promotion and you have an ultimatum. Brett, Camille and maybe even Mustapha are up to something here."

"You think Mustapha has something to do with this too?"

"Who the heck knows, but we need to figure out how we're gonna tackle all this, I think."

"We?" Jacob asked.

"Sure!" Suma yelled out smiling. "We are friends and friends help friends, right? And you, my friend definitely need help."

Suma and Jacob sat together for the rest of the day and into the night. Customers came in and out of Happy Suma's but Suma let Lilianna take care of them so they could work on putting together a plan.

Suma explained. "The first thing we need to do is find girls for Brett. Then, after Ana has calmed down a little, you need to try to talk with her to find out exactly what happened that night."

Jacob really liked how Suma kept saying "we". He finally had someone on his side to help him, and it felt good. They decided that Suma would put the word out to the foreign students, who came into Happy Suma's, that they were looking for exotic dancers and Jacob would get Gabriela to help recruit at Gulf Coast Jobs.

Gulf Coast City had many gentlemen's clubs and the beautiful Russian and Eastern European girls could easily just walk in anywhere they wanted, but they didn't know which ones were safe and which ones were not. Jacob decided the service Gulf Coast Jobs was going to provide would assure these girls that they wouldn't be forced into prostitution and drugs, and the owner wouldn't force himself on them. Jacob was sure Camille would cut off Brett's balls if he ever messed around.

In addition to all this, they could save the girls the hassle of having to pound the pavement going from gentlemen's club to gentlemen's club. The girls could make an appointment with Jacob for an interview, and if they qualified he'd drive them over to Exotic Beauties where Brett and Camille would be waiting.

Suma and Jacob talked all night and into the early morning hours. They analyzed all the details then put together their plan of action. Jacob went home feeling confident for the first time since he'd been in Gulf Coast City that maybe his life was going to get better.

CHAPTER 15
GULF COAST JOBS

"I've never seen so many muchachas bonitas in one place!"
—Mexican Hotel Laundry Attendant

About five days after Suma and Jacob had their long meeting at his restaurant, Gabriela got her first phone call from a Russian girl asking if this was the place that was hiring exotic dancers. Laughing her head off as Gabriela always did, she managed to say, "Yes, it is. Would you like to come in for an interview?"

Less than an hour later, three tall thin Russians stopped by the office. Showing bright colored bra straps and wearing miniskirts that showed plenty of leg, they were there to apply for exotic dancer positions. By the time late afternoon rolled around, Gulf Coast Jobs was jammed packed with young luscious girls all wearing sweet smelling perfume, hoping Jacob could help them.

When one of the Mexican hotel laundry room workers came into Gulf Coast Jobs to get his paycheck, he gasped and cried out, "Oh dios mio! I have never seen so many muchachas bonitas in one place!" Gabriela looked at him and laughed.

For the next couple of weeks, Russian and Eastern European girls kept piling into Gulf Coast Jobs. There were so many hotties coming into their employment agency, Jacob lost count. He kept in touch with Brett and when he felt like he had some really good candidates for him to interview, he gave him a call.

Brett was always happy to hear the good news. Gabriela set a time for the girls to meet Jacob at Gulf Coast Jobs then they all got into the minivan and he drove them over to Exotic Beauties. He felt like he was delivering these girls to the devil but he was too afraid to stop.

Depending on how the girls looked and whether they wanted to take off their clothes or not, Brett divided them into different groups. Brett and Camille were hiring bartenders, door greeters, hostesses, hot tub girls, waitresses and of course exotic dancers. Obviously, the top priority for Brett and Camille was finding exotic dancers.

Working at Exotic Beauties was a chance to make big money. It seemed like every Russian and Eastern European girl Jacob met wanted to work there, but not all of them were willing to take off their clothes. They either told him that they were too shy or this was against their religion or principles. Brett needed girls for just about every position, but dancers, as Brett and Camille insisted everyone call them, were the most in demand.

Now that Jacob was working for the devil, he continued to put the real reason he was in Gulf Coast City out of his mind. And even though the Bible verse from Romans kept coming into Jacob's head, *"and those who are in the flesh cannot please God"*, he was able to block it out.

And as promised, Brett was paying good money. Jacob was finally able to get together enough cash to buy a nice looking used car so he gave his bicycle to a Mexican landscaper and bought himself some better wheels. He now had a used Pontiac Grand Am so he no longer felt embarrassed to have to get on his bicycle or call a taxi every time he wanted to go somewhere. Everything was falling into place for Brett without Mustapha and Ada around. And as long as they didn't come back, Jacob would be able to continue feeding the devil.

***

About a month after they'd started recruiting for Exotic Beauties, Jacob was sitting in his office typing on his computer, when Gabriela called back to him, "Jacob, you have a visitor."

His first thought was *Oh shit its Winston!* So he asked, "Who is it?"

"Karina."

Jacob jumped up in his seat. He'd given up on the soft-spoken Belarus girl with long dark hair, whom he'd spent one romantic weekend with, then a couple of days later shot him down. His mind started racing as he looked in the mirror and combed his hair with his fingers. *I wonder why she's here. Does she want a job? Is she still dating Sergei? Is she interested in me?* He knew they'd only shared a small amount of time together, but he never stopped thinking about her. He was so busy trying to decide why Karina was here that he forgot to respond back.

Gabriela yelled again, "Jacob, what do you want me to do?" She was laughing and no doubt knew he'd been up to something with her.

"Send her back," Jacob insisted as his face flushed.

When Karina walked into his office he felt like she lit up the entire room. She was so radiant, maybe the most lustrous young lady he had ever seen, and during the past month he'd seen a lot. The feelings he'd suppressed about her, and the time they'd spent together, came rushing back to the surface. She seemed sad and her brown bedroom eyes were looking down at the floor. Jacob's heart was racing, but he tried to keep things professional until he determined why she'd come to see him.

He took a deep breath. "Hello, Karina. Have a seat. How can I help you?"

She looked up and said with her seductive Belarus accent, "Hi Jacob. You look nice today."

"Why, thank you. What's going on?" Karina didn't answer but her eyes started to mist. He could tell she was fighting back tears and he wanted to walk around his desk and give her a hug and tell her not to cry. "What's wrong?" he asked.

She responded as a tear rolled down her face. "Jacob, I don't have job. Half the summer is over and still, I don't have work. I paid all my money to come to USA and now I can't pay my money back. My mother is sick in Belarus and I wanted it for her…" Karina couldn't continue because the tears were really flowing now.

He didn't know what to do. He felt so bad and he really wanted to embrace her. He thought, *I will walk around the desk and try to hold her hand, then see how she responds.*

He got up and moved towards Karina, then sat on his desk in front of her. He reached out his hand and put it on her hand. She was no longer crying but her pretty face was still glistening from the tears. She looked up at Jacob then put her other hand on his. Then she pulled his hand towards her cheek so he leaned in closer. This was the response he wanted. Karina and Jacob both moved towards each other and both directed their lips towards the other's lips. Now they were kissing. He ran his fingers through Karina's hair and breathed in her vanilla perfume. He suspected maybe she was just giving in because she needed a job, but he didn't care because this felt amazing and he didn't want it to stop.

Then Jacob and Karina heard Gabriela clearing her throat and both jumped back away from each other. "Um... sorry Jacob, but Brett is on the phone and he says it's urgent."

He walked back around to his side of the desk as Gabriela began studying Karina's face, looking for clues to determine what was going on. "Thank you, Gabriela," he said, trying to sound authoritative like Mustapha would do. "I will take the call in here and you can go back up front."

Gabriela smiled, then took one last long look at Karina to see if she could pick up any more information about what she'd just seen, before heading back to her desk.

Karina and Jacob both sat down acting like nothing had just happened between them, and Jacob picked up the phone. "Brett, let me call you right back."

He hung up on Brett as he was saying, "No, don't hang up, I need to talk to you now…"

Jacob looked across his desk at Karina, who was trying to fix her hair. He told her he had a contract now with Exotic Beauties. She said she already knew. "You are becoming famous in Gulf Coast City because everybody knows this." Jacob's face beamed. He was happy that he could impress the super sweet Karina, but he also felt ashamed.

Karina told him she'd really like to work at Exotic Beauties, but insisted she could not and would not take off her clothes. "Jacob, I can never be stripper. I am just too shy and what if my mother finds out from back in Belarus. She will be sad. Can you find job for me as waitress?"

At this point, he would do anything she asked. He really wanted to be the one that put a smile on her face and solved all her problems. But he did not want to send her to the strip club. "No, I can't send you there. You really don't wanna work there."

"I know, you're right, I don't, but I really need money…" Karina stopped for a second thinking she might start crying. "... for my mom."

He reached out and took Karina's hand. "Look, I have some money saved. You can have it. I wanna help you. No strings attached."

"No Jacob. Thank you but no. I cannot take your money. If you want to help me, please get me job at Exotic Beauties."

"Why don't I get you a job at one of the hotels? You will feel much better about yourself there."

"No, I'm running out of time before I have to go back and I need to make money. Please Jacob, will you help me?" Karina looked up at him with her sad eyes and his heart melted.

He really wanted to help her, but he also knew Brett was maxed out on all his staff right now except for strippers. The only way Brett would hire Karina would be if Jacob told him that she wanted to start as a waitress then move over to exotic dancing after she got the feel for things. Even though he knew Karina would never become a stripper she could work through the summer as a waitress before Brett pressured her into stripping. By this time, she would be back in Belarus.

Jacob put his hand back on top of Karina's and said, "This is what I'm going to do. I'll tell Brett that you're interested in becoming an exotic dancer but you wanna take it slow and get the feel for things by starting out as a waitress."

Karina looked up at Jacob with her big brown eyes and said, "Yes, but I don't want anyone to think I'm going to be stripper."

He responded by saying, "You will never have to be a stripper. I'm just gonna tell Brett this so you can get your foot in the door."

"Yes, but I'm ashamed Brett thinks I am type of girl that wants to be stripper."

This took a little convincing from Jacob, but she finally agreed to go along with the plan. He felt guilty that he had to put Karina through this, but he convinced himself this was the best way and the only way she'd be able to make money.

When Jacob had everything set with Karina, he called Brett back and he answered immediately. "This is Brett." Jacob cringed at the sound of his voice.

"Yes Brett, what do ya need?"

"When are you gonna have more dancers for me?" Brett sounded irritated.

"Well Brett, I'm actually working on that right now. I have a very attractive young lady in my office with me from Belarus--"

"Belarus? Where the fuck is that?" Brett asked, and seemed disgusted. Jacob knew he was going to be even more disgusted when he found out she wasn't going to take off her clothes.

"It's one of the countries that borders Russia." Jacob had the feeling he would have to sell Belarus to Brett then he'd have to sell Karina. Then he had to tell him Karina wasn't going to take off her clothes. "The girls there look and act just like Russian girls," he said. Then he looked at Karina and she was giving him a harsh look back because he'd just insulted her and her country.

Brett jumped in because he knew Jacob was probably going to babble on all day. "I know where Belarus is, Jacob. I'm just fuckin' with you."

"Oh." Jacob's face flushed because Brett had insulted him and he had insulted Karina.

"I've had girls dancing here from Belarus, Russia, Colombia, Mexico... everywhere. Send her over and Camille and I will take a look." Brett was finally starting to lighten up. "I need more dancers than that one, though, so keep working on it. I gotta go."

"Hold on, Brett. This girl wants to take things slow."

"What the fuck does that mean?"

"As you know, none of these girls have done exotic dancing before so she wants to start as a waitress and get the feel for things before she jumps into dancing."

"Fuck Jacob. Now thanks to you, I have more fuckin' waitresses than I need. What I need are dancers that can start on day one. I'm gonna have to say no to this. Tell her to come back when she wants to perform."

Jacob looked over at Karina's sad face and he knew he couldn't give up. "Brett?" he asked, checking to see if he was still there. "Brett?"

"What!" Brett yelled.

"She's my girlfriend and I was hoping you could help her out on this one. She's very beautiful and you don't even have to pay me my commission." Jacob looked at Karina and saw a little hint of a smile.

Brett loosened up. "Aw shit, Jacob. Okay sure. Bring her over. Camille and I'd love to meet her." Jacob's face brightened. Then Brett said, "She better not be a dog."

Jacob looked over at Karina and saw her smiling. They both got up and gave each other a quick hug and a quick kiss. He didn't know how much she was happy about getting a job, and how much she was happy he called her his girlfriend.

They walked out of Jacob's office and into the front reception area. Gabriela was sitting at her desk chomping on some potato chips, trying to pretend like she hadn't been listening to Jacob's conversation. He told her she was in charge for the rest of the day because he was taking Karina to Exotic Beauties for a job interview. Gabriela smiled and looked at him as if to say, *You are one dirty dog, Jacob.*

Jacob and Karina were just about to walk out the door when a tall slender Turkish lady walked in as a taxi drove off with X-man driving and honking his horn. She had a ton of stuff with her; maybe five suitcases and some boxes.

Gabriela, Karina and Jacob all stopped and looked her up and down. She was stunning and exotic. She had dark skin and dark slanted eyes.

"Hello," Jacob said. "Can we help you?"

"Are you Jako?" She asked with a harsh Middle Eastern accent.

"Yes, I'm Jacob. Can I help you?"

"Don't you recognize me, Jako?" He didn't know if she was going to laugh or cry but he could tell she was very excited. He had no clue who she was but was very curious, as were Gabriela and Karina.

"I'm your fiancée Yousra!"

It instantly came back to Jacob. The first night at Happy Suma's, Mustapha and Ada showed him Yousra's pictures. He remembered that she was Ada's sister, and Mustapha and Ada had asked him if he wanted to marry her. After that night, he never thought about her again because he was too busy worrying when Brett was going to have him put in jail, or when Winston was going to break into his place. Jacob looked around the room and saw a big smile on Yousra's face that he was sure was about to turn into a frown. Gabriela was loving the excitement and laughing at him, and Karina was gritting her teeth.

He had to think fast so he said the first thing that came into his head. "Yousra, welcome to Florida. Did you just arrive today?" He didn't want to hug Yousra because he could feel Karina's eyes burning a hole in the back of his head, but he knew Yousra was demanding it. He gave her a quick embrace and apologized that he had an emergency which required him to leave right away. "You can stay here and tell Gabriela everything. It's great to see you but I gotta go."

Jacob rushed outside as quickly as he could and Karina followed. They both got into his car and drove away. He knew Karina would be demanding an explanation so he spoke up.

"That was kinda weird. Don't you agree?"

She tensed her forehead and was silent as if she didn't want to waste any time talking when she could be listening to Jacob's explanation. He said, "That is not really my fiancée, by the way."

"That?" Karina asked.

"I mean *she* is not really my fiancée."

He could feel Karina's eyes boring into the side of his face. He kept looking straight ahead as if he had to put all his effort into concentrating on the busy road.

"But you know her, right?" she asked.

"Well, yes and no." Jacob gave Karina a quick glance and saw her studying his face. "I have never met her but I've seen a picture of her."

"Who is she?"

"I believe she's Ada's sister from Turkey."

"What is she doing here and why does she think she's the fiancée?"

Karina was asking a lot of questions. He assumed she was trying to gather all the facts. Then she was going to decide if she wanted to try to make a relationship work between the two of them. He knew he had to be careful with what he said and how he said it. Calmly he asked, "Do you remember the first night we all went to Happy Suma's together?"

"Of course, that's the night you gave me such wonderful kiss."

"That's right." Jacob grinned and was glad Karina still thought about that. "Well, do you remember when Mustapha and Ada were showing me the pictures of Yousra and they were saying I should marry her, and it would be a business arrangement and all that silly stuff?"

Karina said she did sort of remember something like that but really didn't recall much of the details. She told Jacob that her English was not as good back then as it is now because she had just arrived in the USA.

"Well, I never thought much about that conversation either, but Mustapha must have used me somehow to get her over here."

"Did you help Yousra apply for fiancée visa?" Karina asked. She didn't seem as surprised as when she first saw Yousra, but Jacob could tell she was still a little uneasy about the whole thing.

"As I said Karina, I never thought about that conversation since that night." He gave her another quick glance, trying to get a read on her emotions. She was looking out the window now.

They were almost at Exotic Beauties, so he said he'd introduce her to Brett and Camille then call Gabriela to find out if she'd discovered anything else. One thing he knew about Gabriela was she loved to get into other people's business, so she very well might have all the information he was looking for by the time he called her. Karina agreed that was a good idea but she also didn't want him to leave her alone with Brett and Camille. So now Jacob wasn't sure what he was going to do because he couldn't saw himself in half to keep Karina happy.

When they finally arrived at Exotic Beauties and walked inside to meet Brett and Camille, Karina's hands were shaking but she told Jacob she was determined to do this. He could tell she felt a lot of pressure to earn money for herself and her mom. But he told her if she wanted to quit she could call him anytime day or night and he would come get her.

"Well hello, Jacob. How you doing and who's this?" Camille ran up to them and asked as if they were old friends. She even gave Jacob a small kiss on his cheek which he knew was totally fake.

"This is my girlfriend, Karina," he answered proudly.

About that time beefy Brett waddled up sweating and puffing from only walking a few steps. "Let's all go back to my office and chat," he ordered.

As they walked back to Brett's office, Camille said to Jacob. "It's about time you found yourself a girlfriend, Jacob. She is very bonita." She smiled at Karina, but Jacob wasn't amused by her fake friendliness.

He thought, *How am I supposed to go looking for a girlfriend when I'm too busy getting blackmailed by you and your nasty husband? And how am I supposed to find a girlfriend when I can't get any sleep from fear of having Winston break into my townhouse every night?*

On the surface, it appeared that Brett, Camille, and Jacob were all good friends who enjoyed doing business together. But underneath all the fake kindness, Jacob really despised them. On that day especially, he was determined to get his revenge. Karina seemed to be somewhat comfortable with Brett and Camille because she didn't know the real history they all had.

After they sat down in Brett's office and got through the small talk, Jacob told them he had to call Gabriela to check on some things back at Gulf Coast Jobs. Brett and Camille seemed happy to see him leave so they could interrogate Karina.

"Gulf Coast Jobs, how may I help you?" Gabriela answered.

"Gabriela, it's me."

She started laughing. "You loco Jacob. What did you tell this girl? Is she really your fiancée?"

"No! Of course not!" he yelled down the phone.

"Well, she says you ask her to marry you."

"That's not true."

"She's been showing me letters that you sent to Turkey for her."

"What? What kind of letters?"

"I don't know… love letters, I guess."

"What are you talking about Gabriela?" Jacob was getting annoyed and a little worried.

"She told me you guys have been sending each other love letters all summer. She has lots of pictures here of you too and she says you ask her to come over to Gulf Coast City to get married. I don't know, Jacob. This is what she say, but you are in big trouble, boy." Gabriela was still laughing but Jacob could tell she felt this was serious and was concerned for him.

He knew only one person who could be behind this. "This is all the work of Mustapha!" he yelled.

"Mustapha?" Jacob didn't think Gabriela was totally convinced but he was. "Yousra said you applied for a K-1 Fiancée Visa for her so she can come over here to marry you."

"Yes, I know it was him. He was always asking me to sign things and was always sneaky about it. I know he used me to get her over here."

"Well, this girl thinks she gonna be living with you and you guys gonna get married."

"Is she still there?"

"No, she went outside to smoke."

"She smokes? No way!" Not only was she going to come live with Jacob but she was going to smoke in his townhouse as well. "I gotta go Gabriela."

"What should I say to Yousra?"

"Just tell her I have to work and I'll see her when I'm done."

"I think she wants to go lay down because she says she's really tired from the trip over here from Turkey."

"Well, I would say take her to my townhouse but my doors are locked, obviously. I tell you what, tell her to hold tight and I'll be there as soon as I can."

Jacob hung up with Gabriela then went back to check on Brett, Camille, and Karina. When he got to Brett's office they were all laughing and having fun. Karina was dressed in a skimpy waitress uniform which was an all-white revealing lingerie outfit with white gloves. Jacob thought she looked like an angel. Karina seemed a little self-conscious but cheerful, so he was pretty sure Brett and Camille had given her the job.

He told Brett and Camille he had to get back to Gulf Coast Jobs right away to take care of some urgent business so they said okay and told Karina they'd see her tomorrow night for work.

Karina changed back into her clothes and they were just about to walk outside when Brett called Jacob back. "Let me talk to you in private for just a minute." Jacob turned around and followed Brett but told him he was in a hurry. "This will only take a minute," Brett responded, and they both walked back towards his office. "Karina seems like a really nice girl," Brett said. "Thanks for bringing her to Exotic Beauties. We'll take care of her and I think the customers are gonna love her."

Jacob was not happy about Brett having so much power over Karina. Also, he didn't want to think about all the aggressive customers, who were going to be hanging all over her, but he nodded his head to Brett in approval. Then Jacob asked, "What will it take to get you off my back Brett? I've come through for you pretty good this summer and we're over halfway through the tourists season. I know you're not gonna be pressuring me forever, are you? When will my debt to Ana be paid, and you and I can just do regular business together without the threat of you running to the police hanging over my head?" Now that Brett and Camille seemed happy with how their business was going, Jacob felt like he had a good shot at talking some sense into them.

Brett scratched his exposed belly and responded, "You know what Jacob, you're right. You have come through really good for us. Exotic Beauties is packed every night with great looking girls which means we are packed with lots of customers. Camille and I are making pretty good money and you are too, right?" Brett lowered his hand to straighten his crotch. "I tell you what, if you can find me one more absolute knockout and super exotic girl, like none of the customers have seen before, I will let you off the hook for good and we'll wipe the slate clean." Jacob rolled his eyes and Brett responded with, "Trust me on this Jacob."

Jacob couldn't decide if Brett was telling him the truth or not. But he figured, as usual, Brett was not going to give him a choice on this anyway. So he nodded in agreement and they shook hands and said goodbye.

Karina and Jacob got in his car and headed back to the Gulf Coast Jobs office. He told Karina he needed to be alone to sort things out with Yousra. He explained what Gabriela had told him and convinced her that if Yousra believes she's over here to marry him, then she's going to be in a world of hurt when she finds out this is not true. Jacob told Karina that as much as he wanted to spend time with her, he didn't think it would be fair to Yousra to bring her along to break the bad news. He asked Karina to trust him just like Brett had asked. And Jacob thought Karina trusted him as much as he trusted Brett.

CHAPTER 16
JACOB'S TOWNHOUSE

"Exotic dancing? Is that like belly dancing?"
—Yousra

Jacob pulled into the parking lot of Gulf Coast jobs and dropped Karina off. He asked her to leave quickly so Yousra wouldn't get suspicious. Then Jacob walked inside the office. Of course, he got one last kiss, in his car, before they said goodbye. And it was spectacular. Jacob smiled to himself because he hoped this time they were going to start something really special.

Yousra and Gabriela were inside the office waiting for Jacob. He could tell Gabriela was trying to make small talk with Yousra, but had run out of things to say and was grateful he'd arrived. Now that Karina wasn't there to judge him, Jacob gave Yousra a kiss on the cheek and tried to figure out his next move.

Yousra responded with a big smile, and as he absorbed her face he realized she was absolutely breathtaking. The photograph Jacob had first seen did not do her justice. With her long dark hair, deep walnut eyes and smooth brown skin, in person she was much more desirable than the picture Mustapha and Ada presented a few months back. Yousra told Jacob how excited she was to finally meet him and she couldn't wait to see where he lived.

He was in shock. He was sure that Yousra actually thought this whole situation was real. She actually believed they were going to get married. He didn't want to hurt her so he said, "My place is nothing special."

She replied, "Jako, I've been looking forward to moving in with you ever since you first asked me to get married." What Jacob couldn't quite get his head around was how Mustapha had convinced Yousra, *he* was the one writing her all the letters.

He had no idea what he was going to do and was just going through the motions now. Yousra got inside his car and he drove her over to his townhouse. He kept thinking over and over, *How can I get out of this without hurting this poor young lady?*

When they arrived at Jacob's small beach townhouse and walked inside his messy place, Yousra said, "Wow, your house is really nice." He was surprised, but Yousra was really excited about everything he'd showed her so far. Then she said, "I guess I should call this *our* place, right?"

Jacob told Yousra she should go lie down because she must be tired. She went upstairs to lay in his bed, but not before she gave him a long kiss and whispered, "I'm going think about you when I take my shower." He blushed and his whole body tingled.

He didn't know if this kiss was an invitation to join her in the shower, or just her way of saying I'm happy to be with you. So since he didn't really know what to do, and didn't want to do anything that might hurt Karina, he decided no move would be the best move. He sat on the couch and listened to the shower running as he imagined how it would feel to rub on her large breasts as the water splashed down on them. When he realized he'd stiffened in his pants, Jacob got up and cracked open a beer, blushing with shame.

As the sun went down and Yousra took her nap, Jacob sat on the couch drinking more beer and listening to music. He was pondering so many ideas of how he could get himself out of this situation without hurting Yousra or Karina.

Now that Jacob had a nice little buzz going from whiskey-shot-number-two and beer-number-five, he was too far gone to make a decision. As he was sipping down beer-number-six the words from Brett came back to him. *"If you can send me one more dancer, who is really exotic and really special, I will wipe the slate clean with you and your obligation to me will be done."*

That's it, Jacob thought, *Yousra will be my special dancer to give to Brett. No one here has ever seen an exotic Turkish woman like her, I'm sure. After this, he'll no longer hang Ana over my head every time he wants something from me. No, I can't do this to this poor young lady. And what about Mustapha, he'll kill me if he finds out I've mistreated his sister-in-law.*

About that time, Jacob heard Yousra moving around upstairs and he guessed she was probably done with her nap. She called down, "Jako, are you coming up or do you want me to come down?"

"You come down," Jacob replied.

So Yousra came down wearing her pajamas. She wasn't wearing a provocative negligee, but she still looked seductive. Her pajamas consisted of silky long pants and a tight little pink t-shirt that conformed to her slender body. Jacob breathed in the smell of fresh soap and could feel the excitement coming back in his pants.

Yousra asked in her sweet voice, "What would you like to do on our first night together, Jako?"

He was starting to fidget because he had the feeling Yousra wanted them to have sex. The thought made his heart race, both from excitement and fear. She was so confident and sexy and he had zero experience in this department. He asked a question trying to slow her down. "Were you thinking about working here in Gulf Coast City, Yousra?"

"I love how you talk, Jako."

Jacob could tell Yousra was wound up and more than likely desiring for him to make a move. He responded by saying, "I love how you say my name, Yousra." He cracked open beer-can-number-seven.

Yousra smiled and asked, "Gabriela told me you send girls to do exotic dancing. Is that like belly dancing?"

Feeling the effects of his seventh beer and third whiskey-shot, Jacob laughed and said, "You could say that, yes."

"That's great because I used to belly dance in Turkey a lot. I even took lessons when I was younger." Yousra pranced in closer to Jacob while fixating on his face. "Would you like me to show you, Jako?"

Of course he would! "No thanks. I'm kinda tired and I bet you are too."

"No, I had a great nap, Jako. I'm ready to dance."

Yousra continued to stare into his eyes and started wiggling her hips and dancing around his couch. Jacob slunk down as he sat and absorbed the action. He was listening to Van Halen in the background and wondered if anyone had ever belly danced to their music before.

Jacob knew Brett would be enthralled with Yousra, but he didn't want to send her there. He told her, "That's real impressive dancing."

"I'm glad you like it, Jako." Yousra smiled.

"The only thing Yousra is, exotic dancing is a little different than belly dancing." Yousra continued wiggling her hips around Jacob as he tried to explain. "When a girl does exotic dancing, she can belly dance but she has to add a little extra to her routine."

Yousra seemed a little puzzled but didn't stop performing. "What do you mean, Jako?"

"Well, with exotic dancing the girl has to remove some of her clothes during her performance."

"Do you mean like this?" Yousra asked as she started to take off her pajama top. Jacob's eyes widened as he focused on her perfectly shaped breasts with just a hint of a tan line. He didn't realize that Yousra knew exactly what exotic dancers did, and enjoyed teasing him.

"Yes, like that but you don't have to show me," Jacob said as his voice cracked as if he was a pubescent 14-year-old.

"Do exotic dancers take off their pajama pants as well, Jako?" Yousra asked as she slowly pulled her pants down a couple of inches so Jacob could see she was not wearing any panties.

"Yes," he said nervously. "Taking off your pants is a requirement, yes. But you don't have to take off your panties."

"But Jako, what if I'm not wearing any panties?" Little-Miss-Innocent

Yousra asked as she pulled her pajama pants down to her ankles then put them on top of Jacob's head. When he saw that she was completely shaved below he thought he was going to burst through his pants.

Jacob's heart was beating too fast for him to talk without sounding silly, so he pushed Yousra away before she could try to kiss him. But this was pointless. She just moved in closer and kissed the top of his head. She was completely naked and Jacob was at full attention but was fighting this with everything he had.

He said, "Don't you think we should get some rest?"

"I don't think I can sleep until I have been with my handsome fiancé." Yousra kept coming after him and he kept trying to push her away. But every time he pushed her off, she just came back stronger. Jacob put his hands on her shoulders, trying to push her back, but she fell down to her knees right in line with his crotch. "I want to see what my fiancé has waiting for me in his pants," Yousra said as she glided her hands up his inner thigh. Jacob had been playing defense now for a long time and he was starting to tire. He was only young and human and couldn't hold out much longer. He tried to stand up, but Yousra grabbed the bottom of his pants and pulled them down. Now he was standing in his underpants and Yousra was licking her lips. "One more to go then you can have me all night, Jako." Yousra put her hands right in the place that would neutralize any man, let alone a 21-year-old virgin who'd been surrounded by exotic dancers every day for months.

What happened next was probably the best minute and a half of ecstasy he had experienced so far in his life. It took him thirty seconds to take off his underpants, shirt and socks, then thirty seconds to figure out how to penetrate Yousra. After squirming around trying to get inside, she finally guided him in. He saw her eyes roll back into her head. He was trying to decide if she was feeling pleasure when something came over him. He felt the room spin with a feeling of ultimate pleasure, almost an out-of-body experience. His back ached slightly so he pushed harder inside her. All the beautiful girls who'd come into Jacob's office over the past week, and all the time he'd spent at Exotic Beauties watching the dancers perform, and all the time he'd spent thinking about Karina finally came to a wonderful climax.

Yousra whispered, "Yes, that's it. Don't stop Jako." Jacob pushed inside her then pulled out. He pushed back inside again and she squealed. He pulled out and when he tried to go back in he was limp. Yousra wanted more but Jacob was done. He pulled up his underpants and wiped the wetness from his fingers.

This was his first time and would always be a great memory for him … all one and a half minutes. Yousra and Jacob soon fell asleep on the couch and didn't speak until the next morning.

When Jacob woke up the following day, he felt uneasy. His guilty mind took him to the book of Hebrews which says, *"Let marriage be held in honor among all, and let the marriage bed be undefiled, for God will judge the sexually immoral and adulterous."* Jacob had just had sex out of wedlock and this was considered a sin. At first, he tried to soothe his guilt by convincing himself that Yousra was his fiancée. But Jacob knew this would not fly in the eyes of the Lord. He thought about Karina, and was consumed with guilt. He prayed that she wouldn't get hurt by this.

He needed to get out of his townhouse to breathe, so he told Yousra he had to go into work but would come see her around lunchtime. She smiled and said, "I will be looking forward to seeing you again, Jako."

CHAPTER 17

JACOB'S CAR

"Did you tell her she is not really your fiancée?"
—Karina

Jacob went into work, on his first day of no longer being a virgin, and felt like the whole world probably knew his sexual status had changed. Even though this had been a very pleasurable experience, the guilt was eating at him.

He told Gabriela he'd be back in his office. "So don't disturb me unless something important comes up." He escaped behind his desk all morning and relived last night's events.

Around lunchtime Jacob left work to go see Yousra. But first, he had to get Karina so he could take her to her first day of work at Exotic Beauties. He drove over to the big house on Oak Street, trying hard to forget the memory of seeing her there with Sergei, only a couple of months earlier. When Karina got in his car, he could tell she was looking for clues about last night's events. Jacob knew if he told Karina the truth he'd probably lose her forever. So even though he knew the Bible said *"Lie not one to another,"* he did it anyway. And to make matters worse, very soon both Karina and Yousra were both going to be inside his car.

Karina sat still on the way over to his townhouse but took this alone time to ask him some questions. "Did Yousra sleep at your townhouse last night, Jacob?"

He was sure she already knew Yousra was there so he couldn't lie on this one. "Yes she did," he answered confidently, as he looked straight ahead at the road. He didn't want to reveal the tension he felt in his neck.

"Did you tell her it was all a big mistake and that you are not really her fiancé?"

This question was a lot more difficult to answer, so Jacob replied, "I wasn't able to tell her that yet, but I'm going to tell her today." He was very careful to speak with conviction. Otherwise he knew Karina would know he was lying. "I'm going to tell her I didn't write those letters and I'm only interested in you."

"Do you think she will be sad?" Karina asked, which made Jacob realize that Karina cared for this young lady's feelings.

"Yes, I think she will be very sad. This is why I'm so reluctant to tell her."

"I understand. Please be gentle to her."

Jacob was happy to see that Karina cared about Yousra's feelings. He thought, *I might actually be able to pull this off.*

However, when Yousra walked up to his car and saw Karina sitting in the front seat, he was not so sure. If looks could kill, Karina would have been dead. Yousra cut her a look as if to say, *I'm Jacob's fiancée so why are you sitting in the front seat?* The entire ride up to Exotic Beauties was mostly in silence. When Yousra first got in Jacob's car she leaned forward and gave him a kiss, which made Karina grit her teeth. Jacob peeled out onto the road so Yousra had to sit back and leave him alone.

This was going to be Karina's first day as a waitress. Even though he felt terrible about sending her there, he was excited to see how she was going to look in her skimpy little white lingerie outfit and white gloves. When he parked the car in the Exotic Beauties parking lot, he could tell Karina was annoyed because she stormed out of the car and walked inside without saying a word.

This left Jacob alone with Yousra, so she climbed over the seat and sat up front. He looked at her sitting there in her miniskirt with her legs crossed and a naughty smile on her face. He wasn't interested in playing his secret game of guessing what color panties girls were wearing, because he knew he had more important things to do. His eyes wandered up from her skirt and he thought, *Every blouse she owns must be a size too tight.* Then she climbed onto Jacob's lap and attacked him with a long kiss.

Yousra said, "Hello fiancé I missed you. Did you have fun last night?"

Yousra's crotch was burning into Jacob's. He didn't want her to know he'd been a virgin up until last night because he was embarrassed. He told her, "Yes, it was great. What about you?"

She smiled and said, "Yes, of course, my handsome fiancé."

Jacob knew he had to tell Yousra right now so he said, "Look, I need to talk to you about something."

She kissed him leaving her lipstick on his cheek. "I want to talk to you about something too."

"Well, let me go first."

"Why can't I go first?"

"Okay, you go first, but I have something serious I want to talk to you about."

"I have something I want to talk to you about. I really want to work at Exotic Beauties. Will you get a job for me?"

Jacob paused as he thought about what he was going to say. He was still trying to form the words in his head when Yousra got out of his car and ran towards the Exotic Beauties entrance. He jumped out and chased after her but he was too late. Yousra had already gone inside.

When he entered Exotic Beauties, Brett was there to greet them. "Well hello Jacob and who is this you have with you?" Brett started acting silly the way men do when they see a really pretty girl.

Jacob was all business. He wasn't sure what to say, so he said, "This is Yousra, from Turkey. She recently applied for work at Gulf Coast Jobs."

"Hello Brad," Yousra said, and no one tried to correct her.

"Why hello Yousra!" Brett said as he began undressing her with his eyes. "So you wanna be an exotic dancer, huh?"

She gave him a devious smile and said, "Yes Brad."

Brett started licking his lips as he stared at Yousra's breasts. "Well, Camille's around here somewhere helping Karina get ready."

Yousra's eyes were jumping around everywhere, super excited. She looked as if she couldn't wait to get up on the pole and dance around for everyone. She kept trying to hold Jacob's hand as they walked around, so he kept giving her irritated looks.

When Camille walked past with Karina, Brett said. "Hey Camille, this is Yousra. Why don't you take her with you so you can train her and Karina at the same time." Jacob knew Karina was not going to be happy with this but there was nothing he could do.

Now that Jacob was alone with Brett he figured he'd at least ask. "So what do you think?" Maybe letting Yousra work here wouldn't be such a bad thing. She'd have a job and she didn't seem to be shy about performing.

When Yousra was out of sight, Brett's demeanor turned arrogant again. "What do I think about what?"

"What do you think about Yousra?"

"I think she looks good, but I think your girlfriend, Karina, looks better."

"Okay, but don't you think Yousra is that sexy exotic lady that you said I need to bring you to finalize our deal?" Brett gave him a puzzled look so Jacob explained. "You know, you said if I brought you one more super exotic lady, you'd wipe the slate clean with all this Ana business and you and I could just do business normally. Yousra is a beautiful young lady from Turkey. I bet you've never had a Turkish dancer in your club before. She'll be a big hit and she does a fabulous belly dance routine where she takes off her clothes and I just know all your customers are gonna love it."

Seeing Jacob desperately trying to make the Yousra sales pitch, Brett wasn't going to give him the satisfaction. He looked at Yousra, who was across the room, talking with Camille and Karina and asked, "Why does Yousra look all excited and Karina looks like her dog just died?"

Jacob was angry. He shook his head. "I don't know Brett, maybe

Karina is just a little nervous since it's her first day."

Brett scratched his hairy belly that was hanging out of his shirt then paused to stare at him and said, "You know what Jacob, I could say your obligation to Ana is finished or your obligation is still in effect, but the real person you need to satisfy is Ana, not me."

Jacob's face tensed. He shook his head again. This was not the answer he was looking for and he was getting angrier and tired of Brett's condescending attitude towards him. He looked back at Brett and said, "Well, I'd like to think you'd go to bat for me with Ana and at least try to help make things right between us."

Brett put his hand on Jacob's shoulder as if he was comforting an old friend and said, "I tell you what, Jacob, why don't you come out to Exotic Beauties tomorrow night and you and I can have a chat with Ana to see if we can smooth things over between the both of y'all."

Jacob was repulsed from Brett's touch, so he pulled away. This wasn't what he wanted but he figured it was a step in the right direction. He was tired of having to put up with Brett's bullying, especially since he felt like he had really helped Camille and him get their business back on track.

He was about to tell Brett that he'd see him tomorrow night and make a quick exit, when the club DJ made an announcement over the loudspeaker. "All dancers, come on out to Runway one."

As Brett rudely walked away without saying goodbye, Jacob noticed the girls were going to start practicing their dance routines. Then over twenty breathtaking girls walked out of the changing room and onto the stage. Jacob realized that almost all these girls were from Gulf Coast Jobs. He was sure that most of Brett and Camille's dancers and waitresses had been recruited by Gabriela and him. Ana was still here of course and there were one or two other veterans still around, but Gulf Coast Jobs was the reason Exotic Beauties was doing so well. Brett and Camille owed Jacob and Gabriela everything because the adult entertainment business in Gulf Coast City was very competitive and they had worked hard to give them the best-looking girls in town.

Jacob was enjoying watching the girls twirling around the poles practicing their acts when he felt Brett's fat hand smack down on his shoulder. "Didn't you say you have somewhere you need to be?"

Jacob jumped up startled. He replied, "I was just leaving."

He went home that night to an empty townhouse. Yousra and Karina would be working to the early hours of the morning so he wouldn't be able to see either one of them. He poured himself a Jack Daniels and Coke and sat alone wondering when he'd see Mustapha again.

CHAPTER 18
ATLANTIC CITY, NEW JERSEY

"Hit me."
—Mustapha

Seventeen hours away from Gulf Coast City, Florida is Atlantic City, New Jersey. Mustapha was here gambling his ass off without any concern for his business back in Gulf Coast City.

"Hit me," Mustapha said to the dealer. He'd already lost a ton of money and he'd lost Ada too. As it turned out, Jacob's suspicions about Mustapha and Olga having an affair, were true. Mustapha started having sex with Olga about a week before Jacob met the three Belarus girls. This is why he walked into their motel so confidently without ever knocking on the door. He invited her to come with him and his family on their trip so he could continue having sex with her. He had to give Ada an excuse so he said, "Since you're pregnant, Olga will be our nanny to take care of our children."

Ada caught them having sex the same night Mustapha lost $50,000 in the casino. This was all the money they had. She took the kids and Mustapha's SUV and left him stranded with Olga. This is when Mustapha started bouncing checks on the Gulf Coast Jobs account. Mustapha did so much gambling in Atlantic City that he continued to lose money he didn't even have. He kept trying to get his money back but he needed money to do it. So he wrote checks on the Gulf Coast Jobs account and continued to write checks until all that money was gone as well. This didn't stop Mustapha. Since the funds were now depleted, he just wrote checks that bounced. The Gulf Coast City police put out a warrant for his arrest which pretty much assured he would never come back to Florida. This left Gabriela and Jacob alone to run the business. At the time, they were oblivious to everything Mustapha was doing. They continued their usual routines and when the checks, from Gulf Coast Job's customers came in the mail, Jacob deposited them into the bank. And when payday came around each week, Gabriela processed the checks for their forty or so employees. They didn't have access to the bank statements, and had no idea what the balance was. They didn't know that very soon Gulf Coast Jobs would be out of money and their employees would not get paid.

"Don't you think you've done enough gambling for one night, sir?" The casino dealer took pity on him.

"No I don't," replied Mustapha. He sat at the blackjack table just as he'd done every night since they'd arrived.

"Well, I think you've had enough and I'm going to kindly ask that you cut your losses and head out for the night."

Mustapha knew he was completely broke and couldn't even pay for another night in a motel. He no longer had his SUV, and he couldn't afford to feed Olga and himself. But Mustapha was a smooth talker and Olga was totally smitten with him. It didn't take long for him to convince her to start working at one of the Atlantic City gentlemen's clubs. This gave Mustapha a steady stream of cash to fund his gambling habit.

Olga worked all night doing couch dances and Lord knows what, while Mustapha gambled away her previous night's earnings. This continued night after night until finally, Olga had had enough. She came home from stripping one night absolutely exhausted just to find Mustapha drunk on the bed of their shitty motel.

"Why don't you help me?" Olga asked as a tear ran down her face. She stood there helpless, still wearing her naughty schoolgirl outfit, the uniform of her job.

"Help you with what?" Mustapha slurred his response under his whiskey breath. He was sprawled out on the bed too intoxicated to make an effort to get up.

"Help me with..." she paused for a second to think of the English word, "with everything! We are supposed to be the couple!"

"I don't know what you're so mad at me about..."

"All you will do is gamble, gamble, gamble!" Olga screamed. This was not the life she'd imagined for her and Mustapha. She was in love with him and didn't feel any remorse for Ada and the four children who'd just lost a husband and a dad.

If Mustapha wasn't already a psychopath when he left Gulf Coast City, he certainly was one now. He held out his hand and asked, "How much money did you make tonight?" He had no concern for Olga's or anyone else's well-being except himself. And he was only nice to people when he thought he could get something from them. Olga had not figured this out yet, but was getting very close to her breaking point.

"Is that all you want me for... to make money as your whore so you can go gamble?" Olga was hysterical.

Mustapha was drunk and didn't care. "I don't know what you're so mad about. Gulf Coast Jobs is an unlimited source of money and we can tap into it anytime we want."

"Then why the hell we don't go back to fucking Florida?" Olga screamed.

"I told you we can't go just yet because things are a little shaky down there with my business operations."

"You mean things are little shaky with Florida police!"

Olga hit a nerve with Mustapha and he snapped. His gambling and his temper were two things that he could not control. He stood up and swung at Olga with all 275 pounds of his weight. His fist connected with her face and she dropped to the floor like a sack of potatoes.

When Olga woke up the next morning with a broken jaw, Mustapha was gone. The motel room didn't have a trace of his existence. He'd cleaned up all the evidence, packed up and gotten the hell out of there. Olga's jaw was really sore. She knew she was in bad shape, so she stumbled out the motel and walked down the street looking for a hospital. She didn't know how to use the pay phones in the USA and she didn't have a car. The only possession she had was $225 from stripping last night. But when she looked for it in her purse it was gone. "That motherfucker Mustapha!" Olga yelled out in the middle of the busy street. She knew the last thing he did before abandoning her in the motel room was steal the hard-earned money from her purse.

CHAPTER 19
GULF COAST JOBS

"Everybody says they have bounced checks."
—Gabriela

Today was probably the hottest and stickiest morning Jacob had experienced since moving to Florida. He instantly started dripping with sweat as soon as he got out of his air-conditioned car in the parking lot of Gulf Coast Jobs. He couldn't wait to get inside and splash some cold water onto his face. He looked around and noticed maybe ten foreign students hanging around outside the building. One was Sergei, Karina's x-boyfriend, and another was Karina's friend Lilianna. He recognized the other students as being employed by Gulf Coast Jobs. The young men were standing straight with their fists clenched and faces tight. All the young ladies had an I'm-not-gonna-take-any-shit look on their faces. Jacob sensed they were angry. Yesterday was payday for them, so he assumed maybe there was some minor issue like there always was. Maybe someone was short a couple of hours on their paycheck or maybe someone wanted to know why so much tax had been deducted. He casually walked towards the students. When they saw him, he asked, "What's going on guys?"

They were not pleased. Sergei and the other students gave Jacob a hard stare and Lilianna spoke. "None of us got our money this week and we are all upset… very upset."

This didn't make sense to him so he asked, "What do you mean? I saw you guys get your checks yesterday."

Lilianna responded with her Belarus accent while the other students closed in on Jacob. "Yes, we get check but then we go to bank and they don't give us money. I ask lady at bank why she does not give me money and she says Gulf Coast Jobs has insufficient funds. We don't know what that means so all students came here."

This got Jacob's heart pumping, because he knew exactly what insufficient funds meant. He was not sure what was going on, but he knew he had to keep the students calm while he sorted things out, so he said, "Don't worry guys, this happens all the time with the bank. I'll call Mustapha and get this straightened out."

Sergei moved in closer, looked down at him and said with his deep Estonian accent, "You better straighten out or there will be problems for you." Jacob could tell Sergei was serious and when he looked around at the other students, they were clenching their fists and scowling at him too. Sergei was full of muscles and a lot larger than Jacob. In fact, his nickname at the Sea Biscuit Inn, where he worked, was *"Big Russian,"* even though Sergei was Estonian.

Jacob could feel his legs start to weaken. He didn't want to appear afraid so he casually said, "Okay Sergei, okay guys, let me go inside and see what's going on." He quickly walked away and disappeared inside the building. He could sense the students were all watching him as he walked through the door of Gulf Coast Jobs. Sergei said something in Russian which he was sure translated into, *If I don't get my money I will kick the shit out of that son of a bitch Jacob Carmichael.*

The situation was even worse inside. Jacob counted twelve Hispanic laborers, who worked for Gulf Coast Jobs, and they were all yelling at Gabriela. He didn't need to speak Spanish to know what they were saying.

Gabriela looked up from her desk and was relieved to see him. He'd never seen her so frazzled. The portable TV she usually used to sneak peeks of her favorite Puerto Rican soap operas was all tucked up in her desk drawer. Usually Gabriela could handle anything the employees threw at her, but today she was outnumbered by the hostile crowd.

"Jacob, I'm so glad you're here," Gabriela cried out. "Everybody here says they have bounced checks. I don't think Mustapha has any money in his account."

Now Jacob was pretty sure that on payday all the Hispanic workers had better English speaking skills than on the other days of the week. And he knew if they found out there was no money in the Gulf Coast Jobs account they wouldn't be amused. Their reaction could be anything from everyone quitting their jobs, to a full-scale riot with Jacob being their intended target. He knew he had to think fast and he knew he had to make sure Gabriela didn't keep saying *Mustapha didn't put any money in the account.*

So he asked Gabriela if they could speak privately in the back office. She put her hands up to indicate to the workers that that they didn't have to worry now that Jacob was here. Then she and Jacob slipped off to his office.

When they were alone she said she'd told everyone, in Spanish of course, that he was going to get them their money. This made Jacob's pulse race even faster. He said, "Gabriela where the heck am I gonna get the money to pay these people?"

Now Gabriela's voice was shaking and her eyes were twitching. She said, "I don't know Jacob, but if you don't pay these Latinos, they gonna hurt you. They say they know where you live and they're gonna come to your place."

"Damn it," he yelled. He knew it was super easy to break into his townhouse and the last thing he wanted was a repeat of when Winston and the other guy broke in. "What am I supposed to do Gabriela?" he asked as a new layer of sweat started to bead up on his forehead. Back in the days when he was interning at his church in Tinsley, South Carolina he wouldn't have to ask this question. He'd find a way to get everyone the money or he'd give it to them himself. But now things were different. Jacob was a resident of Gulf Coast City and every day he was becoming more and more like them.

"Well Jacob, I know you get a lot of money from Brett because I've seen your checks. Maybe you should pay these guys with that." Gabriela was right. He was making a lot of money from sending girls to Exotic Beauties but he wasn't sure if this would be enough.

When they walked back into the waiting room, the Hispanic workers kept cutting mean looks at Jacob and outside the students didn't look like they had plans to leave any time soon. He was sweating and shaking. He gave up trying to act as if he wasn't scared because this wasn't fooling anyone anymore. But these guys didn't care and they weren't going to back down. They'd worked hard all week in the hot sweaty laundry rooms washing bed sheets and towels. Or they'd baked outside in the hot sun raking the golf course sand traps or picking up heavy palm branches at some dirty landscaping job. Needless to say, they were not going to start feeling sorry for the operations manager and back off on the pressure they were putting on him.

He made one last attempt to quiet down the angry mob by saying, "Gabriela please tell these guys that I am not the owner of Gulf Coast Jobs, Mustapha is. I'm just an employee like they are and I didn't receive my paycheck either, so I can't pay them."

Jacob listened as Gabriela spoke to them in Spanish then they replied back in Spanish. Just like everything else they'd said today, Jacob didn't have to speak their language to know they were not happy. The fierce looks they were giving him were enough to send shivers down his spine.

He had only asked Gabriela to interpret two sentences but she was talking to them forever. She said something to them then they yelled something to her. Then she said something back to them, then they yelled even louder at her.

This went on and on until Jacob interrupted and said, "What the heck are they saying?"

Gabriela looked up at him and said, "They say they don't care if you are the owner or not. You are the manager and you are responsible for your employees. And if Mustapha is not here then you have to pay them."

"With what?" Jacob pleaded. "I don't have that much money."

"They say you get a lot of money because you are the manager here. You should pay them with that. A lot of the men say they'll put you in the hospital for disrespecting them. They say the Latin people come over here and work hard and make a lot of money for you, Jacob. They say that they work very hard and you get rich from doing nothing. They are saying they will hurt you unless they get their money." Gabriela looked at Jacob to see if she was convincing him. "These people are loco and they blame everything on you."

Jacob bit his bottom lip so he wouldn't start yelling at Gabriela. He still wasn't sure whose side she was on. He decided he'd try to put some blame on her and see if he could get her to help him the way she seemed to be helping the employees. He said, "Gabriela, your job here is more than just being an interpreter. I need you to explain to them this is Mustapha's problem, not mine. How much money I make and how hard I work is irrelevant." As Jacob explained, Gabriela didn't seem overly motivated to help. She kind of looked at him and showed just enough interest to keep him from getting more irritated with her.

He continued, "I know these people are upset and I feel bad for them, but it is not my responsibility to pay them. Even if I wanted to, I don't have that much money in the bank."

Gabriela told Jacob what he wanted to hear. "I have been trying to tell them this all day but they don't want to listen to me. When I tell them this is not your business they say they don't care because you are rich and you are white so you need to pay them." Whether what she said was true or not, Jacob would never know because she spoke to the employees in Spanish.

Just when he thought things couldn't get any worse, Sergei, Lilianna and the other students came into the already overcrowded waiting room. Now the place was absolutely crammed packed with angry people and they were all directing their rage towards Jacob. Sergei could tell the Hispanic workers were just as upset with Jacob as the students. He decided he'd get a little physical with him to show the Hispanics that the students wanted their money too. He walked towards Jacob and grabbed a hold of his shirt. And even though Jacob stood 6 feet, Sergei was looking down at him as he pulled him around the room. First, he pulled Jacob towards him, then he pushed him up against the wall. He looked straight into his eyes and with everyone watching and supporting him said, "Why are you still here talking? You need to go to bank and get money." Everyone was cheering for Sergei so he looked down at Jacob and yelled, "You go now!"

Jacob wanted to argue his case but everyone could see he was shaking and embarrassed because he'd been made a fool of. He said to everyone, "Why don't y'all come back at 5 pm and I'll have your money."

He figured this would buy him enough time to get in touch with Mustapha and hope and pray that he'd put some money in his account. If that didn't work, then Jacob would go to the bank by himself and try to work something out. If those two options failed, then he'd have to pack his bags and get the hell out of Gulf Coast City. Gabriela got rid of everyone and Jacob started dialing Mustapha immediately.

He called Mustapha all morning but all he got was *"The voice mailbox you are calling is full and cannot accept messages at this time"*. This sounded like Mustapha hadn't answered his phone in a long time and was not a good sign. Who knew where Mustapha was and if he'd ever see him again? He called Mustapha every ten minutes all the way up until 12 pm.

With no sign of Mustapha, Jacob told Gabriela, "I need to get out of the office to clear my head." He needed to decide what he was going to do. "I'll be back around three."

Gabriela laughed when she found out that Yousra was working at Exotic Beauties as well. "How did you get your fiancée to work at Exotic Beauties? Is she a stripper?"

Jacob was a little embarrassed, but answered, "She said she wants to try it and says she thinks she might like it because she likes belly dancing." That was enough to keep Gabriela from asking more questions which gave him time to get out of the office.

CHAPTER 20
GULF COAST CITY JAIL

"... I brought someone to keep you company."
—Corporal Hunter

Jacob got in his car and started driving so he could clear his head. As he drove up and down the coast on the Gulf of Mexico, he was thinking how much his life had changed over the past several months. The summer season was coming to an end and this had been the most exciting time of his life. This was a far cry from the quiet life he'd lead as a student at Bob Jones University. He thought about X-man, the taxi driver, and thought he should call him so he could say that everything he'd told him about Gulf Coast City and Gulf Coast Jobs was true. Jacob now realized what X-man meant when he said, *"If the tourists knew what really happened in Gulf Coast City they'd never come back"*.

He thought about Mustapha and for the first time since he'd left Gulf Coast City, wished he would come back. With Mustapha out of the way, Jacob was able to run Gulf Coast Jobs the way he needed to. Looking back now it seemed odd that Mustapha had never bothered to call to check on his business. But all summer, Jacob was so focused on keeping Brett happy that he never took the time to try and get in touch with his boss. Maybe

Gabriela, had spoken with him, he didn't know.

He spent the next three hours driving around the beach trying to decide his next move.

***

When Jacob pulled back into the parking lot of Gulf Coast Jobs he still had not made a decision. If he paid the employees, with his money, he was more than likely going to lose everything he had. If he didn't pay the employees, he didn't even want to think about the repercussions. It was 3 pm, two hours before all the disgruntled workers would be coming back to collect their paychecks, and this time they would not be so patient if their checks bounced. *"A lot of the men say they'll put you in the hospital for disrespecting them. They say the Latin people come over here and work hard and make a lot of money for you, Jacob. They say that they work very hard and you get rich from doing nothing. They are saying they will hurt you unless they get their money. These people are loco and they blame everything on you."*

When he walked through the office door, he saw Gabriela all alone with her head down.

"Hey Gabriela, were you able to get in touch with Mustapha?" He had to at least ask.

Gabriela shook her head and continued to look down at the floor. She was not laughing at all today. "No, Jacob. I tried calling him all day and all I got was the mailbox is full. It looks to me like people have been calling him for a while and he's not answering."

"Well that's just great," he snapped at Gabriela.

Gabriela didn't seem to mind. "What are you going to do?"

"Well, I guess I'm gonna have to pay them with my money and try to get the bank to overdraft the rest."

Gabriela smiled. Jacob could tell she was relieved to hear this. "That's good. I'm glad you're gonna get them paid. I was worried they'd hurt you if you didn't."

"Well let's just hope Mustapha gets back here soon to reimburse me."

"I hope so too."

He asked Gabriela what the payroll was this week for forty employees and after looking up the figures she told him it was a little over twelve-thousand dollars. He had less than half of this in his savings account. If he was to cover payroll, Jacob was sure that he'd have to put every penny of this into the Gulf Coast Jobs account. Then he'd have to try to negotiate some sort of overdraft until he could contact Mustapha. This would be almost impossible to pull off.

Nevertheless, he felt like he had to try. And, he didn't feel as if he had much of a choice if he was going to get out of all this unharmed. Jacob was scared of Winston, but forty angry employees as well as additional boyfriends and husbands was even worse. He told Gabriela, "I'm heading to the bank to try to straighten things out."

* * *

When Jacob got to the bank the problems started immediately. The elderly female bank teller wasn't very helpful because Jacob's name was not on the account. He asked her, "Can you give me the balance on this account please?"

Her reply was, "I'm sorry sir, I cannot give out that information because your name's not on the account."

His reply was, "Ma'am I'm not trying to take money out, I just wanna see how much is in there so I know how much I have to put in. I need to cover a twelve-thousand-dollar payroll so can you at least let me know how much I need to put in to cover that?"

Her snappy reply again was, "I'm sorry sir, but I can't give out that information because your name's not on the account."

Jacob's fuse was short today, and he was already starting to get annoyed with the bank teller. He argued back. "Ma'am, you don't seem to understand. I have forty employees who need to get their paychecks; if I don't pay them they're not gonna be too happy with me." As he tried to explain his situation to the bank teller he was thinking how his employees thought his life was so easy and going to the bank to get their money would be so easy too. His pulse was racing and he was sure his blood pressure was climbing off the charts.

The bank teller's unemotional and slightly condescending reply to Jacob was, "I'm sorry sir, I can't give out this information. Why don't you ask the owner of Gulf Coast Jobs to come in here and I'd be happy to speak to him."

After hearing this, he really lost his temper and barked back, "Look lady, if I knew where the owner was I wouldn't be here myself would I?"

The bank teller shook her head and said, "I'm sorry sir but there is nothing I can do here to help you. Now if you will please move along because other customers are waiting."

Jacob hit his breaking point and all the day's events came boiling to the top. He was no longer in control of his actions. His hands were shaking. Not wanting to let her win this argument, he wanted to yell something back. But he knew the bank teller was just following protocol so no matter what he said she was going to win. This caused him to snap. He picked up the glass candy dish from the counter and threw it against the wall of the bank. It made a loud smashing sound, and everyone in the bank got quiet.

This was all it took for the bank teller to press the silent alarm. Immediately, the bank manager and the police were notified and Jacob was in a hole he'd have a hard time getting out of. The bank manager, an older man with grey hair in a pinstripe business suit, calmly made his way towards Jacob. He pressed his hands together then said, "Sir, is everything okay over here?" The manager looked at the bank teller and said, "I'll take it from here, Betty."

Jacob tried to explain the situation to the bank manager but his response was the same as the bank teller's response. "I'm sorry sir, we can't give that information unless your name is on the account. Just as you wouldn't like anyone knowing how much money is in your account, I'm sure your boss wouldn't want us to give out information about his account."

The bank teller looked at him and smiled like a twelve-year-old whose parents had just taken her side. "Yeah," Jacob said, "but I don't like the bank teller's attitude."

The bank teller continued her smug look behind the bank manager's back so Jacob said, "This lady is the worst excuse for a bank employee I have ever seen."

After hearing this, the bank manager completely changed his attitude. "Okay sir, I think it's time you left." As he was trying to get Jacob to leave, the police walked inside. It was Officer Paula and Corporal Hunter.

Corporal Hunter came up to Jacob first. His short sleeves were rolled up and his biceps were bulging. He said, "Well how ya doing Mr. Carmichael?" He seemed to be taking pleasure in this.

Officer Paula, as always, was a lot more sympathetic. "What's going on here Jacob?" She stayed with him while Corporal Hunter went over to talk to the bank manager and bank teller.

"Paula, all I was trying to do is find out how much money I need to put into the payroll account so I can get all my employees paid."

"Where are you getting the money from to pay your employees?" Officer Paula asked as she took notes.

"Mustapha's business account is low so I was trying to deposit my own money into his account so the employees at Gulf Coast Jobs can get their weekly paychecks."

Paula looked up from her notepad. "Have you spoken to Mustapha about this?"

"No, I can't get ahold of him and my employees are all making threats to me if they don't get paid." Jacob said this with some emphasis hoping Officer Paula would take pity on him.

Paula gave him a sympathetic look but she had to do her job. "Do you know the whereabouts of Mustapha?"

"I'm guessing he's either in Atlantic City or Columbus, Ohio."

"Why do you think he's there?"

"That's where he told me he was going."

Officer Paula stopped writing notes and looked up again. She put her pen back into the top pocket of her shirt. "Jacob, there's a warrant out for Mustapha's arrest. He's been cashing checks on his Gulf Coast Jobs account and they've been bouncing all over Atlantic City. I seriously doubt you'll see him again anytime soon. But if you do please call me."

Jacob began thinking, *I should get some kind of reward from the police because I have to call if I see Winston and now I have to call if I see Mustapha.* Of course, he just nodded his head and didn't say anything except, "Okay, I will."

"Jacob, if you'll excuse me for a minute, I need to speak with Corporal Hunter to see what we need to do next. Just sit tight for a second please." He sat down while all the bank customers and employees looked at him as if he'd just tried to rob the place.

Officer Paula went over to speak with Corporal Hunter, the bank manager, and the bank teller, then came back over and said, "Jacob, I'm sorry but I'm gonna have to place you under arrest."

Then Corporal Hunter walked over flexing his muscles. Jacob could tell he was hoping he'd try to resist so he could get into a fight. Jacob leaned against the wall as Officer Paula frisked him. Then she put the handcuffs on and the two police officers took him to jail.

He had to go through the long booking and fingerprinting process. By the time Corporal Hunter led him to his cell, he was sure it was way past the 5 o'clock meeting time that he'd set with the employees to get their checks.

As he sat alone in a claustrophobic jail cell with two beds and a small toilet, Jacob thought about what had gone on at Gulf Coast Jobs with all the angry employees. He breathed in the smell of urine and wondered if they'd harmed Gabriela. Had they burned down the place? He was sure that they had no idea he'd been arrested while trying to put his own money into the payroll account. They were never going to believe he tried to help them. He was sure some or all of the employees were coming after him. Ironically, he felt as if the safest place to be right now was probably exactly where he was.

Corporal Hunter walked towards Jacob's cell with another prisoner. As he heard them getting closer, Jacob hoped like hell that the prisoner was not going to be coming in with him but no such luck.

"Jacob, I brought someone to keep ya company," Corporal Hunter announced with a grin on his face. "I wouldn't want ya to get lonely in here."

Jacob wasn't amused and was hoping he wasn't some big burly guy coming inside to rape him. Then the prisoner walked in as Jacob was looking down at the floor, too terrified to make eye contact. This was the first time he'd ever been arrested and he was terrified of everything.

Then Jacob heard, "Is that the kid from South Carolina?" It was X-man, the taxi driver, Jacob's mobile psychologist. It seemed he hadn't seen him in such a long time. His hair was quite a bit longer and he looked like he probably hadn't brushed it since they'd first met back in April.

Jacob was happy to see him. "Yep, it's me," he said with a little bit of a smile.

X-man came over and gave Jacob a fist bump and Corporal Hunter shook his head and said, "I'll let you two love birds be alone."

When Jacob was sure Corporal Hunter was out of earshot, he asked, "What are you doing here?"

X-man seemed as happy to see Jacob as he was to see him. "Cops slapped me with another DUI."

"Oh no!" Jacob said. "Were you in your taxi?"

"Of course," X-man responded. "I eat, sleep and drink in my taxi. Sometimes I even do some work in there too." They both laughed. "What about you? What brings you to the Gulf Coast City Hilton?"

"I broke a candy dish at the bank."

"You did what?" X-man started laughing. "That's against the law?"

"Evidently so, X-man. Why else would I be in here right? It's not for the view or the smell, I can tell ya that." They both laughed again.

X-man asked. "So how's it been going at ole Gulf Coast Jobs?"

"I've been working there for over four months now." Jacob sat up straight on his jail cot.

"Wow, that long huh? What did you say your job was again?"

"I'm the operations manager," Jacob said with pride.

"Now that's impressive!" X-man smiled, and Jacob recalled he was missing his two front teeth. X-man fumbled around in his pockets for his chewing tobacco and thought for a moment before asking. "What does an operations manager actually do anyway?" Then X-man seemed to remember that his tobacco had been confiscated during the booking process.

Jacob remembered that X-man was not the smartest guy in Gulf Coast City but he looked up to him regardless. "An operations manager manages the operations," he answered.

X-man chuckled and said, "Well that makes sense. How about all those Russian stripper girls-- have you met them yet?"

Jacob was sure X-man wasn't expecting quite as impressive an answer as he was about to give him. "I've been recruiting and managing Russian strippers all summer. I actually have a contract with Exotic Beauties."

X-man was really impressed now. "Wow, that's super cool dude! How many of those gals are ya bangin?" X-man looked at Jacob with a sly grin.

"Funny you should ask because I'm dating one and living with the other," Jacob bragged.

"Get the fuck out of here!" X-man yelled.

"That's right, and you know, everything you told me on the ride to the Shady Tree motel on my first night in Gulf Coast City has actually turned out to be true."

"I told you this is a fucked-up place man. Do I know this town or what?" Before he could answer X-man asked, "I still don't get why you're in here. Now I know you said you broke a candy dish but something tells me there's much more to this story."

Jacob told X-man everything that had happened to him over the summer. He told him how he'd hit Ana, and he told him how Mustapha had abandoned Gulf Coast Jobs and now the employees had not received their paychecks. He told him that he'd hoped Gabriela would've talked to the employees and made them realize he was not responsible for getting them paid.

When Jacob started talking about Gabriela, X-man stopped him and said, "Hold on a second. Are you talking about that Puerto Rican gal? She's always smilin and she's kinda fat?"

"That's her."

"Yeah, I've heard some things about her."

"Really?" Jacob sat up and focused his eyes on X-man.

"Yeah, I heard that she ain't so innocent as everyone thinks."

"What do you mean by that?"

"Well I've heard some things you know." When X-man saw Jacob looking at him in anticipation, he knew he had him hooked. "I'm sure you know all about that guy, I think he's a Mexican, that sells those fake green cards to all the other Mexicans around here. Well I heard that Gabriela gets a piece of that money."

"Really?" Jacob was shocked.

"Yeah, Gabriela gets money every time she refers an illegal to this guy. You know, like a Mexican that's tryin' to get his papers so he can apply for Gulf Coast Jobs. You know, that kinda Mexican."

This made a heck of a lot of sense to Jacob because from what he'd seen, every Mexican and Central American worker Gulf Coast Jobs hired had the paperwork they needed. Everyone knew the green cards and social security cards were fake, but they were enough to keep Mustapha and Ada out of trouble with the government. He asked, "What else do you know about Gabriela?"

"The thing I heard about Gabriela is that she looks all sweet and innocent and a little stupid, but she's got plenty of street smarts. She has that job at Gulf Coast Jobs just like you, and y'all think well, how does she survive on that little paycheck? I believe she has a kid and maybe even a sister or someone like that living with her. But what you guys don't realize is Gabriela is the slider queen."

Jacob was having a hard time keeping up so he asked, "What in the heck are you talking about?"

"Don't you know what a slider is, man?" Before he could answer, X-man continued, "A slider is a kickback. I think you bigshot operations manager college types would call it quid pro quo or something like that. Gabriela sets up sliders all over the place. Let's say you're a Mexican, okay, and you need a job. You go up to Gabriela and you say, '*Me need workie Gabriela*'." X-man was doing a terrible impression of a Mexican accent. "Then Gabriela says, '*Well, me need money*'. You see how that works now?" As usual X-man didn't wait for him to answer. "The Mexican needs a job so he pays Gabriela a little slider and next thing you know the Mexican has a job."

Jacob didn't really have a huge problem with what Gabriela was doing, although he did recall some Hispanics applying for work and suddenly leaving the office in anger. They'd had a lengthy and loud discussion, in Spanish of course, with Gabriela, then they bolted out the door in a huff. But then he started to think, what about the bounced checks? What was Gabriela's role in all that? As Jacob replayed the events of the day he realized that with Gabriela speaking Spanish to the Hispanic employees she could have said, *"I will tell Jacob you are going to hurt him really bad, so he will be so scared that he will pay you out of his pocket."* He pictured all the Hispanic workers snickering as Gabriela laid out the plan. *"Mustapha will never pay you, so we should pressure Jacob. You guys just stand there and look really mean and angry and I'll take care of the rest. Now if Jacob pays you guys, you all need to give me my slider for helping you out."*

"X-man, I know exactly what went down today, and I know that Gabriela found a way to make money from it. I bet no one harmed her at all when I wasn't there, but I bet they all sat around putting together another plan to scare me into paying them. Gabriela probably told them since Mustapha isn't here we should threaten Jacob."

"Man, I bet you are 100% right on this one, dude."

Jacob chuckled at X-man then he sat on his cot gazing at the wall. His mind wandered, and he thought how embarrassed he'd be if he was back in Tinsley right now. *All the members of the church, his sister, and Pastor Mike, would know that he was in jail. After Sheriff Crepps would arrest him for breaking a glass dish at Tinsley State Bank, he'd have to lock him up. Then Mary Lois would get on the phone and call Miss Annie and Miss Annie would tell all her customers. In less than an hour's time, the entire town would know what he'd done.* Jacob blew out a sigh of relief. He was glad that he was in Gulf Coast City.

Even though the two of them were sitting in jail, Jacob felt really comfortable talking to X-man. So comfortable, in fact, that he decided to ask about Carl and Sue Ellen Dooley. "X-man, I gotta ask you a question."

"Yeah, what else you need to know?" X-man leaned back on his jail cot as if he was the wisest man in Gulf Coast City.

"Do you know a guy called Carl Dooley?"

"Carl Dooley?" X-man stiffened up.

"Yes, Carl and Sue Ellen Dooley."

"Son, everyone knows Carl fuckin Dooley and his wife Sue Ellen. Carl was totally crazy and Sue Ellen is so sweet and nice. He used to beat on her and folks said he'd rape her and all kinds of shit. Now she can't get a job on account of what her old man did." X-man stood up from his cot and started pacing nervously up and down the cell. "Why do you wanna know?"

Corporal Hunter showed up before Jacob could answer. "Well, one of you ladies gets to go home if you're ready to whip out your credit card. I'm willing to bet if Jacob here was gonna drop twelve grand to pay a bunch of dumb Mexicans and stupid Russians, he'd be willing to bail himself outta jail."

"How much is bail?" Jacob asked. Part of him didn't want to get out because he couldn't stop thinking about all the unhappy Gulf Coast Jobs employees that were on the outside waiting for him.

"Now how the fuck should I know? Do I look like a fuckin bail bondsman to you?"

"No, you don't," Jacob answered, embarrassed.

"Do you wanna get out of here or stay with your boyfriend X-man?"

"I'm ready to leave," Jacob said, but wasn't totally sure this was a wise choice.

"Well, then get your dumb ass up because the clerk leaves at ten."

Corporal Hunter took Jacob out of his cell to a room where he got back his wallet, belt and other belongings. Then he escorted him to an office where he had to whip out his credit card to pay bail. The clerk handed him a receipt through the glass window that had a court date on it. He had to appear in front of a judge in eight months to answer to a charge of *disorderly conduct*.

When he walked out of the police station he felt a sense of relief that he was free again, then a sense of fear that any second one of his employees was going to see him and attack. His car was still at the bank and the police only provide a taxi service to the jail, not from the jail. He thought for a second that he should call X-man to get a ride, then he remembered that he'd just said goodbye to him in the jail cell.

Jacob had to walk to the bank to get his car. It wasn't far away, but the whole time he was terrified that one of his many enemies was going to see him walking down the sidewalk. Every time a car drove past, he looked away hoping no one would recognize him. When he finally got to his car he was way too scared to go home because he was sure that the Gulf Coast Jobs employees would be waiting for him.

He remembered Brett had said yesterday that he'd arrange a meeting with Ana to help straighten things out. After all Jacob had been through today, the conversation with Brett yesterday seemed like ages ago. He got in his car and headed towards Exotic Beauties.

But first Jacob decided to drive past Gulf Coast Jobs to see if it was still there. When he pulled onto Third Avenue South, ice entered his veins. He decided he wouldn't get out of his car no matter what. As he got closer to Gulf Coast Jobs, he saw that the building the office was in was still there. No one had burned it down. A sense of relief came over him, but then he saw the glass door had been smashed. Someone must have thrown a brick through the door.

Against his better judgment, Jacob parked his car and got out. As he slowly walked towards the broken glass, he realized that he was shaking. *What if someone is in there waiting to pounce,* he thought, but he still continued to move towards the door, then stepped inside. As his feet walked over the broken glass, he looked around the lobby where Gabriela used to sit. He smiled as he remembered her either watching her Puerto Rican soap operas or helping people find jobs. The lobby was not so cheery now. The temp staff had obviously vandalized the place while Jacob was sitting in the jail cell. If they'd only known he was trying to help them, maybe they wouldn't have done this. It was too late now, and it looked like his days at Gulf Coast Jobs were over.

He walked back to his office which was sure to be vandalized too. He opened his office door and saw that the most damage was here. He was sure that his office was their biggest target just like he was. All his papers and office supplies were scattered everywhere. There was some writing spray painted on the wall written in Spanish. The only words he recognized was "Jacob Carmichael" but he was sure that nothing nice was there about him.

He knew he could never come back to work after this. At least not at Gulf Coast Jobs. This chapter in his life was over. All he could do now was try to move forward. Brett had promised him a meeting with Ana. Even though he didn't think there was much of a point in going now, he got in his car and headed to Exotic Beauties.

CHAPTER 21
EXOTIC BEAUTIES

"Brett and Winston are evil and Camille helps them, so she is evil too."
—*Ana Bautista*

When Jacob walked through the main entrance of Exotic Beauties, strobe lights were flashing and the place was rocking. In addition to Karina and Yousra, all the Gulf Coast Jobs girls were prancing around the club. Jacob looked around and spotted Brett and Camille. They were grinning from ear to ear, no doubt happy with all their new waitresses and dancers. Brett's brother, Jamie, was behind the bar serving drinks as he was being bombarded with customers. The word was spreading around Gulf Coast City that Exotic Beauties was the place to be.

All the stress of the day seemed to seep away as Jacob sipped down a Jack and Coke and looked at the all the erotic girls performing. They were everywhere, it seemed. All three dance runways were packed with girls dancing around the poles. All their practices that Jacob had briefly enjoyed watching was paying off for them. And the customers were loving every minute and pumping the money onto the stage.

Jacob desperately wanted to see Karina. He was really missing her all day. He wanted to see Yousra too so he could see if she and Karina had talked.

Jacob looked around the packed club for Karina and Yousra and saw Winston! He was all dressed up in a velvet red suit as if he were a pimp. Jacob's jaw dropped and he froze. *I need to call the police!* He pulled out his wallet and got Officer Paula's business card. He was so nervous that he dropped the card on the floor a couple of times before he got a firm grasp. He grabbed his cell phone and punched in the numbers, then got ready to run outside where it was quiet. He had to get the cops here quickly to make the arrest. Jacob's heart was pounding in his chest. *What if Winston sees me go outside and follows me? He might beat me up or even kill me before I can make the call.* Jacob snuck out the door, keeping a close eye on Winston.

When he was outside, Jacob ran into Corporal Hunter, who was walking in wearing his night-on-the-town clothes. Wearing a black silk shirt with the sleeves rolled up to show off the biceps, of course, he looked way different from just a few hours earlier back at the police station.

"Oh thank God you're here, Corporal Hunter!" Jacob was so relieved.

"Hey calm down. What's going on?" Corporal Hunter asked while he flexed his muscles then looked around to see if anyone was looking.

"I just saw Winston. He's inside Exotic Beauties right now!"

"Okay, take it easy." Corporal Hunter was so relaxed; Jacob couldn't believe it. He didn't run in there immediately with his gun drawn. He didn't pull out his cell phone and call for backup as Jacob expected. He just shook his head and said in his usual annoyed tone, "Winston is no longer wanted in connection with the Food Chief robbery."

"What?" Jacob asked. He almost said, *But I was there and I saw the whole thing.*

"Just as I said, Jacob. There was some kinda error with the handling of evidence, so Winston can't be charged."

"But, but... what about breaking into my townhouse?"

"But nothing." Corporal Hunter cut Jacob off. "Now, if you'll excuse me I'm off duty and wanna go look at some pussy."

Corporal Hunter went inside and left Jacob out on the sidewalk. *What a nasty guy,* Jacob thought. *How could this happen? How could they mishandle the evidence? Chief Joe White and Officer Paula know it was Winston. Why don't they just arrest him?*

Jacob decided, *You know what, I'm off duty too. I'm gonna go get another drink.* When he got back inside the music was pumping and the club was even more packed. This allowed Jacob to hide from Winston, which helped him relax. At least he wouldn't have to worry about his employees being here. They couldn't afford this place.

The DJ stopped the music and made an announcement over the loudspeaker. "Everyone please make your way over to the Runway one bar and see Jamie. He's got half price drinks for everyone to welcome back my man Winston."

Jacob looked over at Winston while the customers made a dash for the bar. He was standing there with a proud look on his face as if he was the one who owned Exotic Beauties. None of the customers were paying attention to anything else except getting their half price drink. Jacob continued to watch Winston and noticed he was walking around all the tables where the dancers had been sitting before the rush to the bar. Then he observed him take out what looked like a sugar packet and began pouring the contents in all the girls' drinks. *This is not right! What the heck is Winston doing?*

Winston looked up and made eye contact. Jacob's heart froze; he quickly backed up and headed to the other side of Exotic Beauties. He ran into Ana. She was dressed in all black lingerie and had glitter all over her face. Her appearance was dazzling, but her mood seemed depressed. Since everyone else was busy getting their half price drink to honor Winston, the former fugitive and current pimp, Jacob had time to speak with her.

"Hey Ana, how's it going?" he asked, hoping she was not still angry at him.

"I'm fine. How are you?" she replied, but Jacob could tell she wasn't fine. Something was bothering her.

"You don't seem to be fine. Are you upset with me?" It was really dark. With the exception of when the strobe light hit someone's face, they really couldn't be seen. Jacob focused on Ana's face and when the light hit her for a split second he noticed something unusual. The black eye that he'd given her, what seemed like a lifetime ago, had gotten worse. It appeared as though someone had hit Ana again because her cheek was purple, black and puffy. He could tell she was trying to cover it with makeup.

Jacob knew he had to be gentle when he asked, "Ana, it appears that your black eye has gotten worse. Did someone hit you again?"

Her bottom lip began to shake then her eyes filled with tears. Jacob could tell she was keeping something inside. "I can't talk to you here," she whispered as a tear spilled onto her face.

"Can you meet me after you're done?" Jacob asked.

"Okay," Ana replied as she brushed the tear from her cheek. She looked around nervously then said, "I have to go," and quickly disappeared.

Jacob knew he couldn't pursue Ana any further while she was at work, so he focused his attention back to searching for Karina and Yousra. He went to the bar to get another Jack and Coke, then looked all around but the place was so large and so full of customers and dancers that it took him quite a while before he found Karina. She was waitressing near Runway three and Jacob was at the bar near Runway one. She looked amazing, he thought, in her all white lingerie outfit and white gloves. His heart started beating faster when he saw her talking to customers and laughing at the silly things they were probably saying in a poor attempt to flirt. Jacob made his way over to Runway three and sat down at an empty table. Karina saw him and came over.

He knew he wouldn't be able to talk to her for long. He also knew giving her a kiss in front of the customers would get him in trouble with Brett. So Jacob politely said, "Hey, how's it been going tonight?"

Karina smiled and said, "It's been going good… really good, Jacob. I've made a lot of money from tips and the men are very nice to me."

Jacob felt like saying, *They're nice to you because they all want to take you to bed.* But he restrained himself and just gave Karina a smile and said, "That's great to hear. I'm glad you're doing well."

"You look nice Jacob and you smell nice too. Have you been working hard today?"

He wanted to tell Karina that he'd just been released from jail and the temp employees vandalized Gulf Coast Jobs and were all after him. But he knew this was not the time nor the place, especially after he saw Brett glaring at them from the across the room. His arms were folded, and he was giving Jacob a disgusted look, probably wondering why he was interfering with his employee. So Jacob leaned in closer and whispered into Karina's ear, "I had a really tough day today. I'll tell you about it later because Brett is watching us now, so I better leave."

Karina appeared downhearted and said, "How will I get home tonight? Are you going to drive me?"

"I wish I could Karina, but I will probably be home in bed."

"Can I come see you tonight after I get off work?" Karina gave Jacob a tempting look.

Ever since Jacob met Karina that day at Gulf Coast Jobs, he had always dreamed that these words would come out of her mouth. Now she was actually asking him if she could come over to his townhouse, which would probably be around 4 am. There was only one reason why she'd want to come over at this hour and it wouldn't involve talking. Jacob had wanted this to happen all summer and now that it actually was, he had to tell Karina, "No, you can't. I'm sorry, Karina, but Yousra will be there and I think it'll be weird." After Jacob said this he knew he'd probably ruined everything.

Karina's smile instantly dropped and she said, "Okay, well I better get back to work." She turned around and walked away quickly; with all the loud music playing Jacob couldn't say *goodbye or I'm sorry or let me explain.* He just had to let her go and hope that she'd come back to him again.

Knowing he wouldn't be able to talk to Karina anymore tonight, he moved away from Runway three and went back to Runway one. He sat down at a table, hidden in the back, so he could wait for his chance to speak with Ana.

As Jacob sat feeling a nice buzz from his latest Jack and Coke, he looked around the room at all the young Russian and Eastern European girls that were brightening up the place. He could barely see Karina over in the distance, but her long brown hair and athletic body still looked amazing. He focused his attention on the blonde stripper dancing on Runway one. She was struggling to keep her audience engaged. Jacob looked around at several groups of men sitting around him. They were talking and drinking and occasionally looking up at the girl. He had sent so many girls to Brett that he wasn't even sure if she was from Gulf Coast Jobs or not.

The club DJ made an announcement over the music that echoed through the large room. "Welcome to Exotic Beauties, the world's largest gentlemen's club. We have a special treat for you tonight. Every man's dream has come to Exotic Beauties all the way from the Middle East, recently released from her master's bottle. Gentlemen please make some noise for Genie!" The DJ played the *'I Dream of Jeannie'* theme song. The song played for a while, then he switched it to the song by Tone Loc called *'Wild Thing'* and out came Yousra. She was all dressed up in a skimpy genie costume, when they started spraying smoke on the stage it looked as if she had just come out of her bottle. Everyone who had been sitting around jumped up and rushed closer to the stage to see Yousra perform. Then the DJ said, "Give Genie a tip and she will grant you three wishes."

Jacob thought, *She already granted me my wish.* He blushed as he replayed his first real sexual encounter she'd given him. He kept thinking, *If the guys here knew what I did to her the other night, boy would they be envious.* He had to get closer to Yousra. She looked really sexy; knowing he'd been inside her only two nights ago, made her look even better.

He emptied the rest of the Jack and Coke then put the glass down. He got up from the table and totally forgot that every time he was at Exotic Beauties he was actually here in a business capacity. He could never fully act like the actual customers here, who were mostly tourists from out of town. He totally forgot that all the staff and owners of Exotic Beauties knew him and he had to act respectable. He staggered towards Yousra and was totally taken in by her seductive dancing. Her genie outfit was way sexier than the one Barbara Eden wore in the show *'I Dream of Jeannie'* that was filmed in the 60's and 70's. Underneath her pink see-through costume was a satin purple bra and satin purple thong panties. Yousra was putting on a tantalizing act and everyone was totally captivated, Jacob included. She was making eye contact with every customer that gave her money and looked like a real professional exotic dancer. If this week really was her first time performing, you'd never know it.

When Jacob got about two feet away from Yousra, he looked up at her and was about to say, *Hi* when she made eye contact with him and yelled out, "Jako, get out of here! I don't want you watching me. Get away!"

The customers laughed and he was thoroughly embarrassed. He had no choice but to turn around and stumble away as the rowdy men closed in on his spot. He felt humiliated. His brain, numb with whiskey, was thinking he was going to be special up at Yousra's runway because he'd had sex with her the other night and he was even her fiancé. It's a good thing the place was dark because his face was completely red.

Now he felt really out of place. He couldn't go to Runway three because Karina was there and he couldn't go to Runway one because Yousra was there. Fortunately, Exotic Beauties had three runways, so Jacob didn't have to go outside to wait for Ana.

Once again Jacob slithered off and found a quiet table near Runway two. He asked the pretty waitress to bring him a Jack and Coke. She smiled and said with her Russian accent, "Thanks so much for getting me job. I make great money here." Jacob forced a smile and told the waitress he was happy for her.

It was getting close to 3 am. As he sipped on his final Jack and Coke, he decided to see if he could spy on Karina. It wasn't long before he spotted her at a table with four drunk middle aged men dressed as golfers. Gulf Coast City was famous for its golfing vacations and most of the tourists, who come down for a week of golf and nightly partying, were middle aged and married. Jacob felt like these guys wouldn't bother Karina too much because they were professional businessmen with wives and kids at home.

It was the locals that worried him. They were usually single, a little younger, but a lot more desperate to find a girl from a gentlemen's club that they could take home with them. These men wanted to live the same dream as Brett, and would do or say anything to the girls to make it happen.

Jacob's eyes followed Karina's curvy body as she glided around the room going from table to table, always smiling at everyone she served.

There was one guy sitting in Karina's section who was all alone and watching every move she made. His eyes never seemed to leave her cute backside. *Now, this is the sort of guy I need to worry about,* he thought. *This is the Gulf Coast City local who is here on a hunting mission and my girlfriend, or whatever she is, might be his intended prey.*

He got up from his table and moved in closer so he could get a better look. As he got close enough to get a better view, but not so close that Karina would be distracted by him, he realized that he knew who this guy was. It was Hamid the Mustache, his new landlord and big shot business owner who had pulled up in his brand-new BMW at the beginning of the summer that night at Happy Suma's. *This is just great,* Jacob thought, as he remembered Hamid's behavior at Happy Suma's. His mind replayed how Hamid had given Lilianna a $100 tip before she even finished serving them. He remembered how everyone laughed because they knew that married man Hamid was trying to buy sex from her the first night they met.

Jacob focused all his attention on Karina, and felt like he had to protect her from all deceptive men like Hamid. But there really wasn't much he could do without getting himself in worse trouble than he was already in. So when Karina walked up to Hamid's table and asked him what he'd like to drink, he sat helplessly and watched the whole thing. It was killing him, trying to stay calm, but he was doing a pretty good job, at least until he saw Hamid handing Karina some money. He was sure this was a $100-dollar bill. He knew exactly what this meant and he wanted to jump out of his skin when he saw it. Karina smiled at Hamid, but she seemed embarrassed. Jacob knew there wasn't anything he could do now and tried to convince himself Karina would be safe inside the walls of Exotic Beauties. He was definitely going to speak to her first thing tomorrow about exactly what that $100-dollar tip meant.

* * *

Around 3 am, Jacob went outside to the parking lot of Exotic Beauties and got inside his car. He considered driving home for a while but knew his alcohol level was too high to risk it. He sat in his car and waited for Ana to appear. He had to be careful that only she saw him. If Winston, Brett or Camille spotted him, there's no telling what they might think or what they might do. Less than an hour later, Jacob saw Ana walking outside in a great looking pair of *Daisy Duke* shorts and a T-shirt that had Gulf Coast City written on it in some fancy writing.

Jacob jumped out of his car and Ana spotted him. She motioned for him to come over to her red sports car. He walked over and got inside. The car looked like it was about five years old but was still in good shape. Inside the car smelled really great, just like Ana's floral perfume. Jacob was able to get a better look at her bruised face. He could tell she'd probably been crying off and on all night.

Ana drove out of the Exotic Beauties parking lot and found a quiet place to park so they could talk. Jacob started the conversation by saying, "Ana, I just want you to know that I'm really sorry about hitting you. I didn't do it on purpose. In fact, I don't even remember doing this to you--"

She was fighting back tears when she interrupted. "Just stop talking Jacob. I know you didn't hit me. I know you didn't give me the black eye."

"What?" he asked. Now he was confused.

"Just stop talking altogether Jacob, and let me explain."

"So I didn't do it? I don't understand."

"If you shut up for a minute, I will explain but if you repeat what I'm about to tell you, they will take it out on me." Ana took a deep breath and looked suspiciously out her car window. She still had glitter on her face which looked out of place now. "Brett and Camille blackmailed my sister, Lydia, and me a long time ago. Now I don't know what to do, and I don't know how to stop them. Camille keeps telling me if I don't do what they say they will turn me in for prostitution and drugs, and they say I'll be deported and I won't see my baby…" Ana had to stop because her emotions took over.

Jacob felt really bad for her. He put his hand down on the console of her car. He wanted to gently touch her to show he was on her side but he didn't dare. "I'm so sorry. I didn't know any of this."

Still sobbing, Ana said, "Brett makes me deceive people all the time."

"How, I mean why does he make you do this?"

"It's his way of getting control of people so they'll do what he wants. He deceived you so you'd bring him more girls. He always does it the same way. He gets Winston to drug people by putting something in their drink. Then they act crazy, and the next day all they remember is they were out of their mind, but they don't remember what they did. Brett makes up some story and they always believe him."

"How did you get the black eye?"

"Winston punched me in the face."

"No fuckin' way!" Jacob could not believe it. He was relieved that he wasn't the one who hit Ana, but he still felt sorry for her. She'd been through so much. "I'm so sorry for my language, Ana. Who else has Brett done this to?"

"Brett trapped Corporal Hunter last week. He knew the police were about to arrest Winston, so he blackmailed him. He told him that I'd tell the police that he hit me unless he got rid of the evidence from the Food Chief robbery, and your townhouse break-in that Winston and his cousin DeAndre did. Corporal Hunter went down to the police station and ruined the film of Winston pointing the pistola, I mean gun, at the Food Chief cashier."

Jacob could not believe it. *If they could get to Corporal Hunter, they could get to anyone.* "That's why Corporal Hunter didn't arrest Winston tonight. This explains a lot." It was all starting to make sense. "We gotta do something, Ana. Brett can't treat you like this anymore."

Ana looked up at Jacob with her beautiful brown eyes, still soaked with tears, and said, "Jes, I know but how?"

"You gotta tell me everything. The more I know the more I can do something to help. Police Chief Joe White and Officer Paula seem like honest cops. Maybe they can help." Jacob really didn't know what to do, but he definitely wanted to be the one to stop Ana's tears.

"Brett and Winston are evil and Camille helps them, so she is evil too," Ana explained.

"Why, what do they do?"

The more they talked the more Ana's fear of Brett diminished. She trusted Jacob and seemed to think he could help get rid of the mess her life was in. He was sure that after all this time, Ana was happy to tell someone about what she'd been going through. She opened up and told him everything.

"Brett and Winston get these girls addicted to drugs. Winston crushes up painkillers and sneaks them into their drinks when they're not looking. He did the same to me in the beginning. I was always drinking alcohol, so I thought it was this that was making me so relaxed and feeling so good. Then I got more and more dependent on it so Winston kept increasing what he put in my drink. One day I caught Winston putting it another girl's drink and I told Brett. But of course, Brett already knew all about it because he was the one telling Winton to do it. Winston was doing this to my drink for a long time, so I was addicted by now. Instead of telling Brett to make Winston stop, I begged Brett to give me more. Winston did this to me and he does this to all the girls. When the girls beg Brett for more drugs, he makes them pay through prostitution acts with Exotic Beauties VIP pyramid customers."

"Are you still addicted to painkillers?" Jacob asked. He was too embarrassed to ask if she was doing prostitution, but he remembered that not long ago she had fooled around a little with him, during his couch dance, before he'd had the bad trip.

"Yes, but not as bad I was. I'm trying to quit completely."

"Okay Ana, I'm gonna help you." Jacob was determined to assist Ana and the old feelings from his life as an aspiring pastor crept back up inside him. He saw Ana give him a little smile so he continued. "I'm not sure what I'm gonna do yet, but I'm gonna help you." The sun was starting to come up so Ana drove Jacob back to his car in the Exotic Beauties parking lot.

CHAPTER 22
HAPPY SUMA'S

"Brett is pulling all the strings and Winston is his little puppet."
—Suma

The next morning, Jacob was stretched out fast asleep in his bed. He slowly awoke then panicked, then remembered he had nowhere to go. There was no need to go into Gulf Coast Jobs anymore. He relaxed, then turned over and saw Yousra's bare-back. He didn't want to wake her so he slipped out of bed quietly, chugged down six aspirins, then got out of there as fast as he could.

He hopped into his Grand Am and drove around Gulf Coast City trying to decide what he was going to do next. What he wanted more than anything was to make things work with Karina. But first, he had to get Brett and Winston off his back. He figured whatever plan he decided had to include the police. So he set out to look for Officer Paula. Jacob knew she'd more than likely be at Gulf Coast Jobs surveying the damage so he headed in that direction. He drove past the vandalized office but didn't see Paula or the police anywhere. He decided to go to Happy Suma's for brunch. Maybe Suma would have something to say about all this new information from Ana.

As if Suma had a sixth sense that let him know when Jacob was coming to his restaurant, he was waiting for him at the door. "Hello, Mr. Jacob! Welcome to my humble little business!" Suma yelled out with a smile on his face.

"Suma, I really need to talk to you," Jacob said, trying to ignore his throbbing headache. Suma's face turned serious as they went to the table they always sat when they had to talk privately. Suma shouted to Lilianna to bring out some coffee and English muffins, and they both sat down.

"Okay, Jacob, you have all my attention. What's going on?"

Jacob told Suma everything Ana had told him last night. He laid everything out about Brett, Camille, and Winston, and how they had taken advantage of so many young women. He told Suma he really wanted to help Ana and he really wanted to get himself out from under Brett's clutches. Then Jacob sat back and listened to what Suma had to say.

"Okay, Jacob this is what I think," Suma said after he bit into his muffin. "Brett has had you bent over a barrel for a while now. Brett is pulling all the strings and Winston is his little puppet. Maybe Camille's pulling Brett's strings. We'll probably never know."

"So what do we do?" Jacob asked anxiously as the pain continued to knife him in the forehead. He struggled to eat his English muffin, scared his hungover stomach might reject it.

"Patience, my dear friend," Suma said with a warm sympathetic smile. "Just like you, I too do not have all the answers. I will say this, though. As much as you don't like Corporal Hunter, I think you should get him involved. You and he share the same problem, so getting rid of Brett, Camille and Winston will benefit you both."

Jacob didn't want to be around that overly zealous, malicious cop so he said, "I'd rather work with Officer Paula or even Police Chief Joe White."

But Suma said, "That's not a good idea, Jacob. If you get Paula or the chief of police involved, they will do everything strictly by the book. And if Brett makes them think you have broken the law, my friend, they will not hesitate to arrest you. Leave it to me and I'll try to get Corporal Hunter over here so you two can have a chat."

"Suma, I really don't feel comfortable around that guy," Jacob pleaded.

"Don't worry," Suma tried to calm him, "I will be there as well for support. Besides, people can say what they want about Corporal Hunter's methods, but he gets the job done. If he didn't go around cracking skulls and bending rules, Gulf Coast City would be overrun by criminals, I can tell ya that." Suma looked at Jacob to see if he approved, but his face still wore a look of disgust. "Just come back to Happy Suma's tonight around seven and I'll try to have Corporal Hunter here for you."

Jacob thanked Suma for all his help and headed back to his townhouse to lie down and nurse his hangover.

* * *

Around 6 pm he woke up, hit the shower then headed out the door to see Suma and possibly Corporal Hunter. When he arrived at Happy Suma's, to his surprise and for the first time, Suma was not at the door to greet him with his, *"Welcome, Mr. Jacob, to my humble little business"*. When he got inside, he realized why. Suma was already sitting down talking with Corporal Hunter. Tonight, he was wearing his bicep-showing police uniform. He looked serious and Jacob was already getting intimidated. He knew he couldn't let Corporal Hunter detect how he was feeling because he'd start bullying him like he always did. He took a deep breath and thought, *This is just a short insecure guy who uses his uniform to gain power over other people. Don't let him intimidate you.*

Suma and Corporal Hunter spotted Jacob, so he walked over to their table and whispered, "Hey."

Suma yelled out with a smile, "Come on Jacob, sit down. I've been filling in Corporal Hunter on what you told me about Exotic Beauties and Ana. I hope you don't mind."

He did mind because he wasn't so sure he wanted to tell Corporal Hunter the whole story. He really didn't trust this cop and wished Officer Paula was here to help protect him. Still, he felt like he had to respect Suma's advice that it was best to keep Paula away from this one because he could get himself in more trouble. So Jacob said, "No, I don't mind you telling him Suma, and thanks for setting up this meeting."

"You're very welcome Jacob, my friend," Suma replied while Jacob looked at Corporal Hunter's face as he gave a callous look back. Corporal Hunter was a little more fidgety than normal tonight. Jacob sensed he was worried about how Brett was blackmailing him, and probably a little embarrassed too.

Suma continued, "Now Jacob, Corporal Hunter is obviously relieved that he wasn't the one to strike Ana. But he's still very concerned because Brett forced him to misuse his role as a police officer to destroy evidence." Jacob was envious of how Suma knew exactly how to talk to Corporal Hunter.

Corporal Hunter did not seem happy that Suma was belittling him this way so he interrupted, "Suma, we don't need to get into my role in all this. What I need is a statement from Jacob that corroborates your statement. This way I'll have more evidence on Brett, Camille, Winston and the whole Exotic Beauties operation."

Jacob knew Corporal Hunter was trying diligently to hide his shame and wanted to make the whole situation look like he was investigating a high-level case against Exotic Beauties. But even with the huge chip Corporal Hunter had on his shoulders, he couldn't hide the fact he'd been made a fool of by Brett. And if the real story ever came out that Corporal Hunter destroyed the Food Chief robbery tape, that showed Winston pointing a gun at the poor innocent cashier's head, his career would be finished. Not only would he lose his job, he'd also be going to prison. Jacob quite enjoyed thinking about how tough guy Corporal Hunter would survive in prison with hundreds of other prisoners who absolutely hated cops.

He started to smile while he thought about this, then Suma chimed in. "Jacob, I'm going to leave you in the capable hands of Corporal Hunter. I suggest you tell him everything you told me, and he's promised that he'll treat you fairly. What he wants is for the two of you to work together to obtain the same goals. Remember, you gentlemen are both in the same boat. You both want to take down Brett, Camille, and Winston and help Ana with minimal embarrassment to yourselves."

Suma shook Corporal Hunter's hand and thanked him for coming, then disappeared into his kitchen. As Suma walked away, Jacob wished Corporal Hunter would show him the same respect he showed Suma. It seemed as if Suma could say whatever he wanted and he wouldn't say anything disrespectful back. Of course, when Corporal Hunter spoke to Jacob he was rude and condescending, and Jacob was always terrified of what he was going to do.

When the two of them were left alone to talk, Corporal Hunter totally changed his demeanor. Jacob was sure he wasn't going to let him think he had any power over him. He gave Jacob a piece of paper that said at the top *"Witness Statement"*. Then he took out a pen from his uniform shirt pocket and said, "Write down everything and don't leave anything out. I need to know everything you know, ya understand?" He definitely didn't say anything like *Please write down all the terrible things that Brett and Winston have done to you and thank you for helping me save my butt.* He just gave him a pen and paper and said write it all down.

Jacob was worried about doing this, but felt like he didn't have a choice. Now Corporal Hunter had all this information about his side of the story and Jacob had nothing on him. Corporal Hunter could use this witness report to his advantage without needing to help him in return. But feeling like he didn't have a choice, Jacob wrote down everything Ana had told him, every single word.

When he was finished, Corporal Hunter asked, "Did you leave anything out?"

"No, that's all I know."

Corporal Hunter said, "Look Jacob, I haven't had time to come up with a plan of attack on this, but I'll be in touch with you when I do. In the meantime, I'm gonna instruct you to maintain your relationship with Brett just as you always have. I know you fucked up the employment agency but I still want you to act like nothing has changed. You understand?"

"Sure."

"I don't want him to suspect a thing. You think you can do that?"

Corporal Hunter asked in a condescending manner as if Jacob was some idiot that he had no choice but to be involved with to solve this case. Before he could answer, Corporal Hunter continued, "The Gulf Coast City Police Department is ramping up its efforts to prosecute Winston and Brett, and we are focusing our resources on Winston's wife, Lynn. We're hoping she will help us gather enough evidence to make an arrest."

Jacob thought, *Yeah, you guys are focusing your efforts on Winston's wife because you ruined the Food Chief robbery tape.* He wondered how happy Police Chief Joe White would be to hear that Corporal Hunter was the one who destroyed the tape. Of course, like always, he just sat there and let Corporal Hunter dictate the conversation.

Corporal Hunter continued his line of bullshit by saying, "When I'm at Exotic Beauties, I'm usually in an undercover capacity. This is why you saw me last night out of uniform. I'd appreciate it if you don't come running up to me yelling Corporal Hunter, Corporal Hunter! I don't need idiots like you blowing my cover, you understand?"

That's it, Jacob thought, I've heard enough. So he spoke up, knowing Corporal Hunter was going to bust his butt. At this point, he had had it with Corporal Hunter's macho bullshit, so he said sarcastically, "How can you be undercover when Brett, Camille, and Winston know you're a cop? I don't get it."

Corporal Hunter was angry now and Jacob was glad to see it. He snapped back, "I'm not talking about Brett, Camille and Winston! I'm talking about the employees and customers at Exotic Beauties. I don't need to explain this to you. You want me to put the cuffs on you right now? You wanna go back to jail?"

"No," Jacob replied as his heart rate increased.

He could tell Corporal Hunter was loving the power over him. And Jacob knew he would never say these kinds of things to Suma. Corporal Hunter stood up and said, "I have to get back on patrol. Keep your mouth shut about anything that has to do with me, you understand? Suma is not always gonna be around to protect you." Then Corporal Hunter walked out of Happy Suma's and got into his patrol car and left. As he drove off, Jacob shot him the middle finger… making sure he didn't see him of course.

CHAPTER 23

GULF COAST CITY POLICE STATION

"Y'all think you can pimp me out over a coke and a cup of ice."
—Lynn Brown

It all started when Winston's wife, Lynn, was taken to the police station, a couple of weeks after Jacob's meeting with Corporal Hunter at Happy Suma's. The Gulf Coast City police were trying to make one last attempt at getting Winston behind bars, and were hoping Lynn would give them some dirt. Lynn was an unattractive white woman in her 30's. She may have been pretty once, but the years of drug use and regular beatings from Winston had turned her face into an old leather baseball mitt. Since chasing drugs and taking drugs was her top priority in life, things like taking a shower and regular grooming rarely happened. This left her once shiny black hair a greasy grey. Winston and Lynn had two children; the girl was still in diapers. She would regularly sit for hours in her own feces, waiting for Lynn and Winston to come down from their high. Of course, the police were never made aware of this.

Officer Paula was in the interview room but Corporal Hunter led the questioning. His main goal was to get Lynn to give him something that would allow the police to file a domestic violence case on Winston. Corporal Hunter continued to pressure Lynn to admit that Winston beat her on a regular basis, but Lynn would not betray her husband.

Corporal Hunter began, "Now Lynn, you know why I asked you to come in here and you know you can leave at any time, right?"

"Yeah, I know why I'm here," Lynn replied, already irritated and giving plenty of attitude. "Y'all want me to give y'all some shit on Winston so you can arrest my baby daddy. Then when y'all have him arrested y'all gonna rag on him until he gets mad and beats up a cop."

As a high school dropout, Lynn may have been dumb by academic standards, but she had plenty of street smarts. Winston had assured her of this. So even though Lynn was exactly correct in her deduction of what the police were planning on doing, neither Corporal Hunter nor any of the other cops were going to admit it.

Corporal Hunter responded by saying, "Lynn, the only reason we are asking for your help is we're concerned for you and your babies. One of these days Winston is gonna take to whaling on you so bad that your babies ain't gonna have a momma."

The door opened and Police Chief Joe White walked into the room. He handed Lynn a Coke and a cup of ice. "Lynn, Corporal Hunter and the rest of the Gulf Coast City Police department are concerned for your safety." He gave Lynn a smile and looked at her the same way a proud caring father might look at his daughter.

Lynn smiled back bashfully and blushed.

Chief White continued. "Everyone here knows Winston suffers from drug addiction. What do you say you let us take Winston into custody and get him the help he needs?"

Lynn smiled again, "That's okay I'm straight." She picked up her Coke, took a long sip, then put down her drink and smiled. "Y'all think you can pimp me out over a Coke and cup of ice."

After hearing Lynn's comment, full of attitude, the police knew they were not going to have any success getting her to cooperate, so they let her go. Lynn was in such a hurry to leave that she left her cell phone on the table in the interview room. When Corporal Hunter saw the phone, he thought this just might be something he could use to his advantage. He snatched it up quickly before any of the other police officers noticed.

***

Twenty minutes later, Corporal Hunter was banging on Jacob's front door. Yousra was at Exotic Beauties so he was alone. He opened the door and Corporal Hunter barged inside.

"I have Lynn's cell phone," he said proudly.

"Who's Lynn?" Jacob asked, rubbing his eyes, startled to see him.

"Winston's wife."

"Okay?" He really didn't know what to say.

"How 'bout you make me some coffee and I'm gonna tell you what we gonna do here."

Still confused, Jacob set up the coffee pot.

Corporal Hunter sat on Jacob's couch without asking permission. He crossed his legs and got comfortable. "Lynn was at the police station and we were trying to press her for information about Winston. I thought the whole thing was a lost cause, then I saw that she left her cell phone on the table in our interview room." Jacob looked at him as if he didn't have a clue what this was all about so Corporal Hunter continued. "Let me tell you something about Winston. He's a nasty street thug. He steals everything and anything he can get his hands on. He's big time into drugs. He never has any money and he beats and he cheats on his wife. But in some fucked up way, he still seems to have the hots for her and is jealous as shit of every move she makes. I know because I've been to their house a whole bunch of times on domestic disturbance calls."

Still not knowing what all this had to do with him, Jacob said, "Okay, so what?"

"You sure are dumb aren't you, Jacob? I'm surprised you made it to college. Where'd you say you went again? Some Christian college, wasn't it?"

"Yes, Bob Jones University."

"Well, did they teach you how to send texts at Bob Jones University?"

"No, not really. We studied theology and Christian ministries where we learned things like how to manage a church congregation." Jacob was trying to make Corporal Hunter feel silly. But all this did was make him angry.

"I don't care about all that shit, Jacob! I'm talking about the real world here, where people fuck people over every day just to survive. You college boys don't know shit about that I guess."

Jacob started pacing the floor anxiously. He was annoyed with Corporal Hunter for coming in his townhouse uninvited and insulting him. "What are you talking about?" he asked.

"I'm talking about setting up Winston and finally nailing his ass."

"Why didn't you just say so in the beginning?"

Corporal Hunter hated it when Jacob acted condescending towards him. "Is that coffee ready yet?"

"Yes, it is."

"Then pour me a cup black."

While Jacob poured his coffee, Corporal Hunter laid out what they had to do to set up Winston. "Jacob, you're gonna send Lynn some text messages from your phone and I'm gonna send you some from her phone. We're gonna make Winston think that you're having sex with his wife."

"Oh no!" Jacob cried out. "No way! Winston will kill me for sure."

"No, he won't. Don't be a pussy."

"No way, I won't do it."

"Oh yes, you will Jacob! 'Cause if you don't, maybe I won't tell the judge you were cooperative when I had to arrest your ass up there at the bank."

"What?"

"That's right, when you go to court in a few months, I'll be sure to tell the judge that you were talking all kinds of shit about going back to the bank and causing trouble."

Jacob knew Corporal Hunter was mostly bluffing but didn't want to get into any more trouble than he was already in. He argued back, "But you can't expect me just to walk around waiting for Winston to kick the crap out of me. Plus, the guy's got a gun. Don't you remember the Food Chief robbery?"

"Look Jacob, quit being a pussy. I'll have your back the whole time. Before Winston even reads the texts, I'll have my eye on him. I'll follow him and arrest his ass before he gets anywhere near your townhouse. All I need is to get him on attempted burglary and he's finished."

"But what about Brett? Won't he tell Chief Joe White that you hit Ana?"

"Look, once I get Winston in the cell, I'll get him to confess to all the drug activity he's involved with at Exotic Beauties and make sure he implicates Brett. Before you know it, Brett'll be locked up too and you'll have nothing else to worry about except whether you wanna fuck Karina or Yousra."

Jacob stopped pacing and looked at Corporal Hunter who was still sitting comfortably on his couch. "I'm gonna have to pass on this," he said.

Corporal Hunter's eyes turned red and he jumped up from the couch. Jacob started to back up and Corporal Hunter chased after him. He caught him in the kitchen and grabbed his arm. He twisted it behind his back then said, "I wasn't asking you if you wanna do this."

Jacob felt a jolt of pain as his arm was being pulled up behind his bacak. He felt like it was going to snap any minute. "You can't do this," he screamed. "That really hurts."

"It's gonna hurt even more," Corporal Hunter said. "Now give me your fuckin phone."

He struggled to get away, but it was pointless. Corporal Hunter reached into Jacob's front pocket and pulled out his cell phone. Then he kneed him in the testicles and he fell to the floor in agony.

Corporal Hunter started typing texts into Jacob's phone, then he typed some texts into Lynn's phone. He was trying to simulate a conversation between the two of them. This is what he wrote:

Jacob: "I want u to come to my house tonite."

Lynn: - "who dis?"

Jacob: - "Jacob Carmichael"

Lynn: - "What 4?"

Jacob: - "I will pay you to suck my DICK :-)"

Lynn: - "Sounds good!!"

Jacob: - "Be here @ 10 tonite."

Now that Corporal Hunter had the messages logged in the phones there was nothing Jacob could do to reverse it. As he slowly peeled himself from the floor, Corporal Hunter explained that he was going to get Lynn's phone over to Winston's house. And he had to keep Lynn away from Winston. There's no telling what Winston would do to Lynn when he found her texts. Jacob was the one he wanted Winston to come after, not Lynn. Corporal Hunter walked out of Jacob's Townhouse with Lynn's phone. The last thing he said was. "Don't even think about telling anyone else about this."

***

Corporal Hunter began his search for Lynn and found her walking near the beach. He pulled his patrol car over and starting talking to keep her occupied. He told her that Winston had been arrested in Alabama and she needed to come with him immediately. Lynn said her kids were at her mother's house so she didn't have a problem heading out of town. For most normal wives, hearing that your husband had just been arrested would cause a lot of stress and anxiety, but this obviously wasn't the first time Lynn had heard this. She got into Corporal Hunter's police car the same as anyone else would get into a taxi.

While Corporal Hunter had her out of the way, he had a local crack addict break into Winton's house and plant the phone. Breaking into Winston's house was easy. The frame around the back door was completely rotten so the crack addict easily pried his way in without breaking anything. He left Lynn's cell phone on the kitchen table and got the hell out of there, forgetting to pick up Winston's gun.

Corporal Hunter called Jacob to say that he'd spoken with the crack addict and he had successfully planted the phone. He wasn't happy to hear the news. Corporal Hunter said Winston was under the pier smoking crack so he'd be tied up for hours. He told Jacob not to worry because he'd be back at his place before Winston found the phone. The truth is Corporal Hunter didn't see Winston all day. At the time, Jacob didn't know this, but Corporal Hunter figured it didn't matter where Winston attacked him. It could be at his townhouse or while Jacob walked down the street. No matter where Winston assaulted or shot him, as long as there was a witness, Corporal Hunter could still make an arrest and get what he wanted. It was starting to get dark and Jacob was sure Winston was just moments away from coming home and finding his wife's phone.

CHAPTER 24
JACOB'S TOWNHOUSE

"You gonna die tonight fo fuckin my wife!"
—Winston Brown

Now it was pitch black outside around 10 pm. Jacob had been sitting in the dark petrified for two hours. Corporal Hunter hadn't called like he said he would, and no one was around to protect him from Winston's imminent attack. Jacob decided he had to take matters into his own hands so he grabbed a large kitchen knife and prepared himself for battle. With the exception of taking a swing at Carl Dooley, Jacob had never been in a fight in his life. So his experience defending against a jealous husband high on crack was zero. He could only rely on his adrenaline and desire to stay alive to keep him from getting killed.

Jacob hadn't prayed all summer because he still felt like God had abandoned him. But tonight, he got down on his knees and asked Him to come back into his life.

"Oh Heavenly Father, I open up my heart to You. It's been much too long since my last prayer and for this I beg You for Your forgiveness. You put me on this earth to spread Your word and to teach Your children about Christianity, but I failed You. You gave my parents life and it was Your will to take it away. You gave my sister life and it was Your

will to put her in danger..." Jacob brushed away a tear, took a deep breath and continued. *"Lord, I don't know if this was a test You gave me to determine my faith but I know I failed You. I now live among many sinners and I too am now a sinner."* Jacob stopped for a second because he thought he heard a strange noise, then continued. *"Dear Lord, if You can get me through this night and keep me safe, I will try to turn my life around and get back to serving You on the road to sal--"*

In the middle of his prayer, while Jacob was still down on his knees, he heard his back window smash. He knew it was Winston. This time there was no doubt about whether someone was breaking into his place. This time Jacob could hear Winston as he was jumping through his window and making his way up his stairs. Winston wasn't trying to sneak his way up like last time. This time he didn't care if Jacob heard him or not.

"You gonna die tonight, Jacob! You gonna to die tonight!" Winston yelled out as he got closer to Jacob's bedroom door.

Jacob raised up his knife ready to fight. Two seconds later Winston kicked the door down and they were both standing next to each other ten feet apart.

Winston pointed his pistol at Jacob's head and yelled, "You gonna die tonight fo fuckin my wife!" He was drunk and high. His eyes were bright red and full of rage.

Jacob's hands were shaking so badly he couldn't hold onto his knife. Winston slowly squeezed the trigger. The hammer of the gun fell onto the bullet and Jacob heard a *click*. The pistol had malfunctioned. Winston took a step closer towards Jacob and squeezed the trigger again. The gun did not go off.

Winston threw the pistol at Jacob's head. He turned to the side and it hit him in the ear. When the gun hit the floor, it fired and let out a loud bang. Jacob fell down and Winston jumped on top of him and began wailing away. When Jacob covered his head for protection, Winston punched him in the stomach. When he tried to cover his stomach, Winston hit his head. He kept punching Jacob until he lost consciousness.

When Officer Paula arrived, he was out cold on the floor of his bedroom and Winston was still on top of him punching away.

"Freeze right there, Winston!" Officer Paula yelled out with her gun drawn. "Get away from Jacob and get down on the floor!"

Winston was exhausted from running over to Jacob's townhouse, then beating on him for ten minutes. He collapsed onto the floor and Officer Paula put on the hand-cuffs. Then she looked at Jacob's bloody unconscious face and radioed into dispatch.

Five minutes later an ambulance showed up and whisked Jacob away to the hospital as swarms of police descended on his place. Corporal Hunter was one of the cops who arrived on the scene. Since he was the ranking officer he made an announcement to the other police officers.

"Everyone listen up! I don't want anyone going upstairs until I say it's clear. I don't want anyone contaminating the crime scene. Do y'all understand? I'm gonna head up there now and I don't want any of y'all following me up here. Paula stay down here and guard the stairs."

As two cops walked Winston down the stairs, Corporal Hunter walked up. He looked at Winston's exhausted face and said, "Who's first string now bitch?" Winston was too tired and too defeated to respond.

Winston had walked past Hunter so many times on the Friday night football field and rarely acknowledged him. But Corporal Hunter was going to make sure he acknowledged him tonight. Winston could no longer walk off the football field with the fans going wild, with Hunter sitting on the bench waiting and wishing the coach would put him in. He rarely did, and on Monday morning at North Dothan High School, following Friday night's big game, Hunter would walk around invisible while Winston was treated like a celebrity. Girls wanted to date him and guys wanted to be like him. Tonight was Hunter's payback; he was going to enjoy it to the fullest.

When Corporal Hunter got to the top of Jacob's stairs he yelled down to Officer Paula, "Get me one of those evidence boxes."

Officer Paula was confused. "What do you need that for?"

"I need to get the gun to the crime lab immediately to find out who tried to shoot who here."

Officer Paula felt like Corporal Hunter was not following protocol, but she was outranked on this one and had to do as she was ordered. "Okay,

I'll get it," she said, then went outside and asked if anyone had a crime evidence box. One of the cops said he had one in his trunk. He went to his patrol car and brought it upstairs to Corporal Hunter.

Instead of saying thank you to the young policeman, Corporal Hunter yelled, "Didn't I tell y'all not to come up here!"

"Sorry, sir." The policeman gave him the box then ran back downstairs.

Corporal Hunter quickly boxed up the pistol and a baggie of Winston's pills he'd found on the floor, then took the box outside to his patrol car. "Paula, I'm heading to the station with the firearm. You're in charge of the scene now."

"Was there any other evidence besides the pistol?" Officer Paula asked.

"No, just the pistol."

Officer Paula nodded to Corporal Hunter as he walked past her and whispered under his breath, "Don't fuck it up."

Corporal Hunter drove off with the evidence in his trunk. Instead of heading to the police station, he headed to Exotic Beauties so he could plant the baggie of pills. Just like he had told Jacob, he was still intent on framing Brett. Jacob was now laying in the Intensive Care Unit at Gulf Coast City Hospital, still unconscious. Corporal Hunter didn't care about him. As long as he could frame both Brett and Winston, he'd be in the clear. As a nice bonus, he could settle his old high school jealousy with Winston, as well.

* * *

When Corporal Hunter arrived at Exotic Beauties, he told Brett and Camille he was looking for Winston and had reason to believe he was hiding inside Exotic Beauties.

Brett responded with, "You're walking a thin line, Hunter," as he gave him a disapproving look to say, *Don't make me send Ana to the police station with her black eye to turn you in.* Brett, of course, was oblivious to the events of tonight. And he had no idea Winston was currently sitting in a jail cell about to be interrogated by the police.

Corporal Hunter reassured Brett by saying, "Just let me act like I'm looking around here, then I'll be out of your way, okay?"

"Okay, fine." Brett walked away and left Corporal Hunter alone.

Now Corporal Hunter was free to plant the baggie he had hidden inside his shirt. He walked around, and when he was sure no one was looking, snuck inside the dancers' changing room. When he walked back out he no longer had the baggie with him.

***

When Corporal Hunter got to the police station he was anxious to start interrogating Winston. As far as he was concerned his plan had worked perfectly. Never mind the fact that Jacob was clinging to his life. Hunter was able to get Winston behind bars and plant the illegal drugs at Exotic Beauties, thus tying Winston to Brett. All he needed now was some kind of confession from Winston and he could get a search warrant for Exotic Beauties.

The first thing Corporal Hunter noticed when he walked into the interrogation room was Winston had sobered up and he looked scared. This was a good sign he thought. *Now I can get him talking.* Corporal Hunter looked at Winston and said, "So Winston, how ya feeling tonight cuz?"

"I'm feelin' like you need to take these here handcuffs off, so I can whoop yo ass!"

"Now is that anyway to talk to your ole buddy Hunter?"

"You ain't never been my buddy. You's always been jealous of me ever since high school and you know what, I ain't never given a fuck about football… you could a been the first-string halfback… I ain't never cared."

"This ain't about football Winston. In football, you can always go home, win or lose. This is about you never going home unless you cooperate with me."

"You ain't scarin' me, Hunter. You know how many times I done been locked up in here?"

"Were you ever locked up for murder?"

This woke Winston up. "That bitch Jacob Carmichael ain't dead. You ain't scarin me, Hunter."

"He ain't dead yet, Winston, but he will be soon."

"That bitch deserved it fo fuckin' my wife!" Winston was fuming.

Corporal Hunter asked calmly, "Have you seen your wife lately?"

"Hell no, but when I do I'm gonna cut her ass too."

"Your wife has been with me all day today."

"You lyin', Hunter."

"No, I ain't lyin'. I told your wife you were locked up in Alabama. Then I drove her around in my patrol car pretending to take her to see you. I told her you were arrested in Alabama for attempted murder, and I had to bring you back to Florida to stand trial. She was so upset she begged me to help her get you out of jail. I told her I'd only help her if she helped me first. You know what I'm saying?" Corporal Hunter gave Winston a sly smile.

"You a lyin' dog, Hunter. I don't believe your shit."

"Okay, well if I'm lyin' then how come I know about that little heart Lynn has tattooed just above her pussy? Don't it say WB on that cute little thing?"

"You motherfucker!" That was all it took to set Winston off again. He took a swing at Corporal Hunter and connected right on his jaw. Hunter fell down to the ground and Winston tried to finish him off but he still had one hand cuffed to the table.

Hunter grabbed his jaw and said, "Attempted murder and assaulting a police officer. Now you have two charges against you."

As he walked out of the interrogation room, he heard Winston yelling and screaming. Hunter gave a little smirk and closed the door as he walked towards Police Chief Joe White's office.

Winston had been fooled twice. This evening he read the text messages that Corporal Hunter had sent from Jacob's and Lynn's phones. Tonight Corporal Hunter fooled Winston again after he'd read a text earlier from Lynn to Winston saying, "I can't wait for you to see my new heart tattoo. I had the guy put your initials on there so you'd know how much I love you."

***

Corporal Hunter knocked on Police Chief Joe White's office door. "Come on in Corporal."

"Thank you, sir." Corporal Hunter walked inside the chief's large and very impressive office. The chief sat behind a large freshly polished oak desk. His walls were covered with pictures and awards all nicely framed, showing off what a powerful individual he was.

"No, I should be thanking you, Corporal. You finally nailed Winston. That slick cat has been eluding us for as long as I can remember." The chief scratched his chin for a second to think. "You know, I really thought we finally had him after the Food Chief robbery. Now wasn't that evidence mishandling the darnedest thing?"

"Yes, sir it was." Corporal Hunter was starting to get a little uneasy.

"I wonder what those big city police departments would say if they knew we ruined the only tape that would've put Winston away for a long time?"

"They'd probably laugh at us, sir."

The chief looked up from his desk and gave Corporal Hunter a commanding look as if to say, *I'm still the boss here and only I can make the jokes.* Corporal Hunter tried to swallow a large lump in his throat. "Why don't you have a seat so we can have a little chat." Corporal Hunter sat down and tried to look relaxed. "Corporal, I'm gonna put you as the lead man in the Winston investigation. We need to get all the evidence in line for the Carmichael assault." The chief stopped abruptly and stared at Corporal Hunter. "How'd you get that bruise on your jaw?"

"I was assaulted by Winston, sir."

"Goddamit. Are you serious? How'd that happened?"

"I was interrogating him, just now sir, and he hauled off and hit me."

The chief shook his head and said, "Ya know, this guy is a real animal and the sooner we get him locked up the better."

"Yes, sir."

"I'm sorry you had to go through all that Corporal. You know one day we are gonna have enough money in the budget to put cameras in the interrogation rooms. What do ya think about that?" The chief didn't wait for

Corporal Hunter to answer. "By the way, you've been doing a great job for the police department."

"Thank you, sir."

"Corporal, I'm gonna assign Officer Paula Schmitt to assist you with this investigation. You need a second set of eyes and ears. I don't want you getting caught off guard again when you're trying to do your job. Take Paula with you everywhere you go. And next time you interrogate Winston, make sure she is with you to watch your back, ya hear?"

"Yes, sir." Corporal Hunter was not happy to hear that super straight Paula was going to be following him around everywhere he went. He knew this was going to put a real cramp in the way he did his dirty police work.

"Hey, I almost forgot. Here's your search warrant for Exotic Beauties. Judge Stump just signed it right before you got here." Chief Joe White slid the paper over to Corporal Hunter. "Now get on out there and make sure you dot all your i's and cross all your t's. By the time Winston goes to court, I want you to have an airtight case against him for breaking and entering, and attempted murder."

"Yes, sir."

"You know there's one thing I don't understand. Winston brought his loaded pistol over there with him, yet when Officer Paula arrived on the scene he was assaulting Mr. Carmichael with his fist and the firearm was on the floor. You have any idea why he'd do this?"

"No sir," Corporal Hunter responded, as his heart started racing even faster than it already was.

"Oh yeah, that's another charge we'll put on him. Illegal firearm."

CHAPTER 25

EXOTIC BEAUTIES

"... maybe you don't trust yourself alone with all those gorgeous half naked girls."
—Corporal Hunter

Corporal Hunter hopped in his cruiser and got away from the police station as fast as he could. He high tailed it to Exotic Beauties, but before he arrived he got a call on his cell phone from Officer Paula.

"Where are you?" Paula asked.

"I'm heading to Exotic Beauties." Corporal Hunter detested her voice.

"Were you gonna call me? Chief White says you and I are supposed to work the Winston case together."

"No, Chief White said I'm the lead and you gotta assist me."

Paula was used to being pushed around by the mostly male populated police department so she didn't get too annoyed by Corporal Hunter's comments. "Okay, whatever. I'll meet you over there soon." Paula pulled out in her police cruiser to keep an eye on Corporal Hunter.

When Corporal Hunter arrived, it was past 2 am and the place was still packed. Cars were spread out all over the parking lot, and he could barely find a place to park. He elected to leave his police cruiser right up front where Brett had just started a valet parking service. He got out of his car and dared the valet parking boy to say something. He was a pimple-faced Estonian sent from Gulf Coast Jobs only a couple of weeks earlier.

Inside, the girls were entertaining and the music was pumping. Corporal Hunter walked through the door and pushed his way through the crowd until he found Brett's brother, Jamie. "Where's Brett and Camille?" He asked.

Jamie replied, "They ain't here." He was looking Corporal Hunter up and down, annoyed to see him because he already knew Winston was in jail.

Corporal Hunter was glad to hear this. *This is great,* he thought. *Brett and Camille won't get in my way, just that annoying Paula. Wouldn't that just suck if all my surveillance and all my hard work came to a crashing halt because Paula got me on some technicality? I can just see her running to Chief Joe White saying, "Chief, the pills were at Jacob Carmichael's townhouse first, now they're at Exotic Beauties. Corporal Hunter must have stolen them from there."*

He looked around while he waited for Paula to show up. Jamie kept asking questions so Corporal Hunter explained the police were trying to make a case against Winston, and he had no choice but to help them.

Jamie didn't like seeing Corporal Hunter involved because he knew all about Brett's seedy business. "Brett ain't gonna like this at all Hunter."

"I don't give a fuck what Brett does and does not like, you hear me, Jamie!"

"Yes, sir." This was the first time Corporal Hunter had ever raised his voice to Jamie, and he suddenly felt intimidated.

When Officer Paula arrived, they both got down to business. Paula asked. "What's your plan of attack here Corporal?"

Corporal Hunter knew Paula was no dummy so he was very careful with his words. "I suspect Brett is not completely innocent on this one, Paula."

Paula looked confused. "You think Brett had something to do with the assault on Mr. Carmichael tonight? I'm not seeing that."

"Well, maybe this is why I was assigned the lead and you just gotta assist me!" Corporal Hunter snarled back.

"No need to get testy, Corporal."

"Why don't you follow me and the less said the better." Corporal Hunter headed back to Brett's office and began looking around.

Jamie followed them into Brett's office. "Can I help y'all?" Jamie was worried because he knew his brother was no angel.

Corporal Hunter yelled back, "I already told you what's going on Jamie. How many times do I gotta explain?"

Jamie was embarrassed, and Paula interrupted. "Corporal Hunter, have you shown Jamie the search warrant? We don't want Chief White on us for attaining unlawful evidence. I know you haven't forgotten the outcome of the last Winston case?"

Now the veins in Corporal Hunter's head were bulging out because Officer Paula was beginning to jab him in the side a little more than he liked. But he knew she was right. "No, I haven't forgotten the last Winston case. Jamie, here's the fuckin' search warrant so get out of my face!"

Jamie reluctantly held out his hand to receive the search warrant. He knew Corporal Hunter was not giving him a choice. Since Brett was not here for Jamie to ask what to do, he had to step aside. This was all Officer Paula and Corporal Hunter needed to begin looking around. Corporal Hunter had already planted the drugs in the dancers' dressing room, but couldn't go over there immediately. He had to make the search look realistic, especially for Paula. There wasn't much to look at in Brett's office so Corporal Hunter walked out and headed towards the dressing room.

Paula started huffing again. "You wanna tell me how going into the female dressing room of a gentlemen's club is going to get us evidence against Winston?"

Corporal Hunter was angry but he knew Paula was right. He had to be convincing or Paula would know this was a setup. "Jesus Christ, Paula! Whose side are you on anyway?"

"I just don't see why we have to bother these girls so you can look around."

"Okay, Jamie, would you mind asking whatever girls are in there to please either leave or put on some clothes."

"Alright," Jamie reluctantly replied.

Paula still wasn't satisfied and was demanding an explanation from Corporal Hunter so he obliged. "Have you ever spent any time in here Paula?" She shook her head so Corporal Hunter continued. "I didn't think so but I have. I've done surveillance on this place and I can tell you Winston spends more time in the dressing room, supplying these girls with drugs, than anywhere else. But you wouldn't know that because you think I'm just trying to get a cheap thrill from checking out the strippers in the changing room. If I wanna see the strippers strip, I can just go out to the front of the club and see the act there." Paula was embarrassed, but Corporal Hunter wasn't finished. "Or maybe you just don't think you can trust yourself alone with all those gorgeous half-naked girls."

Jamie chuckled, and Paula's face flushed. She backed off of Corporal Hunter and let him look around wherever he wanted.

Corporal Hunter barged into the changing room without knocking. Two partially clothed strippers grabbed their boobs, startled to see the two police officers start snooping around. Corporal Hunter knew Winston's drugs were hidden behind Ana's locker, but be had to make the search look realistic, so he didn't rush directly over there. Paula didn't seem to have too much interest in looking around because she felt it was pointless. She mainly kept an eye on Corporal Hunter.

After searching in some drawers, under sinks, and in the showers, for a convincing amount of time, Corporal Hunter made his way over to Ana's locker. He pulled out his flashlight and looked up and down the front. Then he walked around to the back of the lockers and shined his light into the dark spaces. Then something caught his eye, and Corporal Hunter ramped up his acting skills.

"What's this?" He focused all his attention on a trash bag at the back of Ana's locker. He bent down to pick it up but couldn't reach it. "Paula, your arms are smaller than mine. Would you mind reaching down and seeing if you can get that bag?"

What Corporal Hunter really meant was Paula's arms were longer than his, but he was too embarrassed to say it. Paula stuck her hand behind

Ana's locker and picked up the bag. It was much heavier than Paula expected. "Wow, that's heavy!"

The tension still remained as Corporal Hunter looked at Paula and said, "Well, why don't you open it up? But for God's sake, don't touch anything so we can get prints."

Paula pulled out a handkerchief from her pocket and opened the bag to find a whole stack of pills.

"Bingo!" Announced Corporal Hunter, as he grinned from ear to ear. He knew he'd done a great job acting surprised. Now he had the evidence to show Brett and Winston were linked together. "We'll be taking these with us, Jamie. If Brett wants them back, he can come down to the police station."

Jamie was starting to panic. "Brett ain't gonna be happy to hear this, Hunter."

"I don't give a shit if Brett's happy or not Jamie! Now get the fuck out of my face!"

Corporal Hunter and Officer Paula walked out the door of Exotic Beauties with enough evidence to put a hefty charge on Brett. Jamie watched helplessly knowing Brett and Camille were going to go ballistic when they found out.

CHAPTER 26
GULF COAST CITY HOSPITAL

"It's quite possible that God uses suffering to do good."
—Pastor Mike

After 24 hours in the hospital, Jacob finally opened his eyes for ten minutes before slipping back into unconsciousness. He was pumped full of morphine and in and out of consciousness for the rest of the week. He had severe internal bleeding, and his brain was so swollen that he was having terrible migraines. This made him want to drift off every time he woke up.

On the seventh day of lying in the hospital bed the nurse said, "Jacob, you have a guest waiting for you outside."

"Who is it?" he whispered.

"It's your pastor from South Carolina."

"Pastor Mike?"

"Yes; do you feel strong enough to see him?"

"Sure." Jacob was happy to hear Pastor Mike was here. *Had he come all this way just to see him?* He wondered how Pastor Mike knew he was in the hospital. He hadn't seen or heard from Pastor Mike or his sister Tamar since the day they gave him some money and put him on the bus to Gulf Coast City. He had been doing his best to block his past out of his mind.

The nurse walked outside Jacob's room and brought Pastor Mike in.

"There he is!" Pastor Mike announced with his arms extended and a warm smile on his friendly face.

"Hey," Jacob said in his weakened state.

"Well long time no see. How ya doing, Jacob?"

"I'm okay. What are you doing in Gulf Coast City, Pastor Mike?"

"I came to see you." Pastor Mike said as he sat down next to his bed. "Everyone back at Tinsley Baptist Church misses you a whole lot Jacob. And I miss ya too."

"I miss y'all too." Pastor Mike squeezed his shoulder and Jacob asked, "How did you find me?"

"Well, it wasn't easy, I can tell you that. First, I found Sue Ellen Dooley's house then I worked my way out from there. I found the motel you were staying at, then I found your townhouse. I went over there and Lord have mercy, there was one of those police tapes around your door. You know, Police Line Do Not Cross. So you can imagine my fright, Jacob. I went to the police station and they told me what happened to you."

After hearing this Jacob's eyes started to mist and all the emotions from recent events came flooding back. "It's great to see you Pastor Mike." A tear ran down his face.

"Hey now, don't be upset." Trying to lighten things up, Pastor Mike asked, "Hey did ya hear the one about God, the canoe, the boat and the helicopter?"

"No," Jacob replied, and gave a hint of a smile. He tried to sit up in his bed but he couldn't.

"Okay well, a very religious man was once caught in rising floodwaters. He climbed onto the roof of his house and trusted God to rescue him. A neighbor came by in a canoe and said, *The waters will soon be above your house. Hop in and we'll paddle to safety.*

The religious man replied back, *No thanks. I've prayed to God and I'm sure he'll save me.*

A short time later the police came by in a boat. *The waters will soon be above your house. Hop in and we'll take you to safety.*

No thanks, the religious man replied again, *I've prayed to God and I'm sure he'll save me.*

A little time later a rescue services helicopter hovered overhead, let down a rope ladder and they said, *the waters will soon be above your house. Climb the ladder and we'll fly you to safety.*

No thanks, replied the religious man, *I've prayed to God and I'm sure He'll save me.*

All this time the floodwaters continued to rise, and soon they reached above the roof and the religious man drowned. When he arrived in heaven he demanded an audience with God. Once he was in God's throne room he said, *Lord, why am I here in heaven? I prayed for You to save me and I trusted You to save me from that flood.*

Yes, you did my child, replied the Lord. *And I sent you a canoe, a boat and a helicopter. But you never got in.*"

Jacob gave a little bit of a chuckle and said, "It's great to see you, Pastor Mike."

"It's great to see you too, Jacob. So recent events aside, how do you like it here?"

"It's okay, you know. I'm kinda glad to be away from Tinsley and all the bad memories."

"I understand. You needed a break from your Christian studies, and you needed a change of scenery."

"Can I be honest with you about something, Pastor Mike?"

"Why sure."

"I'm not so sure I have faith in God anymore."

Pastor Mike was silent for a moment and looked around the room, then looked back at Jacob and said, "I see."

"I know this probably isn't what you wanna hear, but it's true."

"Why do you say this Jacob?"

"Well, I just don't see any good in the world."

"Jacob, I know you've been through a bad time with what happened to your parents and your sister but you'll get through this."

"I'm talking about more than just Tamar and my parents, Pastor.

Everyone I know is evil. Well, almost everyone. People use people every day and nobody cares. How am I supposed to keep my faith in God and how am I supposed to remain a good person when this is all I see?"

"Well, why don't you give me some examples so I can understand where you're coming from." This is what Jacob always liked about Pastor Mike. Even though he was a pastor he always listened more than he preached.

"Okay, well, I've been working at this employment agency all summer and my boss just leaves town and gambles away all his employees' money. They worked their tails off all week and when they came to pick up their checks, there was no money in the bank. I'm sure he doesn't care that he hurt them either."

"I see. Well, that's not good."

"And these other two guys, the one who put me in the hospital and the guy who owns a gentlemen's club. They are evil people too. They get girls hooked on drugs and they drug people to get them to do what they want."

"Wow, Jacob! I see what you mean."

"There's even this cop here that goes around breaking the law just so he can get what he wants. If I gave you the details, Pastor Mike, you wouldn't believe me."

"I don't know. You are telling me some crazy things tonight."

"There's even a guy here who had three of his fingers cut off for stealing. Anyway, the only person I have met since I've been here, who seems really decent, is a girl from Belarus."

"Okay, well this is good. What's her name?"

"Her name is Karina, but she hates me I'm sure, because we were gonna start dating but instead I decided to move another girl into my townhouse."

"The girl you live with wouldn't happen to be Yousra would it?"

"Yes, how do you know?"

"I met her at your townhouse. She said the police want her to live somewhere else but she wasn't gonna leave because she's your fiancée. What's that all about?"

"You wouldn't believe me if I told you, Pastor Mike."

"Well, I'll tell ya one thing, Jacob, if you were hoping for a different life out here in Gulf Coast City it sounds like you got it."

They both laughed. "I guess you're right." Jacob's face relaxed. "Now do you see why I have lost my faith?"

"Not really Jacob. And I'll tell you why. King David, sinned too. He committed murder when he killed Goliath and he committed adultery when he laid with Bathsheba. Yet David became the King of Israel."

"Okay, Pastor Mike." This wasn't what Jacob wanted to hear. "But how does this apply to me?"

"Well, I get this question from time to time from my congregation and it's a hard one to answer, as I'm sure you know. Ultimately your faith is only something you can decide... not your friends and not your pastor. Not even God Himself can make you have faith in Him. But your question to me is, should I believe in God when there is so much suffering in the world. Or if you still believe in God, you might ask, why does God allow so much suffering?"

"That's right Pastor Mike, so what's the answer?"

"Well Jacob it's quite possible that God uses the suffering to do good. In other words, *He produces patience through tribulation.* That's Romans 5 verse 3. Or He may desire to save someone through it. Take for example the account of Joseph who was sold into slavery by his brothers. What they did was wrong and Joseph suffered greatly for it. But, later, God raised up Joseph in Egypt to make provisions for the people of that land during the coming drought of seven years. Not only was Egypt saved, but also his family and brothers who originally sold him into slavery. Joseph finally says to them in Genesis 50, *You meant it for evil, but God meant it for good.*" Pastor Mike looked at Jacob with a warm smile. "Of course the greatest example of God using evil for good is the death of his only son, Jesus Christ. Evil people brought Him to the cross, but God uses that cross as the means to save the world."

"Okay," Jacob said with a yawn. He was getting sleepy.

"Well, I know you're tired Jacob. I didn't mean to lay it on you so thick."

"No no. Thank you, Pastor Mike. You gave me a lot to think about."

"Before I go, I'd like to ask, if I may, did you ever make contact with

Sue Ellen Dooley?"

"No, I didn't. I just couldn't bring myself to do it. I almost made it to her house once but the police chased me away. I did try to ask some people about Sue Ellen though. You know, some people who knew her."

"What did these people say about her?"

"They kinda implied she was a victim."

"Well if she's a victim, and your sister's a victim, don't you think the two of you should meet?"

"I guess you're right Pastor." He yawned again and Pastor Mike felt it best to let him get some rest.

Pastor Mike left the hospital room and Jacob sunk off to sleep. When he awoke, the next day, he started thinking about what Pastor Mike had said. *"It's quite possible that God uses suffering to do good."* A lot of people had suffered this summer, that's true, but this was no reason for him to give up his faith. He was once a really good person, who spent every hour of every day truly trying to help other people. After moving to Gulf Coast City and being around so many temptations and bad influences, Jacob had easily fallen down the wrong path. He was only young and human after all, and anyone else put in his situation would probably do the same. Maybe lying here in the hospital was a turning point. Maybe it was just the heavy medication talking, but he felt like God was giving him a second chance to get back out there and get back on the road to salvation.

He pressed the button to call the nurse. "Yes, Mr. Carmichael. Is everything okay?" The middle-aged nurse with large brown glasses asked

"Were you on duty last night?"

"Yes I was. Why do you ask?"

"I wanted to ask you if my visitor left any information about how I can contact him while he's in Gulf Coast City."

"Which visitor are you referring to?"

"My pastor from South Carolina, who I was talking with last night."

"I'm sorry Mr. Carmichael, but the doctor is not allowing you to have any visitors while you're in the ICU. He says you're too weak to handle any excitement."

Jacob was surprised. "You must be mistaken ma'am. I was speaking with my pastor for over an hour last night I'm sure of it."

"No Jacob, I was here with you all last night and you slept the whole way through."

"No, that's not true." At least, Jacob thought this wasn't true but he wasn't sure. *Maybe Pastor Mike came to him in a dream. Maybe God was using Pastor Mike to pass along a message.* Jacob was exhausted from all the excitement and fell asleep for another few hours.

The next week, he was released from the hospital.

CHAPTER 27
EXOTIC BEAUTIES

"Screw Corporal Hunter and screw my drink!"
—Jacob Carmichael

The nurse wheeled Jacob to his car and he drove to his townhouse. It was the first time he'd been back since the Winston attack. He wasn't sure if Yousra was going to be there. He didn't think she knew he'd been in the hospital because surely she'd try to visit him. No one had been to see him, except Pastor Mike, and his visit probably wasn't even real.

No one was home. Jacob could tell Yousra was still living here because her clothes and underwear were scattered everywhere. He assumed she was already at Exotic Beauties. He didn't know what had happened since his attack. Winston might be in jail or could still be looking for him. Exhausted, he took a nap until the sun went down, then showered and decided to head out to Exotic Beauties in search of Karina and Yousra.

It was starting to get chilly at night so Jacob put on a light jacket as he headed out the door. He was just about to get in his car when Yousra pulled up in a taxi. "Wait for me. I need a ride to work."

Yousra got in the back seat and Jacob could tell she was annoyed. It appeared that something was troubling her. He was curious so he asked, "Did you know I was in the hospital?"

"Yeah, I heard that black guy, Winston, beat you up."

Hearing this from Yousra made Jacob feel weak and he could tell she was no longer impressed. "That's right," He argued back. "But he didn't just beat me up. He came after me with his gun because he was trying to kill me."

Yousra clenched her fists and scrunched up her forehead. "Well you deserve it for screwing his wife!"

Then it hit Jacob. When Corporal Hunter came up with the plan to make Winston think Jacob was having sex with his wife, he never considered how Yousra would feel if she heard the same story. Then Jacob started to panic. *What if Karina has heard the story too?*

"Yousra, I didn't have sex with Winston's wife."

"That's not what everybody is saying, Jako." Yousra's face was tense.

"Who is everybody?" he asked.

"Hamid the Mustache, Camille, Jamie--"

"Oh well, those are some really reliable people," Jacob said, hoping to convince Yousra of his innocence. He couldn't believe it. Here he was trying to convince his fake fiancée that he wasn't cheating on her.

Yousra eyes cut Jacob like a knife. "Hamid told me Corporal Hunter showed him some text messages that you sent Winston's wife. And she was going to come over to our townhouse to give you a blowjob!"

Corporal Hunter had really done Jacob dirty but he didn't have the strength to argue. He decided he was going to save his energy to focus on Karina.

Jacob wanted to spend a little time watching Karina glide around the club in her skimpy white lingerie waitress outfit with the white gloves. Then he'd try to have a quick conversation with her… maybe get her to feel sorry for him for almost getting killed.

Yousra ordered Jacob to drop her off at the back of the club so none of her customers would see her. Now she was ashamed to be seen with him. After she got out of the car, Jacob parked, then headed into the *world's largest gentlemen's club*. Since it was October, the place was a lot quieter and empty.

Jacob liked it this way because he had given up drinking and was only here to see Karina.

He sat down at a table in the back of the room. When Ana spotted him, she came over and gave him a huge hug. She was smiling from ear to ear when she said, "Thank you so much Jacob! You have given me my freedom. When I heard from Jamie, I was so happy that Brett and Winston are in jail. Nobody knows that you were behind this, but I do. Thank you."

Jacob was really proud to be the hero. As much as he enjoyed getting a hug from sparkly faced Ana with her black lacy negligee and floral perfume, he really wished it was Karina. She didn't know what Jacob had been through over the past few months. She didn't know Brett was threatening him and Winston was trying to kill him. She didn't know Corporal Hunter was applying all kinds of pressure, and she didn't know the employees at Gulf Coast Jobs wanted their money. All she knew was Jacob was a manager at an employment agency that sent people to hotels, restaurants, golf courses, and Exotic Beauties. He really didn't think she would ever be as impressed with him as Ana was right now. Ana said she had to get back to work so she gave Jacob a quick kiss, leaving her red lipstick on his cheek, then walked away.

Jacob heard the DJ make an announcement over the loudspeaker. "Welcome to Exotic Beauties, the world's largest gentlemen's club. Coming up on stage right now for your entertainment is the amazing and incredibly sexy… every man's dream... Genie!" As the music from *I Dream of Jeannie* played, then cut into Tone Loc's '*Wild Thing*', Jacob started to get a sick feeling in his stomach. Just the thought of Yousra and her new conceited attitude started to make him nauseous. The fact he hadn't had a drink for over a week didn't help either. He'd gone from drinking almost every day for ten months to morphine every day in the hospital to cold turkey tonight. He had told himself because God was giving him a second chance, he wasn't going to drink anymore. He had to find Karina. She was the only one that could make him feel better.

Jacob looked around the room and locked eyes with Corporal Hunter. He came over in his street clothes, which to Jacob appeared to be not too far off from what John Travolta would wear at the club in *Saturday Night Fever*. Corporal Hunter was smiling. His eyes had a blank glare and Jacob could tell he was already a little wasted. He held out his hand and Jacob reluctantly shook it. "We did good," he said. "We finally got those sons-a-bitches." Jacob could smell the gin on his breath and the sick feeling in his stomach intensified. It was a combination of alcohol craving and disgust from seeing someone he detested.

Karina walked by and looked at Jacob with a cold stare. Corporal Hunter noticed her and snapped his fingers. "Hold on baby, where you running off to?" He was behaving drunk and obnoxious, and Jacob was worried he might take it too far.

Karina didn't seem too offended by his remarks when she asked, "What can I get for you Corporal Hunter?" This made Jacob laugh because he remembered how a little over a month ago, Corporal Hunter bragged how he was working undercover at Exotic Beauties. He thought, *If even sweet innocent Karina knew he was with the police, then everyone must know.*

Hunter slurred his words and tried to put his arm around Karina. All the while he never took his eyes off her breasts. They were standing up nicely for everyone to see but Corporal Hunter was taking it too far. She discreetly moved out of his way. "Get me a Gin and Tonic and get him a Jack and Coke. You think you can do that baby?"

Jacob could tell Karina felt uneasy, but she was doing a great job of keeping it professional. When she was at the bar getting the drinks, he told Hunter, "I'm not drinking tonight. I'll be right back."

Corporal Hunter grabbed Jacob's arm as he tried to leave and said, "Isn't she one of your girls? Are you banging that?" Jacob walked away, shaking his head, but could still hear him saying, "Nice piece of ass, Jacob. You done real good there, son."

When Jacob caught up to Karina, he knew she was going to say, *Jacob, I'm working, and I'm too busy to talk*. But he was not going to let her get away. "Karina," Jacob said firmly. "I need to talk to you about us and I can't wait until you get off work."

Karina looked at Jacob and was almost crying. "Jacob, I'm working and

I have to get you and Corporal Hunter his drink."

Still feeling jittery, Jacob fired back, "Screw Corporal Hunter and screw my drink! You and I are much more important than him." Jacob looked at Karina and realized he had her attention so he kept going. "I want you to move in with me Karina. I wanna be with you. I don't care about anyone else but you."

When Karina's eyes began to fill with tears, Jacob thought, *I'm winning her over.* So he kept going. "Karina, I know you're at work now and I know customers are all around listening to me, but I don't care."

A tear fell down Karina's cheek and she put her hand on Jacob's lips and said, "Stop Jacob, please stop. It's too late. If something was going to happen between us it would have already happened. Every time I get close to you, I find out you are with another girl. There's no need to force this."

Jacob shouted loudly and was starting to make a fool of himself, "I want to force this! I want to force this Karina!"

Karina looked at Jacob and what she said next broke his heart. "Jacob, Hamid the Mustache told me about you and Winston's wife." Black eye-liner-filled tears spilled onto her cheeks. "First Yousra then Winston's wife…" Karina had to stop to compose herself and wipe away her tears. "Hamid knows someone in Miami who is going to get me modeling job. I know what you're thinking, so don't even say it. I know you think Hamid is bullshit man..." She had heard Jacob call him this. "And he drives around in his BMW like he's a bigshot." She had heard Jacob say this as well. "But I won't be working for Hamid. I'll be working at his friends' modeling agency in Miami. I have already spoken to them on the phone and Hamid sent them my pictures. I know they're serious because they bought me a plane ticket to Miami and I'm leaving tomorrow morning--"

Karina stopped talking because her boss, Jamie, suddenly appeared. He didn't say anything, but she knew she had to get back to work.

Now Jacob was stuck listening to Jamie as he watched Karina bring Corporal Hunter a Gin and Tonic then stand there while he flirted with her. Jamie shook his hand and said, "I'm sure you heard my brother and Winston are in jail, huh?"

Uninterested, Jacob replied, "Yes, I heard."

Then Jamie looked at him and started smirking. "That motherfucker over there was here last week with some short-haired woman cop and I know he planted them drugs behind Ana's locker. He did a good job of fooling the lesbian cop but he knew they was there the whole time."

Jacob asked, "Then why are you smiling?"

"Because Karina is taking Corporal Hunter a nice little drink of Gin and Tonic with just a little extra drop of acid in it."

"What?" Jacob said. He couldn't believe it. *Was this ever going to end?* Brett and Winston were in jail. They had already got Corporal Hunter once with the acid in the drink, now Jamie was doing it again out of revenge. Jacob knew there wasn't much he could do to help Corporal Hunter, even if he wanted to. Besides, Karina had just broken his heart and this was taking its toll. Jacob told Jamie, "Look, I don't have time for this crap right now, I gotta go."

As Jacob was walking away, he noticed Corporal Hunter was already feeling the effects of the LSD in his drink. He was starting to wobble around the dance floor with his eyes nearly hanging out of his head. Jacob got away from there so he wouldn't be connected. He headed upstairs towards the hot tub rooms because he figured this would be the best place to lay low for a while. Also, you could look through the windows down onto the entire club and see all the action. Jacob was sure Corporal Hunter was about to put on the same show that *he* had at the beginning of the summer.

He climbed the stairs, then went through the doors of the hot tub room hoping to find a quiet place to observe Corporal Hunter's antics. Instead he ran straight into Yousra, who was in the jacuzzi going up and down on some 60-year-old balding man. Jacob was sure he was inside her. When Yousra saw him, instead of jumping up off the man she yelled, "What are you doing here? Get the hell out!" He ran out of the hot tub room and Yousra continued riding up and down on her customer.

By now the club bouncers were all over Corporal Hunter and were about to throw him out. Jacob ran down the stairs and out the main door. He didn't stop until he was inside his car. He started up the engine and drove straight to his townhouse. When he got home he didn't bother writing Yousra a note. He just packed her bags and threw them outside the door. He couldn't stop thinking about Karina, so he jumped back in his car and headed to the airport.

CHAPTER 28

GULF COAST CITY AIRPORT

"We didn't run out of feelings for each other, we just ran out of time."
—Jacob Carmichael

When Jacob got to the Gulf Coast City airport it was almost 5 am. He looked at the departure screen and saw there was only one flight to Miami in the morning and it left at 6:20. He grabbed a cup of coffee and waited for Karina to arrive. He thought about what he'd say and prepared his speech in his head. So far he had, *Karina, I never got the chance to make things right between us. We didn't run out of feelings for each other, we just ran out of time. Now you are going to Miami and we may never see each other again. I'm not asking you not to ever go to Miami. I'm just asking for more time. If this agency wants you to model in Miami now, they will still want you in six months. I want you now too Karina, just like the Miami modeling agency. If you wait I might just go with you. I also need a job now that my only customer is in jail.*

Jacob kept playing everything in his head over and over as the passengers started to arrive for the Miami flight. Gulf Coast City only had one security check-in area, so it was easy for him to keep a look out for Karina. He had to stop her before she went into the terminal and disappeared from his life forever.

More and more people started to arrive and now there was a long line at security. Jacob thought, *This is good because it'll slow Karina down if she doesn't want to hear what I have to say.* The passengers kept arriving and the line kept getting longer but there was no sign of Karina. Then the number of passengers arriving started to slow down and the line started to get smaller. Time was running out for Karina to get here, but there was no way Jacob was going to leave until that plane was in the air with or without her.

Finally, Jacob heard some good news on the loudspeaker. "*Final boarding call for Delta Flight 391 to Miami. Please proceed to departure gate 9 immediately.*"

The whole morning, Jacob had been nervous but now he was starting to feel a little bit of relief. *Maybe Karina was not going to Miami after all. Maybe she'd changed her mind and decided to stay here. This would be great. Jacob could tell Karina he put all Yousra's stuff outside, and he could ask her to move in.*

If anyone had been looking at Jacob at this point they would have wondered why this crazy man was sitting there with a big smile on his face. But Jacob didn't care and he was getting more and more cheery as the time for the Miami flight got closer.

Then Jacob saw someone arrive and walk through the glass doors into the airport. She had a ton of bags with her and she was hurrying towards the security check-in. It wasn't Karina. It was Yousra. Jacob was surprised, he walked towards her until she recognized him.

"Get out of my way Jako, I can't miss my plane!"

He asked, "Where are you going?"

"I've been offered a modeling contract so I'm going to Miami. I know you don't want me because you put all my stuff outside."

He had never seen Yousra so determined. Their fake engagement was definitely over now. And he felt guilty for not telling her the truth when she first arrived. He was sure she'd only had sex with that dirty old grandpa in the hot tub to get her revenge.

Jacob wasn't sure if she wanted to leave him because he caught her having sex last night, or because he put her stuff outside. *Maybe she had the trip to Miami planned all along.* And he still wasn't convinced this was even a legitimate modeling agency.

He had to find out so he asked, "Why'd you decide to leave today?"

Yousra looked at him in her new condescending way and said, "I'd already planned to leave in November. But after you caught me with Steve in the hot tub, I knew you wouldn't want me anymore. I called Hamid the Mustache and told him to give me Karina's plane ticket so I could leave immediately."

"And he agreed just like that?"

"I can make a man do anything, Jako."

After Jacob heard Yousra say this with so much arrogance, he knew there was no way she'd ever forgive him. He just put his hands up and said, "Whatever Yousra, have a nice flight."

Yousra disappeared through security and Jacob thought, *I will never see her again.* As she walked away without looking back, he recalled when she first arrived, how much she loved being here and how happy she was to be with him. *Was it an act?* he wondered. *Was their night together also an act?* Jacob hoped it wasn't. He knew her sexual experience with him, all one minute of it, was not going to be as memorable as his. But for some reason, he secretly wished she felt some tenderness from that night too.

CHAPTER 29
MIAMI INTERNATIONAL AIRPORT

"Hey lady we are not baggage handlers."
—*Mehmet*

A few hours later, Yousra's plane landed at Miami International Airport. When she disembarked with so much pride in her step, you would have thought that the entire city was about to bow down to the new future supermodel who had just arrived to take over the city. Wearing a miniskirt and a super tight pink blouse that showed off plenty of cleavage, she glided through the airport to the baggage claim area. Her face appeared disappointed that there wasn't a porter to pick up her luggage. She saw two middle-aged out of shape Libyan guys wearing jeans and wrinkled T-shirts out in the main terminal. One of them was holding up a sign that said *KARINA*.

Yousra thought, *these silly chauffeurs still think Karina is coming.* She walked towards them and said with some attitude, "Guys, you need to change your sign. I'm Yousra, not Karina. Karina won't be coming here to model."

The Libyan guy, whose name was Mehmet, didn't seem impressed to see her and his reply showed it. "Karina, Yousra. What's the difference?"

Yousra rolled her eyes and responded, "Be careful with my luggage. There's a lot of fragile makeup in there."

Mehmet, tensed his forehead then fired back with, "Hey lady, we are not baggage handlers." So Yousra had to carry her bags with minimal help from her new escorts. When she got to the parking lot, she was disappointed to see an old beat-up minivan. This was not what she was expecting. Yousra thought, *If this is really a high-class modeling agency, as Hamid the Mustache described, then there should be a fancy limousine waiting for me.*

Young attractive Yousra got into the minivan with the unshaven pot-bellied Libyan men and they headed out of Miami International. She was a little suspicious of her two companions, who didn't look professional at all. But outside the dirty window of the old minivan was Miami. She had never been here and was excited to see the large buildings and hundreds of cars on the road as the hot sun beat down.

The driver, whose name was Omar, kept heading down the interstate as Mehmet talked to him in Arabic and ignored Yousra. As she continued to look out the window, in silence, she wondered why didn't they at least ask her if she had a nice flight or was she looking forward to working in Miami? Instead, for the most part, neither one of her new companions said anything to her at all.

They'd been driving down the road for over half an hour when Yousra saw a sign that read, *Now entering Alligator Alley*. "Wow, that's an interesting name for a street," she said, trying to strike up a conversation.

Omar looked straight ahead and said with his harsh accent, "It's not a street it's the interstate." Mehmet, the other Libyan, snickered as Yousra sat fidgeting with the twenty rings she was wearing.

They'd been driving now for over an hour with Yousra looking out the window the entire time. She wished she was anywhere but in the minivan with these two creepy guys. When she saw another sign that said *Florida Everglades,* she went from fidgeting to planning her escape. *Where the hell are we?* she thought in a fright. *Are they going to take me into the swamp? Are they going to drive down a desolate dirt road, rip off my clothes and have me? Yousra pictured the two hairy men taking turns with her, not looking her in the eye, drool coming out of their mouths. She'd try to push them away but she couldn't. She'd have to keep wiping her face because her attacker's saliva would keep landing on her cheeks and her lips. Mehmet would go first and he would be brutal with her. After he relieved himself, Omar would jump in next. He wouldn't care that Mehmet had already left his seed in her. He would just jump right on top and use her body for his pleasure. Afterwards, they'd argue in Arabic, no doubt trying to decide who and how they'd kill her. Omar would lose the argument and would go to the back of the van to get the crowbar. Yousra would try to run but Mehmet would grab her and start laughing. He'd ask where she thought she could escape to way out in the swamp.*

Yousra's body started to shake. Her exposed legs, from wearing just a mini skirt, had goose bumps all over them even though the minivan was boiling hot. She thought, *Either these guys don't believe in air conditioning or it doesn't work inside this piece of junk.*

Mehmet and Omar continued to talk in their language. *Were they planning the best place for her rape or did they already have a place picked out?*

She couldn't stay silent because she was way too frightened. "Where are we going?"

Mehmet answered, "We are taking you to your modeling job."

Realizing that she was in the Florida Everglades and no longer in Miami, Yousra nervously cried out, "I thought the modeling job was in Miami."

Mehmet reluctantly replied, "It's close to Miami."

"How far away from Miami is it?"

"Why don't you sit back and relax. Everything will be fine."

Yousra felt as if she didn't have a choice, so she sat back and didn't ask any more questions. She tried to relax but clearly could not. The minivan continued its path along Alligator Alley which took them deeper and deeper into the Everglades.

After about two hours of driving, she saw a sign that said *Naples 10 miles*. What a relief that was. *Well, at least we're leaving the Everglades. So they are probably not going to rape me and kill me, then leave me in the swamp.* She began breathing normally again but was still nervous about what waited around the corner for her.

As the minivan continued on its course, Yousra finally relaxed enough to realize she had to urinate. She asked, "How much longer because I have to go to the restroom?"

Mehmet answered, "Not much further. We will stop up here."

The van continued along interstate 75 until she saw a sign that said *Fort Myers 12 miles*. Her panic jolted back again so she asked, "Which city are you taking me to?"

"We have an agency in Fort Myers."

Fort Myers? Not Miami? "Well, I really need the toilet. Can you pull over before we get there?"

Even though these were two tough guys, they were not going to deny a young lady the chance to relieve herself. Omar pulled over at the next exit and drove to the nearest gas station. Yousra felt humiliated when she had to get out of the minivan and asked the cashier for a key to the restroom while Mehmet and Omar, two complete strangers, sat there and watched.

When she got back into the minivan Omar said, "We're almost there now."

This had no effect on Yousra. She was worn out and really wished she was still in Gulf Coast City right now. Inside the walls of Exotic Beauties felt much safer than out here. She had no idea what was going to happen next, and these guys were a lot more intimidating than Brett and Camille.

The minivan got back on interstate 75 and continued north. When they got to the Dr. Martin Luther King Jr. Boulevard exit, the minivan got off and headed into Fort Myers. The closer they got to their destination the worse the area looked. Yousra could certainly imagine the minivan fitting in perfectly here. Billboards lined the street advertising bail bondsmen and lawyers -- all the different ways they could help you get out of jail. This was the business of the area. The inhabitants walked up and down the sidewalk interacting with each other. Were they looking for jobs, drugs? It was hard to tell, but if they were looking for jobs they hadn't dressed the part. Homeless people pushing shopping carts were at one corner and trash was piled up on the other. For the first time, she felt safer inside the van than out.

When the minivan reached a sign that said *Free HIV Testing*, Omar turned right off of Martin Luther King. About a block away was a small degenerate house in desperate need of paint with uncut grass in the front yard. This is where the minivan turned in and parked.

"We are here," Omar announced, and he and Mehmet got out. Of course, no one even thought about offering to help Yousra with her luggage so she had to do it herself. This was not the type of modeling agency she was expecting, and not the type of place Hamid the Mustache had described.

"Let's go," Omar shouted to Yousra, so she followed orders and walked into the odious house.

When Yousra got inside, she saw that it was just as untidy inside as out. Pizza boxes and beer bottles filled the tables and jam packed cigarette ashtrays were scattered about. No one had the courtesy to clean up for their new guest. She thought about running out the door, but the residents of this neighborhood didn't look like the type that would be willing to help her. The people she saw walking down the street, looked like the mean streets had toughened them up so much they would never help a complete stranger like her. So she stood inside the filthy living room and waited for her next directions from Omar and Mehmet.

"Follow me," ordered Omar, so Yousra followed him back to one of the bedrooms. "You can sleep here tonight. Then tomorrow you will start your job." Omar walked out of the bedroom and left her alone.

Yousra looked around and saw there were two single beds. She sensed that someone else was living here too. Woman's clothes, bras, and panties were scattered all over the bedroom. The carpet looked like it had never been vacuumed so she was scared to take off her shoes. She desperately wanted to take a shower. She imagined the hot water, with the steam rising up, while she spread some melon flavored soap all over her body. She would scrub away until she'd washed Fort Myers and this whole experience off of her. But when she went across the hall to the bathroom she found the door lock was broken. She wasn't going to risk it so she went back to the bedroom.

When she felt like no one was going to come disturb her, she sat on one of the beds and began to cry. Here she was in Fort Myers. Hamid had promised her she'd be picked up by the agency's driver then be taken to an ocean front condo on Miami Beach, where she'd stay with other fashion models. She was not expecting what she actually got, which was to be picked up by two scruffy potbellied Libyan men, who drove her to the ghetto.

After about twenty minutes Mehmet knocked on Yousra's door. "I have your supper."

She opened up and let him come in. The so-called host handed her a plate with a sandwich, then turned to walk out. But not before Yousra asked, "What about a drink? Don't I get one?"

"Be patient lady. I will bring your drink later."

She wanted her drink now but it didn't arrive until after she finished her supper. Ten minutes after Yousra consumed her plain and unexciting sandwich there was another knock at her door. "I have a drink for you."

Mehmet gave her a glass of Gin and Tonic and a bottle of room temperature water. *It would have been nice if they had given me a choice*, Yousra thought. But no such luck. She smoked a cigarette and drank her cocktail. Soon after finishing her drink she laid on her unsavory bed and fell asleep.

* * *

The next morning Yousra woke up looking wan and bleary-eyed. A freight train was passing through her head and her throat tasted like manure. She ran to the bathroom. *What's going on? Why do I feel so sick?* She began to panic. Thoughts kept entering her head. *How will I go to the doctor if something is really wrong with me, and how will I tell these horrible men that I cannot stop going to the toilet?* Thinking about this made her feel physically sick so she leaned over the toilet and vomited.

As she was just about to flush she heard Omar say, "Keep it down in there." Yousra felt sick again and threw up what was left of her stomach contents. She felt sick and she was scared. This was not what Hamid had described. But what choice did she have? She was in a ghetto prison inside a strange city. She could only hope that since this was only her second day here, things would get better. Yousra went back to her bedroom and laid on the filthy bed.

Around 3 pm, there was a knock on the door from Omar. He came inside Yousra's bedroom and said, "Put this on." He gave her a mini skirt and a tank top blouse.

"What for?" she asked.

"You are coming with us for a photo shoot."

Yousra was nowhere near as excited as she thought she'd be when the time came for her first modeling job to begin. This was so much trashier than she'd expected. But she wasn't a model now. She was a prisoner, so she did what she was told, then went outside and reluctantly climbed into the dingy minivan. Omar and Mehmet got in with Yousra, gave her a cold-hearted look, then drove away from the house.

"Where are we going?" she asked.

Sitting in the van, Omar and Mehmet were already angry. It was as if they were tired of doing this job. Maybe they'd been doing this for a long time. Maybe they were tired of hosting young ladies after picking them up from the airport. Maybe their entire lives revolved around taking models to photo shoots and keeping them in their house. Omar looked at Yousra and asked, "Why do you always have to know where we are going and what we are doing? Can't you just relax and enjoy your new job?"

Yousra didn't feel like this was a job. She felt more like a hostage so she replied, "I just met you people and you are not exactly doing a great job of entertaining me. Hamid told me the job was in Miami but now I'm in a dump of a place in Fort Myers."

Omar was disgusted with the way Yousra was speaking to him. So he yelled back, "You know what, why don't you get the hell out of my van!" He slammed on the brakes and pulled over to the side of the road.

"Gladly," Yousra yelled back. "Your van is a piece of shit anyway!"

Omar was furious now. "How dare you insult your host! I pick you up from Miami. I drive you three hours to my house. I feed you and you disrespect me?"

Yousra wanted to tell Omar that his hospitality was no better than a prison guard's, but she was too scared of how he'd react. She'd never seen anyone get so upset over a simple comment. She was sure he'd hit her if she continued to talk, so she got out of the minivan and walked back towards Omar's house.

CHAPTER 30

FORT MYERS, FLORIDA

"I came here to be a model."
—Yousra

Yousra spent most of the next week laying in her room looking up at the ceiling. She wanted to escape her surroundings but she felt physically sick and anxious. Her stomach kept shooting sharp pains up into her throat. Most of the time all she wanted to do was lie in her filthy bed because she didn't have the strength to move. Omar and Mehmet left her alone except when they brought her a sandwich and a drink. Some mornings she would wake up and have to rush to the toilet from her uncontrollable diarrhea. This worried her but she was too frightened and too weak to do anything about it.

One morning, while Yousra was lying in her bed she saw her bedroom door open and a young attractive lady walked in. She was blonde, pretty, but very skinny.

When she saw Yousra she jumped back. Her pointy nose twitched and she said in a harsh Russian accent, "Oh I did not see you."

Yousra rubbed her eyes trying to wake up then asked, "Who are you?"

"I'm Svetlana. I live in this room. Who are you?"

"I'm Yousra."

Svetlana and Yousra looked up and down at each other. Both sizing the other one up. When they both determined that the other was not going to be a threat, Svetlana asked, "How long have you been here?"

"A week, I think. What about you?"

"Four months."

"Are you a model too?" Yousra asked.

Svetlana laughed as she realized that Yousra was her, four months earlier. "Yes… well I thought I was going to be model. Now I don't know what I am."

"What do you mean?" She was curious to find out everything about Svetlana. It was obvious that she was going through the same journey as Yousra, but was four months ahead.

"Well, I was promised model job in Miami, but instead I come to Fort Myers. I do modeling but it is always Omar and Mehmet who take my pictures."

"Do they pay you?"

"Of course." Svetlana looked at Yousra as if she'd just asked the most ridiculous question. "But as you can see it is not life of glamour."

"You can say that again. I feel sick all the time--"

Svetlana cut Yousra off. "I felt sick too in beginning. I think it's just change in environment and having nerves around new people."

"I think it's more than that," Yousra snapped back. She wanted to tell Svetlana that most mornings she had terrible diarrhea but felt ashamed.

"I don't know but I don't feel bad anymore," Svetlana replied.

Yousra was pleased to have someone she could relate too. More than anything she wanted to get out of this house and get her life back. Svetlana and Yousra talked the rest of the morning until Mehmet came in with their lunch.

Mehmet handed the two girls a tray, then looked at Svetlana and said, "Do you like your new friend?"

"Yes." Svetlana giggled as she batted her eyelids at Mehmet.

Yousra wasn't sure but she had a feeling something was going on between the two of them. They both looked at each other a little longer than normal. Also, they both giggled like they were enjoying the secret that they were both having sex. Yousra, obviously, was disappointed to see this because now she didn't know how much she could confide in her new roommate. For the rest of the day, she was careful with the questions she asked, because she wasn't sure whose side Svetlana was on.

Yousra asked, "Do you like living here?"

Svetlana smiled at her and answered with her Russian accent. "Well no, not really but pay is good. I was making good money before, but this is much better."

"What did you do before?"

"I was dancer in gentlemen's club."

"Me too, but I thought being a model would be more glamourous."

Yousra and Svetlana both smiled at each other and Svetlana said, "Yes, for me the same. I met this guy in a gentlemen's club and he told me I could make much more money in Miami, so I came to here. I thought it would be more of the glamour, like you say, but I'm saving my money and will not work here forever."

Svetlana patted her bed as she explained and Yousra was sure that all her money was under her mattress. Yousra thought, *What a silly place to put your money. You work hard for four months and Omar and Mehmet can easily steal everything right before you leave.* Wanting to change the subject, she asked, "When is your next photo shoot?"

"It's tonight. Mehmet and Omar want you to come but they are afraid to ask you."

Yousra was a little shocked. "Afraid to ask me? How could they be afraid of me?"

"They said you shouted at them last time they wanted to drive you to photo shoot so now they leave you in the room."

"That's silly," Yousra said, and was sure Mehmet and Omar had misled Svetlana on purpose. "I will go with you tonight." Yousra hadn't been in the mood to do any modeling with Omar and Mehmet around. She wasn't ecstatic to do it tonight, either, but the thought of getting out of this house really motivated her to say yes to Svetlana. She was curious to see if this modeling job was for real.

***

When the sun went down the excitement started to pick up for Svetlana and Yousra. Mehmet came into their room bringing them large glasses of a Mojitos. The girls were happy to start drinking, so every time their glasses were empty Mehmet brought them more. They were getting in the mood for their modeling shoot, and both enjoyed helping each other put on their makeup. They continued listening to music and having fun until Mehmet brought in more drinks and told them it was time to leave.

Yousra and Svetlana were tipsy when they piled into the minivan with Omar and Mehmet. Omar pulled out of the driveway and they headed into town. Yousra had no idea whether they'd be heading towards a legitimate studio or another dump just like the house she was staying in. As Omar drove them down Martin Luther King Boulevard, she hoped the scenery would get better. It was dark, and she didn't like what she saw on the side of the road. Hookers and homeless were walking up and down the street and drug dealers were on every corner. Everyone on the outside looked scary to Yousra, and she was glad they were in the safety of the minivan.

After driving about five miles, Omar pulled into the parking lot of a strip mall. They were still in the bad part of town. Fortunately for Yousra, she was still feeling the calming effects of the alcohol, so when Omar said, "Everyone get out," she didn't feel frightened.

They exited the van and walked into a small photography studio. The sign outside read, *Downtown Fort Myers Photography Club*. Written on a piece of paper on the glass door was, *Studio Rentals $20 per hour.*

This was hardly the high-class photography studio that Yousra had pictured when Hamid the Mustache described the trendy modeling scene in Miami. She had pictured limousines but they arrived in a minivan. She had pictured beautiful girls from all over the world, but all she saw was the dregs of society. She had pictured five-star hotels and restaurants but she saw Pop Eyes Fried Chicken.

When they got inside the studio, Omar said, "Okay, let's hurry up. We only have an hour to get things done."

Mehmet started setting up the studio and moving the lights and backgrounds into place. Then Omar told the girls to stand here and there while he clicked his camera. It was all amateurish, and Yousra was not impressed, but she was having fun because Mehmet kept topping off her glass.

Omar brought some outfits for the girls to put on. It was a good thing Yousra was intoxicated because if she wasn't, she'd surely have something to say about having to wear wrinkled up lingerie that had been stuffed into Mehmet's imitation leather suitcase. If Mehmet and Omar had been photographing models for a long time, surely they were not going to buy new lingerie every time a new girl showed up. The contents of Mehmet's suitcase reaffirmed this.

After Yousra and Svetlana put on their wrinkled and faded lingerie, they danced around Omar, as he took their picture. They were having fun, and Yousra was able to let her guard down for the first time since arriving in Fort Myers.

It seemed like they had just started when Omar said, "Our time is up girls. We gotta go." Two chubby girls were waiting outside to get in and have their pictures taken by an older man who had all his camera equipment with him. Svetlana and Yousra walked out disappointed, and got into the minivan.

***

When the girls got back inside Mehmet and Omar's filthy house they continued drinking. Svetlana was drunk by this time and no longer hid the fact that she and Mehmet were an item. They both whisked back to her bedroom and closed the door.

This left Yousra alone with Omar. She was drunk too, and Omar saw this as his chance to make a move, just as he'd been secretly fantasizing ever since she arrived. Omar cranked up his stereo and asked her if she wanted to dance. Enjoying the music and the alcohol in her system, Yousra was ready to forget about the repulsive looking guy in front of her.

She fell back into the stripper routine that had gained her so many fans back at Exotic Beauties. As a form of escape from this terrible place, she took her mind back to Exotic Beauties and imagined Omar to be one of her customers. He, of course, saw this as an invitation to make his move.

Yousra closed her eyes and got into the music while she danced and began to slowly unbutton her blouse. Omar was loving every minute and, of course, misunderstanding her signals. Intoxicated, Yousra opened her eyes and motioned for Omar to come closer to her, just like she always did with her high paying customers at Exotic Beauties. Omar did what Yousra asked, but of course, he was in his house, not Exotic Beauties. So the gentlemen's club rules didn't apply here. At Exotic Beauties, the customers knew they could look but don't touch. Omar figured since he was in his house he could look and he could touch. And that's exactly what he did.

He grabbed Yousra's buttocks and didn't let go. She tried to pull away but he pulled her closer. She opened her eyes, startled, and slapped Omar across the face. He responded by kissing her on her lips and grabbing her breasts. She was now repulsed and quickly came back to the reality of where she was. She yelled out, "Let me go, you creepy man!"

Omar responded by lifting Yousra's miniskirt and trying to pull down her panties saying, "You know you want it, bitch!"

"Don't you ever call me a bitch!" Yousra yelled.

Omar pushed her onto his grubby couch and began to unzip his pants. She cringed and prepared herself as she watched him getting closer. He moved towards her and said, "You're gonna get it now, bitch!"

Yousra kicked her foot up into the air as hard as she could. She connected right in the middle of Omar's testicle sack and he let out a little girl's scream as he fell to the floor.

She got up and bolted out of Mehmet and Omar's house and disappeared into the darkness. She left all her belongings inside and was now running down the street all alone in the middle of the night. She had no idea where to go, or what to do, but she knew she couldn't go back to that house. She headed towards Dr. Martin Luther King Boulevard. When she got to Martin Luther King she turned right, only because this was the way they'd turned to go to the photography studio.

It was way past midnight when Yousra walked down Martin Luther King. Things were pretty quiet except for an occasional creepy guy lurking around in the shadows. Yousra was so upset that she didn't realize her blouse was still unbuttoned. She continued to walk down the inner-city street for over an hour. She was exhausted but didn't want to stop until she reached somewhere that looked safe and clean.

She continued to stumble down the sidewalk until she heard a car following behind her. She was too scared to turn around so she kept walking, hoping the car would lose interest in her and leave. But the car kept following. Then the car got closer to Yousra and she realized who it was. It was the Fort Myers police.

The young handsome policeman pulled up to the side of Yousra and lowered his window. "Is everything alright, ma'am?"

She stopped walking and looked over at him. She was too tired to speak and too tired to react.

The policeman stopped his car and turned on his flashing light. He got out and walked towards her. He wasn't sure what he was getting into. *Is this a victim or some hooker strung out on drugs*? He shined his flashlight on Yousra's face and asked, "Ma'am, where are you headed tonight?"

Yousra collapsed onto the asphalt and started crying. The young policeman now knew he was dealing with a victim, not a criminal. He radioed in, "Officer Taylor, I'm 10-23 on the side of MLK and Tamiami Trail."

"Copy that, Officer Taylor," dispatch responded.

Officer Taylor continued to shine his flashlight all over her sweaty body. He was looking for clues to determine what had happened. He observed her unbuttoned blouse and tearstained face. He asked, "Ma'am, are you hurt? Do you need me to call an ambulance?"

"No," responded Yousra with a weepy voice.

"You wanna tell me your name?" asked Officer Taylor.

"Yousra," she whispered.

"I'm sorry ma'am, can you repeat that?"

"Yousra."

"You-as-ara?"

"Yes, Yousra."

"Well, that's a very pretty name," chiseled-faced Officer Taylor said with a smile.

"Thank you," she replied with just a hint of a smile. But this was enough to get Officer Taylor's heart beating a little faster. Of course, he kept his cool and professionalism on the outside.

"Yousra, you wanna tell me why you're wandering around here all by yourself at 4:30 in the morning?"

"I don't have anywhere to go," she said as she started to cry.

"I see." Officer Taylor gently put his hand on her shoulder. "Do you live around here? Are you on vacation?"

"Vacation?" Yousra started to laugh and cry at the same time.

"Yes, ma'am. Are you vacationing in Fort Myers?"

"No."

"Can I ask what you're doing here?"

"I came here to be a model." Tears rolled down her face as she looked up at Officer Taylor with her sad, dark brown eyes.

"I see. Well, you definitely have the model look." Officer Taylor quickly realized what he had just said and his face turned red. "If you don't mind me saying so."

"Thank you," Yousra whispered. "That's what Hamid the Mustache said too and that's how I ended up here."

"I see. Well, is there anywhere you'd like me to take you?"

"I need to get my stuff from Mehmet and Omar's house."

"Can I ask, who is Mehmet and Omar?"

"Yes, they are the creepy guys I had to stay with while I waited for my modeling job."

"Okay." Officer Taylor was not exactly sure what was going on but he knew things were not on the up and up. "Yousra, why don't you hop into my car and we'll head over to Mehmet and Omar's house so I can have a little chat with them."

"Okay." She walked to the passenger door of Officer Taylor's patrol car and waited for him to open it. He did gladly, showing Yousra the gentleman that he was.

When they were both inside the police car heading back towards Mehmet and Omar's house, Officer Taylor could not believe how far she had walked. She gave directions all the way back to the seedy house where she'd felt like a prisoner. Officer Taylor asked Yousra to tell him her story. She explained everything all the way back to when Hamid promised her a glamourous job as Miami fashion model.

When they pulled into the driveway of Mehmet and Omar's house, Yousra noticed the minivan was gone, but her heart was still thumping. "I don't think they're here," she said.

"Do you have a key?" Officer Taylor asked.

"No," she replied.

"Well, why don't you knock on the door anyway," Officer Taylor said as he looked over at Yousra and saw she was frightened. "I will walk up there with you, so you'll be fine."

She gave a slight smile and got out of the police car. Officer Taylor followed, as he radioed in his location. "Officer Taylor, come back."

"Go ahead Officer Taylor," Dispatch replied.

"I'm 10-7 at 5501 Santos Street."

"Did you say Santos Street?"

"10-4. It's a couple of blocks off of MLK."

"Stand back for a second, Officer Taylor." Dispatch ordered. "I'm not pulling that address up."

"Ah, shoot." Officer Taylor was a little frustrated. He wanted to help Yousra and dispatch was not allowing him to go up to the house. "It's behind that big HIV Testing sign on MLK."

"10-4. Stand back for confirmation."

Officer Taylor and Yousra waited for a couple of minutes for dispatch to give the go ahead, but they never responded. Officer Taylor didn't want to look incompetent so he said, "Let's go ahead, Yousra. I'm sure they'll figure out where I'm at soon enough. Besides, I'm sure you won't hurt me."

Yousra smiled. She liked having Officer Taylor flirt with her. They both walked towards Omar and Mehmet's house. When they got to the front door Yousra checked to see if it was unlocked. And it was.

They both walked inside after Officer Taylor nodded at Yousra to give her the go-ahead. When they got inside the house, everywhere was dark and quiet. Officer Taylor flicked the light switch and led the way. "Where's your bedroom?" he asked. She pointed to her room down the hall. "Stay here for a second," Officer Taylor ordered as he walked around with his hand on his gun holster. He checked all the rooms then waved Yousra forward when he deemed the place was empty and safe.

Yousra went to her bedroom and gathered her belongings. She carried them out to the car and Officer Taylor helped. She went back to her bedroom with Officer Taylor to check that she hadn't left anything.

Before she left for the last time, Yousra looked over to Svetlana's side of the room and thought about what she had said about her money as she patted her bed. *"I am saving my money and I will not work here forever."* She had to check to see if Svetlana's money was under her mattress. She looked over at Officer Taylor, who was watching her every move.

He asked, "Is everything okay?"

"Yes," Yousra answered. "I just have to check something." Then she walked over to Svetlana's mattress and lifted it up. Officer Taylor and Yousra looked down and saw pile after pile of dollar bills. They were all in different denominations. The two of them stood there and secretly tried to calculate how much money was there. Neither Yousra nor Officer Taylor said anything out loud, but they both decided Svetlana must have had at least five thousand dollars stashed away.

Yousra never once thought about taking the money. Even though she could have told Officer Taylor the money was hers, there was no way she was going to do this to Svetlana. She put the mattress back down and walked out of the room.

Officer Taylor asked, "Whose money was that?"

"It belongs to a girl who lives here with me."

"What was going on in here?" Officer Taylor had his suspicions that maybe Yousra was a prostitute after all. Just as he'd originally thought.

"I told you, I came here thinking I was going to be a model, but things didn't turn out the way I planned."

Officer Taylor didn't say anything, but he was highly suspicious that something illegal was going on. He took the lead and began looking around the house.

He walked back to Omar's master bedroom and she followed. This was the first time she'd ever been inside this room and the first thing they both noticed was the place was a mess. Just like the rest of the house, papers and boxes were scattered everywhere.

Officer Taylor opened one of the boxes. Inside he saw dozens of computer disks. Each one had a female's name on it. *Dina, Olga, Yulia, Natasha K, Natasha P, Oksana, Tatiana, Natalia, Lyuba, Lidiya, Elena, Vera, Veronika, Daria, Inna, Nadia S, Nadia D, Svetlana and Yousra.* Officer Taylor picked up the disk that said *Yousra* on it and asked, "Do you know anything about this?"

Yousra was surprised and answered, "No, I don't."

"Well, would you like to see what's on it?" Officer Taylor asked.

She grabbed the disk from Officer Taylor. "Yes, I most certainly would!"

Yousra and Officer Taylor continued to look through the rest of the boxes. Each box contained computer disks and each disk had a girl's name on it. And most of the names were Russian. Yousra held onto the disk that said *Yousra* and the one that said *Svetlana*.

Officer Taylor looked at her and said, "No one from dispatch has responded back to my check-in. So I don't think anyone knows where the heck I'm at. I'm not so sure taking you to the police station right now is such a good idea. They will interrogate the crap out of you for sure."

She looked up at Officer Taylor with her big brown innocent eyes and asked, "Where will you take me?"

"I think we should go to my place. I have a computer there that we can use."

Yousra didn't hesitate because she liked what Officer Taylor had just said. "Okay," she quickly answered.

They both walked out of the house with the disks and got into Officer Taylor's car.

CHAPTER 31
GULF COAST CITY

"Get fucked out of here..."
—Sergei

Jacob Carmichael left Gulf Coast City Regional Airport with a sense of relief. Karina was still in town. He headed straight to the house on Oak Street where she was living. When he arrived, Katrina was inside but Sergei was at the door. The sight of him made Jacob panic, but he did his best not to show it.

"Karina does not want to see you and you owe me money. Get fucked out of here before I kick your ass," Sergei said with his harsh accent.

Jacob was squirming at the thought of going inside. Sergei and the other students, no doubt, still wanted to hurt him over their bounced checks. He got out of there quick and hopped back into his car. He sped off towards his townhouse. He figured he could hold out until tonight, then he'd go to back to Exotic Beauties and talk to Karina there.

* * *

When the sun went down Jacob got in his car and headed to Exotic

Beauties. He knew he was running the risk of Camille coming after him for what he did to Brett and Winston. But he was willing to take the chance so he could see Karina. All he needed was a few minutes alone with her. But when he arrived at Exotic Beauties, to his surprise, he was not allowed inside.

Jamie was the bouncer at the door. "I'm sorry Jacob, but you ain't allowed in here no more."

"Why? What's going on?"

"You fucked Winston's old lady. Camille said you're the one that got Brett locked up, so you gotta go dude."

"Come on Jamie, let me in man."

"Can't do it, Jacob."

"Ah shit." This was going to really hurt his chances of getting to see Karina. Jacob couldn't go to Karina's house because Sergei was there, and now he couldn't go to Exotic Beauties because Camille was there. "Jamie, you and I have always been cool, right?" Jacob asked.

"Sure dude."

"Well when you see Karina, can you tell her to please come to my place? It's important that I talk to her. Tell her that she owes me this, at least, because I'm the one who got her this job."

"Okay, dude."

"But be careful how you tell her okay, Jamie?"

"I will but you gotta go."

Jacob left Exotic Beauties and didn't go back. For the next several weeks he mostly stayed inside his townhouse. He only left during the hours that he thought Karina might be leaving to go to Exotic Beauties or she might be coming home. But he never saw her.

About a month had passed when Jacob decided he couldn't just stay in his townhouse forever thinking about his problems. With the money he'd saved from the summer slowly running out, he decided he'd pay a visit to the closest person he had to a friend, Suma.

***

When he walked through the door of Happy Suma's, Suma was sitting alone at one of the tables in his restaurant.

"Hey Suma," Jacob announced.

"Well, hello Mr. Jacob!" Suma came over and shook his hand. Even though it felt like he was going to break his bones with his strong grip, it felt good to see him again. "It's good to see you're still in one piece. That was a terrible thing that Winston did to you. I called your cell so many times, but you never returned my calls."

It's true. Suma did call and leave a lot of voicemails, but Jacob hadn't wanted to talk to anyone over the past couple of weeks. Now he was finally trying to make his move back into society. "I know, Suma. I know you called and I'm sorry for not calling you back. I wasn't in the mood to talk to anyone."

"I understand, my friend. You don't have to apologize."

"Thanks, Suma. By the way. Where's everybody?"

"Where is everybody? The season is slowing down, my friend. It's almost December so we won't get many customers for a while."

"What will you do during the slow time?"

"You know, the same as everyone else… clean up, take some rest and plan for next season."

As soon as Suma said *"plan for next season"* a light bulb went off in Jacob's head. *I need to plan for next season too.* "Suma, you know, you and I should talk about some opportunities that are out there for next season."

"Okay sure... like what?"

"Well there's a bunch of hotels and restaurants out there that are looking for an employment agency to do business with. You know, now that Mustapha split town."

Suma's eyes lit up. "You know what Jacob… even better than that. I hear there's a gentlemen's club in need of a lot of help too."

"Really?" Jacob was sure Suma was talking about Exotic Beauties. "Are you talking about Brett and Camille?"

"I sure am."

"Why, what have you heard?" He was curious.

"I heard that with Brett looking at prison time, Camille is looking for some quick cash and of course she can't manage that huge place with just Brett's older brother, Jamie."

"Is she looking to sell it?"

"I think she is. Or at least I think she can be talked into it."

Jacob liked what he was hearing and he'd love to take over Exotic Beauties. *The thought of the employees being treated the way Ana had described, haunted him. If he took over Exotic Beauties with Suma, he could treat the girls the way they deserved to be treated. He would never be able to do away with gentlemen's clubs, and he could never stop young girls from going after the money. But he could keep them safe inside the walls of his business.* "So what are you thinking?" he asked.

"I'm thinking if we approach things the right way with Camille, we can steal Exotic Beauties from under her."

"Sounds good. But how?"

"I don't know exactly but I think we can figure something out."

"Okay… so what should we do first?"

"Well Jacob, let's look at what we've got… Brett's in jail waiting on a court date for having those drugs at his place. Winston's in jail for assaulting you and he's connected to Brett's drug charge. If things go the way they should, both these guys will be out of our hair for a long time. Brett's older brother, Jamie, is too simple minded to help run the show over there, so that leaves Camille. Of course, she's gonna run whatever we tell her by Brett when she goes to see him."

"Okay, so what do we do with this?" Jacob asked, getting excited about what he was hearing.

"Well, there's more to it than this, and Camille knows it. If Brett is found guilty for having the drugs, he is looking at prison time yes, but nothing major. But Corporal Hunter and Officer Paula are still searching for more evidence. And this, my friend, is Camille's biggest fear. What if the cops find out about everything that Brett and Winston were up to? I'm sure you know more about this than I do."

"Yes, I do." Jacob was starting to see some possibilities. "Suma, I know a little bit about a lot of stuff that Brett and Winston were up to."

"Okay this is good."

"Yeah, but y'know what's better? I know someone that knows everything."

"Who?"

"A dancer at Exotic Beauties. Her name is Ana."

"I see." Suma's eyes brightened. "Well, we need to have a talk with Ana. Don't you think?"

"Yes we do, Suma."

"And y'know who else we need to talk to? Corporal Hunter."

Suma always had to bring Corporal Hunter into the mix. "Oh no. Why do we have to do this?"

"I don't mean at the same time, but I think we should meet with both these guys to see what they can offer us, don't you think?"

"Well that's the last thing I'd suggest, but if you want to."

They agreed that Suma would set up a meeting with Corporal Hunter and Jacob would set up a meeting with Ana.

* * *

The next day Jacob's cell phone woke him up. Suma was on the line and he said, "Corporal Hunter is here at Happy Suma's now. Can you come over?"

"Sure, I'm on my way." This was not going to be his idea of a pleasant morning, but it would be the first time he'd seen Corporal Hunter sober since his assault. Jacob was curious to see what he had to say.

He headed over to Happy Suma's without getting in a shower or shave. When he arrived, he saw Corporal Hunter all decked out in his police uniform. Jacob knew he'd be in his usual condescending mood. He was sure he'd start bullying him if Suma left them alone.

Suma saw Jacob's car pull into the parking space and walked outside to greet him. "Jacob, come on in. I've been chatting with Corporal Hunter all morning and he wants to help us."

"That's good," he replied, but he didn't have the same enthusiasm as Suma.

When he walked inside, Corporal Hunter stood up and shook his hand.

"Jacob, it's great to see you. You look great."

Jacob was shocked to hear a compliment coming from him. "Thanks," he replied. This was nice to hear but he was still suspicious.

Corporal Hunter looked him up and down and said, "Jacob, I'm gonna get right to the point here because I ain't got a lotta time. The Gulf Coast City police department is conducting a thorough investigation into Brett and Winston's illegal activities. What this means is a lottastones are gonna be overturned and a lotta private activities are gonna come out."

"Okay," Jacob said, still suspicious of Corporal Hunter and not sure where he was going with this.

"I'm gonna let you sit there for a second Jacob and think about some of your recent activities…" Hunter paused for a second. "Now, is there anything you can think of that might be a little embarrassing for you to have come to the attention of the police?"

Jacob was starting to get nervous. "No," he replied. "I can't think of anything." He looked at Suma, who was sitting there silent. He gave him a nod as if to say, *Everything's going to be okay.*

Corporal Hunter was not as supportive. He looked at Jacob with his callous face and said, "Let me see if I can refresh your memory. Do you remember any text messages that were sent to Winston's wife's phone?"

"Yeah but you--"

"Yeah, but they came from your cell phone. Am I right?"

Now Jacob was really nervous. His mind was racing as thoughts of him sharing the prison with Brett and Winston kept blowing through his head. He had to ask, "Why are you telling me all this?"

"Why?" Corporal Hunter looked at Jacob as if he was stupid. "Have you been listening to anything I've been saying?"

Suma finally spoke up as he put his hand on Corporal Hunter's shoulder to quiet him down. "Jacob, what Corporal Hunter is trying to say is all three of us would really like to see the Brett and Winston case end quickly. Meaning we don't want to drag this thing on long enough for the police to dig up more evidence on you and Corporal Hunter." Suma gave Corporal Hunter a stern look. He was challenging Hunter to argue with him. Corporal Hunter, of course, knew he was the one who sent the texts to Lynn even though they came from Jacob's phone. Jacob was sure there were many other things he'd done that would get him into plenty of hot water with Police Chief Joe White.

So he said what he had to, to keep Corporal Hunter off his back. "Okay, I'll keep my mouth shut."

Corporal Hunter exhaled in disgust and shook his head. "You can't just say I'll keep my mouth shut and expect me to do all the work."

"Okay," Jacob said, a little shocked. "What do you want me to do?"

"Suma told me you're gonna speak with Ana."

"Ana? What does this have to do with Ana?"

"Ana has been interviewing with me and Officer Paula and is ready to testify against Brett and Winston."

"That's great." His eyes lit up.

Corporal Hunter rolled his eyes. "Suma, I told you this guy was a dumbass."

Suma came to Jacob's rescue. "Now Hunter, is that necessary? We are all on the same team here. Why don't you just tell Jacob what you told me."

Corporal Hunter looked as if it was killing him to have a conversation with Jacob. "Ana is terrified of Brett and Winston and I'm not so sure she's even gonna show up for the trial. When you speak to her, you need to convince her that everything is gonna be okay. Y'understand?"

"I guess so."

Corporal Hunter shook his head again. "Don't just say I guess so! If she doesn't show up for the trial, or if she gets cold feet on the witness stand, then Brett and Winston get a mistrial and they walk free. Is this what you want?"

"No." Jacob was scared but trying not to show it.

"Then like I said, you need to tell Ana everything will be okay and no one is gonna hurt her and no one is gonna deport her Mexican ass."

"Okay," Jacob said, "I got it." He was trying hard to get Corporal Hunter off his back.

"And let's not forget Winston's wife's text message exchange. Don't you even think I'm gonna take the blame if that comes out." Corporal Hunter pounded on the table.

"What do you mean?"

"If I go down, I take you down with me. That's what I mean." Corporal Hunter was not holding back. Suma was still there but it seemed like Hunter was so desperate, he wasn't afraid to threaten Jacob in front of him.

As he suspected from the beginning, Corporal Hunter was at this meeting to save his butt, not Jacob's. He was worrying that the fake text messages would come out in court and he'd be implicated. He was also scared that when they came after Jacob he'd tell them what a crooked policeman he really was. Also, he was sure that Ana knew that Brett had made him destroy the Food Chief tape and he didn't want her to tell Officer Paula. Corporal Hunter couldn't say all this in front of Suma but Jacob knew this was the reason he was here behaving like this.

"Okay, I'll talk to her," he said, hoping this would get rid of him.

Corporal Hunter jumped up out of his seat. "Well I gotta get going." He shook Suma's hand. "Suma, nice seeing you again." Then he glared at Jacob and walked out of Happy Suma's.

When Corporal Hunter was outside Jacob looked at Suma and yelled, "Man I hate that guy! He never gives me any respect. What kinda cop is he?"

Suma gave him a sympathetic look. "He's a crooked cop, that's what he is. But I think you and I need him on our side if we are going to take over Exotic Beauties. Don't you think?"

"Not really," Jacob answered.

"Well, I'm pretty sure that without Corporal Hunter's dogged determination those two scoundrels would be walking the street right now. So you have to decide Jacob, do you want a nice cop around or a nasty cop that gets things done."

"I guess you're right," he said, hating to admit it.

"Let me tell you something, Jacob, as an older maybe more experienced businessman than you. I don't mean any disrespect, because I think you have done a great job managing things at Gulf Coast Jobs. But sometimes you have to work with people you absolutely can't stand to get what you want."

He knew Suma was right, and even though he hated to admit it he said, "You're right again, Suma."

"Why don't you go look for Ana." Suma smiled. "I tell you, there's a lot worse ways to spend your time than looking for a beautiful creature like her."

At first, Jacob was surprised that Suma even knew Ana, then he remembered Suma knew everyone in Gulf Coast City. Suma told him again he was glad that he was back after his assault, and he had a good feeling that the two of them would be doing some great business together. They said their goodbyes and Jacob set off to find Ana.

CHAPTER 32
ANA'S HOUSE

"Jacob you are so loco."
—Ana Bautista

A couple of nights later, Jacob was walking around the beach when he ran into X-man. He walked up to his taxi and X-man rolled down his window.

"Hey X-man, just the guy I need to see."

"What's up buddy? You been in the slammer lately?"

"No." Jacob laughed. "You wouldn't happen to know one of the dancers from Exotic Beauties called Ana, would you?"

"Yeah, that hot Costa Rican gal? I just saw her not too long ago."

"You did?" Jacob's eyes brightened. "Hey, you wouldn't happen to know where she lives would you?"

"I sure do," X-man answered proudly. "I know where all the strippers live. I just wished they'd invite me over to see them." He laughed at his own joke.

Jacob smiled and asked. "Could you give me her address?"

"I can do better than that, my man. Hop on in and I'll take ya there."

This was great. He got in X-man's taxi and they headed down the road.

He stretched out in the back seat. *It was good to be back.* He asked, "What about Karina? Have you seen her?"

"Naw, man. She went back to Russia last week."

Jacob's heart sank. "How do you know?"

"'Cause I took her to the airport."

"Was she with anyone?"

"Yeah, some big Russian guy."

Jacob was sure he was talking about Sergei from Estonia. "Did she say anything to you?"

"Like what? About you, Jacob? No, she didn't say nothin'."

"You sure she didn't say, see ya next year?" He was desperately hoping.

"Naw, man. She just said thank you for being a great taxi driver. You know, stuff like that. I will say this. She's a very classy young lady and you kinda fucked up lettin her go, son."

He knew he'd messed up. X-man didn't have to remind him. He hoped like hell she'd be coming back next season. She never told Jacob what her plans were and when she left, she was mad at him. Trying to change the subject, he asked, "What about Yousra. Have you heard anything about her?"

"Yousra, who's that?"

"Never mind." Jacob wasn't going to get into the details of her once being his make-believe fiancée. "How about Brett and Winston? Do you know the latest on them?"

"They're outta jail. I can tell ya that."

"Really?" Jacob raised his eyebrows.

"Yeah man, they're both out on bail. And I believe they're both on house arrest. You know, the ankle bracelet and all that shit. I think they have a court date comin up real soon, but I'm pretty sure Brett can't go inside Exotic Beauties until after the trial."

"Oh, okay. I see." He was relieved because at first, he thought X-man meant they were both out of jail for good.

The evening was quiet, with the exception of a couple thousand crickets chirping in the grass. Ana lived a long way from the beach in a predominantly Hispanic neighborhood. When they pulled into the dirt driveway of her small house, it was completely dark outside.

X-man tried to turn on the dome-light in his taxi. The light was falling apart just like the rest of his car and just like X-man, himself. He pulled out his cigarette lighter and flicked it a couple of times until the fire burned. He fumbled around through his messy glove compartment until he found a stack of business cards. He handed one to Jacob and said, "I tell you what. I'm sure you lost my card so here's another one. I'll wait for you to see if she's home. If she is, I'm gonna head to the store to get some chew. Just call me when you need a pick up."

"Thanks, X-man. Thanks a bunch for helping me like this." Jacob really appreciated his efforts.

When he walked up to the door, he couldn't stop fidgeting and had no idea what was waiting for him on the other side. He rang the doorbell then combed his blonde hair to the side with his fingers. A few seconds later Ana appeared.

"Jacob, why are you here?" Ana asked, with her Latina accent, which he thought sounded sweet. She looked a lot different without her makeup and exotic dancer outfit on. She still looked pretty, but now she looked a lot more normal. She looked a lot smaller too. The reason was she didn't have on her stiletto heels tonight.

"Hey Ana, I wanted to talk to you about some things." Ana looked at him and he could tell she was considering whether to let him in, so he said, "It's about Brett and Winston's court date. I'm sure you're worrying about it and I want to help."

Ana thought for a second then stepped aside to let Jacob enter. Her house was small and old but she still took pride in her home. The inside was very clean and well decorated with pictures of Costa Rican beaches. She lived in the poor part of town, but she had some new furniture and a nice TV in her front room. At first, Ana appeared to be alone, then he noticed there was a young girl sitting on the floor watching TV.

"This is my daughter Paola," Ana said as the little girl looked up at Jacob and said, "I'm five."

"Hello, Paola." Jacob's mind flashed back to the children he'd ruined Christmas for only a year ago. He quickly brushed the thought under the carpet. "Where's Paola's daddy?" he asked.

Ana looked a little embarrassed and answered, "Paola's popito is back in Costa Rica. Paola has never met him."

"I never knew you were married." Jacob's Christian ideology was still with him.

"Jes, well, Paola's father is still in Costa Rica and we'd love for him to come here but it's hard."

He could tell he was getting too personal so he backed off. "Ana I wanted to talk to you about what you're gonna say at the trial."

"You mean about Brett and Winston?"

"Yes."

"Officer Paula and Corporal Hunter have been talking to me about that. I know a lot of things Jacob, but I'm es-scared because I'm illegal here and even though Brett may go to prison, Camille will still be here and she's my boss." She looked at Jacob with her troubled face. He could tell she was feeling a lot of pressure to stay employed at Exotic Beauties. He assumed she was worried about how she'd take care of her daughter if she lost her job. "I keep worrying that after the trial, Camille will fire me no matter what happens to Brett because she doesn't trust me."

Once again Jacob felt like he had to rescue Ana. He got the feeling that she didn't have many friends. He assumed it was because of her profession. "Ana, I've been talking with Suma at Happy Suma's, about maybe taking over Exotic Beauties."

"Wow!" Her face lit up. "That would be great!"

"Yeah, but I don't think we can do it without your help."

"Me, what can I do?"

"Well, you play a big part in whether or not Brett and Winston go to prison for a long time. Did you know this?"

"Jes, I guess so."

"Well Camille knows this too, so we are gonna use this as leverage to get Camille and Brett to sell the business to us for a cheap price. You understand?"

"Jes, I think so. But what do you want me to do?"

"If you tell the jury the truth about everything, and I mean everything Brett and Winston got up to, you'll be helping me and all the other employees." He looked at Ana a little longer than customary to make sure he stressed his point. Ana, still worrying, looked down at the ground. "Now, for me to negotiate a cheap price for Exotic Beauties, I'm gonna lie to Camille and tell her I can influence what you say in court."

Ana was surprised. "How are you going to do this?"

She had a point. He couldn't just walk up to Camille and say Ana is going to do whatever I tell her. "Well, I could always tell Camille that you're my girlfriend." After Jacob said this he almost wished he could take it back. Then he waited to see her reaction.

"Wow, Jacob!" Her face turned red. "You must really want Exotic Beauties bad."

"Yes, I do want Exotic Beauties bad. And not just that, I think Brett deserves to lose it."

Ana looked confused. "You want Exotic Beauties so you ask me to be your girlfriend? I don't get it."

Jacob wasn't sure he got it either, but in the short time he'd been over at Ana's house talking with her, he decided this was the best plan of action. "The way I see it, Ana, if you're my girlfriend, I can convince Brett and Camille that I can influence you to say whatever I want to put Brett in prison. This will be enough to deceive them into selling Exotic Beauties to Suma and me. Then when I have ownership of Exotic Beauties, you can have a management job there for life."

She smiled and said, "That is either the craziest or nicest thing I have ever heard."

"So will you do it?"

"As much as I'm flattered that you would ask me this, and as much as I know you would help me, I have to say no. Sorry Jacob, but I can't be your girlfriend."

"You're right Ana, I would help you," he answered, feeling silly that he'd asked this in the first place.

Ana gave him a sweet smile and said, "I can still pretend to be your girlfriend."

He blew out a sigh of relief. "That's really nice of you, Ana." He smiled back. Then there was an awkward silence as they both started thinking.

"Jacob, I still don't know why you tell me all this."

He explained. "Brett doesn't think I'm a threat to him. He thinks I still believe that I hit you, way back when I first came into Exotic Beauties. And he doesn't think I can talk you into telling the truth about him. If he thinks we're dating, then he will be really scared that you'll say and do anything to keep me happy, including testifying against him in court. Get it?"

"Jacob, you are so loco!"

"I know I'm loco, but what do you think?"

"You know what? I think I like being your girlfriend… I mean, pretend girlfriend." Ana smiled. Then they both started laughing. When he left Ana's house, he had X-man drive him straight over to Happy Suma's to tell Suma the good news.

CHAPTER 33
EXOTIC BEAUTIES

"I just made the biggest mistake of my life!"
—Ana Bautista

Jacob felt like he needed to check in with Suma and let him know they now had Ana on their side. When he walked through the door of Happy Suma's, Suma was sitting all alone reading a magazine. He looked up and smiled.

"Hello, Jacob Carmichael, my friend."

Jacob proudly announced, "I found Ana and she's on our side. She's gonna do whatever it takes to help in court and do her part to put Brett and Winston in prison. She says she's super nervous, but she's still gonna do it. Also, she'll play along with anything we tell Camille when we try to pressure her to sell out."

"That's great! How did you manage that?" Suma asked.

"Well X-man, the taxi driver, took me to her house just now and her and I had a long talk. I actually convinced Ana to pretend to be my girlfriend when she's around Camille."

"You sly little dog, Jacob!" Suma yelled out, then asked, "Are you happy, my friend?"

"I will be Suma."

"You will be? What do you mean?"

"I will be when you and I take over Exotic Beauties and we can run things the right way."

"I will be happy too if that happens." Suma put his hand on Jacob's shoulder and looked him in the eye. Of course, only one eye looked at him and the other one looked away, but Jacob was used to this by now. "But if it doesn't happen, I will still be happy. And I hope you will too."

"When do you think we should try to get a meeting with Camille?" Jacob asked, anxious to get things going.

"Well, I don't know," replied Suma. "You see, I've just received some bad news. My father is dying back in Turkey."

"Oh… I'm so sorry Suma," Jacob said softly.

"I'm going to try and leave tomorrow and spend some time with him. He's in the hospital and the hospitals there are not like they are here. I will have to bring him his food and help him stay comfortable."

"Sure, I understand Suma. If you need anything from me, you know, like helping out at Happy Suma's or your motel, I hope you know that I'm always here."

"Thank you, Jacob. I will let you talk to my wife about that."

The next day Jacob drove Suma to the Gulf Coast City airport. Suma hopped on a plane to Ankara, Turkey and didn't return until March. Suma's father passed away due to complications from lung cancer. He smoked 2 packs a day for over 50 years, even after he received the diagnosis.

Jacob spent the rest of the winter helping Suma's wife, Azra, run Happy Suma's. Most of his time was spent cleaning and picking up supplies. He didn't mind, and Azra was happy to pay him a small wage.

Then one day in March while Jacob was cleaning off the tables at Happy Suma's, Suma walked through the door.

"Jacob, my friend, has my wife been making you work hard?" Suma laughed.

"Hey, you're back." Jacob put down his wash rag and came over to shake his hand.

"You look good, my friend. How are things here?" Suma asked.

"You know, kinda slow."

"What about our friend Mr. Brett; have you taken his business from him yet?" Suma asked with a grin.

"No, not yet. I've been waiting on you."

"Well, I'm here now."

"Okay cool. When you wanna go?"

"I guess we need to go soon, and now is a great opportunity with Brett sitting in jail."

"Actually, Brett is out of jail, but he's not allowed inside Exotic Beauties," Jacob interrupted. "Remember? I told you this back in December."

"You're right. I'm sorry Jacob my mind was on other things back then."

"No, you know what, I'm the one who should be apologizing to you. I never told you I was sorry to hear about your dad."

"Thank you, my friend. My father was an honorable man and I owed him for saving my life back when I was a kid. I'm sure I told you the story." Suma looked at Jacob and he nodded back. The story of Suma getting his fingers chopped off by the Turkish police, then stowing away on an Air Force transport plane, was one that Jacob would not soon forget. "Anyway, what do you say we cut all the formalities and get to work on more important things like Exotic Beauties."

"I'm ready to go tomorrow if you are," Jacob replied.

"That sounds good." Suma scratched his wiry white hair and stared off into space for a second. Then he said, "We'll go to Exotic Beauties and lean on Camille since Brett won't be there. We'll convince her we can do what's best for her." He looked at his watch, then continued. "Why don't you swing by Happy Suma's tomorrow and pick me up and we'll head over to Exotic Beauties."

"Do you want to rehearse what we're gonna say?" Jacob was already starting to fidget.

Suma shook his head. "No, I'm sure we're both ready. I think it's better if we go in there unrehearsed and see if we can put a little pressure on Camille. I'm sure she'll be worried when she finds out the key witness against her husband is now with you."

Suma asked Jacob if he wanted to stay for a late-night supper, so he did. He offered to pay but Suma refused. Suma and his wife Azra never let him pay for any of the tasty Turkish dishes they served. After supper, he said goodbye to Suma and they both agreed they'd meet at Happy Suma's tomorrow then go to Exotic Beauties for their chat with Camille.

***

The next morning, when Jacob arrived at Happy Suma's, he could see Suma through the window so he waved and Suma waved back. He came out the door soon after he finished giving his wife Azra a kiss and some last-minute instructions, then got into Jacob's car.

Suma reclined the car seat way back and stretched out as they both headed down the road. Jacob was really anxious now, so he asked, "Are you nervous at all?"

"Nervous? No, why are you?"

He lied and said, "No, I'm not nervous." He couldn't believe how Suma could be so calm and cool when they were about to go inside Exotic Beauties and try to steal the business away from Brett and Camille. He knew Camille was going to fight them tooth and nail to hold onto her livelihood, and this terrified him.

When they pulled into the parking lot of Exotic Beauties, Jacob saw Ana's car was already there. His stomach was so jumpy, he thought he was going to vomit. He couldn't say anything of course, because he felt like Suma would lose confidence in his future business partner. And this made his gut churn even more.

Before they got out of the car, Suma said, "This is what I think we should do. Ask Camille to give us a price to buy the business from them. Then, of course, we'll try to negotiate this down. When we agree on a price, we'll tell her that I'll write a check for half and you will make payments to them every month out of the company profits. What do you think?"

Jacob couldn't answer because he felt the morning's breakfast coming up his throat. Then he ran out of his car and puked all over the parking lot.

"Are you okay?" Suma asked. "You poor guy. You must have partied too much last night, huh?

Even though Jacob was sure Suma knew the real reason, he responded back by saying, "Oh yeah, I guess I did."

"We can always do this another day," Suma said, trying to calm his nerves.

"No, let's do it now." Jacob felt a little better after he'd upchucked and he wanted to get this meeting over. He walked up to the glass front door of Exotic Beauties and waved at Suma to follow him. When Suma caught up, he pushed it open and they stepped inside. It was early, maybe 1 pm, so there was no need for a bouncer on the door. Before their eyes could adjust from the bright sunlight to the dark cave, Jamie was on them. "Dude, you can't be in here. Who's this you're with?"

Jacob put his hands up in defense and explained, "This is Suma from Happy Suma's."

Then he looked over Jamie's shoulder and saw Camille walking quickly towards them. When she got within earshot she nervously asked, "What are you doing here?" Jacob could tell she was uptight. She looked at Suma. He was dressed very casual in his shorts and t-shirt as if he had no desire to impress anyone. In contrast, Jacob was dressed to impress, in slacks and a button down red shirt. He had a much better look for their meeting wearing his business casual attire. Luckily for Jacob, it was dark inside and the specks of vomit did not show on his shirt.

He stepped forward and formally announced to Camille, "This is Suma from Happy Suma's. We'd like to sit down with you and have a chat."

Suma extended his hand for a handshake with Camille but she looked away. "Brett is here. Wait here and I'll ask him what he wants to do."

Camille walked off and Jacob looked at Suma and whispered in a panic, "Brett's here?" *So much for X-man's idea of staying home with the ankle bracelet.* This was not going as smoothly as he'd hoped.

"Patience, my friend," Suma replied. He still was not the least bit nervous.

They both looked around Exotic Beauties while they waited. Because it was early in the day, there was only a handful of dancers and only a handful of customers sitting around. Jacob saw Ana in the distance leaning over whispering in a customer's ear. They both got up and headed towards the stairs that lead to the couch rooms and hot tub rooms. Jacob wasn't jealous, and he knew for Ana, this was only business. Now if he'd ever seen Karina doing this, he'd want to punch the customer smack in the face.

About the same time as Karina came into Jacob's mind he looked over and there she was! His heart instantly ratcheted up to full speed. She looked so radiant; Jacob was over the moon to see she had come back to the United States.

He was enjoying looking at Karina in her all-white lingerie waitress outfit with the white gloves, when Ana appeared. She gave him a kiss on the cheek. She was pretending to be his girlfriend just like they'd discussed. Then she said, "I was missing you, Jacob. I'm glad you came to see me." Still putting on a tremendous act, Ana gave him a hug. Jacob was way too nervous to get excited and wanted to push her away, but he knew this would not help his cause. While they were embracing, she whispered in his ear, "How am I doing?"

"You're doing just fine." Jacob could barely speak. He felt anxious and sick. He could feel the vomit creeping back up into his throat. He reciprocated Ana's hug because he had to continue the act. As they held each other, he looked around the room and locked eyes with Karina. *Oh no,* he thought. *This can't be happening.*

He pushed Ana away and was about to walk towards Karina to explain, when enormous Brett appeared. His face was red with anger and he was already sweating. "You got a lot of balls coming in here!" Jacob took a couple of steps back then stopped when he realized he was trying to hide behind Suma. Brett was clenching his fist when he demanded, "What the hell do you want?"

Jacob was so nervous all he could say was, "I.. I.."

Seeing Jacob couldn't answer, Suma stepped in. "Hello Brett, I'm Suma. I have a business in Gulf Coast City as well, called Happy Suma's.

It's not as big as this one but--"

"Yeah, I know who you are, Suma." Brett was still annoyed.

Suma continued. "Brett, I was hoping we could sit down and talk about how we can all help each other."

"I'll give you two minutes and we stand right here." Brett obviously was not going to give them the satisfaction of going back to his office.

"Okay, Brett." Suma was still relaxed, while Jacob felt like he was about to have round two of his vomit fest. "I'll cut to the chase because I know you've probably got a lot to do today." Suma paused for a second just to subtly show Brett that he was not going to be intimidated. "Jacob and I obviously know that you're having some legal problems and we'd like to help you out." Suma stopped talking because he knew Brett wouldn't be able to stand the silence and would have to speak.

"Okay, I'm listening," Brett responded, then glared at Jacob as if to say, *I'm going to kick your ass later for bringing this Suma guy over here.*

"Brett and Camille, I'm sure you guys have a lot of legal expenses, so Jacob and I'd like to help out." Brett's face got redder and more sweat popped out onto his forehead. Jacob was sure he was going to punch Suma any second. But Suma continued. "And God forbid, if you have to go to prison, Jacob and I can help you continue a source of income."

More blood pumped into Brett's face until he exploded. "You get the hell out of my business, Suma!"

"As you wish," Suma replied calmly, and slowly turned to leave.

"Jacob, you get the hell out too and take your fuckin' new girlfriend with you!" Brett was really angry and started following after Jacob and Suma with his fists clenched.

Even though Jacob wanted to run out of Exotic Beauties, he kept the same pace as Suma. As he was walking out he saw Karina and realized she'd heard everything. This meant that now she was sure that Ana was his girlfriend. Suma and Jacob walked outside, then someone else rushed out the door behind them. At first, Jacob thought it was Brett coming out to fight in the parking lot, then he realized it was Ana. She had just been fired.

Tears were pouring out of her eyes and she started yelling. "What in the hell have I done? Why did I pretend to be your girlfriend?" Jacob was embarrassed, but Ana wasn't finished. "I just made the biggest mistake of my life! Jacob, you told me being your girlfriend would help me. You said you would be the new owner at Exotic Beauties and I'd get a manager job for the rest of my life. Do you remember you said that?" She was screaming and crying hysterically. Jacob knew he'd let her down as he looked away, unable to face her. Ana was obviously terrified now about how she was going to take care of her little girl. Since she was here illegally, she couldn't just walk up to any business in town and ask for another job. He tried to put his arms around Ana to comfort her, but she pulled away and ran off. The last thing she said before she got in her car was, "Don't follow me! I don't ever want to see you again!"

Suma looked at Jacob comfortingly and said, "Give her a little time to cool off and she'll be fine." They got in Jacob's car and headed back to Happy Suma's. Neither one said much to the other on the drive back because they both were embarrassed by how unsuccessful their visit to Exotic Beauties had been.

CHAPTER 34
GULF COAST EMPLOYMENT SOLUTIONS

"What is name of club?"
—Russian J1 Visa Student

For the next few weeks, Jacob barely left his townhouse. If he ate, which was seldom, he'd have a pizza delivered. If he wanted to move on with his life, the voices in his head would convince him to stay put. Inside the walls of his townhouse was the only place he felt safe from the outside world that was always planning its attack.

On the day he left Exotic Beauties with Suma, he was sure that he had put the final nail in the coffin of a potential relationship with Karina. Now it was almost a year since they'd first met. In that time, she'd witnessed Jacob's fiancée arrive. Then she saw the sexual text messages with Winston's wife. Then she saw Ana's public displays of affection that were good enough to convince her that she was his girlfriend. Karina must have thought he was the worst man alive. Now she was back at Exotic Beauties and Jacob couldn't get her out of his mind.

Ana was now unemployed and living off the money she'd saved as an exotic dancer. She continued to search for work but was always unsuccessful. He went over to see her occasionally. She was civil but he could tell she still blamed him for losing her job.

Jacob spent the rest of March sitting around his townhouse doing almost nothing. One day, his cell phone rang and it was the manager of the Sea Biscuit. This was one of the hotels that they had sent housekeepers to last season. The Sea Biscuit manager had heard Gulf Coast Jobs was out of business and wanted to know if Jacob knew where they could get hotel staff for the upcoming season. Even though he didn't have a clue what his future held, he told the Sea Biscuit manager that he was taking over. A few days later another former customer of Gulf Coast Jobs called Jacob. Then another and another. Jacob's cell phone number was still on the Rolodex of most of his customers, and they all wanted to do business with him again.

When Jacob met with Suma to get his advice, he said, *"Open your own employment agency. Why would you turn away business? Tell them you can do whatever they ask, then find a way to do it."*

Suma was right, Jacob thought. And this could be the firecracker that got him back out into the world. He went to see Ana and offered her Gabriela's old job. With her strong work ethic and Spanish knowledge, Jacob couldn't think of anyone better suited. After a little convincing and apologizing, Ana got on board and the two of them got to work. They hit it hard, getting things ready to open up again.

As luck would have it, the prior office location of Gulf Coast Jobs was still available. The landlord for the office, of course, was Hamid the Mustache. After Jacob promised Hamid he'd pay for the vandalism from his employees, the Mustache handed over the keys.

Jacob got the workers comp and required insurance and set up a relationship with a payroll company, lawyer, and an accountant. Ana even put some of her hard-earned cash into building some working capital for their new business. They cleaned the office up nicely, painted the walls and bought new office furniture. Ana and Jacob proudly hung a sign outside with the name of his new company. *GULF COAST EMPLOYMENT SOLUTIONS.*

Now it was April first and they were ready for business. Ana was sitting where Gabriela used to. Of course, the place looked a lot classier than it did before. And Ana looked a lot classier than Gabriela too. Ana traded in her exotic dancer outfits for elegant looking business suits, and she really fit the part.

On their first official day of business, the phone rang and it was the Sea Biscuit. They were looking for twenty extra staff for housekeeping and laundry to help them get through the busy season. Ana would be spending the rest of the day bringing in applicants to interview for the new jobs.

Since almost all the applicants were Hispanic, and Jacob didn't speak Spanish, he decided to head over to Happy Suma's for lunch. He told Ana he was leaving her in charge and promised to bring back some food. She didn't argue, happy to have the responsibility. After the high stress Brett and Camille used to put on her back, this job was a breeze.

Suma didn't know Jacob was coming over and was pleasantly surprised. "Come inside my humble little business. How've you been? Is your employment agency up and running now?"

"Funny you should ask Suma, because we got our first order for temp staff today. The Sea Biscuit wants twenty housekeeping and laundry staff," Jacob announced proudly.

"Wow, twenty housekeepers and twenty laundry staff? That's really great!"

"No Suma, ten housekeepers and ten laundry staff."

"Oh, twenty total… I see. Well, that is still great! And the spring break season hasn't really started yet."

Jacob's face now had a constant gleam. He and Ana were getting along great. The working arrangement they had was going well. Ana forgave Jacob for costing her the Exotic Beauties job, and now she was way more to him than just an office receptionist.

Jacob forced Karina as far out of his thoughts as he could. He knew it would be a long time before he lost his feelings for her, but as long as he kept busy he was sure he could slowly forget.

He asked Suma, "Do you ever regret that we never got to buy out Exotic

Beauties? I mean this would've been a great business venture. We could've helped the girls and been super successful at it too."

"Yes, I do," Suma replied as he rolled around the hand with the missing fingers. "I don't have many regrets in life. You know, maybe I didn't show it, but I was really excited about the possibility of squeezing Brett and Camille into selling us the business. Especially since Brett was so nasty with you. Yeah it would have been sweet--"

Jacob's cell phone rang and interrupted Suma. "Excuse me just a second, it's Ana." Jacob put his finger up and said, "Hi Ana." Suma got up to give Jacob some privacy and do a little work back in his kitchen.

"Hello, you won't believe who is here at Gulf Coast Employment Solutions."

Jacob could hear young ladies talking Russian in the background. "Russian students?"

"Students, yes. But you know these students. They're the Exotic Beauties girls from last year. They came back Jacob, and they want us to send them over to Exotic Beauties."

"How many are there?" Jacob asked, in a higher pitched voice than normal.

"Maybe twenty or twenty-five… I don't know."

"Why did they come to our office? Why didn't they go to Exotic Beauties directly?"

"I don't know. They said that they came here first the last time and we arranged everything for them, so they came here again."

"Okay, this is really good!" Jacob would have jumped up and touched the ceiling if he could. Instead he gave two thumbs up while he looked at himself in the reflection of the Happy Suma's window. "And how well do they get along with you Ana?"

"They get along with me great. They all love me. I was their floor manager remember? Why do you ask this?"

"Okay, don't let them leave! I'm coming over right now. Don't let them leave!" Jacob was so excited that he forgot to say goodbye to Suma.

He jumped into his car and began planning what he'd say to all these girls. He knew Brett and Camille wanted them and he had them. There had to be a way he could keep them away. He kept tossing around all kinds of different ideas in his head. When he pulled up to the parking lot outside Gulf Coast Employment Solutions, he had a plan in mind.

Jacob confidently walked through the door and said. "Hello, everyone. Welcome to Gulf Coast Employment Solutions." The room got quiet, and twenty plus sexy young Russians dressed to impress and smelling great, focused their attention on Jacob. "I have some good news for you all." The girls started to cheer then quickly got quiet to hear what he had to say. "I know everyone is here to make as much money as you can before you go back to Russia, right?"

The girls looked up at him and said, "Right!" as they flashed a flirty smile.

He looked over at Ana and saw her eyes bearing down on him. He knew he had to make this a great sales pitch. "I'm proud to announce to everyone that we have a much better gentlemen's club to send you to this year. The pay will be much more. There is a much better split with the tips and a higher pay ratio between the dancers and club owners. And you all can do your job without worrying about being mistreated."

Ana was squirming in her seat but the girls bought into it. They started clapping at the great news, so Jacob continued. "I want you ladies to all get down to the beach and stay there. Get really tan, then come back here two weeks from today and Ana and I will send you all over there."

One of the girls looked suspiciously at Jacob and asked with her strong Russian accent, "What is name of club?"

Jacob almost thought he'd gotten away without someone asking this question. "Come back in two weeks and I'll tell you." When he saw that they were all sufficiently satisfied, he motioned for everyone to leave.

The girls walked out the office smiling, then Ana asked, "What are we going to do in two weeks? We don't have another club to send these girls to." Jacob could tell Ana was worried. "These girls trust me Jacob. We can't deceive them."

Jacob stood confidently in front of Ana. For a split second, he felt like he had turned into Mustapha. "Don't worry. In a couple of weeks, we'll have a club for them."

"How will you do this?"

"Look Ana, I have twenty-five beautiful young Russian girls depending on me to find them employment. But the last thing I want to do is send them to Brett or any other club for that matter. I just don't want anyone to take advantage of them like they did you."

"You're still trying to get Exotic Beauties away from Brett and Camille, aren't you?" Ana gave Jacob a sly smile.

"I'll never tell," he responded and gave her a wink.

The spring break season was starting to pick up now and the rumors Jacob was hearing about Brett and Camille were good. They were having a lot of trouble finding girls to work for them now that they no longer had Jacob to help recruit. Most of their full-time girls had heard the stories about dancers being drugged, and were scared to work for him too.

Now was the time, he thought, to put the squeeze on Brett and Camille. His trial with Winston was coming up in a matter of weeks. Jacob was sure Brett wanted to get his business back on track before this all began. He got on the phone and called him.

When Brett answered Jacob's call he thought, *This is a good sign*, because he was sure he recognized his number on the caller I.D. "This is Brett."

"Brett this is Jacob, how ya doing?"

"Yeah Jacob, what do you want?" Brett didn't sound as enthusiastic as he used to when Ja would he would call.

"Brett, my offer to help you still stands."

"You mean your offer to blackmail me with your new girlfriend still stands," Brett snarled down the phone.

"Well I wouldn't call it blackmail, Brett, but if Ana testifies in your favor, I think you would owe me some gratitude, wouldn't you?"

"Ya know, you're just lucky that you're not standing here in front of me, 'cause I'd punch you right in your mouth!"

Jacob bit his lip and couldn't believe Brett wasn't at least a little curious to see what he had to say. He didn't bark back. "Well, I'm sorry you feel like that Brett. I'll just tell Ana to speak from her heart when the prosecutor wants to know what you got up to at your club."

Brett slammed down the phone. Jacob could tell he was livid and his pride was not going to allow him to try to work something out. So he forgot about Exotic Beauties for the next few weeks and focused on the staff at Gulf Coast Employment Solutions. Ana and Jacob were engulfed with helping their customers. Now they had contracts with hotels, golf courses and landscaping companies up and down Gulf Coast City.

Whenever the Russian girls would come back inquiring about their new exotic dancer jobs, Jacob would tell them they were still too pale. *"Go back to the beach and try to get a little darker. Then come see me in a week or two."* Some of the girls went back to the beach, and some found jobs on their own.

Ana and Jacob kept their heads down and focused on building the new business until the trial of Winston, Brett, and Winston's cousin DeAndre rolled around. And when that day finally arrived, they had to put things on hold.

CHAPTER 35
THE TRIAL (Day One)

"We have a young policeman, who isn't married, volunteering to spend his free time at a gentlemen's club."
—Attorney Dennis Candy

The bailiff asked everyone to rise for the judge, then be seated. In walked Corporal Hunter shortly after, looking very well dressed. He had on his police uniform and appeared as if he'd stayed up all night polishing his badge and ironing his shirt and trousers.

"Do you swear to tell the truth, the whole truth and nothing but the truth, so help you God?" The bailiff asked.

"I do," Corporal Hunter responded with confidence.

The courthouse was erected in the 1800s and hadn't changed much since. The inside had wooden creaky floors and nicely polished solid oak chairs. The large room was very pleasing to the eye, and a joy to experience if you were an American history buff. Winston wasn't thinking about any of this because he was on trial for felony human trafficking for commercial activity in the first degree. Just days before the trial was to begin, Jacob had been notified that all charges of attempted murder had been dropped against Winston. The reason - mishandling of evidence, specifically Lynn's cell phone. It appeared that Winston was going to slip through the cracks once again. Brett was also on trial for felony human trafficking for commercial activity in the first degree. And Winston's cousin DeAndre Brown was on trial for felony possession of an illegal controlled substance.

The prosecutor's name was Harold Potsuk, a slick looking well-dressed, older gentleman from North Florida. He boasted confidence as he walked around the courtroom in his dark navy pin-striped suit and nicely polished shoes. He'd been putting criminals away for a long time and now his hair was completely grey. But he still seemed to have a lot of class and perfect suntan to match. Jacob thought about two things as he waited for the trial to begin. *How did Mr. Potsuk maintain such a great tan if he worked indoors all day and how great was it that he may finally get satisfaction against Brett and Winston?*

The nameplate on the judge's desk said Stump, but the name didn't fit the man. He was by no means sturdy like a tree stump. He looked more suited for the 65 and older communities of North Florida than the judge of a major felony trial. In fact, he looked like he'd be one of their senior members. This probably explained why such a messy trial was about to take place.

Jacob quickly looked over and saw Brett fidgeting in his seat. Then he looked around the gallery and spotted Camille. She looked even worse than Brett. He noticed her hands shaking, then she slid them under her legs as if hoping this would help. Jacob almost felt sorry for Brett and Camille, but he quickly remembered how they'd made the threats for beating up Ana. He remembered how Camille, who liked to act innocent, yelled at him and said, *"What kind of a man hits a woman?"* She knew that it wasn't Jacob who hit Ana, yet she still had no problem making him suffer.

"You may proceed," Judge Stump announced.

"Thank you, Ya Honor," replied Mr. Potsuk as he approached Corporal Hunter. "How are you doing today Corporal?"

"Fine, sir."

"That's good..." Mr. Potsuk looked at his notes, straightened his reading glasses, then said. "'Cause I'd been checking in with you from time to time over the past year, and boy did you look tired."

"Yes sir," responded Corporal Hunter.

Mr. Potsuk continued to look down at his notes. "May I ask why you looked so tired?"

"Yes sir." Everyone, the jury included, looked at Corporal Hunter's proud expression. "From March 1995 to October 1995, I logged between seventy and eighty hours a week on patrol."

"Seventy and eighty hours a week, wow. Now everyone's probably wondering why a police officer would work so many hours, so Corporal Hunter can you tell us all the reason?" Mr. Potsuk paraded around the courtroom as if he was anxiously waiting for Corporal Hunter's reply.

Corporal Hunter tried to look calm and cool, but Jacob could tell he was eating up the compliments. "Because I volunteered to do some undercover work in addition to my uniform patrol duties."

Mr. Potsuk pointed over to Police Chief Joe White and said, "He volunteered to do some detective work and Police Chief Joe White gave him permission. Isn't that right Chief?"

Judge Stump banged on his gavel and said, "Please don't address members of the gallery, Mr. Potsuk. Also, can you pick things up a little here."

"Yes, Ya Honor," Mr. Potsuk responded. "Corporal Hunter, can you briefly describe your detective duties from the time period of March 1995 to October 1995?"

"Yes, sir." Corporal Hunter sat up in his chair and Jacob could tell he was about to lay out a line of bullshit. "During the early part of this year, I had several meetings with Police Chief Joe White and other members of Gulf Coast City law enforcement. We mapped out a plan to do surveillance on the defendant, Mr. Winston Brown, due to a highly-suspected increase in his drug activity and violent crime."

"Let me stop you there, Corporal Hunter," Mr. Potsuk interrupted. "So we can comply with the court's request to speed this up a little, let me ask you this. Where or what location did this surveillance always lead you to?"

"Exotic Beauties, sir."

"Objection!" Defense attorney Dennis Candy responded. Everyone stopped what they were doing or thinking to look at him. He was wearing a navy-blue blazer, khaki pants, and Docksides leather shoes. He was casual and barely presentable in the courtroom. What killed it for him was the white socks, a huge fashion mistake when you wear brown leather shoes.

"Judge, why is the prosecutor trying to bring Exotic Beauties into all this?" Judge Stump checked his watch, then looked down at Attorney Candy. He turned up his nose when he noticed Mr. Candy wearing the same casual attire that he was known for. "Just because a suspected criminal happens to go into Exotic Beauties doesn't mean you have to slander this business in a court of law. Did Mr. Brown go into Walmart during this time period? Did he go into McDonald's? Maybe you should tell the court about this?"

Judge Stump banged on his gavel and said, "Okay that's enough Mr. Candy. We get your point."

Mr. Potsuk smiled and said, "Nice of you to join us Mr. Candy."

"Mr. Candy, I won't allow you to go on a tangent with your objections," barked Judge Stump. "Just object, then state the reason. I won't listen to a long presentation from you."

"No, no the defense attorney is right," Mr. Potsuk said. "Why did Corporal Hunter spend so much time at Exotic Beauties? I tell you what, I have the log sheets right here, so why don't we take a look." Mr. Potsuk thumbed through some papers pretending like he was searching for the answer. "Aha!" he yelled out as if he'd just solved the whole case. "I think I know why Corporal Hunter brought up Exotic Beauties now. In fact, I *know* why Corporal Hunter brought up Exotic Beauties." Once again, came another dramatic pause trying to build the suspense. "Every single day and every single night Corporal Hunter was at Exotic Beauties, with the exception of only a handful of days, Mr. Brown was there too."

Mr. Potsuk looked at Corporal Hunter and asked, "Can you tell me, sir, what sort of activity you witnessed Mr. Brown engage in? I don't care if it seemed illegal or legal. Just kinda give the members of the jury a feel for what Mr. Brown was up to when he visited Exotic Beauties all those days and nights for seven months."

"Yes sir," Corporal Hunter responded, clearing his throat. "From the dates you mentioned earlier, I engaged in hidden surveillance of Exotic Beauties. I observed many days of suspicious activity during non-business hours that involved Mr. Winston Brown, and Mr. DeAndre Brown entering and leaving the business--"

"Let me stop you there, Corporal Hunter," Mr. Potsuk interrupted. "Did you say during non-business hours?"

"Yes, sir."

"Okay, let's go back a little here. And just to make sure we're all on the same page with the jury, let me ask you this, Corporal Hunter. What type of business is Exotic Beauties?"

Judge Stump interjected, "Mr. Potsuk, do I have to warn you about dragging things out again? Everyone here knows what type of business Exotic Beauties is. This isn't the only trial in Gulf Coast City, you know."

"Yes, Ya Honor." He took his time just to show the jury that Judge Stump had not intimidated him.

Corporal Hunter asked, "Do you still want me to answer the question?"

Mr. Potsuk paraded around, then looked at the jury and said, "If you wouldn't mind, sir."

"Exotic Beauties is a gentlemen's club."

"Thank you, Corporal Hunter." Mr. Potsuk acted as if no-one in the courtroom had previously known that. "Now, let me ask you this. After surveilling Exotic Beauties for over seven months, do you think you can tell us what sort of business hours a gentlemen's club like Exotic Beauties would keep?"

"Yes, sir. Exotic Beauties usually opens at 12 pm but doesn't really get busy until 8 pm, and it closes around 3 am."

"Okay good, thank you Corporal Hunter. Now, if this is a gentlemen's club, I assume the gentlemen go there to observe the ladies. Do they not?"

Dennis Candy jumped up and yelled, "Does the city pay this guy by the hour or what?"

Judge Stump banged on his gavel. "That's enough Attorney Candy."

But Mr. Candy wasn't finished. "Can we get past this? Everyone in this room knows that men go to gentlemen's clubs to look at ladies, do they not?"

Judge Stump looked at Attorney Candy again and said, "I feel your concern, Mr. Candy, and I'm trying to push the prosecution along too. So settle down and let me do my job."

Mr. Potsuk continued, totally unfazed by the interruption. "So Corporal Hunter, did you observe any female staff at Exotic Beauties during non-business hours?"

"Very rarely, sir."

"Okay, let's see what we have so far, shall we Corporal Hunter?" Before Corporal Hunter could say *Okay*, Mr. Potsuk continued. "Exotic Beauties is a gentlemen's club. The gentlemen who go in there go for the explicit reason to see ladies, am I right?" Once again Mr. Potsuk didn't wait for Corporal Hunter's answer. "Now, you observed Mr. Winston Brown going in and out of Exotic Beauties mostly during non-business hours, correct?"

"Yes, sir."

"So what was he doing there during these times?"

"Well, sir--"

Mr. Potsuk interrupted Corporal Hunter. "Don't answer that just yet, Corporal. We've established that no ladies were in Exotic Beauties during non-business hours; yet you just said Mr. Brown was in there during non-business hours." The courtroom gallery began to chatter, so Judge Stump did a light tap with his gavel. Mr. Potsuk put his hands in the air to celebrate as if he just blown the case wide open and said, "Now, if Mr. Brown was going to Exotic Beauties to see the ladies then I'd say why didn't he go there during business hours? Mr. Candy thinks I'm picking on Mr. Brown and wants me to ask, why did he go to Walmart or why did he go to McDonald's?" Mr. Potsuk gave another dramatic pause. Jacob had lost count of how many this was by now. "My answer to Mr. Candy is, I would ask what Mr. Brown was doing at Walmart or McDonald's if he spent many hours in there when they were closed." The gallery began to chatter, and it looked like Mr. Potsuk had won the first round of the battle he was having with Attorney Dennis Candy.

As Mr. Potsuk paraded around the courtroom as if he was seeking applause, Judge Stump asked, "Is the prosecution finished with the witness?"

Mr. Potsuk stopped and walked back towards Corporal Hunter. "Just a few more questions, Ya Honor."

Judge Stump said, with a bored look on his face, "Okay, but let's keep the theatrics to a minimum."

"Yes, Ya Honor." Mr. Potsuk looked at Corporal Hunter and asked, "Corporal Hunter, I'm sure the members of the jury would like to know why Mr. Brown was at Exotic Beauties when there wasn't an exotic beauty in sight."

This was Corporal Hunter's cue to present the results of his investigation. He sat up even straighter than he already was. He gave his bicep a little flex, cleared his throat then said, "Well sir, after logging hundreds of hours of surveillance on Exotic Beauties, we found several key correlations. One was, as you already pointed out, Winston Brown spends a lot of time at this place of business during non-business hours. Another similarity is whenever we see Winston Brown enter or exit the business, DeAndre Brown is not far away."

Mr. Potsuk interrupted, "Okay, now this is getting interesting. Winston Brown has a long rap sheet of arrests that we'll be getting to later. But the only person I can think of in Gulf Coast City who has a *longer* rap sheet is his cousin DeAndre." Winston's cousin DeAndre sat next to Winston with a proud expression on his face.

Mr. Potsuk glanced at the judge to see if he had offended him, then focused back on Corporal Hunter, and nodded for him to continue. Jacob was sure that the two of them had probably rehearsed these questions quite a few times before they came into court today. Corporal Hunter continued, "That's right, and if you look at some of the surveillance photographs you'll see Winston sneaking packages under his arms into the Exotic Beauties rear entrance."

"Objection!" Attorney Candy obviously heard someone say something bad about Brett's business, so he spoke up. "Sneaking something in, Your Honor? This is the opinion of this police officer is it not? Winston could be delivering food or office supplies. So why is the witness accusing him of sneaking?"

Judge Stump looked in the direction of the jury and said, "The jury should disregard the witness's last statement because this is just the opinion of the police officer." Then Judge Stump looked at Attorney Candy as if to say, *Are you happy now?*

"May I continue?" Mr. Potsuk asked.

"Please do," Judge Stump said sarcastically.

"Okay, Corporal Hunter, let's explore this a little. Attorney Candy says that Winston may have been delivering food or office supplies. Now, did this ever dawn on you that maybe this is what he was sneaking... sorry, delivering under his arms?"

"Yes sir, it did."

"So did you follow up on this?"

"Yes sir, I did."

"Corporal Hunter, please tell the court what you did just to check and see if Winston was maybe delivering food or what was it again? Oh, yeah, office supplies into Exotic Beauties." Mr. Potsuk smirked at Attorney Candy and Attorney Candy glared back.

Corporal Hunter proceeded, "Well sir, I was never able to get a search warrant on DeAndre, so I couldn't just enter his vehicle to search for contraband."

Mr. Potsuk nodded his head and said, "Sure I understand. So what did you do?"

"Well sir, earlier in the day I was interviewing Winston's wife, Lynn, with Chief Joe White and Officer Paula Schmitt. At the conclusion of the interview, Lynn failed to retrieve her cell phone, so I had it in my possession. My patrol route went past Exotic Beauties, so I decided I'd look for Winston since he's always there."

"You're right about that," Mr. Potsuk chimed in.

"I figured I could give Lynn's cell phone to Winston and possibly get him to engage in some non-intrusive conversation with me." Corporal Hunter paused to look around and scratch his scalp after he told his lie. "And as a result, I'd try to question Winston about why he's in Exotic

Beauties at this time. This is what we call field interviewing, and it's pretty much standard procedure for all police departments." Corporal Hunter let out a nervous cough. "So when I pulled into the parking lot of Exotic Beauties, I observed DeAndre sitting in his car. I decided I'd ask him if he knew where I could find Winston."

"Okay, sure. Sounds all pretty routine, right?" Mr. Potsuk looked at the jury to see if they were on board. "What happened next?"

"As I approached DeAndre's car on foot, he started the engine. I was a little concerned to see this so I told DeAndre, *Hey I just wanna talk here*. When I got about twenty feet from his vehicle he drove towards me at a high rate of speed. I jumped out of the way and in the process dropped Winton's wife's cell phone onto the ground." Corporal Hunter looked up to see if anyone was contesting his statement.

"Okay, now we are getting somewhere." Mr. Potsuk was trying to keep the story as exciting as he could, so he could keep the jury interested while annoying Attorney Candy at the same time.

"Yes, sir," Corporal Hunter responded as Mr. Potsuk motioned for more. "I got into my patrol car and engaged in pursuit of Mr. Brown for about four blocks before he crashed his vehicle into a street light."

Mr. Potsuk put his hand over his heart and pretended to be shocked. "Oh my! Well, this is not good. Then what happened?"

"I called for backup and approached DeAndre Brown's vehicle on foot. When I was a couple of feet away, I smelled a strong marijuana odor. This of course, gave me probable cause to search his vehicle after I made the arrest."

"Okay Corporal Hunter, very good. Now did you find anything inside the car that might be of interest to the jury and Attorney Candy?"

Judge Stump looked down at Mr. Potsuk, covered his microphone and said, "Watch yourself, Mr. Potsuk."

Mr. Potsuk put his hands up in the air and said, "Ya Honor, don't cut me off now, we're finally getting to the good part."

Judge Stump's veins in his forehead started to pop out. He said, "I'm not stopping your questions, but I will tell you this Mr. Potsuk, if you continue these little underhanded jabs at Attorney Candy, I will shut you down. You hear me?"

"Yes, Ya Honor."

"Okay, please proceed with some professionalism from now on."

"Yes, Ya Honor." Mr. Potsuk turned his attention back to Corporal Hunter and asked, "Please tell the jury what you found inside DeAndre Brown's car."

Corporal Hunter looked at the jury proudly and announced, "We found a couple of baggies containing controlled substances and other contraband." DeAndre's proud expression was gone and his jaw dropped.

"Okay, controlled substances and other contraband, you say?" Mr. Potsuk asked, acting as if this was the first time he'd heard this. "Can you tell the members of the jury what type of controlled substances and contraband you found in these baggies?"

"Yes, sir. The contents of the baggies were later identified in the lab as containing Lysergic Acid Diethylamide, Rohypnol, and Percocet."

"Okay great! Now, Corporal Hunter, would you mind explaining what these drugs are, and what they do? Maybe if you give us the street name, we'll be more familiar with them."

"Sure," Corporal Hunter replied with confidence. "Lysergic Acid Diethylamide is LSD. Some people call it acid. Rohypnol is known as the date rape drug. Some people like to call them Roofies. And Percocet is a strong pain med that can only be obtained legally by a doctor's prescription."

Mr. Potsuk walked up to the jury and said, "Okay well, then, Mr. DeAndre Brown is done here right? I mean there's no getting out of this." DeAndre looked as if he wanted to put his head on the table in front of him, but he kept his face an unemotional blank just as Dennis Candy had instructed him to do. Mr. Potsuk continued. "What I don't understand is, why did DeAndre plead not guilty? I'm sure we have the evidence to back all this up. Am I correct in assuming this Corporal?"

"Yes, you are sir. We have pictures of the accident scene where DeAndre's vehicle hit the street light and we have photographs of the baggies at the crime scene as well as back at the police lab."

"Okay thank you, Corporal. Great work here." Mr. Potsuk did his victory parade around the courtroom then stopped and said, "You know what, I bet the jury would love to see these pictures don't you think?"

Corporal Hunter didn't answer but Mr. Potsuk went back to his table and put down his notepad. "Permission to approach the bench judge."

Judge Stump, looking uninterested and probably hoping it was getting close to lunch, grunted, "Permission granted."

Mr. Potsuk walked up to Judge Stump and said, "I'd like to enter into evidence exhibits 1 through 8."

"Permission granted," Judge Stump replied, then instructed the bailiff to hand Mr. Potsuk the photographs.

"Thank you judge," Mr. Potsuk replied. "Members of the jury, I'd to ask you all to take a look at the pictures I have here of DeAndre Brown's vehicle as well as the illegal narcotics the Gulf Coast City police department recovered from inside his car." He walked over and handed the pictures to one of the jury members and motioned for him to pass them around. "Members of the jury, after you've looked at the pictures of the wrecked car that we know belongs to Mr. DeAndre Brown, and you've seen the pictures of these baggies that contain very dangerous drugs that are pictured inside DeAndre Brown's car, I want you to answer the question that's been buggin' me for a long time. Why in the heck is Mr. DeAndre Brown pleading not guilty? Does he think the jury is blind? Does he think the jury is stupid?"

"Objection!" Attorney Candy yelled out. It was obvious that Mr. Potsuk had hit a nerve, or Attorney Candy felt like Mr. Potsuk was going to hurt Brett-- the only client that was paying him. "How on earth can the prosecution know what my client thinks?"

"Sustained," announced the judge. "Mr. Potsuk, once again I'm going to instruct you to keep these proceedings professional. You've been doing this a long time and I know you know the rules here."

"Yes, Ya honor," Mr. Potsuk replied, unfazed. "Members of the jury, please look at the photographs and determine if it looks like this shows sufficient evidence that the defendant did in fact fail to stop for a marked police car, and was in fact in possession of large quantities of illegal controlled substances. And if you do see what everyone else at the Gulf Coast City Police Department sees, and find the defendant guilty, I can save you a lot of time and get you all back to your family and friends a lot sooner."

"Objection!" Attorney Candy screamed. "Judge, I'm sure there's a law against the prosecution blackmailing the jury."

"What are you talking about, Attorney Candy?" Judge Stump asked.

"What the prosecution is saying here is if you find the defendant guilty you can all go home to your family and friends, but if you don't, I will make you stay longer and torture you some more."

"He has a point there, Mr. Potsuk," replied the judge.

"Ya Honor, I'm just trying to state the obvious here about DeAndre Brown. If you ask me he's just wasting the court's time."

The judge grumbled something under his breath. "That's for the jury to decide, sir. What do you say we get moving here. The jury can answer your question about innocence and guilt after they've seen all the evidence that's presented to them."

Mr. Potsuk played some more with his cuffs, refusing to make eye contact with the judge. "Yes, Ya Honor. That's a good idea too, Ya Honor. Why don't we go back to Winston's wife Lynn's cellphone?" Jacob looked over and saw Winston staring at him like he wanted to run over and sock him in the mouth. Jacob was sure that he still thought he'd had sex with his wife. Mr. Potsuk continued. "Corporal Hunter, let me ask you one more question before I let you get back to work. What ever happened to that cell phone after you dropped it in the Exotic Beauties parking lot?"

Corporal Hunter replied, "Sir, I believe it was retrieved by one of the employees at Exotic Beauties." Then he nervously scratched his scalp once again, hoping no one would challenge him on this.

"Really? Okay, that makes sense. Was this one of the employees coming into work who happened to see it on the way in from the parking lot?"

"Yes sir. This appears to be the case."

"Okay," said Mr. Potsuk. "Do you have a name for this employee?"

"No sir, I don't."

Mr. Potsuk snuck a quick glance at Attorney Candy then remarked, "Okay, it doesn't really matter anyway. Corporal Hunter, thank you for taking your time today to speak with the court."

"Your witness, Attorney Candy," announced the judge, showing no interest.

"Thank you, Your Honor." Attorney Candy was licking his lips at the chance to discredit Corporal Hunter. Part of Jacob was actually pulling for Attorney Candy to embarrass Corporal Hunter and make him squirm.

"Thank you for coming in today Corporal Hunter. I won't take too much of your time. I know you have to get back to working eighty hours a week," Attorney Candy said sarcastically. "I just have a few questions okay?"

Corporal Hunter sat like a stone. "That's fine," he replied.

"Okay great, let me ask you a little bit about your surveillance of Exotic Beauties from March 1995 to October 1995. For eight months, you targeted Exotic Beauties and for eight months you spent taxpayers' money staking out this local business in Gulf Coast City. As we heard from the prosecution, you volunteered to spend your spare time prancing around this gentlemen's club." Jacob was enjoying watching Corporal Hunter squirm. "Now let me ask you this Corporal, when you were inside Exotic Beauties doing your surveillance, were you in uniform or plain clothes?"

"Mostly plain clothes, sir," Corporal Hunter answered the question, without showing that he was a little embarrassed.

"Okay, and what sort of surveillance did you do inside Exotic Beauties with all these beautiful half-naked women walking around?" The court gallery gave a little bit of a chuckle because they'd caught on to what Attorney Candy was insinuating.

Corporal Hunter gave a great response, Jacob thought. "I'm not allowed to discuss the details of my surveillance, sir."

Attorney Candy chuckled. "Of course you're not." Attorney Candy looked at some of the men in the jury and smiled. "You know, I'd probably tell my wife the same thing if she asked me why I was at a gentlemen's club every night of the week." The gallery laughed, Corporal Hunter sat there on display, trying to remain unemotional. "Of course, you can't tell me this during the investigation but now we're at the trial, Corporal Hunter. This means under oath you must answer all my questions whether you like it or not." Attorney Candy gave him a stern look, then continued, "Of the entire eight months that you were inside Exotic Beauties, not outside but inside. I'm sure every business has problems with illegal activity happening outside their business and they can't be expected to keep an eye out for this, but inside is different, of course. So inside Exotic Beauties, did you see Brett Olson engage in any illegal activity?"

Corporal Hunter showed a hint of irritation when he responded, "Well, if you read my report you woulda seen that I discovered a large amount of drugs inside Brett's place of business. And the lab identified these drugs as being from the same stash as what we found inside Mr. DeAndre Brown's vehicle at the time of his arrest when he fled from the Exotic Beauties parking lot--"

"You're not answering my question, Corporal." Attorney Candy was talking down to Corporal Hunter even more that Suma did, and Jacob was enjoying it. "I asked you if during all your surveillance inside Exotic Beauties for eight months did you ever see Brett, and I mean actually see Brett with your own eyes, engage in any illegal activity?"

"Not exactly, sir," Corporal Hunter replied.

"That's all I have, judge," Attorney Candy announced in victory

"You may step down, Corporal Hunter," ordered the judge. "And I don't think we'll be needing you anymore today so you can get back to work whenever you'd like."

"Thank you judge," Corporal Hunter replied as he got up to walk out.

While Corporal Hunter was leaving the witness stand, Attorney Candy began a tirade against him. "Well, I don't know what to make of this, ladies and gentlemen of the jury. We have a young policeman, who isn't married, volunteering to spend his free time at a gentlemen's club." The gallery laughed. "I tell ya, maybe I shoulda been a policeman when I was younger. Sounds like a great job, huh?" Attorney Candy looked at the male jury members and winked. "All this on the taxpayers' dime. No wonder this city is going broke." The gallery started to chatter again, so Judge Stump pounded his gavel. Attorney Candy continued without waiting for them to quiet down. "I mean eight months of surveillance and he never once saw my client engage in any illegal activity. Judge, I move to have the case against Brett Olson dismissed. I mean, the prosecution has got absolutely nothing on him, but they're still willing to discredit an honorable business owner in our city."

"Objection, Ya Honor!" Mr. Potsuk had had enough of the slandering Attorney Candy was throwing at Corporal Hunter. "What kind of malarkey is the defense trying to pull here? Is he presenting his closing argument already? Because if he is that'll be just fine with the prosecution."

Judge Stump jumped in. "I think you've said enough, don't you Mr. Candy?"

"Yes, Your Honor." Attorney Candy knew the judge wouldn't let him continue and he was sure he'd inflicted plenty of damage already.

Mr. Potsuk interrupted, "Ya Honor, may I remind Attorney Candy that he has two other clients with him today? He seems to keep forgetting this, and these two clients are interwoven into a series of criminal activity that I have not even begun to scratch the surface of."

"Duly noted, Mr. Potsuk," Judge Stump said. "And no, Attorney Candy, I'm not going to dismiss the case against Mr. Olson." *But thanks for wasting my time,* the judge wanted to say.

"I have nothing further then," Attorney Candy replied.

"Okay good," the judge said. "Why don't we adjourn until tomorrow morning at 8 am. How does that sound attorneys?" The judge got up and left the courtroom without listening to Mr. Potsuk and Attorney Candy's responses.

CHAPTER 36
THE TRIAL (Day Two)

"And even the defense, who argues with everything I say no matter how small, is not refuting Corporal Hunter's statement."
—Harold Potsuk

Day two in court began with one very noticeable difference. Winston's cousin DeAndre Brown was no longer sitting at the defendants table with Attorney Candy, Brett and Winston. Mr. Potsuk had gotten to him and he was now pleading *guilty* to a lesser charge. Mr. Potsuk met with DeAndre and Attorney Candy yesterday, behind closed doors. When Mr. Potsuk showed DeAndre all the drug evidence he had on him, DeAndre knew he didn't stand a chance. Attorney Candy had already demonstrated he wasn't going to break his back defending him. Brett appeared to be Attorney Candy's only concern, and he was willing to lose the case against DeAndre in order to focus more on his paying client.

"Do you swear to tell the truth, the whole truth, and nothing but the truth, so help you God?" asked the bailiff.

"I do," answered DeAndre Brown as he sat on the cold wooden chair in the witness stand. If his cousin Winston was built like a running back, DeAndre was a linebacker. The Brown family had all shown a talent for football. Drugs had ended DeAndre's career, just like Winston's. The only difference was DeAndre began hitting the glass pipe at thirteen, so he never even made it to high school. Growing up around the everyday party life in Gulf Coast City had proved to be too much temptation for him, and today he was paying the price.

"Your witness," the judge said to Mr. Potsuk.

"Thank you, Ya Honor," Mr. Potsuk said as he walked towards DeAndre as if he was a tiger wearing a pinstripe suit, circling his prey. "DeAndre Brown, I have a few questions for you if that's okay, sir."

"Yeah," DeAndre replied. Dressed in his flashy street clothes, he looked very relaxed today. He appeared more comfortable than yesterday when Attorney Candy had forced him to wear a jacket and tie. DeAndre now knew what his future held. Yesterday he was looking at ten years in prison for felony possession of large quantities of an illegal controlled substance. Today, he was pretty sure that he was only looking at three years for misdemeanor possession. Mr. Potsuk had already told him he'd be out in a little over a year with good behavior. What Mr. Potsuk wanted, and needed, was someone to testify against Brett and Winston. And DeAndre had agreed to do it for a lesser sentence.

Mr. Potsuk looked down at his notes then back at DeAndre. "Okay, so DeAndre you are Winston Brown's cousin. Is this correct?"

DeAndre glanced over at Winston then gave another disrespectful, "Yeah." Winston was gritting his teeth and clenching his fists. His eyes were red, Jacob had seen this look before. His thoughts quickly went back to the night Winston had broken into his townhouse the second time with so much anger in his heart.

"Okay, good. And Brett Olson, what is his relationship to you?"

"Relationship?" DeAndre asked.

"Yes," replied Mr. Potsuk. "How do you know Brett?"

"He's just a dude, ya know." Brett was sitting next to Attorney Candy, stone-faced, dressed in a grey suit and yellow tie.

"No, I don't know," Mr. Potsuk snapped back and tensed his forehead. "DeAndre, this court doesn't have all day to play games with you. If this is your intention, I don't think Judge Stump is gonna look favorably on this. Now, I'm sure you understand the question. So I'm gonna need you to answer it."

DeAndre's thoughts of coasting through Mr. Potsuk's questions were quickly coming to an end. "Okay, man. He's a dude who buys drugs from me."

"Objection!" Attorney Candy couldn't say this, but this was not part of the deal he'd made with Mr. Potsuk. The unwritten agreement was DeAndre could say whatever he wanted about Winston but he had to leave Brett out. "I think Mr. Potsuk should ask DeAndre if he ever actually directly sold illegal drugs to my client."

"Which client, Mr. Candy?" Mr. Potsuk asked with a smirk. "You have three... or did you forget?"

"That's enough," Judge Stump jumped in. "You two are starting your scrapping early today and I'm not going to play referee. Mr. Potsuk, if you'd be so kind to answer the defense attorney's question, I think we can speed things along."

"What was the question, Ya Honor?" Mr. Potsuk asked as he leered over at Attorney Candy.

"Mr. Candy, please ask the question again," ordered the annoyed judge.

Attorney Candy arrogantly replied, "You need to ask DeAndre if he directly sold illegal drugs to Mr. Olson."

"That doesn't sound like a question to me, Mr. Candy. It sounds more like a command, and I don't remember being instructed by the court to take orders from you."

The judge interjected. "Look gentlemen, I've warned you both way too often about these petty little jabs you throw at each other. If you two want to argue this case somewhere else in an unprofessional manner, that's fine with me. If you both want to put on the gloves and box in the parking lot, that's fine with me too. But in my courtroom, you will both abide by my rules and you will do it without me having to scold you both." The judge paused to rub his arthritic hands. He scribbled something on his notepad, then looked up from his reading glasses and said, "I'm going to fine you

$500 each on contempt of court charges. I'd like this paid by the end of the day in the clerk of courts office. I know you both know where this is."

"Yes, Judge," both Mr. Potsuk and Attorney Candy replied, like two boys who'd been caught misbehaving by their teacher.

"Now, will you please answer the defense's question Mr. Potsuk, and don't try to dance around it." The judge gave Mr. Potsuk a stern look.

Mr. Potsuk played with his cuff links as he considered making a condescending comment. He knew he couldn't, so he finally did as he was told. "DeAndre, did you ever sell, or did you ever see anyone selling, illegal substances to Brett Olson?"

"Naw," DeAndre answered disrespectfully. He'd been sitting patiently waiting for the two attorneys to finish their childish quarrel.

"Is that a no?" Mr. Potsuk asked.

"Yeah, that's a no."

"Did you ever know of anyone selling illegal substances to Brett Olson? And before you answer DeAndre, remember you're under oath and your answers here will certainly affect your sentencing."

DeAndre slouched down in his chair, looking cool on the outside but Jacob suspected, judging by the fear that flashed over his features, that on the inside he was beginning to panic. He knew he was all alone in this and didn't have Attorney Candy to rely on. So he replied, "Yeah, I know some shi.. stuff."

"Okay, good. What kind of stuff do you know?" Mr. Potsuk gave DeAndre a stare as if to say, *This answer will affect your sentencing also.*

"Some stuff, you know."

"Mr. Brown, please don't make me come down on you every time I have to ask a question. Now, the judge knows you have plea bargained a lesser sentence and he is fine with this. But let me remind you that the judge has only agreed to a lesser sentence contingent on receiving your full cooperation in this trial."

DeAndre scrunched his forehead, wondering what contingent meant, but Mr. Potsuk had already explained to him yesterday that if the judge didn't feel like he was cooperating, he could easily recommend that he receive the full ten-year sentence. "Okay, what do you wanna know man?"

"I'll repeat the question." Mr. Potsuk snapped back. "What sort of drug activity do you know about that involves Brett Olson, and for that matter, Winston Brown?"

"Brett used to buy some shit from Winston, yo." The court gallery began to chatter, and Mr. Potsuk paraded around like he loved doing when things went his way.

Mr. Potsuk smiled at DeAndre. Then he dropped his grin and said, "Information is what we need from you, DeAndre. That's all, and your plea agreement stems on the quality of what you provide us. Do you understand this?" This wasn't entirely true. DeAndre's plea agreement had already been approved by the judge, but Mr. Potsuk certainly wasn't going to tell him this. Attorney Candy only appeared to be looking out for Brett so he didn't seem inclined to help with this either. The only way DeAndre could go back to his original sentence would be if he was found in contempt of court for misbehaving or for being totally uncooperative.

"Yeah," DeAndre disrespectfully replied with his eyes on the floor as he kicked around an imaginary beer can between his feet.

"Okay, good," Mr. Potsuk said. "Let me take you back to the day when you were arrested for having all those pain pills, Roofies, and acid sheets in your car. When you first saw Corporal Hunter and you took off in your car, where were you?"

"Exotic Beauties."

"Okay, good. Now what were you doing in Exotic Beauties?"

"Objection!" Attorney Candy heard Exotic Beauties and immediately leaped out of his chair. "Mr. Potsuk is trying to infer that my client was actually inside Exotic Beauties, and of course he was *not*."

Mr. Potsuk shook his head because Attorney Candy was beginning to wear him down. "I'll rephrase the question, Ya Honor. Where was your car parked when you saw Corporal Hunter and decided to drive away from him?"

"Exotic Beauties, yo."

"Okay, thank you DeAndre. And where was Winston at this time?"

"Exotic Beauties."

"And where was Brett?"

"Exotic Beauties."

"Okay, so I'm starting to see a pattern here. Is anyone else?" Mr. Potsuk looked at the jury as if he wanted an answer, but they all gazed back in silence. "The pattern here is this. DeAndre keeps the drugs inside his car. Winston goes inside and makes the deal with Brett. Then Winston comes out to the car and picks up the drugs from DeAndre and he brings them to Brett."

"Objection!" Attorney Candy screamed out. "Where is the evidence for all this? Mr. Potsuk says he sees a pattern and just like that we are supposed to believe him? No one has said anything about drugs inside Exotic Beauties, and all of a sudden some big drug deal is going on inside there. Your Honor, DeAndre Brown has pleaded guilty to drug possession, but Winston Brown and Brett Olson maintain their innocence. In fact, they are not even being charged with any drug offense. Just because the police catch someone with drugs outside Exotic Beauties doesn't mean everyone inside Exotic Beauties is in on some big drug deal."

Judge Stump rolled his eyes at Attorney Candy and said, "Okay, we get the point." Then he looked back at Mr. Potsuk and asked, "Do you have any evidence to back up your theory here?"

Mr. Potsuk smiled and seemed pleased the judge had asked him this question. "Yes I do, Ya Honor. I'd like to dismiss this witness and call Corporal Hunter back to the stand."

"Thank you, DeAndre," said the judge. "You may step down. Bailiff can you check to see if Corporal Hunter is out there?" The bailiff walked out into the hall and came back with Corporal Hunter following behind him.

As Corporal Hunter tried to get comfortable in the witness chair the judge said, "Let me remind you Corporal, that you are still under oath."

"Yes sir," Corporal Hunter replied.

"Your witness," said the judge.

"Thank you," replied Mr. Potsuk. "Corporal Hunter, thank you for coming back into the court to speak with us." Corporal Hunter nodded his shiny bald head. "The reason I asked you back is the defense seems to think that I am just imagining drug activity inside Exotic Beauties. They seemed to think there is no evidence to prove this, and I thought maybe you could give me your thoughts."

"Absolutely sir." By the smug expression on Corporal Hunter's face, everyone could tell he thought he was the coolest guy in the room.

"Corporal Hunter, soon after you arrested Winston Brown, would you like to explain what you found inside Exotic Beauties?"

"Yes sir--"

"And when I say inside, I don't mean outside in the parking lot. I mean inside the building of Exotic Beauties." Mr. Potsuk gave a quick glare to Attorney Candy.

"Yes sir," Corporal Hunter answered again. "With Officer Paula Schmitt assisting me, we entered the premises of Exotic Beauties."

"Okay, good. When you got inside, did you find anything?"

"Yes sir we did. We found a large bag containing pain medications, Rohypnol tablets and LSD laced sheets."

"Wow!" cried Mr. Potsuk, as if he was hearing this information for the first time. "And you say you found this inside Exotic Beauties?"

"Objection," Attorney Candy interrupted. "Your Honor, haven't we already heard this testimony from Corporal Hunter? I feel like we're going in circles here."

"Overruled," snarled the judge. "Please continue, Corporal Hunter."

"Yes sir we did," Corporal Hunter replied proudly.

"So what did you do after you found these illegal drugs inside Exotic Beauties?" Mr. Potsuk was going to use every chance he could to say illegal drugs and Exotic Beauties in the same sentence.

"We took them to the crime lab for further investigation."

"And what did the crime lab find out about the illegal drugs from Exotic Beauties?"

"They determined the drugs were from the same source as the ones found inside DeAndre Brown's car." Mr. Potsuk paraded around the jury and Attorney Candy's table. Then he walked back toward Corporal Hunter and asked, "So give me your honest opinion as a high-ranking police officer. If DeAndre is sitting inside his car with a huge stash of drugs, then you and Officer Paula Schmitt find the same drugs inside Exotic Beauties. And Winston is inside Exotic Beauties all day every day. And DeAndre is the one who brings him over to Exotic Beauties. And Winston spends most of his time at Exotic Beauties when the business is closed. And Winston and DeAndre have a rap sheet of drug arrests longer than any I have ever seen in my twenty-year career in Gulf Coast City. Would it be safe to say that some kind of drug interaction is going on inside Exotic Beauties?"

"Yes it would," replied Corporal Hunter. Mr. Potsuk and Corporal Hunter both waited for Attorney Candy to object, but he did not. This was a good sign and Mr. Potsuk appeared to sense that this was the beginning of the end.

"Okay, good," Mr. Potsuk replied. "And even the defense, who argues with everything I say no matter how small, is not refuting Corporal Hunter's statement." Mr. Potsuk looked at Attorney Candy, Brett and Winston. They were all staring down at the floor even though, they were trying to play it cool.

"Thank you, Mr. Potsuk. You may step down Corporal Hunter, and thank you again for your time and service in this courtroom." The judge wanted to scold Mr. Potsuk for his theatrical performance, but he appeared more concerned with getting to his afternoon nap.

"Why don't we adjourn for today then reconvene at 9 am tomorrow." Just like yesterday, Judge Stump got up out of his seat before anyone could object to his statement.

CHAPTER 37

THE TRIAL (Day Three)

"Members of the jury, I apologize for having to put you through this."
—Harold Potsuk

Now it was day three and Jacob had gotten almost no sleep the previous night. Ana had called around midnight saying she was having a panic attack and didn't think she'd be able to give her testimony. He tried to calmed her down over the phone, knowing how important it was that she testify on the witness stand, but he wasn't able to help. He had to go over to Ana's house and they ended up spending the entire night preparing for today.

Now Ana was being sworn in and her face was pale.

"Do you swear to tell the truth, the whole truth and nothing but the truth, so help you God?" said the bailiff.

"I do," replied Ana as she stood visibly shaking in a nicely shaped white blouse and navy-blue skirt.

"The prosecution may proceed," ordered Judge Stump.

"Thank you, Ya Honor." Mr. Potsuk gently walked towards Ana, sensing she was uncomfortable. "Good morning, Ana. Thank you for coming in today."

"G'morning," Ana responded softly.

"Miss…" said Judge Stump.

"Jes, I know, Mr. Judge. I need to speak up," Ana said, slightly louder.

"Thank you, Miss." Judge Stump smiled, and everyone could see that he had a soft spot for her.

Mr. Potsuk continued. "Now, Miss Ana, the reason the police and I asked you to come in here is because we need you to tell your story. As you see, Mr. DeAndre Brown is no longer with the defense. And this is because he wised up and decided to change his plea." Ana looked over at the defense table and saw only Brett, Winston, and their defense attorney sitting there with long faces. "DeAndre will still be convicted, but he is going to receive a lesser sentence. I'd be willing to bet that by the end of the day, another one of Mr. Candy's clients will be trying to make a deal as well." Mr. Potsuk walked closer to Attorney Candy then whispered, "And soon there will be one."

"Mr. Potsuk," Judge Stump snarled. "Let's make this your last jab at Mr. Candy for today, okay?"

"Yes, Ya Honor," Mr. Potsuk replied, and everyone knew he had no intention of keeping his promise. He walked back towards Ana and began speaking to her in a calm voice. "Miss Ana, as I was saying, the jury needs to hear your story. DeAndre Brown has admitted to his criminal behavior but Mr. Brett Olson and Mr. Winston Brown have not. And even though the police know and I know that they committed the crime they are being charged with, the jury has not heard any evidence that will convict them of felony human trafficking for commercial activity in the first degree. The law states that in order to be convicted of a felony, the prosecution needs to have a unanimous decision from the jury. This means that everyone here in the jury box has to agree beyond a reasonable doubt that the defendant or defendants are guilty. I know it and the police know it. But in order to get a conviction, we need the jury to know it."

"Judge, can you move the prosecution along for us please?" interrupted Attorney Candy shaking his head.

"Don't even think about giving *me* orders, Mr. Candy," Judge Stump fired back.

It seemed that Attorney Candy was still going to put up a fight for Brett's innocence, and in the process, fight for Winston's innocence as well.

"As I was saying," Mr. Potsuk started again, "your statement is important to us, and everyone here is willing to let you take your time and try to relax as you tell us your story. If you feel like you need to take a break to collect your thoughts, then everyone is fine with that too." Mr. Potsuk looked over at Judge Stump and said, "Right, Judge Stump?"

"That's right, Mr. Potsuk," answered the judge with a hint of a grin. If Mr. Potsuk had asked this for anyone else, the judge would not have been so warm but he was sympathetic to Ana, and Mr. Potsuk knew it. This helped Ana loosen her shoulders and get a little more comfortable.

Mr. Potsuk gave Ana a soothing look and asked, "Are you ready to start?"

"Jes, sir," Ana replied softly, then glanced at Judge Stump to see if he was going to ask her to speak up.

"Okay, great," said Mr. Potsuk. "Ana, you worked for Exotic Beauties for a long time. I think it was 1991 to 1995. Is this correct?"

"Jes, sir."

"Okay, good. Now during this time did you ever witness Brett Olson engage in any illegal activity?"

Ana hesitated for a moment, looked around and locked eyes with Brett. His eyes bore into hers and her heart jumped into her throat, but she replied, "Jes sir."

"And was any of this activity the same activity that Mr. Olson is being tried for in this case?"

"Jes sir."

"Objection!" Attorney Candy jumped in.

"On what grounds?" Judge Stump asked.

"Ana Bautista is not an attorney. How can she decipher if something is legal or illegal?"

"You're really reaching on this one, Mr. Candy," the judge fired back as he continued to stick up for Ana. "Please keep going, Mr. Potsuk."

"Thank you, Ya Honor." Mr. Potsuk looked at Ana and asked, "Can I take you back a couple of years when you first started working at Exotic Beauties?"

"Sure."

"Let's say six months or so after you first began. How were you feeling?"

"I was tired and very dizzy all the time." Ana paused for a second and wiped her sweaty forehead. Then she pushed her long black hair out of her eyes, took a deep breath in and out and said, "I used to black out a lot too."

"Okay. Now, were you sick?"

"No, not really."

"Uh huh. So what was wrong with you, did you know?"

"Not at first, but I later found out I was addicted to pain pills."

"Really? Well, how did that happen?"

"Brett had Winston put pain pills in my drinks when I was at work and I didn't know it. I just thought I was getting tired a lot, but I grew dependent on it--"

"Objection!" shouted Attorney Candy which made Ana jump as if a gun had fired.

"On what grounds?" asked the judge.

"The prosecution is speculating here big time. I mean, a stripper who is hooked on drugs. Well, I've never heard of this before?" Attorney Candy replied sarcastically.

The judge looked at Mr. Potsuk and asked, "Do you have any evidence that Winston put drugs in Miss Ana's drink? And I assume you're going to say that Brett gave the orders. So do you have evidence to support this as well?"

"I do, Ya Honor. And there's a long list of other women who worked at Exotic Beauties that were drugged over time and became dependent. And once they became dependent they were manipulated into doing things they didn't want to by Brett Olson. And some of them did things that to this day they don't even know about."

Attorney Candy shook his head and said, "Give me a break."

"Okay, settle down, Mr. Candy," said the judge.

"May I continue, Ya Honor?" asked Mr. Potsuk.

"Please do."

"As I was saying, these employees of Exotic Beauties all have the same story of being given pain pills and other narcotics such as Rohypnol. Now, if you remember, Corporal Hunter explained earlier that Rohypnol is the date rape drug. And each and every one of these employees have no recollection of how they got this in their system."

"This makes absolutely no sense," cried out Attorney Candy. "These people have drugs in their system so they decide they are gonna blame their employer. This is ridiculous."

"Ya Honor, if I can get through what I'm saying here I can tie all this together. But if Attorney Candy keeps rudely interrupting he's just gonna slow things down, as well as make a fool out of himself."

"I've warned both of you more than enough about the personal attacks," the judge interjected. "And as far as suggesting Mr. Candy stop interrupting you, well I'm sorry but I can't do that. This is how the process works, you know this Mr. Potsuk. I will say this though, to both of you. If Mr. Potsuk can back up everything he's laying out here, then I will instruct Attorney Candy to lighten up on his objections."

"I guess that sounds fair to me, Ya Honor," replied Mr. Potsuk.

"Then you may proceed," the judge fired back.

"Thank you." Mr. Potsuk kindly looked at Ana and asked, "If the jury feels like they would like more evidence that Brett told Winston to put these drugs into your drinks, and other employees' drinks, can you give it?"

"Yes sir, I can," replied Ana. She looked only at Mr. Potsuk now and refused to look in the direction of Brett and Winston. She could only imagine what kind of hate they were throwing her way.

"Okay, good. Well, what makes you so sure that it was Winston and Brett behind this?"

"I saw Winston put some white powder into other girls' drinks."

The courtroom audience reacted loudly, and Mr. Potsuk raised up his hands like he enjoyed doing to say *Hey, I scored another one.* Then he asked,

"Did you say you saw Winston put white powder into other employees' drinks?"

"Jes, sir."

"Well, there you have it. Ana gets hooked on drugs; the other employees get hooked on drugs and Ana sees the whole thing."

Attorney Candy stood up and said, "I never did hear Ana say she saw Mr. Olson put drugs into other people's drinks."

Judge Stump gave Attorney Candy a stern look and he sat down.

Mr. Potsuk continued, "Ya Honor, as I've been saying all along, I'm getting to this." Mr. Potsuk quickly got back to questioning Ana before the judge or Attorney Candy could cut him off. "So Ana, what did you do when you saw Winston putting drugs into the other employees' drinks?"

"I went to Brett to speak to him about this."

"Okay, good. You saw Winston putting drugs into the other employees' drinks so you decided to bring it to the attention of your boss. That sounds like the logical thing to do, right?" Mr. Potsuk looked at the jury for approval even though he directed the question to Ana.

"Jes, sir," Ana answered.

"So what did Brett say? Was he shocked to hear this?"

"No, sir."

"No? Why?"

"He told me to quit complaining and to get back to work."

The gallery started rustling and a few of them cut some harsh looks Brett's way. Mr. Potsuk stopped long enough for everyone to settle down then he continued, "I see; well, this is not good. What did you do, Ana?"

"I'm ashamed to say." Ana looked down at the polished wooden floor.

"Why is that?"

"By the time I figured out what was going on, I was addicted to the drugs that Brett gave me. So instead of turning him into the police, I begged him to give me more." A tear ran down her face.

"Do you need to take a break, Ana?" Mr. Potsuk asked.

"No, I'm okay." Ana wiped her watery eyes then took a deep breath and removed the strand of hair that had fallen on her face.

"Well, that's understandable that you got hooked on these drugs. They are very addictive."

"Jes, sir."

"Did Brett admit to giving you these drugs?"

"Jes, he did." The gallery started chattering again but Ana didn't stop. "He said he does this to control his employees and to make people do what he wants them to do."

"I see. Did you ever tell Brett you were gonna go to the police?"

"I wanted to, but I was too es-scared."

"Scared? Why were you scared, Ana?"

"Because I'm in this country illegally." The noise in courtroom overpowered Mr. Potsuk, so Ana hung her head until they quieted down.

"I see… and we all understand how you feel Ana. It makes complete sense that you were scared."

"Jeah, Jes." Ana hesitated because now she felt like everyone in the courtroom was judging her.

"Ana, you have nothing to worry about from this court. You are not the one on trial here, you understand?"

"Jes, sir," Ana said, but didn't sound like she was convinced.

"Ana, let me ask you about something you just said. When you said Brett told you he got these girls on drugs so they would be easier to control, what did you mean by that?"

"Brett was always es-scared his dancers would leave and go work at another club. And he could never get enough girls to dance for him because his club is such a big place. He was always worried he was going to lose money and stuff like that."

"I see, well, this is not good. Did you ever see these girls acting different or behaving differently after they had been drugged by Winston and Brett?"

Blood was gushing into Attorney Candy's face. He looked as if he wanted to jump up out of his seat every time Ana or Mr. Potsuk opened their mouths. But he was fighting to restrain himself.

Ana cautiously glanced over at Brett to see if he was looking at her. When she saw that he wasn't, she continued, "I used to see Brett and

Winston running out of the couch rooms just as one or two of the dancers were waking up."

"Waking up? What do you mean?" asked Mr. Potsuk. "Did they take naps in the couch rooms?"

"Not really," replied Ana. "Sometimes the drugs that Winston and Brett gave them were so strong the girls would pass out, so Winston or Brett would carry them to the couch rooms so they could sleep it off."

"I see. And what did Brett and Winston do in the couch room with the girls while they were sleeping?" asked Mr. Potsuk.

"I don't know."

"Well, this is not good. This is not good at all." Mr. Potsuk looked down at the floor and shook his head. "This has so much foul-play written all over it that I don't even know where to start. This is all I have for now, Ya Honor," concluded Mr. Potsuk.

"Your witness, Mr. Candy."

Still wearing the same navy blazer and white socks he had all week, Attorney Candy got up out of his seat and said, "You know, we have all sat here listening to this ridiculous story all morning long and have not heard a shred of proof that Brett or even Winston for that matter has done anything wrong." Attorney Candy closed in on Ana and she looked as if she was looking for ways to escape. Then he began his interrogation. "So, Miss Bautista, did you just say you were hooked on drugs?"

"Jes, sir," Ana replied sheepishly.

"And did you ever see anyone put drugs into *your* drinks?"

"No, sir."

"So you just decide you're going to blame your employer?"

"Jes sir, because--"

"No need to answer that miss. We've already heard your testimony." Ana looked down at the floor. "And you also said that you saw Winston and Brett carry these girls into a room that had a comfortable couch so they could sleep off the effects of the drugs they were taking; is this correct?"

"Jes, sir."

"And this makes them bad guys?"

"Jes… I mean no, sir. Not carrying them to the couch--"

"I mean, what do you want Brett and Winston to do when these drug addicts are passing out in the middle of the club, just leave them on the floor?"

"No sir, that wasn't what I meant."

"This is total hogwash." Attorney Candy pounded on the table. "Your Honor, unless Mr. Potsuk can come up with concrete and tangible evidence to back this up, I recommend you strike the witness's entire statement from the record just for wasting everyone's time. My client, Mr. Brett Olson, is an honorable business man here in Gulf Coast City, and Winston Brown was a legendary high school football player."

"Okay, that's enough, Mr. Candy, we get your point. If you're not going to ask the witness any questions, then you need to dismiss her." The judge jumped in as Mr. Potsuk smiled in victory. "He does have a point though Mr. Potsuk. I suggest you show the court some tangible evidence, preferably from a qualified witness."

"Yes, Ya Honor." Mr. Potsuk looked down as if he'd been set back but everyone was sure he had more tricks up his sleeve.

Then seemingly out of nowhere, Attorney Candy started rambling about what great citizens Brett and Camille were. "I've gotten to know Brett Olson and his wife Camille pretty well over the past couple of months, and members of the jury you might be surprised to hear that I'm proud to know them." The jury now had their eyes fixed on Attorney Candy. "The whole reason Brett and Camille started Exotic Beauties was so they could be role models for their employees. As a former exotic dancer herself, Camille mentors her young ladies on how to entertain their customers without all the unethical and illegal activity that seems to surround all the other gentlemen's clubs here in Gulf Coast City. And Brett has told me many times that he is proud of his wife, and he has zero tolerance for bad behavior amongst his employees. Now, Mr. Potsuk will tell you Ana is not the one on trial here. But maybe she should be. I can't disclose the details, but Brett has told me that his parting with Ana from Exotic Beauties was very crucial to keeping up the high standards his business demands."

"Attorney Candy." Judge Stump was rubbing his red eyes trying to bring them back to life. He'd been dozing off, and Attorney Candy had taken the opportunity to present his case. "I think I've already warned you about presenting your closing arguments in the middle of the trial."

"Yes, Your Honor," Attorney Candy responded, then walked back to his table.

"Miss, you may step down," the judge said to Ana with his usual smile that he only gave to her. "Please call your next witness, Mr. Potsuk."

Mr. Potsuk stood up from his chair. "Ya Honor, I'd like to call back to the stand Corporal Hunter, if I may."

"Okay," replied the judge. "Bailiff would you mind seeing if Corporal Hunter is out in the hall?"

The bailiff walked out and returned with Corporal Hunter. This time he was carrying a black leather briefcase by his side. Brett and Winston's eyes were all over the place and everyone could see they were terrified.

"Let me remind you you're still under oath," said Judge Stump.

"Yes, Ya Honor," replied Corporal Hunter.

"Please be seated Corporal Hunter," ordered the judge. "You may interview the witness, Mr. Potsuk."

"Thank you, Ya Honor." Mr. Potsuk looked at Corporal Hunter, and they both grinned at the same time. It was as if they both knew that they had arrived at the time where they could finally show the evidence that would convict Winston and Brett. "Corporal Hunter, how are you doing this morning?" asked Mr. Potsuk as kind of a warm up question.

"Good thank ya." replied Corporal Hunter, then went back to wearing a blank look on his face.

"You know I'm doing good too, Corporal. And I'm gonna tell you why. Attorney Candy wants me to provide concrete tangible evidence that the Exotic Beauties dancers were drugged by Winston and Brett. And he wants me to prove that these ladies didn't just get a little wasted and have to sleep it off. And something tells me what you have in your briefcase is gonna give Attorney Candy what he wants."

"Yes sir, I believe it will." Corporal Hunter was trying to remain totally unemotional even though he was enjoying the attention. And it seemed that he was feeling the triumph of finally being able to get payback on Winston and Brett from as far back as his high school football days.

"Okay good," said Mr. Potsuk. "Let me ask you to open your briefcase now and pull out the slides that you have in there."

Corporal Hunter opened his briefcase and pulled out what looked like twenty large slides with pictures on them. Brett's fat face was completely frozen as if he knew what was about to be presented.

"Objection!" Attorney Candy barked. "Judge, what in the heck is Mr. Potsuk doing?" Attorney Candy stood up from his chair. "These slides were not in discovery."

"Why don't you both approach the bench," the judge ordered. The defense and prosecution walked up to the judge. He placed his hand over the microphone and asked, "You wanna tell me what's going on here, Mr. Potsuk?"

"Yes, Ya Honor," Mr. Potsuk answered. "I went by your office yesterday afternoon so I could speak with you but your secretary said you were taking a nap on your couch, so I didn't want to disturb you."

"So you just decide to enter some photographs into evidence without presenting them to me first? Are you looking for another contempt of court charge, Mr. Potsuk?" the judge snapped back.

"No sir," Mr. Potsuk answered, while Attorney Candy smirked.

"Well, are you gonna tell me what this is all about?" asked Judge Stump.

"Yes, Ya Honor. These photographs are a result of a new form of image analysis software that the Gulf Coast City police department has implemented only this week. To make a long story short, the computer software can identify people in photographs, who previously could not be identified, which is very crucial to this case."

"Let me see what you've got," ordered Judge Stump.

Corporal Hunter handed the slides to Mr. Potsuk and Mr. Potsuk handed them to Judge Stump. The judge looked over every slide with a stone face, occasionally taking off his reading glasses to rub his eyes. Then he announced, "Court recessed for one hour. Attorney Candy, you may take these photos with you and review them." Judge Stump banged his gavel then got up from the bench and walked out, leaving Attorney Candy standing there with his mouth wide open.

***

An hour and twenty minutes later, everyone was back in their seats. Mr. Potsuk stood and approached the bench. "Ya Honor, with your permission, I'd like to present these slides to the jury by using this projector."

"You may proceed," replied the judge. "Bailiff, would you mind rolling out the projector and getting it set up for Mr. Potsuk?"

While the bailiff was getting everything ready, Mr. Potsuk began setting up his presentation. "Ladies and Gentlemen of the jury, it's with mixed feelings that I finally give you the concrete tangible evidence that you've all been waiting for to convict the defendants. After seeing these horrific slides, you will certainly be able to convict Mr. Brett Olson and Winston Brown of felony human trafficking for commercial activity in the first degree against over twenty unsuspecting victims. Justice will finally be done but the victims' shame will be with them forever."

The bailiff gave Mr. Potsuk the nod to say the projector was ready for use so Mr. Potsuk picked up his first slide. He was just about to place it on the projector when he paused and said, "Ladies and gentlemen of the jury, and other members of the court, before I present this evidence I have to warn you that these slides are extremely graphic. And I apologize for having to put you through this. But I feel you absolutely must see what's here to be convinced of the terrible nature of this crime committed by Brett Olson and Winston Brown."

Mr. Potsuk built up the suspense to the absolute max, before he placed the first slide onto the projector. When the slide came into focus the courtroom gallery and the members of the jury all gasped. Some of the women put their hands over their mouths as if they were going to be sick, and some of the men's faces turned red with rage. Jacob was sick to his stomach when he realized that the young lady on the slide was Ana. Mr. Potsuk stood in silence as everyone looked up at the large screen and saw Ana lying on the floor. It was obvious that she was unconscious. She was laying on her side and was dressed in only her bra and panties. Her panties were pulled down to her knees and a middle-aged man was standing over her. No one could see his face but he appeared to be an Exotic Beauties customer.

Mr. Potsuk looked at the jury and seemed sympathetic to their disgust. Then he said, "I'm sorry folks, but this is only the first slide." He took the slide off the projector and placed another one down. This one was also of Ana unconscious. This time it appeared that another man was about to release into Ana's mouth as her lifeless body lay on the floor. The jury was even more horrified, and any doubt of Brett and Winston's innocence was now completely gone.

Mr. Potsuk continued to look sympathetically at the jury and said, "Let's take a break from those pictures for a second, shall we?" The jury and the court gallery all looked relieved. Even the judge was giving Brett and Winston a detestable look, and they knew they were both done here. Mr. Potsuk walked over to Corporal Hunter and said, "Corporal where did you get these absolutely horrific and heinous pictures from?"

Corporal Hunter was the only one in the courtroom not showing any emotion. He replied, "I hid a camera in one of the couch rooms, which is upstairs at Exotic Beauties."

The court gallery was chattering so the judge banged gently on his gavel. Mr. Potsuk continued, "Inside Exotic Beauties?"

"Yes, sir."

"Not in the parking lot of Exotic Beauties?"

"No, sir."

"Sweet Jesus!" cried out Mr. Potsuk, trying to make his presentation as dramatic as he could. "What kind of a person would let this go on inside his club?"

"I don't know, sir," replied the stone-faced Corporal Hunter.

"Well, this is not good. This is not good at all." Mr. Potsuk was doing a great job of pretending to hear this news for the first time. "Folks, as much as I hate to do this I'm gonna have to show you more slides."

Mr. Potsuk put another slide on the projector. This one showed a close up of Ana's head with her curly black hair glistening. The Exotic Beauties customer had obviously just finished himself and all that was left was Ana's spattered face. When the court gallery saw what was on the slide, they erupted. Ana's sister Lydia stood up and yelled, "¡Hijo de puta! I'm gonna kill you!" She ran towards Brett and Winston and began swinging at both of them. Three large policemen ran after her and pulled her away.

The gallery was now yelling at Brett and Winston, so the judge banged on his gavel. "Ladies and gentlemen, I realize this is a very sensitive case and a lot of emotional content is being presented today. But this is a court of law. And in a court of law we present all the evidence and then we let the defense present their case. Then the jury decides the defendant's innocence or guilt. Now if anyone here cannot abide by this, then I will ask them to leave or I will have the police remove them. Is this clear?" Everyone watched as the three policemen escorted Lydia, kicking and screaming, out of the courtroom. "Mr. Potsuk, why don't you hold off on the slides for a while?"

"Ya Honor, I'm just getting started here. I have at least twenty more photos just like this one that needs to be seen," Mr. Potsuk replied, as he looked at the judge and pleaded with him. "Ana is only one of many young ladies who has been humiliated by the defendants. If we don't show all these photographs, then this trial will most definitely be compromised."

"Are there more pictures of Miss Bautista?" asked the judge. He was doing his best to protect Ana.

"No, the other photos are of other dancers from Exotic Beauties."

"Okay, I will allow you to present these pictures but let's not make a big production over each one of them, okay?"

"Yes, Ya Honor." Mr. Potsuk walked back to his pile of slides and put another one onto the projector. The court gallery, the jury and Jacob all sat there horrified and too shocked to react as Mr. Potsuk continued to put slide after slide on the projector. Each one had a different male customer engaging in some kind of indecent act with an unconscious exotic dancer. They looked at photos of fourteen other exotic dancers. Jacob recognized every one of them because, with the exception of Ana, they were the Russian and Eastern European girls who he'd sent to work at Exotic Beauties. He hung his head in his hands as the guilt rushed over him.

Judge Stump took about as much as he could stand then he spoke up. He was visibly upset and probably wanted to say something like, *You know ladies and gentlemen of the jury, I've been sitting on this bench for over thirty years now, and this is probably the worst depiction of human cruelty I have ever seen. You must convict Brett and Winston and make sure they never see the light of day!* What he really said was, "Mr. Potsuk, why don't you distribute your hard copies to the jury for them to review."

"Certainly, Ya Honor," replied Mr. Potsuk. Then he asked, "Is it okay if we put back the first slide? I need go over some things with Corporal Hunter."

The judge paused for a moment to remove his reading glasses and rub his eyes. "Okay, Mr. Potsuk," he answered reluctantly.

"Thank you, Ya Honor." Mr. Potsuk put the slide back up on the projector for everyone to see Ana lying undressed and unconscious while the man stood over her. "Corporal Hunter, was the Gulf Coast City police department able to identify the individual pictured here?"

"Yes sir, we were."

"Okay, good. And where is this individual now?"

"This individual, as well as the other suspects who were pictured, were arrested soon after we arrested Brett, Winston, and DeAndre. They are currently locked up at the Gulf Coast City jail awaiting trial for felony sexual assault."

"Okay, well this is good," Mr. Potsuk replied as the noise from the gallery once again began to rise. "Now, Corporal Hunter, I count two people in this picture. Ana Bautista and the attacker. Do you see anyone else?"

"Yes sir, I do. If you look closely at the far wall you can see a little round silver button looking object."

Mr. Potsuk tried to squint so he could see the slide better, then he said, "I'm not sure if we can all see that, Corporal. Let me get another slide that has a close-up of that wall." Mr. Potsuk picked up another slide and put it down on the projector. This slide showed the silver button on the wall magnified, so Mr. Potsuk asked, "What is that on the slide, Corporal Hunter?"

"It's a peephole," Corporal Hunter replied.

"A peephole?"

"Yes sir, a peephole."

"Why is there a peephole looking into the couch room?"

"Well, a lot of gentlemen's clubs have them in their couch rooms for security and safety of their dancers. I'm sure you can understand that."

"I sure can and I think it's a good idea." said Mr. Potsuk. "Especially after seeing the sort of activities that go on inside the Exotic Beauties couch rooms." Mr. Potsuk was doing an excellent job of being shocked and outraged at the pictures he was presenting. "Okay, so Corporal Hunter, I asked you if you saw anyone else in the couch room and you showed me a peephole. Is there any reason for this?"

"Yes sir, if you put up the next slide you will be able to see a more magnified version of this picture. And this picture shows a close-up of someone's eye who is looking through the peephole."

The bailiff put up the slide and everyone in the courtroom gasped as they saw a large picture of someone's eye.

Mr. Potsuk walked up to the slide projector then looked back at Corporal Hunter and asked, "Corporal Hunter can you identify whose eye this is?"

"Yes sir, with the new image analysis software we got this week, the crime lab can now do this."

"Okay good, and have you identified whose eye this is?"

"Yes sir, we have."

"And the person, who belongs to this eye, obviously saw everything that went on inside this couch room, did he not?"

"Yes sir, I believe he did."

"Okay Corporal, now for the million-dollar question: whose eye is this?"

"Brett Olson."

"Objection, Your Honor!" Attorney Candy jumped up and cried out as the congregation went wild. "Mr. Potsuk is trying to make it look like Brett

Olson was behind this. Maybe Brett saw what was going on in the couch room and came running in to stop it. As Corporal Hunter just told the court, these peepholes are put in place for the safety of the dancers. Quite possibly Brett saw what this man was doing and came running in to help."

"Okay settle down, Attorney Candy," responded Judge Stump. "You'll have plenty of time to cross examine the witness, as well as bring in other witnesses to rebut the prosecutor's statements."

Mr. Potsuk continued, "Ya Honor, I can address Attorney Candy's objection right now."

"As you wish."

Mr. Potsuk continued, "Before I respond to Attorney Candy's ridiculous comment, I'd like to say one thing. Every one of the pictures that I have shown you today has two other pictures with close ups of the peephole and the eye that is looking through the peephole. Each one of the photos of the eye was taken to the Gulf Coast City police department crime lab for identification. And each picture with the eye came back from the Gulf Coast City crime lab with the identification of Brett Olson." The gallery began to stir, but Mr. Potsuk kept going. "Attorney Candy is right, maybe Brett did run into the room to stop these heinous crimes each time this happened. But as everyone can plainly see, what's going on here is not something that a club owner should take lightly. He should obviously know that this is a police matter and should immediately call them if he sees this." Mr. Potsuk paused for a couple of seconds, then looked over at Corporal Hunter and asked, "Corporal Hunter, are your photos time and date stamped?"

"Yes sir, they are."

"And Corporal Hunter, on the dates that these pictures were taken, did the Gulf Coast City police department receive any phone calls from Exotic Beauties about a sexual assault?"

"No sir, we did not."

Jacob and the court gallery wanted to cheer, but they daren't for fear the judge would kick them out. The prosecutor looked at Corporal Hunter and said, "Well done, Corporal."

"Your witness Attorney Candy," announced the judge, ever so slightly shaking his head.

Attorney Candy stood up and approached Corporal Hunter. "Things are not always as they seem, am I right Corporal Hunter?"

"I suppose."

"These strippers sure take a lot of drugs, am I right Corporal?"

"Yes sir, they do."

"And is it your testimony that every single time they take drugs, my client is forcing them to do it?"

"Well, I wouldn't say forcing them. I'd saying sneaking it in their drinks."

"Well, what I want to know Corporal is where's the proof? These women posed for photographs pretending to be asleep and all of a sudden my client put them to sleep? Where's the proof? What everyone needs to remember here is these women work in the sex industry. They put on an act every single night when they dance and take off their clothes and Lord knows what else behind my clients' backs. Now would it be so outrageous to say that all these pictures are just an act?"

"Well, that's not my opinion."

"Of course your opinion is everyone is guilty, Corporal Hunter. You're a police officer. Your job is arresting people then the attorneys have to sort out whether they're innocent or guilty; isn't this correct?"

"I suppose."

"Where are the rest of these women who are on these pictures to give their story? They are not even here--"

"Okay, Mr. Candy," the judge interrupted. Attorney Candy had recently discovered that none of the other witnesses were in the courthouse. In fact, none of them even knew the court case was going on. The other young ladies in the pictures were either back in Russia or Eastern Europe, or working at another gentlemen's club or laying on the beach waiting for Jacob to find them a job. Attorney Candy now knew this and he was going to use it to tear apart the prosecutor's case. Brett knew these foreign students would not cause any problems for him because their visas demanded they go back. This was definitely why he used them in the first place. The only witness standing in his way was Ana, and Attorney Candy would certainly continue to throw everything he could at her to destroy her credibility.

Attorney Candy was about to get started again when the judge interrupted, "You know what, this seems like a good time to recess for the day. Why don't you make your closing statement, Mr. Potsuk, then we will reconvene tomorrow morning at 9 am."

Mr. Potsuk seemed happy to have the floor one more time before the day's court session ended. "Thank you, Ya Honor," Mr. Potsuk responded. "Before we leave today I'd like to ask Attorney Candy to ask his client, Mr. Brett Olson, about the pyramid." Mr. Potsuk looked around to see if the jury had their eyes fixated on him. When he saw that they did, he looked over at Attorney Candy who was writing *what is the pyramid?* on his notepad before passing it over to Brett.

Then Mr. Potsuk continued, "We will get into this in more detail tomorrow and I will be bringing in witnesses to corroborate this. But for now, let me just give you all a brief description of the pyramid." Mr. Potsuk paused and looked around while everyone was anxiously waiting to hear more. "The pyramid is something that Brett uses at Exotic Beauties to feel out his customers to see if he can trust them. As they build their trust with Brett they climb the pyramid. And as they climb the pyramid they get more and more sexual privileges from the dancers. And of course, as they get more privileges, Brett gets more money." Brett's face turned pale. "Members at the top of the pyramid get to do what you all saw today during our horrific slideshow. And by the way, these upper tier pyramid members are all in jail awaiting trial. What this means is all these guys will be looking to cut a deal to receive a lesser sentence. So please keep this in mind Mr. Candy, tonight, and try to think about what they'll say, for us to go a little easier on them. We look forward to seeing you all tomorrow ladies and gentlemen of the jury. Have a good evening." With that Mr. Potsuk, sat down and the judge ended the day's session.

CHAPTER 38

FORT MYERS, FLORIDA

"Is this what you girls were doing inside this house?"
—Officer Brad Taylor

When Yousra arrived at Officer Taylor's ranch house in Fort Myers, she felt totally at ease. It was as if she'd already known him for a long time. Walking through his tropical garden onto his front porch, she felt relaxed, like she'd been rescued from all the stress from the past few weeks.

Officer Taylor unlocked his front door and they both walked inside. It was obvious that he lived alone and was not expecting any guests, especially an attractive young lady from Turkey. Otherwise he would have cleaned up the beer cans, pizza boxes and dirty dishes. Yousra didn't mind. To her, this meant Officer Taylor must not have a girlfriend and this she liked.

"Have a seat over here on the couch," Officer Taylor said as he quickly moved some clutter out of the way. "I'll go get my laptop so we can put the disks in."

"Okay," Yousra whispered. Her hands started shaking nervously in anticipation of what they were about to see.

Officer Taylor disappeared and she fidgeted with her rings. Then he returned with his computer. He turned it on then asked, "Which disk would you like to look at first?"

"Svetlana's," Yousra said immediately. She figured she would see what was on Svetlana's disk first before she decided whether she wanted to view hers. When Officer Taylor's computer was up and running, he put in the computer disk that had *Svetlana* written on it in magic marker. Both Yousra and Officer Taylor waited in anticipation of what might be on the disk. After the hour glass finished, for what seemed like forever, a screen menu came up which had five video choices on it. Each video was labeled *Svetlana one* through *Svetlana five*.

"I guess we click on *one* first," Officer Taylor suggested.

"Okay," Yousra replied as she continued to fidget. She tried to take comfort from observing his well-toned biceps. Her eyes roamed up and down his body and stopped at his black sideburns. Yousra tried to smile so she could relieve the tension, but found it impossible.

Officer Taylor clicked on *Video One* and immediately they could see the bedroom where Yousra and Svetlana had been sleeping. It looked different in this video. Yousra's bed was not there and the room actually looked clean. Svetlana's bed was covered with a red velvet blanket and Svetlana was laying underneath, pretending to be asleep. The camera zoomed onto Svetlana's pretty face and pointy nose and Yousra and Officer Taylor could see she'd caked on the makeup.

"That's kinda a lot of makeup to be wearing just to go to bed," Officer Taylor said, trying to lighten up the mood.

"I agree." Yousra forced herself to laugh. The tension in the room was high and both Officer Taylor and Yousra were trying hard to relax. Yousra had just met this complete stranger. Even though she found him attractive, he was still a policeman and they were both watching what Yousra had a feeling was going to turn into a pornographic movie.

The camera focused on Svetlana's face then roamed up and down her body while she lay under the covers. Svetlana continued to act as if she were sleeping. Then the bedroom door opened and Mehmet walked in. He was wearing only his thong underwear which was not a turn-on with his pot belly hanging out. This is what Yousra was thinking as the sick feeling from that house came back to her stomach and started climbing up her throat.

Mehmet pushed the hair away from Svetlana's pretty sleeping face, then slowly pulled down the covers to reveal the rest of her body. She was barely covered by a skimpy little lime green Teddy as Mehmet began to rub his hairy hands up her legs. Then he put his hands on Svetlana's breasts and Officer Taylor clicked pause on the video. "I can see where this is going." He was embarrassed and so was Yousra.

"I can too," Yousra whispered.

"Do you want to see your disk?" Officer Taylor cautiously asked.

"I don't know." Yousra wanted to watch but was afraid of what it might reveal.

Officer Taylor went back into his policeman mode and asked, "Is this what you girls were doing inside that house?"

"No!" Yousra snapped back.

"I'm sorry," said Officer Taylor. "I didn't mean to offend you."

"No, you didn't offend me. I'm just… I'm worried about what is on my disk, that's all."

"I understand." Officer Taylor gently put his hand on Yousra's shoulder and she looked up at him and smiled. *His touch felt good.*

Yousra tried to speak but was having trouble finding the words. "Off.. Officer Taylor, I want to tell you something." Yousra tried to summon the courage to look her companion in the eyes. Instead she looked at his biceps first then moved her eyes over to his broad shoulders.

"Why don't you call me Brad." Officer Taylor moved in a little closer to Yousra and she jumped back. He didn't make her nervous, but the uniform did.

"Brad, I want to tell you something. I'm not an innocent girl. I was a dancer in Gulf Coast City before I came to Fort Myers. I even sold my body once." Yousra wanted to let out her feelings and she felt like Officer Taylor had a kind ear. "It's not what you think, though. I was very angry at my fiancé because I just found out he cheated on me with another woman. The owner of the club told me there was a customer who wanted to pay $1000 dollars to have sex with me in the hot tub. I wanted the money but more than that, I wanted to get revenge on my fiancé, so I did it. This was the first and last time I ever did anything like this. Now I feel ashamed and I'm also ashamed about what might be on that disk."

Officer Taylor could tell Yousra was suffering and he had a soft spot for this young lady. She was different from anyone else he'd ever met in Fort Myers, and this made his heart beat just a little faster. "I tell you what," he replied. "I have to get back on patrol. So why don't I leave you here and you can watch the video in private."

"Okay, that sounds good." Yousra smiled. She blew out a sigh of relief. "Thank you, Officer Taylor."

"Remember, you can call me Brad."

"Thank you, Brad." Yousra was starting to warm up to him even more.

Officer Taylor walked out his front door and got into his patrol car, leaving Yousra all alone in his house. Now that she was by herself, she was ready to see what was on her disk. She popped in the *Yousra* disk and waited for the menu to come up. When it finally did, Yousra saw that it only showed one video. She took a deep breath then hit play. The video came on and she soon noticed it was the same bedroom that she'd been living in. The camera zoomed onto her bed. And to Yousra's horror, she saw that she was laying there asleep. It was obvious in Svetlana's video that she was faking. In Yousra's video, it looked like she was faking as well. Yousra, of course knew that she was not.

Then Omar walked into her bedroom. He was dressed only in his underpants. Mehmet had worn a red satin thong in the video with Svetlana. It now appeared that Omar was wearing the same one. *How disgusting*, Yousra thought.

Omar walked closer to Yousra with his skinny legs and beer belly. The entire time he was looking at her sleeping and licking his lips. Yousra felt sick to her stomach. She wanted to stop Omar, but how could she? This had already happened, she just hadn't known about it.

He started stroking Yousra's face with his hairy hands while she was still out cold. *I must have been drugged*, she thought.

Omar started to pull down the covers and Yousra recognized the bra and panties she'd worn to bed on the second night in that house. *This is why they didn't care if I went on the photo shoots. They were already using me,* Yousra decided and felt her stomach contents rising up.

She continued to watch the video in horror as Omar started massaging her legs. Then he moved his hands up Yousra's body until he had his hands on her crotch. He started massaging between her legs through her panties. When Yousra saw this, she vomited all over Officer Taylor's carpet. But she had to keep watching. She had to find out what else Mehmet and Omar had done to her, no matter how bad it was.

Omar began to unzip his pants. He had a dull gaze on his face, and his tongue was hanging out as he looked at Yousra's sleeping body. When Yousra saw his drool hit her stomach while he was pleasuring himself, she sent out her second load of vomit onto Officer Taylor's computer. She couldn't watch another second, so she ran out of the room.

CHAPTER 39

THE TRIAL (Day Four)

"...Gulf Coast City is now a safer and much more pleasant place to live and visit."
—Judge Stump

Day four turned out to be the final day in court for Brett, Winston and DeAndre. When everyone piled in at 9 am Judge Stump made an announcement. "Ladies and Gentlemen of the jury, the prosecution and the defense met yesterday afternoon and both came to an agreement." The judge no doubt wanted to say, *How the defense and the prosecution agreed on anything I have no idea.* "The defense would like to change the plea of his remaining two clients from *not guilty* to *no contest.* The prosecution has agreed to accept the plea bargain, and they have both come to an agreement on the terms of the sentences for Mr. Brett Olson and Mr. Winston Brown. Let me state now that pleading *no contest* is not an admission of guilt but an admission that the facts and evidence against the two defendants are so overwhelming that Mr. Olson and Mr. Brown, under the advice of counsel, feel it is in their best interest to accept the terms of the reduced sentences I have handed them." Judge Stump looked up to see if everyone was listening to him, and of course, they were hanging on his every word. Brett and Winston had their heads down. Camille looked like she was about to cry, and Corporal Hunter stood there unexpressive. Jacob was sure that, if given the chance, Corporal Hunter would want to jump up and down and pat himself on the back.

Judge Stump continued, "Since the defendants do not wish to proceed further with the trial, I will now go straight into the sentencing phase. After I read the sentences the jury will be free to leave. I'd like to thank every one of you for your time, your patience and your good citizenship towards Gulf Coast City, Florida." The jurors all nodded back at the judge, then he looked down at his notes so he could read out the agreed upon sentences for Brett, Winston, and DeAndre. "DeAndre Brown has pled *guilty* to misdemeanor possession of controlled substances. Mr. DeAndre Brown was very helpful and cooperative in giving the Gulf Coast City prosecution that added extra bit of information to convict the other two defendants. For this reason, I am handing down a reduced sentence to Mr. Deandre Brown of three years in the Florida State Prison. He will be eligible for parole in six months."

Deandre looked relieved that he wasn't going away forever. He looked over at Winston and saw him shaking his head. He was giving DeAndre a look as if to say *I'll get you back when we are both on the inside.*

Judge Stump cleared his throat then continued, "Winston Brown has pled *no contest* to felony human trafficking for commercial activity in the second degree. He is not eligible for parole. The sentence I'm handing down to Mr. Winston Brown is fifteen years in the Florida State Prison in Raiford."

Winston tried not to show it but he felt completely defeated. He started his life with so much talent for football and now he was going to prison and would not be released for a long time.

Judge Stump continued, "The other victims in this case are no doubt back in Russia and Eastern Europe, so we are not able to proceed any further with charges from them. I'm sure this is why Mr. Olson and the Brown cousins inflicted their actions onto these girls in the first place. They assumed they could get away with it if the young ladies were not here to testify against them. Thankfully, Ana Bautista was here and was brave enough to testify. Corporal Hunter, Officer Paula Schmidt, Chief Joe White and the rest of the Gulf Coast City police department should be commended. They worked long hard hours putting this case together and as a result, Gulf Coast City is now a safer and much more pleasant place to live and visit."

Judge Stump looked up as if he was expecting the court gallery to applaud but they did not. Jacob and everyone else wanted to hear what the judge was going do with Brett. Judge Stump wrote something down on his note pad, then continued, "Brett Olson is also now pleading *no contest* to felony human trafficking for commercial activity. His charge will remain in the first degree but he will be spared the life sentence. The sentence I'm handing down for Mr. Olson is twenty years in the Florida State Prison in Raiford. He is not eligible for parole."

The gallery started to chatter and Jacob could tell they were satisfied. Everyone looked at one another to see if they were feeling the same. Judge Stump gave out his final remarks by saying, "Attorney Candy, Mr. Brett Olson and Mr. Winston Brown will now be taken into custody to begin their sentences immediately. Please have Mr. DeAndre Brown report to the Raiford Prison in two weeks before 4 pm. Do any of your clients have any questions?"

"No sir," Attorney Candy answered as Brett, Winston and DeAndre stood silent and defeated.

Judge Stump's final comment was, "Ladies and gentlemen of the jury, thank you for your service. You are dismissed."

For Jacob, this felt really good. He wanted to walk up to them and gloat but obviously could not. He looked around and saw Corporal Hunter. He sat there unemotional, but Jacob was sure he felt a sense of accomplishment as well as relief that he wasn't the one going to prison. As his eyes continued to wander, he saw Camille and she had tears in her eyes. He didn't feel sorry for her because he remembered how she'd been just as devious as Brett. She must have been feeling lucky not to be charged as an accessory.

CHAPTER 40
JACOB'S TOWNHOUSE

"Hamid the Mustache says a vacancy has become available in Miami."
—Karina

About a week after the trial, there was a knock at Jacob's door. When Jacob opened up, Karina was standing there in a cotton T-shirt and denim shorts, looking as radiant as ever.

"Jacob, I wanted to come see you," Karina said softly.

"Yeah, yes." He could barely speak, he was so excited.

"I came here to say goodbye to you. I'm going to Miami."

This was not what Jacob wanted to hear. "No, you can't do this!"

"Hamid the Mustache says a vacancy has become available in Miami at the modeling agency. So I have to fly there tomorrow morning."

No, not Hamid again. "Karina, I have a really bad feeling about Hamid and this Miami modeling agency. How much do you know about this place?"

"I only know what Hamid has told me." She looked up at Jacob with her large brown eyes, almost melting his heart. "But Hamid says if I don't like it, I can always call him and he will send me a plane ticket to come back. Also, I don't feel comfortable now at Exotic Beauties and I think

Camille is going to close the place."

"Yeah but… have you heard from Yousra? How's she doing in Miami?"

"Hamid tells me she's loving it." Karina's face brightened and Jacob could tell there was probably no way he was going to convince her to stay.

Karina kissed Jacob on the cheek and said, "I have to go. I have a lot to do before my flight tomorrow."

He was so happy to see her, but he couldn't think of anything to say to make her change her mind. He could tell she was super excited about her new career move. So when Karina started walking away, Jacob ran after her and yelled out, "At least let me give you a ride back to your house."

"Okay Jacob, but please don't try to talk me out of this."

"I won't."

Karina got in Jacob's car and they drove to her house in silence. When Jacob dropped her off, Sergei was standing in the front yard giving him a hard-bitten look. Jacob couldn't help it; he had to say something to him, so he got out of his car and mouthed off, "What the hell are you looking at?"

Sergei walked towards Jacob's car and Karina started to squirm. "Guys, please don't start anything," she begged.

Sergei got closer to Jacob and said with his strong accent, "I am looking at nothing."

Jacob really despised Sergei. It all started at the beginning of the summer, when he showed the chip he had on his shoulder by insisting that the only job he would accept was a hotel houseman. Then when Jacob thought he was going to have a summer romance with Karina, Sergei was there on the couch snuggling up with her. When all the checks bounced, Sergei was the ringleader who rallied all the employees against him. Now here he was again, standing in the way of Jacob getting his girl.

All the anger surfaced to the top, so when Sergei looked away, Jacob took a huge swing and connected with the Estonian's jaw. Even though Sergei was all muscle and almost a foot taller than Jacob, he fell down to the ground. Karina screamed, "Stop it guys!" Sergei stood back up and lunged at Jacob and wrestled him to the ground. Now Sergei was on top of Jacob and they were both punching and kicking each other. Sergei hit Jacob's nose so hard, he was in excruciating pain and seeing stars. Jacob punched Sergei in the balls and he screamed like a little girl. Jacob eased up for a second to catch his breath, and Sergei punched him hard in his stomach. Jacob could feel the extra thirty pounds of weight Sergei had over him as he gasped for air.

Jacob was choking and about to beg Sergei to stop when he saw a police car coming closer to the house. Sergei didn't see the police, so he kept wailing away. Jacob covered his face as Sergei continued to beat on him.

Several long seconds later, Jacob heard Officer Paula's voice, "Jacob, knock it off. That's enough."

Jacob was happy to cease fire and he'd like to think Sergei was too.

Officer Paula walked up to both of them and even though Sergei and Jacob were far larger than her, they stood at attention and listened to what she had to say. "What's going on here?" she asked.

"Nothing goes on here," Sergei responded. He was breathing hard and Jacob was happy to see there was a small speck of blood dripping from his lip. Jacob didn't look all that great either and his nose, stomach and entire body was killing him.

Officer Paula looked up at the three of them and said, "This is what's going to happen here." Officer Paula pointed at Karina and Sergei and said, "I'm assuming you two live inside with the other students." Karina and Sergei both nodded. "Okay, I want both of you to go inside and don't come out." Sergei and Karina quickly walked off and went inside their house together. This did not turn out the way Jacob wanted.

When he was alone with Officer Paula, she calmed down her tone and said, "How have you been since you got out of the hospital?"

"I'm okay Paula, you know."

"And how have you been after the court case? You know that was the talk of the town around here." Officer Paula smiled at him.

"I'm glad those guys are going to prison."

"That's good, Jacob. I was sorry to hear that you got all mixed up with Winston, Brett and DeAndre. You always seemed like a nice person."

"Thank you, Paula." He could tell she really cared about the community, unlike Corporal Hunter.

"You know Jacob, I'm not sure what went on or didn't go on with you and Winston's wife, but it seems like the right people got locked up at least."

"I guess you're right." Jacob didn't want to say too much.

"You haven't heard from Mustapha lately have you?" Officer Paula asked.

"No, not since he left."

"Well I'm sure you were fighting with those J-1 Visa students over their paychecks, so I'm not going to say too much about that. But if I was you, I'd stay away from that big guy. He's a lot larger than you." Officer Paula gave Jacob a wink.

"I'll be sure to do that." He smiled and said, "Can I ask you a question?"

"Sure."

"How much do you know about this modeling agency that Hamid is always sending girls to?"

When Jacob's question registered with Officer Paula she responded, "All I really know is he's been sending girls there for a long time."

"And has anyone ever complained?"

"Like I said, every summer there's always a fresh crop of new girls coming in from overseas and Hamid always seeks them out. We've had a few minor complaints about him, but there's never been enough for the police to do anything about it." Jacob gave Paula a dissonant look so she continued. "Once we tried to track down the alleged Miami modeling agency but couldn't find any evidence of its existence."

This really worried Jacob. Especially since he knew Karina was going there. "Don't you think that's weird?" he asked.

"Sure, but we never found any evidence of foul-play."

"Shouldn't the police do an investigation?"

"This is more of a Miami problem than a Gulf Coast City problem. You know, since the alleged agency does business in Miami PD's jurisdiction."

"Okay but..."

Officer Paula's radio went off. "I gotta go. You take care Jacob."

"Will do."

She swiftly walked away and got in her car. "Remember, I patrol this area so don't let me see you when I come back here."

"No problem, Paula."

He drove back to his townhouse and thought about cracking open a beer. He had the perfect excuse to start drinking again. Karina was leaving and he had no chance of getting her to stay. He decided against it because he was not going to give up his pursuit. He knew the only way to see Karina again was to get to the airport tomorrow. This would be his last chance to change her mind. He couldn't sit around his townhouse because he couldn't stop thinking about pouring some alcohol into his body. The soothing pleasure of a just a couple of beers would be all it would take to put his mind at ease.

Disobeying Officer Paula's orders, Jacob decided to get in his car and drive past Karina's house. He did this about hundred times, it seemed. He kept circling the block hoping Karina would step outside so he could flag her down and talk to her. But she never did. He drove around all night and kept sucking down imaginary beers in the process.

Now it was 5 am, and Jacob never saw Karina. His pretend twelve pack was gone and he'd drank himself sober. He decided the best thing to do was head to the airport.

He got to the airport around 6 am because Karina said she was heading to Miami in the morning and there were flights heading out around the clock. He sat down in a chair where he could see the security check-in, and waited for Karina to arrive.

He was fast asleep when he heard someone say, "Jacob wake up. What are you doing?" He thought he was either dreaming or dead because he saw the face of an angel. The silhouette of a long brown haired beautiful women, oozing with vanilla perfume was standing over him. He rubbed his eyes. It was Karina. She was nicely dressed in a short skirt and clean white blouse. She had her leather suitcase by her side. Jacob begged and pleaded with her not to go but she insisted that this was the best move for her.

Jacob asked, "Will you give me your address and phone number when you get to Miami?"

Karina coldly replied, "No, I can't."

He asked, "Well can I at least have your mother's address in Belarus?"

"No, Jacob. I can't give you that either."

"Karina, I absolutely cannot allow you to get on that plane because I care about you way too much to let you risk going to Miami by yourself."

Karina looked at him and said, "No Jacob, I'm going to Miami. If you really cared about me, you would not have slept with Yousra or Winston's wife. And you wouldn't have dated Ana."

In the middle of the Gulf Coast City airport Jacob grabbed Karina's arm and yelled out, "I never slept with Winston's wife and I didn't date Ana! I won't allow you to go!"

Karina's mood turned to anger. She screamed, "Let me go Jacob!"

This was all it took for airport security to jump in. The buzz cut airport policeman with the serious look on his face said, "Sir, you are about five seconds from going to jail if you don't leave this young lady alone."

Jacob responded, "I wasn't trying to cause any trouble. I'm just very worried about what might happen to this young lady, that I care about very much. I can't let her get on that plane."

But the two airport policemen were not interested in hearing Jacob's story. One took out his handcuffs and the other put his hand on his truncheon while Karina walked through security and never looked back.

When Karina was out of sight the airport security let down their guard, so Jacob walked back to the parking lot with tears building in his eyes. *Why was I so stupid*, he wondered. *The entire summer I didn't do anything to show Karina how much I really cared about her. I put all my energy into helping Brett and Winston. I was willing to deposit six thousand dollars into Mustapha's account so all the employees could get their paychecks. When Yousra showed up, I gave her a job and a place to stay. But Karina got nothing from me. So now she has to move on and take care of herself because no one else is going to. She's going to Miami and I'm never going to see her again.*

He got inside his car, started up the engine then turned the engine off. *No, I'm not going to let her go like this.* He ran back into the Gulf Coast City airport then marched straight up to the ticket counter. "I need a ticket to Miami," he demanded.

The ticket agent smiled and said, "I think we can do that for you. When do you need this ticket for, sir?"

"Right now."

"My pleasure sir, let me check that for you."

As the ticket agent looked down at her computer screen, the two airport policeman returned. "Didn't we just watch you leave?"

Jacob's heart sunk into his stomach. He looked at them and pleaded, "I'm okay now and my friend has gone. I'm not gonna cause any problems. I just need to buy a ticket to Miami and y'all will never see me again."

Jacob could already tell airport security was not going to allow any of this. "Sir, you know just as well as we do that the young lady is on the other side of the security checkpoint and you just wanna go over there so you can cause some more trouble with her."

He tried to argue back but it was pointless. "No, that's not true."

"Well sir, we don't have time to follow you all around the airport to make sure you behave so you're just gonna have to leave." The airport policeman put his hand on his truncheon, just in case he had to pull it out, so Jacob moped out of the airport again.

He got back into his car and thought, *I can't get a plane from Gulf Coast City airport but the airport in Destin is only 40 miles away.* So he drove to Destin as fast as he thought he could without the police stopping him. He weaved in and out of cars the whole way and was constantly watching for police traps. He got lucky and arrived at the airport in under half an hour.

He spent a ton of money to get a plane ticket for a flight that was about to leave in five minutes, but he didn't care. He was going to get to Miami to see Karina and nothing was going to stop him.

The flight seemed like it took forever, and when the plane finally touched down at the huge Miami International airport, he had no idea where to look for Karina. With all the excitement earlier, Jacob didn't even check when her flight was going to arrive. But he was in Miami and even though this place was absolutely massive compared to Gulf Coast City, he was not going to give up on her. He looked up and down the airport terminal and he looked at all the screens for Gulf Coast City baggage claim. He went to every baggage claim area in the airport but he was too late each time.

He sat down on a bench outside the airport and hung his head in his hands. *What was the point of this whole year?* he thought. *Nothing but trouble has happened and I lost the girl I really want to be with.*

He watched as the taxis pulled in and picked up airplane passengers, then disappeared as they headed into the city. Everyone got on a plane to come to Miami for a different reason. Some came on business, others came on vacation, some were coming here to see family and some were returning home. Karina had come here to start a new life. Jacob was sure she came here to make a lot of money, and of course to get away from him.

He had been there for about thirty minutes when he looked inside an old beat up minivan and was astonished to see Karina inside. With her were two unshaven middle eastern guys and she didn't seem happy to be with them. Jacob was incognizant that Mehmet and Omar were there to pick her up so she could take the place of Yousra. He had to react quickly because if he didn't stop this minivan, it too would disappear out of sight and head into the city, never to be seen again.

Jacob stood up, ran towards the minivan and yelled as loud as he possibly could, "Karina, Karina, Karina!" She saw him and smiled, but the two grubby guys weren't amused and tried to get away from the crazy man. Jacob knew there was only one way he could get Karina back, so he jumped on top of the minivan's hood and looked the driver straight in the eyes. Then he yelled, "Stop right now and let Karina out!"

There was no way Mehmet was going to head into the city with a lunatic on his hood so he stopped the van and put it into park. And no amount of yelling from Mehmet and Omar was going to make Jacob get off.

Airport security came after Jacob and once again he began to panic. The Miami airport police were by no means as polite as the Gulf Coast City airport police, but Jacob wasn't going to back down. He said to them, "I care about this girl and I don't trust the men she's with. I came all the way from North Florida and I'm not gonna let her go with them."

Lucky for Jacob, the Miami police let down their guard when they realized he was just a young man with a silly crush and not a terrorist or someone like that. The older policeman grabbed Jacob's arm and pulled him off the hood. Then the younger policeman made everyone else get out of the minivan.

The older policeman looked at Jacob and said, "I'm afraid it's not your decision to make where or what this lady does." He looked at Karina and asked, "Miss, do you want to get back in that van or do you want to go with Romeo here?"

Jacob's heart was pounding in his chest as he remembered the Gulf Coast City airport police asked Karina the same question, and she decided to get on the plane. Karina looked at Jacob and with tears in her eyes said, "I want to go with him. I wanted to be with him since the first day we met way back at Gulf Coast Jobs and after he kissed me that night, I didn't want to leave him. But I knew if we spent the summer together, I'd never go back to Belarus to take care of my mother so I went back to Sergei because I'd already started dating him before I met Jacob--"

The older policeman rudely interrupted, "Miss, this is Miami, where we have the highest crime rate in the country, we don't have time to be the love police. Why don't you go with your boyfriend and the two of you get the hell out of here."

Karina and Jacob got out of there as quickly as they could, and the airport police focused their attention on Omar and Mehmet. As the young couple disappeared around the corner, more police descended onto Yousra's captors.

Karina didn't care what the policeman had to say and neither did Jacob. They were together now and that's all that mattered. The two of them rented a car and drove back to Gulf Coast City. On the way back, Jacob explained everything that had happened over the past year and told Karina she was the best part of it.

That night Karina stayed over at his place. The next morning Jacob woke up with Karina in his bed and everything felt perfect. He told her he wanted her to move in with him permanently.

Karina answered, "I'd love to. Will you help me go to my house and get the rest of my clothes?"

"Sure." Jacob said, hoping like hell that Sergei wouldn't be there. "Then I need to head over to see Ana at Gulf Coast Employment Solutions."

"It's a date," she said with a smile.

They drove over to the old house on Oak Street and Jacob was already shaking before he got out of his car. It was only two days ago that Sergei and he had fought. And the bruises on his face and stomach still hurt.

When they arrived at Karina's house she asked, "Jacob, do you want me to go inside to see if Sergei is there?"

"No, you don't need to do that," he answered. He didn't want Karina to think he was scared.

"Okay, but please promise you won't beat him up again."

Jacob was really glad to hear Karina say this. *Did she think he was the one who won the fight?*

"Okay, I promise," he answered as he got out of the car to walk into the house and quite possibly an ambush from Sergei. He was really frightened. Maybe Jacob wasn't as scared as when he was waiting for Winston to come over and beat on him, but he was still worried that Sergei would pounce as soon as he walked inside the house. What really terrified Jacob was the thought that if he was inside, Sergei could attack him and he wouldn't stop. Officer Paula wouldn't see them fighting this time, and Sergei would be free to beat on him for as long as he wanted. He'd just been released from the hospital and definitely didn't want to go back.

Jacob was about to walk inside the house when his cellphone rang. He didn't know who it was but he told Karina, "I better answer this." Karina nodded, so he answered his phone. "This is Jacob Carmichael."

"Hello Jako, this is Yousra."

"Yousra, why are you calling me?" He was happy to hear from her but didn't want her to know it. Karina's eyes cut into Jacob so he waved his hands in the air to say, *What can I do? She called me.* Karina stormed off into the house to get her stuff while he talked to Yousra.

"Jako, I'm calling you because I have to tell you something very important."

"Okay what?" Jacob answered, sounding a little annoyed.

"Please don't let anyone else come here for the modeling job. It's not what Hamid the Mustache says."

Jacob knew it. He just knew Yousra was going to tell him how bad it was in Miami, and he knew Yousra was going to tell him Hamid had lied to her. Jacob thought about how close Karina had come to going, and was glad he saved her. He was curious to hear what Yousra had to say but he didn't want her to know. So Jacob replied, "Oh really, why do you say this?"

"I haven't been in Miami. I was taken to Fort Myers in a dirty old mini-van by these two really nasty Libyan guys. They drugged me, and when I was unconscious they filmed me. One of the guys fondled me while I slept."

Jacob was shocked. He never imagined the modeling job was going to be this bad. "Oh my God, Yousra. This is terrible. Are you okay? What are you going to do now?"

"Don't worry about me, Jako. I put the Fort Myers police all over this. They chased after the guys and now they are sitting in jail. The police told me that when they get to prison the other prisoners will make them pay for sex crimes against women."

"What about Hamid?" Jacob asked, because he really wanted him arrested.

"Brad told me he contacted the Gulf Coast City police and they're looking for Hamid too."

Fantastic! Jacob thought. "Brad, who is that?"

"Officer Brad Taylor is my new boyfriend, Jako," Yousra said with pride, and a hint of embarrassment.

"I see." Jacob was happy for Yousra.

"Jako, I know you probably hate me because you saw me having sex in the hot tub but I want to explain this to you."

"You really don't have to." He started to fidget.

"I only did this because I found out that you had sex with Winston's wife and I wanted to get revenge on you."

Jacob didn't know what to say and he didn't know what to feel so he just said, "Yousra, we all had a crazy year in Gulf Coast City but we made it through. It sounds like you're happy now and you've found someone who cares about you."

"Yes, I have Jako. Brad asked me to move in with him and I said yes. I'm going to stay in Fort Myers."

"Well I'm happy for you, Yousra. I really am."

"Thank you, Jako."

Karina walked out the house with two suitcases.

"Do you need help, Karina?" Jacob asked.

"No this is everything," she said with a smile.

Yousra asked, "You're with Karina? I'm happy for you, Jako. I always knew she liked you."

"Thank you Yousra. Listen, I have to go but please keep in touch, okay?"

"I will Jako. You keep in touch too."

"Take care of yourself."

"I will Jako, bye."

Karina and Jacob got into his car and headed to Gulf Coast Employment Solutions. Jacob looked at Karina and said, "I'm glad you're going to move in with me and I'm going to find us a better place really soon, don't worry."

"I'm not worried, Jacob." Karina leaned over and gave him a kiss. "As long as I'm with you, I'm happy to live anywhere."

They pulled into the parking lot of Gulf Coast Employment Solutions and Jacob's cell phone rang again.

"This is Jacob Carmichael."

"Jacob, you need to come to Happy Suma's right now!" Suma cried out.

"Why, what's going on?"

"Exotic Beauties is out of business. Camille is getting rid of all her stuff."

"Wow, fantastic!"

"Come over now, Jacob. We will go meet the landlord of that building and try to take over the lease." Jacob was instantly giddy, he'd never heard Suma so excited.

Three weeks later, Beach Babes opened its doors. The owners, Suma and Jacob, could not have been prouder. The Russian and Eastern European students, who didn't already find a job, had been at the beach now for over a month. They were super tan and ready to start exotic dancing. Jacob finally had a place where he could provide total safety while the girls made bundles of cash.

EPILOGUE
SUE ELLEN DOOLEY'S HOUSE

"... The devil prowls around like a roaring lion, seeking someone to devour."
—1 Peter 5:8

Last Christmas had been a depressing one for Jacob Carmichael in Gulf Coast City. But this year was different, mostly because he had Karina. He still had some unfinished business, and that was to pay a visit to Sue Ellen Dooley. Beach Babes was closed for Christmas Eve, so Jacob told Karina today he was finally going to follow up on Pastor Mike and Tamar's advice.

"Good luck, Jacob," said Karina. "Do you want me to come with you?"

"No, this is something I have to do myself. But thank you for thinking about me." Jacob smiled. "This is one of the many things I love about you."

He got in his car and headed towards Sue Ellen Dooley's house on Oak Street. Christmas time in Florida was a little different than in the foothills of South Carolina. He remembered his Christmases back home with all the houses nicely decorated, as he now looked outside at the palm trees and the bright sunshine. There were decorations here but it wasn't the same feeling when it seemed like summer time outside.

When Jacob pulled into Sue Ellen Dooley's driveway his heart started racing. He imagined Carl inside still beating on his sister Tamar. *I have to do this*, he thought, *I've put this off long enough.*

Jacob got out of his car and noticed that someone had painted over the words, *"LEAVE TOWN BITCH"* on the driveway. He walked up to Sue Ellen's front door, took a deep breath then pressed the doorbell. He wanted to run away immediately but resisted. He waited but no one came to the door. He walked around to the side yard where the grass was up to his knees, then looked through one of the windows. It was dark inside and just appeared to be an ordinary old house. He was searching for clues but wasn't getting any.

Jacob heard the front door open and a small woman walked outside. She was in her early thirties but looked much older. She had huge bags under her eyes and long black hair that looked like it was turning prematurely grey. She said softly, "I've already called the police and they are on their way right now." Jacob froze and the woman continued. "I wish you people would quit vandalizing my house. I'd move away if I could."

He put his hands up to show he meant no harm. "Miss Dooley? I just wanna talk with you if that's okay?"

"Who are you?" Sue Ellen asked.

Jacob wasn't planning on telling her who he was right away because he wanted to ease into things. But now he felt like he didn't have a choice. "I'm um… I'm Jacob Carmichael."

Sue Ellen was silent as she studied his face. He could tell she knew immediately who he was. All she could get out was, "Oh."

"Mrs. Dooley, I'm not here to cause any trouble." Jacob slowly started walking towards Sue Ellen. "I just wanna talk to you. I really just need to find answers, that's all."

"I understand," Sue Ellen answered softly.

"Is it okay if I come inside?"

The houses where Sue Ellen lived were all close together and the neighbors were already starting to stare. Sue Ellen agreed and motioned for him to enter.

When Jacob stepped into the house, he was immediately greeted by a musty smell, as if no one had been in or out for ages. The air was heavy and stagnant inside but the dining room was very tidy. Besides the fact that no Christmas decorations were on display, the room looked normal. Jacob wondered why it looked so clean inside and so overgrown and rundown outside. They walked over to the dining room table and Sue Ellen motioned for him to have a seat. "Would you like something to drink?" Sue Ellen asked politely. "I have some tea."

"Yes, that would be nice."

As Sue Ellen walked away to the kitchen, Jacob thought she was probably once very pretty, but the stress from her husband had beaten away at her now gaunt face.

Sue Ellen came back with a large glass of iced tea and nothing for herself. She sat down at the table with him and said, "I'm very sorry, Jacob. It must have been terrible for you and your sister. I am so sorry…"

"No, please don't apologize, Mrs. Dooley."

"Call me Sue Ellen, please."

"Please don't apologize, Sue Ellen," Jacob said, trying to comfort her. "This is not why I'm here."

"Oh okay, I'm sorry."

Jacob wondered how many times she had to apologize for her husband in the past. "I moved to Gulf Coast City a year and a half ago because my pastor and my sister advised me to do so."

"Oh, I see." Sue Ellen refused to make eye contact with Jacob, her eyes downcast, fidgeting with her cheap wedding ring.

"You see, I'm training to be a pastor at a church. Or at least I was. And my pastor advised me to come see you, so I could get some clarity on the incident with my sister."

"I understand, and I'll help you with whatever you want."

"Thank you Sue Ellen, but I'm not sure what I want. I think what my pastor thought was, if I came to see you, I'd be able to get the thoughts out of my head that your husband was a huge monster."

"Well, I guess I could tell you a little bit about him if you think this would help." Sue Ellen sat back slightly in her chair and tried to relax.

"That would be great, thank you." Jacob took a sip of his iced tea.

"My husband Carl was a lovely, caring, very sensitive man and I loved him very much." Jacob was about to say, *Wait a minute cut the crap,* then Sue Ellen said, "But he was also the most evil man I'd ever met. You see, Carl suffered from schizophrenia, so I never knew who I was going to come home to every day. One day I'd come home from my old job as an accountant and find that Carl had made me supper and bought me flowers. The next day I'd come home and Carl would punch me in the face and rape me as soon as I walked through the door. This went on for ten years."

Jacob took a quick gulp of his iced tea, subconsciously thinking it was Jack and Coke. "I gotta ask, Sue Ellen. Why didn't you leave him?"

"I wanted to but I never did."

"May I ask why?"

"Sure. There were two main reasons I guess. First was, I loved him very much. I mean, I loved the kind gentle man, not the other one. And second was, my priest was totally against it. He told me that God had chosen me to make Carl a better man. And if I failed Carl, I failed God. So I never tried to divorce him."

"I see." He really didn't know what to say next.

Sue Ellen looked him in the eyes for the first time and said, "I'm sure you're wondering why Carl was in South Carolina."

"Yes." Jacob sat up in his chair.

"The last couple of months before Carl left Florida, he used to lock himself in our bedroom and read the Bible all day. Ordinarily, I'd say this was a good thing, but he was obsessed with this. He studied every page and he'd only communicate with me through Bible verses. It was very disturbing."

"Oh, I can imagine."

"Carl told me one day that God had chosen him to roam the earth. He quoted a verse from the book of Peter."

"Do you know which one it was?"

"Oh that's right, you said you were studying to be a pastor." Sue Ellen gave Jacob an approving nod. She looked up at the ceiling trying to think, then said, "No, sorry I don't remember. I have tried to block a lot of that out of my mind."

"Did he say this to you?" Jacob wasn't going to go easy on Sue Ellen because he needed answers. "Be sober-minded; be watchful. Your adversary the devil prowls around like a roaring lion, seeking someone to devour?"

"Yes, that's what he said." A tear rolled down Sue Ellen's cheek. "I am so very sorry Jacob."

"Please, Sue Ellen. You don't have to apologize to me. You did everything you could to try to stop him, I'm sure. You coulda divorced him but you stayed and tried to help him, but he was too powerful."

"That's right." The tears were really flowing now covering Sue Ellen's face.

"Let me ask you one more thing," Jacob said as he scooted his chair closer to her. "Do you have any idea why Carl quoted the book of Peter?"

"Yes, I think I so," Sue Ellen responded. She took a deep breath then looked at Jacob, who was now hanging on her every word. "I think he was trying to warn people to always be wary of other people. I know, the way he did it was wrong, but I believe he was trying to show people that they should always be on the lookout. And that evil can easily be lurking around every corner. He left Gulf Coast City about a month before he arrived in Tinsley. He traveled around to different small towns. I didn't realize it then but now I believe he was mistreating people so that he could teach them a lesson." Sue Ellen paused to see his reaction.

Jacob looked down at the table trying to make sense of what he had just heard. Then he looked up and said, "You know, Sue Ellen I think I get it. Before Carl came into my life, I was oblivious to the opportunists that live in this world. And I believe the entire town of Tinsley was too. But you can bet your you-know-what that they all lock their doors and look over their shoulders now."

"I'm sure you're right Jacob. But I still don't want you to feel like I condoned what Carl did because I didn't."

"No, I have no bad feelings towards you, Sue Ellen. I do have another question though."

"Sure."

"Carl, stole $5,000 from the church and when the sheriff and I caught up with him probably less than two hours later, he still had the bank envelope but there was only $20 left. I have always wondered what he did with the money?"

"My guess is he more than likely just threw the rest into the nearest garbage can. He didn't steal to help himself, he stole to teach a lesson. He probably just took out $100 to get him to the next town and tossed the rest."

"I understand… I mean I don't think I will ever understand, but at least I can see what his motivation was. Let me ask you one last question. Did you ever call the police on Carl?"

"Oh yes. Of course I did." She wiped her moist cheeks with a napkin. "The police assigned an officer to keep an eye on Carl but there wasn't much he could do or really wanted to do for that matter."

"I guess there's no law against roaming the earth, thinking you're the devil."

"No, there's not and once again Jacob, I am so sorry. If there is anything I can do please ask me."

Jacob could see Sue Ellen was truly despondent over what her husband had done. He didn't want to torture her anymore so he asked, "Do you mind if I use your bathroom?"

"Sure, it's right down the hall."

He got up from his chair and walked in the direction Sue Ellen had pointed. He stepped inside her small but very tidy bathroom. He turned on the water and looked in the mirror trying to process everything he had just heard. Then he pulled up the seat to the commode and urinated, feeling as if he was a million miles away. He flushed the toilet and went back to the sink and ran the water again as he gazed into the mirror.

"You okay in there, honey?" Jennifer asked. Jacob froze then rubbed his eyes. "You okay in there, Jacob?" Sue Ellen asked again.

"Sure, I'll be right out," he replied as his mind when back to the night he had hidden in Jennifer's bathroom while she paced up and down outside. *If only he'd walked straight out of there and immediately headed out her door. None of this would have ever happened.*

Jacob dried off his hands then walked out of the bathroom and asked, "You said you were an accountant. Is that right?"

"Yes, I was."

"What do you do now?"

"I cut grass because I was fired from my accountant position."

Jacob assumed Sue Ellen was fired because of her husband, so he didn't pry. "You say you cut grass now?"

"Yes, it's the only job I can get now in Gulf Coast City because everyone knows me here." Jacob turned his head around and looked at the messy front yard. Seeing his gaze, Sue Ellen said, "You're probably wondering why someone who cuts grass for a living has such an untidy yard."

"No, I wasn't thinking that," he lied.

"Well, it's because when I used to go outside to cut my grass my neighbors would throw rocks and beer bottles at me."

Then it hit Jacob like a ton of bricks. Mustapha had told him over a year ago that he paid Sue Ellen peanuts to cut grass because this was the only job she could get. Jacob felt sorry for her. "I see, well that's terrible. Don't they realize that you had no control over your husband's actions?"

"No, they don't." Sue Ellen wiped away another tear. Jacob was sure she wanted to say, *I hope you realize this too.*

He scratched his head, took another sip of tea then said, "Sue Ellen, I own a couple of businesses in Gulf Coast City and we could use a good accountant. Would you be interested in applying for this position?"

"Well I…" Sue Ellen hesitated.

"If you're afraid of what people will say or do I can set you up in an office that's away from them. You can do your work and get paid without being harassed."

Sue Ellen smiled for the first time since her visit with Jacob began. "Can I ask what type of businesses you own?"

"Sure," he answered proudly. "I own Gulf Coast Employment Solutions and Beach Babes."

"I see." Sue Ellen got quiet. She sounded surprised.

"I know what you're thinking," Jacob responded. "Why on earth would a devout Christian own a gentlemen's club?"

"No… I wasn't thinking that," Sue Ellen lied.

"I'm gonna tell you the reason, Sue Ellen, and I have never told anyone this before. Not even my girlfriend. When I was at Bob Jones University, studying to be a pastor, I never would've thought that one day I'd own a gentlemen's club. But now I do and it isn't because I have completely lost my faith and gone in the opposite direction. My faith in God is actually at an all-time high. I now know that I'm in the best position ever to keep an eye on vulnerable young ladies and help protect them. Do you remember the court trial with Brett Olson from Exotic Beauties about six months back?"

"Yes, I remember something about this. A lot of girls were drugged and taken advantage of."

"That's right and I was involved with that. I felt obligated to go to the trial all day every day because the owner of the club had taken advantage of me. At one point in the trial, Brett's lawyer, Attorney Candy, said that Brett and Camille mentor the girls to keep them away from drugs and prostitution. I knew, of course that he was full of baloney, but I said to myself, this is what I want to do for real. I had other reasons for buying into the club but this was a big factor in my decision."

"That sounds very honorable, Jacob--"

A loud knock came from the front door. Jacob had been speaking with Sue Ellen for over thirty minutes and finally the police had arrived.

"Excuse me for a minute," Sue Ellen said politely as she got up.

"Ma'am is everything okay?" the policeman asked and Jacob thought he recognized his voice.

"Yes, I'm sorry, the vandals have gone away."

"Well look ma'am, we can't come out here every time some kid rides by on his bicycle and calls you a name. You're just gonna have to get used to it."

Jacob was sure he knew who the policeman was. He only knew one cop with that arrogant attitude, and that was Corporal Hunter.

"Okay, I understand." replied Sue Ellen respectfully.

"Anyway, I won't be the one coming out here no more. I've been promoted to detective," Corporal Hunter bragged, and Jacob's heart sank.

Sue Ellen closed her front door and turned around to continue speaking with her guest. But Jacob had already stood up to leave.

"Thank you so much for your time, Sue Ellen. This talk was a big help for me." Jacob held out his hand for Sue Ellen to shake. "Please come by my office at Gulf Coast Employment Solutions on Monday. I really want to help you. No strings attached, okay?"

"Okay, and thank you Jacob."

He left Sue Ellen's with a satisfied smile on his face. He got in his car and headed over to Gulf Coast Employment Solutions. The office was closed for Christmas, but Jacob wanted to use the phone.

When he arrived, it was quiet inside and completely empty, perfect for him to call his sister.

"Hello," Tamar answered.

"Merry Christmas, Tamar!" Jacob yelled down the phone. A tear ran down his cheek.

"Merry Christmas, little brother. Oh my Lord, I haven't heard from you in forever. How are you?"

"I'm just great. I'm sorry I haven't called you. I just wasn't in the right place for so long but now I'm doing great. How are you?"

"Well, Pastor Mike told me it was best to give you some time and space so that's what we all did. I'm doing great too, thanks. So tell me, what've you been up to. Anything exciting?"

Thank you for reading my book. If you enjoyed it, won't you please take a moment to leave me a review at your favorite retailer.

Thanks,
David Lloyd.

About the Author

David Lloyd was born in Warrington, England but grew up in Summerville, South Carolina. He attended Francis Marion University and has a Bachelor of Business Administration. After selling his employment agency, David moved as far south as he could. He is now over fifty, happily married and enjoying life in Southwest, Florida.

David enjoys tennis and writing. His first novel, titled *Gulf Coast City*, was influenced from running an employment agency that provided temporary staff for anything from hotel housekeepers to exotic dancers and everything in between. David is currently working on the sequel to *Gulf Coast City*. Publication dates can be found on his web sites.

Web Site: www.DavidLloydNovels.com
Facebook: www.facebook.com/DavidLloydNovels
Twitter: DavidLloyd@DavidLloydNovel

Acknowledgements

I'd like to thank the following people for their generous help with the writing of this book: My beautiful wife Susan; Robin Stover; Cathy Boartz; Scott Balog; Kimberly Common and Mitransh Parihar - Book Cover Design; Deb Rhodes of Better Beta Reads; Starr Waddell, Jennifer, Jessica, Joshua, and Samatha of Quiethouse Editing.

www.ingramcontent.com/pod-product-compliance
Lightning Source LLC
Chambersburg PA
CBHW071229250626
47163CB00001B/108

* 9 7 8 0 9 9 7 8 0 6 9 1 5 *